# THE KATANGA

*American Mercenaries in the African Congo*

# NORMAN KELLEY

outskirtspress

DENVER, COLORADO

The Katanga
American mercenaries in the African Congo
All Rights Reserved.
Copyright © 2016 Norman Kelley
v4.0

Cover Photo © 2016 thinkstockphotos.com. All rights reserved - used with permission.

Outskirts Press, Inc.
http://www.outskirtspress.com

ISBN: 978-1-4787-7599-7

Library of Congress Control Number: 2016907171

Outskirts Press and the "OP" logo are trademarks belonging to Outskirts Press, Inc.

PRINTED IN THE UNITED STATES OF AMERICA

*For my wife, Patricia Ann*

# Prologue

The layover at the mining facility had been unrealistically peaceful. All of the modern conveniences temporarily made up for sleeping in tents, eating beans and rations and tolerating the always-present bugs. We left in high spirits and on a cloudless day, idling slowly down the unpaved road. I figured this couldn't last, and it didn't. This was potentially dangerous territory and we were on full alert. Mike and I were part of a squad that walked ahead along the shoulder, strung out over a quarter of a mile. We carried our FALs and pistols, assuming that the scrub bush and thick vegetation precluded any sniper activity, and it was a comfortable march without all of the specialty gear. But after about eight miles, the trucks slowed and then abruptly skidded to a stop. When anything out of the usual happened, like an abrupt stop on this untraveled road, we knew that something was up. Mainala dropped out of the passenger seat of the lead vehicle and waved to us with a lot of urgency, to come to the front of the truck. We gathered by the fender and looked ahead. Just starting around a curve we saw a small sports car, the top down and the driver's door open. In the Katanga, you didn't just stop and walk away from your car. The adrenalin started pumping as we unshouldered our FALs, chambered a round and the squad followed Mainala. We were all eyes then, alert to possible cover and moving at a good pace. As we reached the car, we saw a thin line of smoke coming from the exhaust and we realized that it was still running! And then, as we came alongside the vehicle we realized that this wasn't a matter of someone stopping to take a leak. There was a trench dug across the road, a common Baluba tactic to stop a lone vehicle and then attack it. Then it got worse. Ten feet from the car was a woman's purse with the contents spilled across the road and we knew something terrible had happened.

A lone woman in a small car in the middle of Baluba country? Mike saw it first. A spiral of smoke several hundred yards from the road, which in this area signaled something very bad. Mainala motioned for us to be silent, sent four guys back to guard the trucks and we followed him. After only a few steps we found a woman's shoe and signs of a scuffle and some red material stuck to a tree. We had only gone about two hundred yards further and saw what we didn't want to see. A Baluba, probably a chief, wearing a bunch of animal skins was frog marching a blonde haired woman ahead to a gathering of about thirty tribesmen. We moved slowly and she became clearly visible in her bright red dress. The Balubas were chanting something and they were focused on her, not our approach. This chief was jerking her around, and kicked her feet from under her, holding her by her hair and she began screaming. This all happened in a second or two and before we could take any action she pushed away from the guy and reached into the top of her dress, pulled out a very small gun, shoved it up against the Baluba's chin and fired. He immediately crumpled and then we watched, stunned as she turned the gun and put it in her mouth and fired. Transfixed for a second or two, we were aghast as the entire tribe attacked the woman, who probably was already quite dead, and started hacking and cutting. What followed was carnage on a large scale. We usually saw the aftermath of these things, but this time the entire episode unfolded right before us. Mainala said "Move!" as he leveled his FAL and fired at the pile of tribesmen. And then we all began firing as we approached the fire. Flesh and blood was flying everywhere, heads exploding as we dropped empty magazines and started all over again until there were several piles of dead Balubas. Well, not quite. One guy lifted his arm and four FALs immediately dismembered him. The damage to a human being by twelve FALs, is hard to describe. Skulls opened with blue-grey matter falling into pools of blood, hunks of flesh and bone everywhere, and then total quiet. We pulled the Baluba's bodies off of the woman who clearly was dead as well. Her little two-barreled .41 caliber derringer had done its job in a way unexpected for such a tiny gun. The Balubas, in only seconds had already managed to almost sever one of her legs. The apparent leader she had killed was equally dead, the bullet having travelled through his mouth and out the top of his skull. At least this time, all of our hi-tech stuff had no place whatsoever.

We stood there, breathless, thinking about the terror the woman must have felt and what might have been if we had arrived only seconds before. Could we have saved her? Maybe, but who would ever know? Our anger quickly turned to the shithead who had allowed her to be out on the open road by herself. As gently as we could, we placed the woman in a poncho and created a makeshift litter. Despite the disaster, we could see that she was young and attractive despite the matted blood in her blonde hair. She had also been very foolish.

All of this had taken place in only about 30 minutes or so as we began the hike back to the road. We left the Balubas for the already gathering crows. Mainala, with tears in his eyes, said "Lets head back to the mine and have a talk with those assholes."

# Chapter 1

M y odyssey started in 1960 when my buddy Mike Genard, who lived about a block away, came running into the backyard waving a piece of paper. Tony! Tony! I immediately sat up because I had never seen Mike move that quickly. He came over to me and threw a small envelope into my lap. No wonder he was upset. The letter was from the local Draft Board and Mike had just been re-classified 1A. A short letter accompanied a new draft card stating that because of Mike's 'discontinuing' Junior College he had been re-classified 1A and could be called for a physical and possible induction at any time. Then it hit me. How about my mail? I had also withdrawn from college at the same time, without really thinking about the consequences. I got up and ran to the mailbox, reached in it and there it was! The identical envelope. And after tearing it apart, there were the identical contents. I just stood there in the hallway and developed a cold sweat.

In retrospect, Mike and I should have known better. Oh, we talked about the draft and all, but as far as we could tell, the local draft board was composed of a bunch of old guys running banks and real estate offices around Bakersfield. Actually, the draft was nothing new, and had been in effect since 1940. The difference was that our new president, John F. Kennedy, was making bold statements about Viet Nam in the wake of the French collapse. Everyone figured that the next step was drafting men into that part of the world, and no one was excited about it. Germany? OK. Vietnam? Hell no! The Korean thing had not gone well, and the jungles of Indochina seemed impossible to imagine.

Like many 21 year olds, we were living in a dream world of girls, beer and hot rods. In fact, we had not actually withdrawn from college, we just stopped going to class! As I recall that day, what ensued was two six-packs of beer and jawboning about these stupid fuckers taking control of our lives, taking away our freedom, while a curtain of fear descended over us, knowing that we had no control over any of this.

In the past, whenever Mike and I had a problem like this, and after priorities like girls, beer and hot rods were satisfied, the fourth thing on our list was shooting. We had somehow fallen into a pattern of solving our boredom or frustration by heading north out of town to the oilfields and going shooting. Mind you, not just any kind of shooting. My dad had given me an old Springfield bolt-action rifle that he had acquired after the war, along with a large supply of 30-'06 ammunition. Dad was one of those workaholics who was never around much, but he had taught me how to handle a gun, starting with a .22 single shot, and a German Walther P.38 9mm pistol which I rarely shot because there was no cheap 9mm ammo. The Springfield was a kind of rite of passage into adulthood, and every time I could, I hopped into my '37 Ford and headed for the oilfields. The target? Jackrabbits. There were thousands of them in the oilfields, eating not only weeds but also small gardens and generally anything organic. Once I took Mike along with me and he was immediately taken away with this new, free hobby, and we developed it into a science. Even back then, no one appreciated us shooting animals except those tending gardens around oil company leased houses and a few people living in shacks trying to lessen their produce bill. To them we were 'The Answer'.

As time went by, we became more sophisticated. I managed to buy a 10x scope for the Springfield and Mike bought several 'spotting scopes' at the surplus store, some which were originally used as tank periscopes. He had found others at a store specializing in telescopes and the like, originally not for shooting jackrabbits but for looking at the stars and bird watching. Somewhere along the line, Mike acquired a Savage bolt-action rifle, not because Savages were all that great but because he was left-handed, and only Savage made an inexpensive left-handed 30-06 rifle. As time went by, we perfected our war on jackrabbits, trying to see how far away we could mow them down. We worked our way up from 400 yards, to 500, 600, and finally 700 yards. That is approaching ½ mile and we felt pretty good about it. Jackrabbits have a habit of being social creatures, and in groups, munched away at whatever greenery they were destroying. Our idea was not to just pick off a single rabbit, but hitting several of them before they knew what hit them. My dad had bought me several boxes of match ammo and we were now perfecting the art of not just blowing these suckers away, but making headshots.

While Mike was a good shot, we accepted that I had the better gun, even though it had probably gone through thousands of rounds. But Mike was a born spotter, using his various scope collection to zero in on a family 600 yards away. Therefore, we set up on a hilltop and Mike surveyed the area out to a range of about 800 yards. The nature of scopes is that the larger the power, the less field of vision, so I concentrated on finding general targets and he concentrated on finding the shot sequence.

So here we were, laying prone on a hilltop and surveying the hilltops, making sure there were no oilfield workers or other folks wandering around. "Tony, look left 30 degrees," said Mike and I scanned the area, finally finding a bunch of rabbits in a small lettuce garden next to a chain link fence. The program here was for me to choose a shot, then for Mike to call out the next one, in yards. I sighted in, paused, exhaled my breath to slow my system down, and gently squeezed the trigger. Before I knew the result, Mike hollered "Three left," and I chambered a round, moved the rifle just a hair to the left and there he was, having lost a brother or a cousin before he knew what had actually happened. Then he was gone. "Nine left," chamber a round, and squeeze the trigger. "Fourteen right", chamber and squeeze again, et cetera until I had exhausted the five rounds. I could see rabbits scampering all over my field of vision, but we had to get up and walk 600 yards to see what we had actually accomplished.

Five dead guys. The first two were actually head shots, but as the shots proceeded and the rabbits became aware that there was something wrong. The last three rounds were a little shaky, becoming body shots. Not much matter to the rabbits as they were all dead. Overall, knowing that even a big jackrabbit was only about 18" in height when he is eating dinner, a head shot was pretty damn good. 'Head shot' is also probably a misnomer, because when a jackrabbit's head encounters a 30-06 bullet, the head just disappears. We did this about twice a week, and only constrained ourselves by the supply of match ammo supplied by my dad. There seemed to be an unending supply of rabbits.

On the way back to town we congratulated ourselves at the excellent shooters we had become, but the reality of the Draft Board letter became the subject. "What the fuck do we do?" said Mike. The next day we were sitting in the backyard nursing a cold beer in an unusually hot Bakersfield winter day. I was reading the want ads in the *Bakersfield Californian* and Mike was looking through a gun magazine. As if getting a job would sever the draft board's control over our lives. Service station attendants, lawn boys, paper deliverers, and the really good jobs that we didn't actually read because it was now setting in that we were only good for the draft. We were smart asses. Dropped out of college.

Then, I saw it. I just about wet my pants! "Newly formed country in Central Africa recruiting sharpshooters with military experience to guard and protect international government facilities. A six-month contract, meals and all support provided, beginning salary commensurate with superior experience." A phone number was provided to us for further information. "Mike, look! An overseas job and no draft board!" We were dazzled, reading and re-reading the tiny ad, until we were sure that we had a job! We ran into the house and called the number and a woman asked what our qualifications were. I explained that we were long-range snipers! She paused for a moment, asked us about calibers and ranges as though she had a prepared list of questions. Apparently satisfied that we had something going for us, she set an appointment in Los Angeles for the following week and she suggested that we thoroughly document our experience. She said that there had to be clear evidence about our being snipers. I wondered, what do we do, bring in some dead rabbits? But the first challenge was wondering if our crappy cars could make it 125 miles to Los Angeles and back.

Later that evening a telephone call came and my dad just happened to answer it. The person on the other end of the line identified himself and asked to speak to Tony Ward. When I entered the room, I heard my dad say, "You are a representative of what country? The Katanga? I've never heard of it. Where?" The conversation went on for a minute or two, my dad throwing visual darts at me all the while, no doubt wondering what his jobless son was up to now. Finally, he handed the phone over to me and a person at the other end of the line identified himself in some sort of foreign accent, as Jules Falques and that he represented the Belgian government. He was responding to my request for a possible appointment. My dad left the room, his head shaking, looking for my Mom. But now, I was gathering my wits and felt free to talk. He asked my age and military experience and I responded that I was 21 years old and had no actual military experience. "Then why are you responding to this advertisement?" he said in a sort of snotty tone. "Well," I responded, "the ad said you were looking for marksmen and I believe that I have those skills." He asked just what skills I thought I had, in an increasingly disinterested tone. I responded, "Today we were shooting 6" x 6" targets at 700 yards." There was a pause and he seemed more interested. "Shooting at rabbits." I said. "Rabbits at 700 yards? With what? Are these paper targets?" So I explained the whole deal about Mike and I, how we had formed a sort of team as shooter and spotter, and that I was using a 1903 A3 Springfield 30-06 with a 10X scope.

When I further explained that these rabbits were not made of paper, Mr. Falques became more respectful. "This I would like to see. Where do you shoot?" So I explained that we did our shooting out in the oilfields near Bakersfield which I further explained was about three hours north of L.A. "So when could I witness this kind of shooting?" Falques asked. Thinking quickly now, with my mother glaring at me through the open door, and considering my tight calendar of beer, girls, and hot rods, I explained, "The only place I know of to shoot is in the vacant land around the oilfields and Mike and I could do this Wednesday or Thursday." "Why Mike?" he asked. "Mr. Falques, Mike and I have worked out our shooting together. We are a team of shooter and spotter." After a pause, he said, "Very well, Mr. Ward, can you meet me at the Bakersfield airport on Thursday at noon? I have an appointment in the evening in Fresno and we can do the exhibition in the afternoon, so bring your gear and rifle with you. You can arrange the location for the shooting." "OK, I said, we'll be there to pick you up. What flight is it?" "I will be piloting a private plane so meet be at wherever the General Aviation terminal is." "OK," I said, we'll see you there."

I hung up and my dad called me into the living room where my Mother, Mike, and his father were sitting. My dad got right to it: "Now tell us all exactly what the hell is going on here."

# Chapter 2

It was a long evening. Mike and I went through the whole thing with our dads. My dad had invited Mike's dad over and they quickly discovered that neither of us had 'dropped out' of college. Their first reaction was that we were a couple of freeloaders. My dad was fuming. "Why didn't you tell us and then go out and get a job? You guys were just clowning around drinking beer and eating our food...just playing around. It doesn't work that way in this house!" Mike's dad grunted his assent. However, after apologizing for the college fiasco, we got into the draft board letter and then the newspaper advertisement. Our parents understood our reluctance to be drafted and shipped out to Vietnam or wherever. But, I suppose that was exactly what would have happened except for this unusual contact. We were definitely not candidates to move to Canada.

Our dads had very good input, which, I suppose, is why they are dads. However, their opinion was that it was OK to go shooting with this person, but we had better find out where the hell The Katanga was and why there was a person from Belgium recruiting Americans. What exactly is the problem that requires mercenaries? We had heard a little about almost all countries in Africa gaining their independence, and how the mix of colonial powers and the western world were confusing the issues, but that was about it. The Katanga? We didn't know that it was even a country.

We figured that we had to develop a sense of urgency to all of this. The recruiter person was due in two days, and that letter from the draft board was not going to sit idly by for very long. As we understood it, once we were called, all options ended. But until then, we were Americans after all, and free to travel. Mike brought up a good point: if we were going to travel overseas wouldn't we need a passport? That seemed pretty obvious so the next day we headed down to the Post Office, had our pictures taken, provided a copy of our birth certificates, paid $12 (at the time) and then headed to the library.

On the way, we decided to drop by the gun store and I picked up two boxes of National Match 30-'06 ammo. To be expected, we were more interested in bullshitting with the guys at the gun store than doing any serious research. The guys at the shop thought that actually getting some exotic overseas job was probably about zero. Eventually, we wore out our welcome handling all of the new hardware, and headed to the library.

The available books were about the huge Belgian Congo, reaching from the Atlantic Coast into the heart of Africa, where we found the Katanga province. We read through some old magazines and found Belgium was the colonial master of the Congo. In fact, in the late 1800s, it was the personal property of King Leopold. Most authors agreed that the fundamental problem with colonial powers was that Europe saw this huge land mass providing an opportunity to extract minerals and other wealth, and they had little interest in developing or educating the population. Therefore, when an international effort got underway to give independence to these countries, they were completely unprepared for these responsibilities. The result was civil disorder, and in most cases, tribal conflict. After all, many of these 'countries' had borders artificially created by their colonial masters, and typically had no relationship to historical or cultural facts. I mentioned to Mike, "Look at this border. It looks like someone took a straight edge and just drew a two-thousand-mile line. Our own borders also had some of the same appearance, but rivers, mountain ranges and so on were at least taken into account. All of this confusion allowed potential new masters, such as Russia, to begin meddling. And where Russia meddled, the U.S. became interested. That seemed to be the pattern.

Mike ventured, "Why the fuck didn't Europe just leave these guys alone?" But what I got was a glare from the librarian. I then managed to acquire a firm grasp of the obvious. Why didn't we leave our Indians alone? And, with untold riches to be discovered in Africa, why bother educating the savages? In High School, I had written a paper about the inequities in South Africa, where a relatively small number of whites ruled millions of blacks. My point was, the only difference between South Africa and the U.S. was that we killed 99% of our Indians, and avoided the entire issue. So how is it that we had any right to criticize South Africa, no matter the grievances?

Beyond books, the other information came from newspapers, and the librarian helped us with working the microfiche machine and loading in the New York Times and other major newspapers. It seemed from these reports that Belgium was ready to give up everything in the Congo except the province of Katanga, for obvious reasons. Katanga had a well-developed mining effort going on which was primarily copper extraction, but there seemed to be other mineral possibilities. But the U.N and internationalists were hearing none of this. It was time for independence and the traditional and arbitrary borders were just the way it was going to be!

The powers in Belgium, being realistic, apparently knew that they could not simply carve out a piece of Africa in the 1960s, and that was when the political issues took shape. At this point, the librarian, who turned out to be one Abigail Fetterton, a tidy and matronly woman who took great interest in any young person actually looking for knowledge, took us aside and gave her opinion. First, she said, a Russian trained ex bank teller, Patrice Lumumba seemed to be the closest thing to a new leader. However, a Mr. Moise Tshombe, with some formal education, had no confidence in Lumumba and with Belgium's support, declared The Katanga to be a separate country. That was a black person declaring independence, not a white Belgium citizen. Ms. Fetterton had other demands on her time, but she told us "Then the problems started. The native population and Baluba tribes had no clue as to the intricacies of forming a country but they hated the Belgium rulers, and any black person seemed preferable. But they also had a vague notion of the Congo and did not like the idea of splitting it up. There were reports of murdering Belgium citizens in remote areas, and while just rumors, there were reports of gruesome ritual torture." We thought about that for a minute and our eyes confirmed that maybe Katanga wasn't such a hot idea after all. But then, Ms. Fetterton continued. "That was only the start. The U.N. got involved with a typically political conclusion that prepared or not, The Congo was to become a country and as for Belgium people, please go home. However, just a day or two after the Congo declared independence, The Katanga declared independence. They technically had just seceded from the Congo. To white people who had lived there for generations, this seemed like an altogether logical thing to do. What emerged was a country recognized by just about no one. Pressure was placed on the U.N. to take the province over with a multi-national force, while the U.S and Russia engaged in the usual east-west intrigue. Meanwhile, Mr. Tshombe stated that he would build a self-defense force."

"Jeez, pretty complex stuff." I said. Mike added "Nothing about any of that in the newspaper ad!" Ms. Fetterton excused herself, and we were left staring at each other. Mike said it: "Looks like a real old fashioned goat fuck." "Yep", I responded, "Is this really something that we want to get involved in?" Neither of us said it, but Vietnam was looking better all the time.

# Chapter 3

On Wednesday evening. Mike and I were in my bedroom cleaning our guns. We had decided to go through with the shooting exercise with Mr. Falques, but we were certainly not ready to make any commitments about signing a contract. My dad dropped in, shot the bull for a while, and asked, "Where is the P.38?" It was kept under the bed and I reached down and gave the old German WW2 pistol to him. He had brought this gun back from Europe and it had a special meaning to him. He sat down by the desk and went to work. Drop the magazine, put the gun on safety, pull the slide back while rotating the take down lever, pull the slide and the barrel off the frame, push the locking block button and separate the barrel from the slide and the result was all of the components in neat order, all in less than five seconds. "Jeez, dad, you really know that gun!" He nodded, and took an oiled cotton swab, ran it through the barrel, oiled the key parts and put all back together in a minute or two, handed it to me, and said "Ready to go." That was as close as I ever got to an endorsement of our possible adventure.Mike stayed over and we talked late into the night, intent on shooting straight but committed to getting answers from this recruiter guy.

# Chapter 4

We started the day talking my mother into borrowing her Chevy. Showing up at the airport in a 37 Ford did not seem like the best way to impress a foreign recruiter. On the other hand, we dressed for the occasion. We were going to be lying in the dirt in prone positions, and jeans, long sleeve work shirts and low-topped boots seemed to fit. We started early and drove through the suburbs, passed through Oildale, a hardscrabble area full of bars, oil workers homes, and many weekend fights. Meadows Field was a couple of miles further out and we drove by a row of small private planes, a few tattered war surplus aircraft with their covering fabric in shreds, and on to the small terminal and parking lot. United Airlines had two DC-3 flights a day from Los Angeles and the waiting room and small grass area also provided an area for visiting private planes to gas up, use the head, grab a sandwich and be on their way. We bought some cold drinks, and sat on a bench outside of the terminal and practiced our game plan.

Which wasn't much. We figured that we would try and be professional and all grown up, take Mr. Falques out to the shooting area, another 4-5 miles, and pump him for information. Of course, anything positive was completely dependent on our shooting ability. Then we wondered how that was going to go. We hadn't even thought about targets, and what if the rabbits didn't show up today? About a half hour later, we saw a twin engine Cessna circling the field, making his approach and touching down to a smooth landing. If this was Mr. Falques, he was not travelling cheap! The Cessna was a neat looking polished aluminum thing as the pilot taxied around to the access ramp, onto the welcoming tarmac and then followed a worker in coveralls over to a parking place and shut the engines down.

In a couple of minutes, the Cessna's door opened and a person dressed in khakis stepped out on the wing and on to the ground. He went around to a cargo hatch, pulled out a canvas bag about 4 'x 4', and looked over our way. We waved and he began walking towards us. Our nerves were twanging like banjo strings! As he approached, we got our first look. Mr. Falques was average height, slim but seemingly fit, in starched and pressed work clothes. We stepped forward, and introduced ourselves, impressed by a very firm handshake. "Good to meet you Mr. Ward and Mr.Genard." "Same here, Mr. Falques. That is really neat, flying up here in a private plane." We were plainly impressed.

Mr. Falques seemed to have no interest in getting on a first name basis. Then or later, I do not think I ever saw him smile. His mouth was as if a surgeon had slit right across his jowls, having closed, narrow lips. He had an aquiline nose, and his eyes focused directly on whoever he was addressing. This was no shrinking violet. He had a close-cut haircut, military fashion, and clearly, the impression he gave was that he just wanted to get on with our exercise. Had he not been destined for Fresno, another 100 miles north, I doubt if he would have even come. We walked over to the car and opened the trunk where our firearms were, and I loaded his canvas bag. It must have weighed 50 pounds! He got into the passenger's seat, and with Mike in the back seat and drove out of the airport parking area and headed north. As we drove, I explained that our experience was to shoot small, live animals at extreme distances, but we had no set targets. I conceded that was a mistake on our part, because rabbits did not congregate for the convenience of their executions. I thought that was pretty funny but he apparently saw no humor in my joke. However, he did say, "No problem, I have brought the targets", which explained the heavy canvas pouch. This guy was very well organized.

Mike asked him exactly whom he represented. Mike said it in a polite way, and Mr. Falques seemed to take it that way. "I am a Major in the Belgium army, seconded to the new Republic of The Katanga.

He reached in his shirt pocket and gave us each a business card, which we only glanced at, but it said something like Jules Falques, Liaison to The Katanga Government, followed by a list of telex numbers, phone numbers, and addresses. He went on and explained that it should be obvious that Belgium has an economic interest in The Katanga. "We take pride in what we have accomplished in the last hundred years and our best avenue to keeping that interest intact is in supporting the new government. We have hopes that this will be the only successful white-black country left in Africa." I nodded. That seemed straightforward enough to me, though probably a well-rehearsed statement. We drove on in silence. I will say, it was intimidating because here we're talking 1:1 with a real major from Africa, and all we knew how to do was shoot rabbits!

We pulled off in the same spot we usually shot from, in the shade of an oil pumping plant. It was now afternoon and the temperature would easily hit 90. Opening the trunk, we took out all of our wares, taking the rifles out of their covers, the scopes, ammo, along with his canvas pouch and placed them all on a concrete pad supporting the oil well. Mr. Falques picked up my scoped Springfield and carefully looked, working the bolt and checking the bore. "I assume this is your rifle, Mr. Ward. It's a real old timer." Falques seemed to admire the condition of the gun, which had developed a certain patina over the years, thinning blue, and a smooth oiled stock. Functionally, about perfect. "You have given it good care." "We also have our side arms and Mike's Savage." Mike had a Browning Hi Power 9mm and of course, I had the Ward family 9mm P.38, but he pretty much ignored them. He checked out the Savage, but clearly recognized that I was the shooter and the Springfield was the gun.

Mr. Falques said, "I am going to set up some paper targets at 100 yard intervals starting at about 400 yards. Is that satisfactory?" "Sure", I responded, "and you can go out further". "How far?" he asked. "How about 700 yards" I responded. I thought I detected a little surprise at that. Small paper targets get very small at that distance. Feeling a little put out by Mr. Falques' coolness, I said, "Go ahead and put the last one at 900 yards." I saw a little shake of his head and maybe just a tiny condescending smile. Mr. Falques proceeded to unzip his bag and take out some really well made target frames that could be pushed into the ground, securely holding the paper targets. He then took a small wheeled device that he said would accurately mark off stations at 100 yard intervals and off he went. As he left us and walked across the very slightly rolling hillside, we got organized. I was pretty much ready to go, laying our ammo out on a section of foam, and placed two plastic mats on the ground. I had a couple small sandbags and a chintzy bipod, and that was it. Mike laid out his two scopes, one 40x with an extremely narrow field of vision, and a more conventional 10x scope. We had done this dozens of times, so it only took a few minutes.

Shortly, Mr. Falques returned, a little sweaty, but seemingly not tired at all. "OK", he said, "What I want you to do is to start at the 400 mark with two shots, then progress with two shots at each target as far as you think you can. I have clearly marked each target with the distance, so that when we are done, we can see what has been accomplished." Then he said, "I'd like to know just what Mr. Genard's role is." I was surprised that he asked, but nodded to Mike for an explanation. "Well, in the real world, these targets will not be stationary in the ground, no matter what we are shooting at, and I can call out the distance, and where the target is to Tony, left, right, up or down. He doesn't really need that if it's a single shot, but if we have multiple targets I can call that out as he shoots." He went on. "Even today, at extreme distances the wind can play an important role, and my hi power scope can detect movement in grasses or trees from the wind and I can call them out as well. It may be quiet here, but not necessarily so at 900 yards." Mr. Falques nodded. He understood. He just wanted to know if we understood.

My primary asset was my 20/15 vision, and even with the naked eye I could see that Mr. Falques' 600-yard target was invisible, not because of the distance but because it was at the bottom of a gully.

He understood. You cannot hit something that you cannot see. I had examined the paper targets and saw that they were conventional bulls-eye paper targets available in any sporting goods store, with the actual black part of the 'eye' about 6" across. The idea, of course, was not only get into the 'eye', but get into the middle of the eye. I dispensed with the bipod and firmly nestled the rifle on some small sand bags, and with the safety on, I loaded five rounds into the magazine and chambered one, then added an extra round, and sighted the first target. Safety off. Mike called out no wind, no problems. I looked through the scope, made adjustments, my breathing, squeezed the trigger and fired. Before looking at the result, I worked the bolt, chambered a second round, and shot. With a 40x scope, Mike could see the result: a single hole, one bullet on top of the other. Move to 500 yards. Chamber, sight, squeeze, shoot. Then again. Mike said "Good shot, same result." I called out to Mr. Falques, reminding him that the 600-yard target was invisible due to the terrain and said I was moving to 700 yards. Load, chamber a round, sight, squeeze, shoot, then repeat. Mike sighted with the 40x scope and said 'The holes overlap about ¾ inch. Not perfect, but at this range nothing is. I rolled over and reloaded the Springfield, inserted one into the chamber, and closed the bolt. Time? About five seconds. We were now at 900 yards and clearly, Mr. Falques did not expect much, but then he was observing with the naked eye and had not actually seen the results of the previous shots. The target was tiny, almost invisible without a scope. Compensate elevation four lines in the scope reticle. Adjust, squeeze. Repeat. I rolled over and laid the rifle down. The entire shooting exercise had taken less than 3 minutes. By the time Mike and I had stood up, Falques was walking away, picking up the targets. Mike said "Tony' that was spectacular! I've never seen you do that well!" "Thanks Mike. I was getting a little pissed at Falques. I don't think he expected this."

In a few minutes, Falques was back from his one-mile hike, shuffling through the targets. "This is very good shooting, Mr. Ward.

Especially with a 50-year-old rifle at these distances. Your team seems to work well." I loved it. Especially the 900-yard target which had both holes about 2" off center. To a live human, or even a rabbit, that degree of inaccuracy would make no difference at all. We gathered up our gear and loaded it up in the trunk of the Chevy. We had a couple of canteens of water and we all took a swig, and wiped our faces with a couple of towels that were stacked by the spare tire. I had the urge to look at Falques' business card but thought that would be a little out of place. We hopped into the car and started the trip back to the airport. Mike asked about how the recruitment process worked, and Falques responded "Very quickly. We will either make a commitment within two weeks or turn you down. However, after seeing your shooting effort, it will be a positive recommendation. If a commitment is made, you will get instructions on how to proceed, but you might be thinking about that. All you need to bring is a carry-on bag with personal heath medicines and the like and any small personal belongings. Everything else will be supplied." "What about the rifles and the handguns?" I asked. "Leave the rifles at home. We will supply custom FN FAL .308 rifles and optics. The .308 has ballistics which are very similar to the 30-06 and should pose no problems for you. We might contract for a Mauser sniper rifle, and we'll have to think about that." Mike followed up. "What about the handguns? My Browning has a 13 round magazine which is a pretty potent gun."

"Mr. Ward, please pull over here. We need a short conversation." I pulled over onto the dirt shoulder and turned the engine off. I had an idea that something serious was about to happen. "You men need to understand a few things. First of all, it is OK to bring your handguns, but the capacity of your magazines is not something that is an issue. The main concern is that the gun carry one cartridge. Just one. That cartridge is meant for you in case you are about to be captured. You do not want to be captured." Our eyes widened but we were 100% ears. "We have a good safety record, but there over a million Baluba tribesmen in The Katanga. They are right out of the middle ages.

They have a few ancient shotguns but they rely on spears and poisoned bows and arrows. They also believe in torture. In addition, they are a lot better than we in travelling through the bush. It is not the point to frighten you or discourage you, but this is something you need to consider. We have absolute proof of the Balubas tying or nailing prisoners to a stake in front of a fire, and hacking off their hands and feet. And opening their chests while the prisoner is still alive and pulling out a beating heart. When the poor chap is finally dead, they eat him. You don't want to be captured. Make sure you have a reliable last bullet." Mike and I must have turned white. All I could say was "Fuck!" Mike swallowed and mumbled "Cannibals?" Almost in unison, we said "Jesus Christ!"

Falques seamlessly went on. "I say these things to emphasize that this is no picnic ground and you should consider the possible consequences while we make our recruitment decisions. We have lost only a handful of men, but for those men, the end was inhuman. Now, we have other problems. These U.N troops. How they fit into this movement, I do not know". We just sat there by the side of the road for a minute or two, until Falques said, "Let's be on our way." We got Falques into his Cessna and watched him take off, then headed for home in silence.

# Chapter 5

Even though Mike was a little under age, there was a bar in Oildale that would sell us beer, and we pulled to a stop in the parking lot. We had not said a word since Falques had taken off. We sat at the end of the bar in an almost-empty room and ordered a couple of Buds. Mike broke the ice. "Well what did you think of that?" I just shook my head. "For Christ sakes, fucking cannibals?" We ordered another round and as usual, that opened up our mouths. I started. "Seems to me that we have a couple of weeks to decide, assuming they even want us. I would say that we should find out a little more about this connection between Belgium and this Katanga place. From what this Fetterton gal at the library said, it's now complicated, not only by fucking cannibals, but the U.N. and who the hell else?" I added that our parents would be impressed to think we were spending time in the library, assuming they didn't know why we were there. That prompted another swig, and a little laughter.

Mike brought up another point. "You know, what I have been thinking about is what a mercenary is like. I think about some French Foreign Legion guy, or a grizzled SS soldier left over from WW2. Shit, we are hardly past the pimple stage!" "True, but apparently taking head shots at 900 yards doesn't grow on trees", I said. "Problem is," Mike added, "Is that we might not be able to keep 900 yards between us and these fuckers! I don't want to end up in a copper pot!"

We drank more beer. "Well, Falques did say that they had a good safety record. Maybe he just wanted to see if we were serious," I said. "I suppose", said Mike. "Oh yeah, what did you think about new FN FAL rifles? And possibly a Mauser sniper rifle? You don't see that kind of stuff at the gun store! It sure doesn't seem like these guys have any financial problems, handing out $1000 rifles, plane tickets, uniforms or whatever, and flying around in private planes and all of that," I said. "How about we go by the gun store and see what those guys know. They read every gun magazine and book published. Then, tomorrow, we could get up fresh and see Ms. Fetterton." We agreed that was about as good a plan as any. I added that we had better update our parents so we do not get into a brouhaha with them. "One more beer and let's head for the shop."

The usual hangers on were on duty at Stewart's Gun Shop. I often wondered how Stew made a living because about all I have ever seen him sell was a box or two of ammo, while the 'customers' handled all of the new guns. We still had our grubby shooting clothes on and Stew remarked that we must have been having some fun today. It was all I could do to keep from telling him the real story. I was checking out the magazines and books and lo and behold, there was an article about 'Emerging Africa'. So I looked through it and there was a picture of Elisabethville, the capitol of the Katanga Province in the Congo. So I read more. The actual article was all about the emerging new countries, or better put, the old countries with new management. But this picture of Elisabethville sort of boggled my mind. When we thought of Africa, we thought of mud huts and thatched roofs, but this picture suggested a modern city. In just this little picture, I could see a big European justice building, a modern looking movie theatre, traffic lights, and paved streets congested with cars! In fact, at least in these pictures, it looked a lot better than Bakersfield! Mike had to remind me that the Belgians had been around since about 1850, and that in turn reminded me of text book images of Shanghai and Hong Kong, with all of the European pillared buildings and historical statues everywhere. It was true, the Europeans took their culture everywhere they went, and pretty much ignored the native system. However, that was about as far as the article went because they were selling guns, not culture. But every time we focused on this African possibility it seemed to get more complex. We fondled some new rifles and read an article about sniper kill at 1700 yards using the new .300 Winchester Magnum cartridge. I wondered if I could make a 1700 yard shot if I had something better than my 50-year old Springfield. After all, earlier today I had been off 2 inches at 900 yards. Then I had to remind myself that the paper target was stationary and there was no stress involved. For the first time, it registered that Mr. Falques was talking about shooting real people.

That evening, we got together with our parents and told them about Mr. Falques flying in with a two engine Cessna and the successful shooting exercise. We let it go at that, saying that Falques would get back to us in a couple of weeks. While our elders were impressed that there was apparently money behind all of this, I doubt if they took any of this very seriously.

# Chapter 6

It was back to Ms. Fetterton the next day. She was so excited about our returning that within a few minutes she had an entire stack of books and periodicals about Africa to look at. She might not have been so excited if she knew that we might be mercenaries shooting people. On the other hand, wasn't that what our government could be drafting us for in Viet Nam? In the event, it took us the better part of the day to grind through the material, and we checked out the more interesting books. As far as Katanga, we learned more about history than the current events. We were again surprised at the modern nature of Elisabethville, but in the outer reaches of the huge province, there were small towns and villages that looked like our old west with false store fronts and straight-as-an-arrow main dirt streets slicing the towns in two. There were Coca Cola and Fanta signs visible in pictures but the rest of the signs were in a foreign language, probably French. The literature talked a lot about the emerging self-rule countries and all of the impossible problems faced by new governments with virtually no education or skills. We read that in Nyasaland, to the south of Katanga, there was only one native medical doctor in an area with a population of seven million. Although we did not know (or cared) much about world events, it seemed like a ripe environment for exploitation.

Later in the afternoon, we stopped at Mike's house and his mother gave us a hand written note from Andy Schmidt who lived the next street over. "Come see me immediately!" Andy was one of those guys who never did anything 'immediately' and we could not imagine what this could be about. However, it was an urgent note, and we walked over and found him on the front porch drinking a beer. From the looks of the empties, it looked like he had been drinking for a couple of hours. "Hey Andy," I said "What's up?" Andy thanked us for coming over and tossed us each a beer from a plastic chest full of ice. "Take a look at this", and handed us an official looking letter.

*To: Mr. Andrew Schmidt*
*2208 Sunset Avenue*
*Bakersfield, California*

*Consistent with prior information furnished, you are directed to appear at the U.S. Army Induction Center in Los Angeles on January, 22, for a physical examination. Transportation is available by bus, to leave the Santa Fe terminal at 0730. Bring this letter, your draft card and any other I.D you have. Lunch will be provided and you will return by bus to the Santa Fe terminal by six P.M. the same day.*

*Claude Pitkin, Chief, Kern County Selective Service Administration.*

It was signed with an artistic flair by the crony in charge of the local draft board, a realtor who every young man in Bakersfield automatically despised. Mike said "Shit!" I added "Fuck!" Andy just looked bleary eyed and asked "What should I do?" "Whaddyado?" I asked. "You better be on that fucking bus!" Easy for us to say, but Mike was looking at me, obviously alarmed as hell, with both of us wondering if we had the same letter waiting for us at home. We carried on the discussion with Andy for another hour, avoiding our own mailbox but waiting until all of Andy's beer was gone. As we walked home, I said, "I cannot imagine Andy Schmidt carrying a rifle!"

We were very happy that we did not have a letter from this draft board asshole, but then the next question came up. It might be tomorrow. Or next week. Mike said it. "We need to get a hold of this Falques guy." As it was, the business card Falques had given to me had gone through the washing machine the next morning and was unreadable, but Mike's was still intact, so we sat down to work out our strategy. We knew that draft names were drawn on some sort of lottery basis and ours might not come up for six months. On the other hand, it might come up next week. We needed to talk to Falques or else return Ms. Fetterman's books and exchange them for information on Viet Nam.

What we did was to sketch out the questions that we wanted to ask Falques, rather than get lost in a fog of foreign government intrigue. So we started:

1.  Explain the draft situation. Let him know that if we did not settle this quickly, the draft board would settle it for us. When can he make a decision?
2.  Why is he even interested in a couple inexperienced young people? What is his rationale?
3.  What are the terms of the contract? He must have done many of these.
4.  What exactly are the duties? Combat? Guarding assets? Patrolling? What is the makeup of the working units?
5.  In case of injury or death, what are the benefits? How many westerner casualties has he experienced?
6.  When does the effort end? It looks like everyone is against what you are trying to do.
7.  All other things being equal, when would we start?
8.  Compensation

We looked at the list and had to admit that this was going to be a very tough conversation. In fact, it looked like we were trying to find an excuse to *not* go. We went over all of this with our parents and after two hours of questions from them, agreement was reached to at least get this information. Even if all was well, we still had the freedom to refuse. And go to Viet Nam! We made an ice tea, realizing we had to be on top of our game. Beer later. It was a toll free number, Friday and 1:00 P.M in Bakersfield. Even if we were calling New York, someone should answer. I dialed and after a couple of rings we had an answer. "Belgium Consulate, how can I direct your call?" a lady said in a kind of sexy French voice. I asked what city the consulate was in. "Los Angeles. Do you have a party you wish to talk with?" "This is Anthony Ward, and can I talk to Mr. Falques, who we met with on Thursday?" "Mr. Falques is in a meeting right now. I can have him call you back in about an hour." "OK, thank you," and gave her my number.

So, we had another hour to stew. My father had an extension phone in his bedroom and Mike and I could see each other between the bedroom and the living room. We also made sure no one was going to interfere with the call, which irritated my mother. We refined our list and did a 'what if?' session. What if he answered all of our questions satisfactorily? Would we commit? A beer would go really well, but we restrained ourselves. At 3:10 P.M. the phone rang. "Tony Ward here." "Yes, good afternoon Mr. Ward, this is Mr. Falques in Los Angeles. What can I do for you?" "I have Mike Genard on the line and something important has come up that we want to discuss with you. If we can get an answer to one question, then we have some other questions to ask." "Well, I am glad that you called because I was just discussing your situation with my superior. So go ahead." I explained the imminent problem with the draft. If we did not settle this right away, there would be no decision to make. I went on to say that if we actually got the notice for a physical, we would go in that direction. Until then, we were still free men. "I appreciate your allegiance to your country. I think that I can forward a proposal to you in the morning, special delivery. So proceed with your other questions."

He explained that we had an unusual situation. It was true that we were young and inexperienced, but that was the reason he had flown to Bakersfield to actually witness the shooting exercise. We claimed that we were marksmen and that is what he had advertised for. "I was very impressed with your shooting skills." With regard to the contract, he said "This is a standard contract, tailored to each individual. We have about 200 of these in effect. The contract is with The Katanga Government. It will specify compensation, travel costs, the chain of command and your duties. We are on a very short timeline here. I am afraid I have to say this will be a take it or leave it situation, but I also think that when you see it, you will realize the terms and conditions are very generous. Keep in mind, I am not the final approval here, but I can get this settled early tomorrow. We will expect your response by Monday." That answered many of the questions.

I asked "When would this start, and when would it end?" Falques explained that he would expect us to be in Brussels by the following Monday for a short orientation program, then on to Johannesburg, and onward to Elizabethville, which would be our base. "I can forward travel documents, tickets and a travel advance voucher next week. As we discussed in Bakersfield. The terms of the contract will be for six months on the ground, with allowance for travel time and expenses." The guy seemed so buttoned down that I was a little shy about compensation, but he seemed to take the question in stride. "I understand that you are a team with Mr. Genard, and we are prepared to honor that relationship. However, in our view, your marksmanship is what we are actually looking for and so there will be a differential in compensation. For you, it would be $350 U.S. dollars per month. For Mr. Genard, $300. The benefits would be identical."

I looked at Mike. Questions, I gestured? No, as he waved his hands…smooth ."I appreciate your response Mr. Falques. If you can get the proposal to us tomorrow, we will respond Monday" Falques said "One more thing Mr. Ward. Do either of you know of any physical disabilities or health problems you might have? If it is possible, we would like you to undergo a physical exam with your own physician, including a panel of ordinary blood tests, and any problems with medicine such as malaria prevention medication and other drugs for living in the tropics. If possible, bring the results with you and we will reimburse you for the costs. If not, we can handle the physicals here, but it is preferable that you do this in Bakersfield. Ordinarily all of this would take place over about 15 days but because of your draft situation, we need to compress some of these things." We signed off and breathed a giant sigh. Mike said "Where is the beer?"

At noon on Saturday we had a contract delivered to the front door.

# Chapter 7

The contract accurately reflected our discussion with Falques. Importantly, it made clear that we were working for the country of The Katanga, but that a number of expatriates, primarily Belgium army officers, acted as training personnel and participated in maneuvers. The arrangement seemed to parallel our planned involvement in Viet Nam and we had no problem accepting that arrangement. It was clear by now that the new country was not merely 'Katanga', but 'The Katanga'. Mike commented. "Do you suppose they think there might be more than one?" It was a long weekend. On Saturday I drove over to Dr. Stockton's office, the family doc on 19th Street and scheduled a physical for Mike and myself on Monday. The Doctor was in the hallway and saw me at the desk and gave me a 'thumbs up'. I supposed that stemmed from a visit I had made to Tijuana with four of my buddies, who decided that ladies and beer was more important than taking our final exams. The problem was, I brought back a very uncomfortable case of the clap, and the Doctor gave me some penicillin pills without notifying my parents. The next day the other three guys came down with the same problem, so I referred them to Dr. Stockton. The Doctor's remark to one of my friends was 'You must have been on the same vacation as Tony Ward!'

The library was open on Saturday and we checked out more books and magazines on The Congo, the UN/US/Russian involvement, all of which that ended up being quite a stack. We sat on our front porch and started reading and taking notes. Every once in a while we stopped and talked about something that seemed important. However, almost all of this material was either history or diplomatic stuff that was way over our heads. But there were two obvious camps: 1) Those who said 'hands off' The Congo, even though those giving the advice seemed to be the ones meddling, and 2) The thousands of Europeans in the Congo, many of whom had families living there for longer than most Americans had lived in the U.S. They wanted to stay. We concluded that we would be somewhere in the middle, between international concerns and the interests of settlers seeking some level of control over their future.

Our parents had two sessions with us, obviously trying to discourage an adventure, but at the same time saying that it was 'our decision'. By Sunday we were though reading and listening. If they would have us, we were going. On Monday, we called Falques and left a message with the same sweet-talking secretary, explaining that we accepted the contract and to please send the final documents as soon as possible. Further, we would bring the results of our physical and to tell us the address in Los Angeles where we should report. Later in the day we got a call from Falques. He confirmed our agreement and said that we should arrive at an address on South Broadway, which was the Belgium Consulate, with nothing more than our physical report, and an overnight bag. If we had decided to bring our side arms, to bring them and he would arrange for their shipment to Elizabethville. Further, he informed us that we would be on the Tuesday flight to Brussels via Sabena Airways, which is the Belgium National Airline. We would be staying in Brussels for a few days. Lastly, we should bring receipts for all of our costs, which he would reimburse. He asked us to immediately inform him if there was any sign of a medical problem, and that if we had passports, to bring them. However, if we did not have them, he would arrange travel documents. All in all, it seemed clear that Falques had done this many times, and had the entire process nailed down. Bakersfield would be history.

All of this led to two things: terror and relief! We had at least decided what to do. Now, it was time to settle our affairs in Bakersfield. I needed to take Loretta, my on-again-off-again girl friend to the movies and let her know what I was up to. That was not going to be easy. She seemed a lot more interested in a long term relationship than I. She had even mentioned marriage a time or two, and here I was, no job and an old car. "Africa !!!" I could almost hear her. "You guys are nuts!" We dropped by Andy Schmidt's house to tell him what we were up to, and he wanted to go too! But it was too late for him. He was going to Viet Nam. The physical exam went off with no problems but we still had no passports. My parents volunteered to drive us to Los Angeles as a final positive gesture, which we thought was very nice. They also had a barbecue for us in the backyard, and quite a few friends came by, amazed not only what we were going to do, but it was going to happen in two days! Loretta was there and already seemed to be warming up to Stan, a sometimes friend who lived in La Cresta, a high-end neighborhood. He also had a practically new convertible, so that loose end was resolved. No doubt, he was the better catch!

At that moment, we seemed more excited about an airline flight to Europe than our eventual assignment. We slept very little that night.

# Chapter 8

At 6:00 A.M on Tuesday, I had my overnight bag in the car and I was ready to go! Despite the sleepless night, I was so pumped up with adrenalin that I could not understand my parents, leisurely eating breakfast and reading the morning paper. And where the hell was Mike? We needed to get this show on the road! I walked out to the garage to make sure the cover was on my old Ford and saw that I had forgotten to disconnect the battery, so I handled that detail, and removed the keys. Even though there was no way my parents would ever drive the car, with all of its idiosyncrasies that seemed routine to me. Then Mike stuck his head in the garage and said, "Let's get going! My folks are out in the driveway." Wow! This was it! Mike's dad had a grim sort of look on his face but gave his son a big bear hug, and his mother gave him a big juicy kiss, which he reluctantly tolerated. "Be sure to send me you address when you get there." That was something I had completely forgotten about. How about correspondence from the draft board? Christ, they would probably send the Marines after me if they could not make contact. And how about our passports, which had not yet arrived? We put our handguns and overnight bags in the trunk and piled into the back seat. My dad got behind the wheel and backed the 58 Ford wagon out the driveway, probably thinking more about a trip to downtown L.A and back in a single day than what Mike and I were headed towards. "Hey dad, if you are having second thoughts about this we could catch the Greyhound Bus." My Mom quickly cancelled that idea and said "Oh no! We want you safely delivered to that consulate office. And we have a lot to talk about!" On the one hand, I think that they were truly apprehensive about our adventure, but on the other hand, they were probably a little pleased at seeing their son finally doing something other than drinking beer, racing cars and chasing girls.

And so it was, driving Highway 99 over the Ridge Route, hearing about brushing my teeth, keeping my underwear and socks clean, eating good food, and all kinds of other advice that I endured. Mike made a lot of faces and generally just looked out the window or dozed off. I finally dozed off too, mainly to cancel my mother's advice, but also to catch up a lack of sleep from last night. When I woke up were in the middle of the traffic on the unfinished Golden State Freeway near Glendale and feeling guilty about not taking the bus. Now my dad had to face the entire trip all over again on the way home. We got off the freeway on Spring Street, drove by the Los Angeles Times Building and jogged over to Broadway. My mother was at it again, saying that we were going into the consulate 'with our boys' just to make sure they were in good hands. Fortunately, my dad cancelled that thought. "Ethyl, they will be just fine. When they get to Brussels they can call collect and assure you of their safety. Besides, I have no idea where I could ever park the car in this traffic mess." So she started up again about our hygiene, staying away from 'naughty girls' and generally treating us like 12 year olds. About 12 blocks from the freeway, we were in a kind of seedy area that was transitioning from department stores to car lots and smaller buildings. And then, there it was! The flag of Belgium, an uncomplicated affair of three vertical stripes, black, yellow and red flying atop of a reasonably modern two-story building. We would become intimately familiar with that flag in the weeks to come. By now, my mother was sobbing and leaning on my dad's shoulder. We said we loved them and be careful driving home, and that we'd call from Belgium. With that, Mike and I hopped out of the car with our bags and the Ford began to move into traffic for the drive back to Bakersfield. I don't know about Mike but I developed a very hollow pit in my stomach. This was beyond yakking and planning. We were actually going to do this!

We straightened our hair and walked into the building, but

found only a directory on the wall. The Consulate of the Embassy of the Republic of Belgium, second floor. No elevator. We walked up the steps and found a locked glass door with a buzzer button and a speaker. We buzzed and explained through the speaker that we were Ward and Genard here on instructions from Mr. Falques. We were buzzed in and entered a pleasant reception area with a very attractive female sitting behind a counter. It was that person on the phone with the French accent, and she asked us to take a seat and she would be with us in a couple of minutes.

What ensued was what I suppose is termed a whirlwind. The lady, Marie Valcet told us that Falques was not there, having been called to the embassy in Washington; that she had all of our travel papers including tickets on this evening's Sabena flight from LAX. She took the handguns, gave us a receipt, and said the guns would be returned when we got to Belgium. We wondered about the physical we received, because we thought this could be a go-no go issue, but she looked over the papers from Dr. Stockton and seemed satisfied. Later, she said that they were mostly concerned about allergic reactions to the malaria medicine that would be provided, and gave each of us a small package of quinine pills, and told us that we should begin taking these this evening. Overall, Ms. Valcet seemed to be running the place, and had answers to everything we asked. She gave us a voucher from a restaurant down the street and told us that a van would leave the consulate at 4:00 P.M. for the airport. She added that there were two other men taking the same shuttle and the same flight. Therefore, we were free to wander around L.A. but to be back promptly at 4:00 P.M. The flight left at 8:00 P.M. But she said, "You never know about L.A. traffic." Finally, we would be met at the Brussels airport and transported to a military facility where we would receive uniforms, and several days of training. The training, she explained was mainly concerned with the political situation in The Katanga and some cultural issues, and that the actual military training would take place in Africa.

We had a big lunch and just killed time until about 3:30 when we wandered back to the consulate. On the sidewalk, there was a guy about 30 years old about to enter the building who was clearly offended and pissed off, saying, among other things, "Fucking misleading bastards" as he headed for the same door, uttering expletives as we walked towards the same office. He looked at us and said "You are fools if you go to Katanga!" Wow! "What's the problem?" "I thought I was going to do some guard duty, offer some protection services, maybe some patrolling of outlying towns. Now, I find out that the U.N has sent troops into Katanga to dismantle the government, and the Congo army is on the march to stop the secession, the Russians and America are involved..... want more? It sounds like a mix-master to me and I'd end up right in the middle of it." I looked at Mike and we both felt panic running through us. He had left out the cannibal problem. But had we been sold a bill of goods with a plane taking off in only a few hours? We followed him up the stairs and were buzzed in. This guy went right at Ms. Valcet. "I am not going. Please hand me my bag and scratch me off your list, and here are your papers and tickets." Startled, Ms. Valcet stood up and defended herself. "Mr. Austin, no one has deceived you. You were told that we were recruiting people to defend the new republic. You read and accepted the contract. Are you now saying that at the last minute you have had some kind of epiphany and blame the recruiter? This is extremely upsetting and it will be expensive to undo at this hour." "Well, I don't give a shit. You are placing people in the middle of some kind of civil war and that is not what I signed up for. Give me my bag and here are your papers," and tossed them onto her desk. Mike and I stood a few feet away, agog at what we were witnessing. She reached behind a partition and put a small bag on the counter. Flushed and angry, she said, "Is that all?" "Damn right," and he stalked out. I was wondering what an epiphany was.

Ms. Valcet looked at us, breathing hard and said, "I am very sad that you had to see this. To the best of our knowledge, no one has misled that person or anyone else. She also got prettier the angrier she became." Mike said "Don't worry about it, we're OK." Much later, we realized that we should have had a longer conversation with this guy. However, we grabbed our bags, admired her profile, and walked downstairs.

Waiting by the curb with a small bag was apparently the other person waiting for the van. We introduced ourselves and I said, "Looks like we're going to the same place." Art Stepan was a good-looking guy, well-tanned and looking like he spent a lot of time outdoors. He was about 6'2", slender in Levis, a polo shirt and tennis shoes. As a nondescript van pulled up, he said he was from Bishop, California. Maybe it was just my lack of confidence, but he clearly looked down on us, as if to say "What are you kids doing here?"

On the Harbor Freeway, Stepan said he thought there would be four of us, and Mike explained the scene we had just witnessed with Ms. Valcet. That surprised him since he thought he had a clear idea of what we were going to be doing. I asked him if he knew about the cannibals! "Yep, but Falques had mentioned that they had spears and bows and arrows and we would have automatic weapons." He just laughed it off. Still, we wondered what in the world that Austin guy had stumbled in to. The traffic was a bitch, and it took 45 minutes before we started west on Century Blvd. Thirty minutes later the van pulled up before the International Terminal that according to the signs, serviced about 30 airlines. One of them was Sabena. The driver dropped us off on the crowded sidewalk into a crowd milling around, all seemingly just as nervous and lost as we were, and then he drove into the crush of traffic.

The three of us stuck together and generally just followed the signs and the crowds. We checked in, and found that we would be stopping in New York for fuel required for the Atlantic crossing but we would stay onboard. We went thru a passport check and surprisingly, the consulate paperwork did the job. Stepan had a passport and a glance at it showed that he had been to many, many countries. We boarded the Boeing 707-320 at 7:30, and at exactly 8:00 P.M. accelerated down the runway and left the ground at an astounding rate of climb.

# Chapter 9

It was mid-morning as we descended to the Brussels International Airport. The flight had been cramped and long, but the stewardesses did a good job of keeping us fed and the drinks flowed in large quantities. There was an announcement that we would land at the Brussels Airport/National Zaventer, whatever Zaventer meant, in ten minutes. Please buckle up. Throughout the night the three of us alternatively dozed and speculated. Dozed and speculated. Maybe this would be just a big vacation at over $300 per month. Or would we get into a firefight and die? And eaten. Why hadn't we heard about all of the intrigue that the complaining guy had brought up? Because we only read the sports page? Because he was just nuts? We learned more about Art who had been in the final days of the Korean War, and when he got out of the Army, he just bummed around Southeast Asia. His jobs all involved firearms, training paramilitary groups, acting as a guard in some obscure country I never heard of, and finally returning to Bishop, bored as hell. In the end, we just fell asleep.I was happy to stretch out of my pretzel configuration, gather up my bag, and join Mike and Art as we began deplaning. We had no baggage to pick-up, so we cleared customs and headed for passport control, which again proved to be a cinch with the papers provided to us. Then we were at the arrival lobby where we immediately saw a guy with sign on a stick that said 'Stepan-Ward-Genard-Austin'. Obviously, he had not received the memo about Austin. Mike said, "This is alright. I had no idea where we were supposed to go when we got off the plane." The greeter was a very short 50-ish man with a cigarette dangling from his mouth who spoke no English. We turned the sign and fingered a cross mark on Austin's name, which he seemed to accept. All we had to do was follow.

We walked to a small van, threw our bags in and took a seat. We were on the east side of Brussels and had driven only about a mile when we pulled up to an old wooden building, which was flying the Belgium flag. The driver pointed at the building and said "German Barracks." After that slick airplane ride, it was a real comedown to realize that out temporary home would be a leftover Nazi warehouse or whatever. A uniformed person appeared at a door, walked over to the van and said "Please follow". Inside, another uniform checked us in, gave us some paper work that looked like a schedule and showed us the old building. It was not so bad on the inside, having a small canteen and cafeteria attached to a long hallway to a meeting room, and what looked like sleeping quarters. He opened numbers 23 and 24 that each contained two beds, a small dresser and a clothes rack. Both rooms were vacant, so Mike and I threw our bags onto the beds, and Art took the room next door. The uniform said "Toilets at end of hall. Welcome to Belgium." He gave us a mimeographed sheet that provided a dinner schedule for 7:00 P.M. and mandatory attendance in meeting room #1 at 8:00 P.M., interesting because we found that there was only one meeting room. We nodded and he turned and left. I assumed that until dinnertime, we were free to do whatever we wanted, but since we were in the middle of a field with no transportation, there was really nothing to do except read the literature they gave us and then crash. The effects of jet lag, a new phenomenon for us, was beginning to set in, we being nine hours ahead of Bakersfield time. So we lay down on the thin mattresses and slept.

Around 3:00 P.M. I started rummaging around in my bag, which woke Mike. We wandered to the end of the hall and found not only toilets but also a community shower, with fresh towels, soap and shaving materials, so we took full advantage. During our showers, another guy walked in, stripped and showered, mentioning something in a language we didn't understand. We put on the same old clothes and I could hear my mother telling us about clean underwear and all of that. 'That' seemed like a year ago on another planet. We wandered around the barracks and just killed some time. We ran into other people, all older than us, and listened to them swapping stories and lies. Around 6:30, we went to the cafeteria, which looked like it was set up for around 50 people. At 7:00 P.M, a couple of waiters started serving food. No choices here...you get what they served or you did not eat. However, the food was not too bad. Some kind of lamb and potatoes, some carrots, and a foo-foo dessert. Interestingly, wine was served, which I guessed was a European tradition. In fact, even when we were in Africa wine was served except when we were in the field. After dinner, the room was rearranged, and a podium was brought in. As we started, I counted 37 other people.

It began with a Mr. Thomas Keith, from the Belgium Foreign Affairs Ministry. He wore a suit and tie, and seemed to be well informed. He welcomed us in clear English and said that we would be here about four or five days. The point of this orientation was to explain what we were doing in The Katanga, and to understand some of the friction points, cultural issues and the purpose of our group. His first point was an apparent stunner for some. "You are not working for the Belgium government. You are working for The Katanga government. If you question that, you should take another look at your contract." Actually, Falques had made that very clear to us, but some of the men looked shocked. "You need to understand that Belgium supports The Katanga's secession from the Congo. That support, briefly, involves professional government support to The Katanga bureaucracy, external governmental support in the United Nations, and military advisory support, the latter of which is the role of this group. However, it is a delicate balance, and all of us are diplomats in one form or another. You are expected to behave in a professional advisory role. As you will learn, advice doesn't always end in talk. On occasions, you will find yourself in a combat role. This is a very complex issue. Even though it is very clear that the Congo is totally ill-equipped to govern 2 ½ million square kilometers of land, the bulk of other nations nevertheless oppose the creation of

The Katanga. This is a very hot political issue. How you folks handle your assignments will, in part, determine how The Katanga washes out in the long run. While there are many nations sympathetic to the secession, not one of them, including Belgium, has yet officially recognized the new State." That boggled my mind. Belgium was organizing all of this but had not yet recognized the new country?

"I want to explain just a little about the many factions you will encounter. Generally speaking, there is antipathy towards any white presence in Africa. On the other hand, we see this as an opportunity to create a partnership resulting in a colorless country. There will be grudging respect for your skills but you may expect doubt about your intentions. That is realistic. We have been there for 120 years and have not done well at all regarding the education of blacks.There are indigenous tribes in The Katanga dominated by the Balubas in the north, numbering about 750,000 to 1,000,000. They are not centrally controlled but operate semi-cooperatively region-to-region. They generally object to any white presence. However, at times they can be cooperative and at other times, they are downright hostile. They are primitive people who technically are in the 1700s. But do not....ever...underestimate them. Then there is the Congo Army itself. This is a rag tag, undisciplined bunch are centered in the capitol at Leopoldville. They and their leaders also object to the secession. And they too have advisors, Russians for the most part, who see The Congo as an opportunity. The United Nations is opposed to the secession, and has a multi-national force present in parts of The Katanga but have orders to only attempt keeping the peace and currently regard the secession as an internal matter. That is naïve, but that, at least for now, is their position, even as many countries want to use these troops in combat against us."

"There are indigenous tribes to the east from Uganda, Rwanda and Ethiopia who advocate an all-black Africa but these people are not actively engaged in our affairs, at least not yet". This guy was feeding us these kernels of information off the top of his head, but I wished we had some pencils and paper to take notes. Each sentence contained all-new information that had to be digested in order to ask questions and understand. He continued, "Now against all of this we actually have some friends". This brought a roll of laughter and relief to an increasingly intense presentation. "To our south we have Northern Rhodesia, Rhodesia, Nyasaland and of course South Africa. However, aside from South Africa, all of the other countries are on track to become independent countries, ready-or-not. Their support will be short-lived. Colonialism is over. In particular, America pushes this independence issue very hard. They take the view that World War Two was not fought so that European countries could restore their domination over other people. Their president, Eisenhower, was particularly hard on the French and is determined to get them out of Indo- China and West Africa. We in Belgium assume that the basic reason for this stems from France's poor performance in the war. On the other hand, it may simply be an anti-colonialism attitude which is understandable, given America's history. Where the new American president fits into this is a critical concern.We in Belgium recognize all of this as an uphill battle. Today, we wish that we had started this effort of independence twenty years ago. However, it is surely worth the effort now. Another ally you will have is the Belgium people themselves. Many of these people consider themselves settlers. Many have parents and grandparents born in The Katanga and have been here long before Americans settled their west."

"I know that in one form or another, you are warriors. However, our success will depend in large part on not only your military skills but also seeing this situation through the eyes of the native people. Now I will stop. Stand up and stretch your legs and I will answer questions informally for the next 30 minutes or so". I looked at Mike and Art. This was a lot to digest.

# Chapter 10

The next morning, we entered the cafeteria at 7:00 A.M talking about last evening's lecture. After the political person left, we had a person talk to us about The Katanga's history and climate. Included were all of the great references to malaria, leeches, giant ants and yep…cannibals! On the door where we entered the dining area was a note stating that breakfast today would be 'Cooked English Breakfast.' That turned out to be half- cooked bacon, watery scrambled eggs, and a stack of toast. Mike commented, "It's nourishment." At 8:00 A.M. the dishes were cleared and a man pushed the podium in place and began talking about today's agenda. "First of all, you will line up at room #3 and the quartermaster will measure you up for uniforms." This came as excellent news because our clothes were getting ripe after a transatlantic flight and two nights in Belgium. "You will then be divided into groups depending on your specialty and assigned to a staff member. You will be tested against your specified specialty." That created a lot of mumbling. What if we failed? "We will then meet here after lunch and I'll give you the afternoon schedule." More mumbling as we headed to room #3, down the hallway.

The 'room' was actually a counter about 50' long, behind which were shelves of clothes and other gear. There were five people serving all of this, so it did not take long. We received a large camouflaged canvas bag, and in it were six changes of underwear, socks, tee shirts, shaving material, soap, a toothbrush and other bathroom stuff. That completed the 'one size fits all' part of the exercise. We were then measured for pants, shirts, jackets, gloves, boots and whatever else was necessary, given a ticket and told to come back after lunch to get the rest of our allotment. It was well organized and looked as if this had been repeated hundreds of times.

A guy at the end of the room called out that when we were done, to come to a warehouse that was actually an extension of the barracks, to receive our 'hardware,' and any stuff we were unable to bring on-board the plane. This was arranged in a similar manner as the clothing, with five columns. When we got to the counter, our eyes lit up. "OK, Mr. Genard. Here is a checklist that I will complete as I give it to you. You will be responsible for this hardware so be sure you are actually receiving this material as I check it off. 1) 1 FN FAL assault rifle, caliber .308 NATO with cleaning kit; 2) five 20 round magazines for the FAL." I was watching Mike as he was receiving all of this and placing it in his open canvas carrier. Like a kid at Christmas. The FN FAL rifle was a dream! The finest military rifle made, and by coincidence, made in Belgium! The person droned on to Mike as if he was dispensing potatoes. "Three, one bayonet and scabbard for the FAL. 4) One knife and scabbard, 5) one emergency first aid kit. Now let's see. I also have a Browning Hi Power pistol to return to you." The Browning had a tag on it signed by that nice looking Ms. Valcet back in Los Angeles. "Mr. Genard, please stay here until I deal with Mr. Ward because you two will have to go to another officer, who dispenses all of the special equipment." I was next. I got exactly the same equipment plus my P.38 and was told to accompany Mike to Mr. Jolly's shop. So we took an approved requisition form to a small shop in the next room. It had a sign on the door that said 'K. Jolly, Chief Quartermaster'. We went into the room and took a seat at a long table. We could look an adjoining door that opened to a work shop area. Jolly turned and saw us and came into the room and looked at our requisition form and introduced himself. "Glad to see you men. I was wondering who was going to receive this amazing stuff. What I have here is some special equipment that is needed for your specialty. You are instructed not to open these packages until you meet with your assigned NCO who will explain the contents, but I guarantee that you will be pleasantly surprised. However, even if you can't see the contents you must sign for them." I supposed that was just a part of the bureaucracy. Sign for something that you couldn't see. The form said: Ward: Special Mauser Rifle. It was in a semi-hard plastic container, weighed about 20 pounds and had a stenciled stamp on it 'Mauser Waffenfabrik, Oberndorf, Germany.' I nervously signed the form and handed it back to Jolly but I was about ready to wet my pants. What could be better than a new FAL? Then he turned to Mike and gave him a large cardboard box that was thoroughly sealed. It too had a stencil on it from Oberndorf, Germany and Mike signed the same kind of form and gave it back, who remarked that our assigned staff member will explain all of this to you. He shook our hands and said "Good luck to you." I sort of wondered what that meant. Did our assignment now rely on good luck? But we couldn't wait to get into those packages.

We stood and I said "Hey Mike… this is fucking for real! What do you suppose is in this case? And look! Here is my P.38!" I thought if only guns could talk. The P.38 had made it through the war, on to the U.S., and now back across the Atlantic not more than one hundred miles from Germany. After about ten minutes a guy came over to us and introduced himself as Sargeant Steven Piquart. He was dressed in full camouflaged military garb with staff sargeant chevrons on his sleeve with 'Piquart' on a patch over his right pocket. Sargeant Piquart was a tall, slender person, about 6'3" and apparently very fit. We shook with a firm grip and he said "Very glad to meet you fellows. We have a special assignment, so get dressed in your new clothes and gather all of your hardware, and I'll meet you down the hall in room #6." The other guys, including Art, were not going anywhere else, so we were a curiosity.

After dressing in all of the stiff new clothes and boots in our room, we gathered up the rifles, the plastic cases, knives, bayonets all of which seemed to weigh about 100 pounds. I was wondering about humping around Africa with this load when you added bedrolls, food, canteens etcetera. We entered the small room the size of our bedroom, furnished with three chairs and a table, and deposited all of our stuff on the table. Piquart said, "What I want to do here is to familiarize you with the special equipment we have here. After lunch, I want you to take all of these goods and return to your room, read all of the manuals, and get some rest. You may not realize it, but you are suffering from your travel through many time zones. I want you to be fresh and ready in the morning, because after breakfast we will travel to a shooting range at another location. This is a crucial exercise for you because you have probably figured out by now that you have been recruited for a unique task. Again, acquaint yourself with the equipment and the manuals and get some rest. Also, I want you to try walking around a bit in your boots and speak up if any of the clothes do not fit. If you have any problems, now is the time to get back to the quartermaster for a better fit."

With that, he took a razor knife from his pocket and opened the cardboard box they had given Mike. Inside, there were three more cardboard boxes that were opened, revealing the contents, carefully wrapped in plastic. As Piquart unwrapped the plastic, Mike became almost apoplectic! What we had were three scopes like we had never seen before. Piquart explained. "The first here is a range finder. This will tell directly the distance to your target." Wow, I thought. I had heard about these things but had never actually seen one. Mike put the device to his eye but Piquart admonished him in a friendly manner: "Not now, Mr. Genard, we'll get into that tomorrow." Then he unwrapped the second and third devices. "The first here is a 50x scope intended for narrow, detailed long range vision. The third device is a conventional 10x30 scope for normal wider field of vision, the same as you would find on a normal rifle. Obviously, your job will be to find a target, detail the target and obtain the range of the target." I noticed that all three scopes had 'Zeiss' inscribed on them. There was no Taiwanese crap here! He then pulled out a wire contraption and mounted all three devices into this device, all very compact.

Piquart continued. "This will allow you to move your vision between all three parameters: wide distance, narrow and detailed vision, and actual distance by moving only an inch or two." Mike blurted "Great! Outstanding." It was now obvious that Falques had cleared us as snipers! I could almost taste whatever was in my sealed case.

At first, I was disappointed. It was a beautiful gun but it was bolt action. However, lifting it from the case I could see that it was no ordinary gun. It carried the Mauser banner on the receiver, and had been fitted with a heavy fluted 26" barrel with a muzzle brake and a bipod. The stock was beautifully oiled with a soft, dull finish and fitted with a thick, soft butt pad. The rifle itself was finished in some kind of dull Parkerized coating. I rolled the rifle over in my hand and looked at the chamber markings. This was no .308! Inscribed was .300 Winchester Magnum. Piquart said "I see that you have noticed the caliber. The .300 Winchester Magnum is effective to 2000 yards" That just boggled my mind. All of this was becoming brain overload to me. New FALs, scope equipment, and best of all, the Mauser. Thousands of dollars were being spent here and I wondered if we were worth it! Or better, just what miracles were they counting on to justify all of this? Piquart added the icing on the cake. "A new cartridge is currently being developed in Finland, the .338 Lapua, and we will move to that round in about a year. It is effective to over 2000 yards with less drop than the .300 Win Magnum. But it will require an entirely different action." Unbelievable.

We shook hands, gathered all of our gear, agreed to meet right after breakfast in the morning, and told that in the meantime, get some rest and familiarize ourselves with all of these new Christmas presents! After depositing the new hardware in our room, we went to the cafeteria. We met Art and compared notes on the stuff we had received. He too was headed to a range tomorrow but with a separate advisor, and with ten other recruits. While eating lunch, a wave of tiredness came over me and I thought that Piquart was absolutely right. We needed some rest before handling all of this gear and I did not want to be tested or graded when I was bone tired. I thought that the clothes were OK and the boots very stiff, but I also figured that all of this stuff would break in. Mike had a problem with his shirt fitting but was back from the quartermaster's room in about ten minutes, satisfied.

Lying on our beds, I said, "This Piquart guy seemed like a good egg, and pretty much treated us as equals." "I agree," said Mike. "Have you noticed that some of these other people have looked at us like what the hell are you kids doing here?" I had seen that attitude too, but in fact, I wondered myself what I was doing here. I rolled over and instantly fell asleep and missed dinner.

# Chapter 11

I was up at 0500 and starving. I headed for the showers, shaved, and was back in the room dressing when Mike rolled over and said "What the fuck are you doing?" "Hey Mike! Get up and let's get organized! This is the big day. I finished dressing, lay down on the bed, and started to re-read manuals as Mike wandered down the hall, grumbling about the early hour. At breakfast, I noticed something was different. It wasn't the watery eggs or the half-cooked bacon either. I looked around and made a head count of the group we had flown in with. There were 6 missing. I leaned over and talked softly to Mike. "What do you suppose happened? All we've done is gather gear and attend a couple of classes. Somehow we are being graded without even doing anything." Later, Sargeant Piquart told us it was attitude. A few of the recruits were acting as though they were bored and not paying attention. Most of the recruits were from northern Europe, and seemed to look down on the Belgians, and that did not go over well. Two people including a Canadian just quit. This guy had a real problem on his hand as he was informed that he would pay for his own way back to Canada. Later in the day, the Canadian apparently re-thought the whole package and was re-admitted, but was told that he would be under close observation. Later, all but one 'of the missing' apparently received 'counselling' and came back on board, giving us 36. What the Belgians clearly did not want were any smart asses or know-it-alls. After breakfast, we were told to stay in place and a Belgium officer came to the head of the room and with no sound system boomed, "I want you all to keep in mind that this is very serious business. We are treating you with respect, but I want you to know that this is no vacation. You are adults. You have a very short time to get ready for the trip to Africa. Make sure that you conduct yourselves with that in mind. Have a good day" and he stalked out of the room.

We hadn't observed any poor behavior, probably because most of the time we were scared shitless. But clearly, there were observers who were trained in the art of attitude and they were not taking any crap. We went back to our room, rolled up our civilian clothes and put them in a bag. We did not know about taking our pistols but we put them in our equipment pouch. By 0745 we took a leak and walked to the front of the building. And there was Sargent Piquart by some kind of a station wagon with a driver at the wheel. "Good morning gentlemen. It looks like a good day for shooting." He got into the passenger seat, we followed into the back seat, the driver fired up the diesel engine, and we headed west. Everything was quiet for a while, but Piquart asked us about our equipment kit, if we understood the manuals, and if we had rested well. Mike nodded affirmatively and I said everything made sense but I explained that the Mauser manual was in German. He chuckled at that but I followed by saying, "But there were a lot of pictures and it all made sense."

We drove through the countryside on an expressway for about an hour, which by my calculation was a good part of the way across Belgium. A large facility loomed ahead and it soon was clear that we were headed to a modern-looking military base. We entered through a guarded gate, and were waved through after looking at the Sargeant's I.D. The guard did not even look at us.We headed around a group of buildings and out to an open field which turned out to be the rifle range. There were some shooting benches, and a variety of tables lined up. The place was deserted except for us. We got out and began to unload our canvas bags on the tables. Piquart then said, "OK, let's take our inventory. Mr. Ward, you place you items on this table and Mr. Genard, you settle in over here. Piquart went to Mike's table and looked things over. "Oh, I see that you have a Browning High Power. Good choice! It was made in Belgium! So let's get the pistols squared away first. Mr. Ward, I see you have an old P.38 . Not so good! It was

made in Germany. We didn't come out very well in that skirmish."
We all laughed at that. This guy had a good sense of humor, given that
the Germans had overrun Belgium in two World Wars. Something a
little more than a 'skirmish!' He placed the pistols in front of himself
and in about two minutes he had broken them down, inspected them
and then instructed us to put them back together. This guy was very
cool. No challenge. We had them back together in another minute!
Very good, men! He reached into a bag and gave us each a box of 9mm
ammo and told us to place the ammo and the pistols back in our bags.
"We're not here to shoot pistols, but I feel certain they will serve their
purpose." Whatever that is, I thought.

"Let's deal with Mr.Genard and his FN first. Please go ahead and
load your magazines." He provided a bucket of military grade ammo
and Mike proceeded to load cartridges into the 20 round magazines,
which took a few minutes. While waiting, Piquart pulled out two
boxes of competition grade .300 Winchester Magnum cartridges and
placed them on my table. Back to Mike. "OK, Mr.Genard we like
to keep the loaded magazines in the canvas bandoleers so go ahead
and do that. Piquart picked up one of the loaded magazines and was
apparently satisfied. While this was going on, I noticed the driver
setting up targets down range. These looked like permanent pop-up
target frames arranged at 100-yard intervals starting at 200 yards and
then starting again at 400 yards and continuing down range until the
driver was almost out of sight. The paper targets were then attached
to these frames. "OK, load a magazine." Mike inserted a magazine.
And Piquart nodded. "Now chamber a round." Mike did that and
placed the FAL on safety. "Very good Mr. Genard, for placing the gun
on safety." Piquart took the gun from Mike and said, "I want to point
out some things here. This selector switch is used to change the semi-
automatic firing to full automatic. Do you gentlemen understand?"
We nodded that we understood but Mike said, "We have never fired
a full automatic rifle." "That is OK. I will demonstrate. But in real
terms, there will not be many times when full auto is appropriate.

You will burn up huge quantities of ammo, you will be unlikely to hit very much because the rifle will 'climb' on you and unless you are shooting pigeons or in a very, very close fire fight, the selector should stay on semi auto."

The sergeant handed out ear protection muffs, made sure that the driver and his helper were off the range and held Mike's FAL to his shoulder. He placed the selector on 'auto' and pressed the trigger. The gun rattled out 10 rounds in about 1 second and it was now aimed up at a 45-degree angle as he applied the safety. He said "Now you try it and he gave the rifle back to Mike. Try and keep the rifle flat." I could see that Mike was nervous as hell but he was also a smart guy. He put the rifle to his shoulder, took the gun off safety, leveled the gun to the first target, sighted through the iron sights and fired. The gun climbed through another 10 rounds in a second. Not quite as bad as Piquart had done, but Mike was obviously holding on very tight. Piquart said nothing but picked up a hand held telescope, looked at the first target and said "Mr. Genard, you have one hit! So tell me the lesson." "There is no doubt. Conserve your ammo, shoot semi auto unless maybe you have a whole herd of enemies coming at you ten yards away." The Sargeant clapped! "Good response."

Mike removed the now-empty magazine and placed it on the table. "Now I want to show you one other shooting lesson that is less obvious. You see that a set of five special targets have been set across the range, anywhere from 50 to 100 yards out. Those are fresh cardboard man-sized targets on those stands. I want you to take one shot at each target as fast as you can. Go ahead and load another magazine." Mike loaded a magazine, charged a cartridge into the chamber and placed the gun on 'safe'. He checked to ensure it was on 'semi'. "I like your safety habits Mr.Genard. The range is clear. Fire when ready. This should take no more than five seconds." That was unexpected. Not only were we shooting for accuracy but time as well. Move right, sight, fire, move right, sight, fire, move right, sight, fire, move right, sight, fire. Stop. Five rounds. Mike pulled the rifle to his chest, placed it on safety and returned to the bench. "That was good discipline, Mr. Genard. You planned five shots and that is what you did. You did not get carried away with the trigger. You constantly moved to the right and did not focus on one target twice. The problem with speed is that is that not only does accuracy suffer, but it could mean that the enemy doesn't go down....he shoots back. Now let us see what you accomplished." The driver went to the cutouts and yelled back "Number 1, one hole, Number 2, no holes, Number 3, one hole, Number 4 one hole, Number 5, one hole." "So you see, Mr. Genard, four holes, five shots. Not perfect but very good. And, you did keep a pretty good pace at 8 seconds." For the first time I saw Piquart looking at a stopwatch! Mike looked dejected. "Now let me show you the problem. Part of this is that you chaps have been using bolt action guns and not concentrating on rapid fire." Piquart seemed to know more about us that we thought. "Now let me have the rifle and I'll show you another approach." The driver placed tape over the four holes Mike had made. "The problem is, especially at short distances, is that when you initially shoot using the sights, then move to target #2, you will always over shoot the target and have to move back. That takes time. It confuses." He gave the stopwatch to Mike and told him to take time.

Piquart stood, aimed the rifle and looked back to us. Notice that I am now sighting through the sights but only for the first round. Then it will be over the sights, not through them. Fire, fire, fire, fire fire. Mike called out "Five seconds." "OK, now let's see about the accuracy. The driver called out "A hole in each target." Piquart looked at us and said, "The idea here is to sight the first target and immediately turn your head to the second, shoot where you are looking, and turn your head to the next target and shoot where your head and eyes already are. Use your head and your eyes, not the sights. Now, Mr. Genard, you try it. It will take some time to get this down, because it is counter-intuitive, but at short range, this is how it's done."

Piquart took the stopwatch back while Mike inserted a fresh

magazine. Placed the gun on safe, and stood and aimed. Charge the first cartridge. Off safety. Fire, fire, fire, fire, fire until five rounds were gone. It was amazing when you know what to look for. You could see Mike's head move simultaneously with shooting the second cartridge at each target. "Excellent, Mr. Genard. You are a very good student. That took 6 seconds. Now let's see about accuracy". The driver called back five hits. "Sensational, Mr. Genard!" Mike had a big smile on his face and Piquart joked, "Now which one of you is the shooter?" We all laughed, but the Sargeant quickly became serious. "You see, it's Mr.Ward here who is the sniper, and Mr. Genard is the spotter. But it does not always work out that way. If the enemy finds where you are, and charges you, both of you better be prepared for some close range shooting, and that is the point of this. You did well, Mr. Genard." Mike beamed. I could see that he loved this Sargeant.

We set up the scopes on the ground. We knew that we would not be shooting from benches, and so we got on the ground, just like we did with the rabbits. Mike had spent a couple of hours yesterday fooling around adjusting the scopes, quickly moving from one parameter to another. "OK to load ?" I asked. He nodded affirmatively but added "One step at a time Mr. Ward." The Mauser did not have a detachable magazine so I turned the bolt upwards and back, took five cartridges from the box and loaded the internal magazine, shoved the bolt forward, and placed it on safety. God, this thing was smooth. I looked back at Piquart and he nodded. This was a different thing than what Mike had gone through. If I took more than one shot per target, I probably would fail. I adjusted the huge 50x scope. Mike was doing the same thing but he had other responsibilities. He had to call out the range, which would cause me to adjust the vertical alignment of the scope in order to compensate for the bullet drop past about 400 yards. Actually, the way this scope worked was that there were a series of horizontal lines below the absolute the cross hairs, each at 100 yards beyond the initial 400 yards. Therefore, if Mike called out 500 yards, I knew I had to sight a line below the absolute cross hairs. That was simply the ballistics of the .300 Winchester Magnum, specifically calibrated into this scope. We had a card that documented exactly the bullet drop at different ranges, but that was more for the FALs because in the case of the Mauser, the scope did it for you. Mike also had other responsibilities. He had to give me left-right adjustments due to wind, which was a visual thing that this hi tech machinery could not help. And he had to be looking around as I shot to find the next target. His equipment helped a lot.

"Are you guys ready to do a short test?" said Piquart. "Mike, will you use your range finder and call out the yardage to each target?" I thought that might be unnecessary because we thought the targets were spaced at roughly 100-yard intervals. He began. 400 yards, 500 yards, 550 yards. 650 yards. 725 yards, 800 yards. I asked "What happened to the evenly spaced targets?" "The reason is that you have to trust your spotter. We deliberately spaced the targets at odd intervals. Trust your spotter. Trust Mike." Lesson learned. It also registered that Mike was now Mike, not Mr. Genard! I liked that.

"OK, shooter, shoot at the first target just to zero in our equipment. Shoot three rounds. Mike called out "No wind" At 400 yards, the target's chest filled the cross hairs of the 50-x scope. Fire. Fire again. Fire again. It was a set trigger, meaning that there were actually two triggers, one to 'set' the trigger and the other to fire. The second trigger had a pull of about one pound, meaning that about all you had to do was caress the trigger. It was just fantastic. Not gritty and undependable like the old Springfield. The driver walked out to the target and came back stating, "There was only a single hole!" I knew what had happened and so did Piquart. The driver thought that I had missed the entire target twice. Not so, three bullets made the same hole. A hole within a hole. The single hole was an inch left-of-center, and I adjusted the scope accordingly. Of course, this was only 400 yards. "Great Shooting" encouraged Piquart, although we both knew that this was just the start.

Piquart told the driver to adjust the targets at odd distances past

400 yards. Through the scope, I could see what he was doing but Piquart said nothing, trying to test us. "Mr.Ward, please take head shots from this point. I nodded and loaded the magazine with five more rounds. I was feeling good about this. "Are you ready, Mike?" I asked. "Yep, but I see wind in the grass at around 700 yards, left to right, so stay alert to that. I reminded Mike that there were not an infinite number of horizontal lines, or elevation correction lines on the scope, so not to get too scientific. Even with all of this equipment, I would have to extrapolate between 100-yard elevation lines. I made sure the bipod was secure and the safety was off and said, "Let's go!" "525 yards, no wind." Fire. God that trigger was sweet and the butt pad and muzzle brake softened everything. This was not a road race. This was slow and deliberate. "625 yards, wind from left, minimal" I sighted the elevation recticle down a space, moved the gun a hair to the left. Fire. "700 yards, wind 5 per" Adjust elevation a half a hair. Fire. 850 yards, no wind. Adjust elevation 1 hair. Fire. 950 yards wind five left. Adjust elevation. Quite a bit more drop at this distance. Compensate for wind. Fire. Exercise over.

The driver was in the SUV was heading out on the range. After all, the last target was well over half a mile away. "Looks good Tony!" Wow! I guess I had joined the club. I was now Tony.

A few minutes later, the SUV stopped at the benches and we checked the targets. The first thing I checked was to see if there was a hole in each target. Then we checked further. There was a hole in each target at about the forehead level. The last one, the 950-yard target, had a hole in the guy's mouth. "Tony, that is incredible shooting! Both of you have done very well. I am proud of you!"

On the way back, Piquart gave us another tip that should have been obvious but it had gone right by Mike and I. "At extreme distances, let's say for argument about 1500 yards, the bullet actually gets to the target about 2 seconds before the sound. It's just like lightning and thunder. Light moves a lot faster than sound, and in our case, the bullet moves faster than the speed of sound. So in this extreme situation, you might be able to get off a second shot before the targets know about the first one. Oh, they will see a guy crumple, but where did the shot come from? So it's always a good idea to have a second shot identified by Mike. You'll have about a 2 second lead." Mike looked at me and simply said "No shit!" I said, "Maybe that explains why the rabbits back in Bakersfield didn't react to the first shot. They just thought that the first guy had indigestion or something!" That brought on a laugh, and Piquart said "I have some more things to show you." More?

# Chapter 12

On the way back to the base, Piquart, with a wink, asked the driver to make a 'detour'. In a few minutes we pulled up to a pub and Piquart said, "I'm buying'. The Belgium beer was stout and wonderful. Mike and I consumed two tall ones and never felt better. A 950 yard shot, two beers, and now we were on a first name basis with our advisor. Life was good! During dinner that evening, Sergeant Piquart embarrassed us by holding up the 950-yard target, a man with a hole in his mouth. Everyone clapped and from that moment on, we were considered varsity players.

After dinner Mr. Campbell, the person who seemed to be in control of overall logistics, gave a short talk and laid out the schedule for the remainder of our stay. He reminded us that the purpose of our stay in Belgium was not to try to make us a cohesive unit, because in The Katanga we might very well be broken into other groups. But he emphasized that the purpose here was basic. Weapon familiarity and practice, issuance of gear and clothing, cultural awareness, a short course on getting to The Katanga and what we can expect when we got there, and other similar orientation issues. He mentioned that we obviously had an international group here, which raises the issue of language difficulties. As a result, if there is a misunderstanding in English, please speak up and we can repeat the matter in French. He went on to explain that training would continue in The Katanga for one to two weeks before we participated in maneuvers.

Campbell seemed direct and honest, stating that "The existence of this group and similar groups already in The Katanga is controversial both in Europe, at the U.N., and Internationally. This is the reason that we are at a remote facility, in order to keep out of the public eye.

You will fly to Johannesburg on a commercial airline, but once there, you will travel to Elisabethville by a private, and I might add, a more primitive airline. Once there, you will be housed in a relatively modern barracks close to town. Some may be assigned to several outlying towns." He went on with some necessary red tape, "We have some legal issues to deal with. I am passing out some forms that will comply with certain legal requirements." He explained that it was necessary to have a contact address and phone number in our home country and, as practical matter, completion of a will and our instructions on how to handle our pay. He stated that using the Belgium State Bank had proven to be useful, as an office in Elizabethville allowed contract employees convenient access to funds, international transfers, etc. "I'll stay here as long as any of you have questions."

As we broke up, we began to talk it up with other recruits, and there was no apparent friction between the young and the old, Germans vs. French, etc. It was clear that we were going to have to depend on each other in an unstable country and petty crap did not fit into that model. Art was working with a group of Englishmen who were about his age but said he was hopeful if he could work with us. Once again, we retired to our rooms, full of questions that we had forgotten to ask.

The next morning, we turned in the paperwork, which was straightforward. Mike and I chose the Belgium banking system just for the convenience. We figured that we could save a lot of money, but at the same time, we wanted to have access to some ready cash. Completing a will was a little disconcerting, but we understood the necessity of it and we both named our parents as beneficiaries.

After the runny egg routine, we met with Sargeant Piquart outside the barracks. He was standing beside the driver and the station wagon so I guessed we were travelling somewhere. He said that we should retrieve all of our arms equipment and bring it to the car, which only took a couple of minutes. Then we were off. "We're going to the same range we were at yesterday. Practice is a good thing and I have some additional gear to provide. By the way, you can call me Steve, and the driver is David. There is no need for formality." On the way to the range, we had many questions and it was a good time to ask. First off, I asked "I notice that you have green cammies and ours are sort of dappled brown and grey-green, and I just wondered about the difference." "Good question. My uniform complies with European NATO design, and more clearly represents the terrain and vegetation in Europe. I will not be travelling to The Katanga. But you will be operating in a much more varied environment. Some of it is almost like a desert, all the way to actual jungle. The uniforms you have are the best mix we have found to fit the environment in The Katanga." Mike asked if he had been there and what it was like. "Oh yes, I have been there for a total of 24 months, dating back to pre-secession days." I asked the obvious question "Can you tell us a little about what it is like?" "Certainly. By the way, they will be showing you a movie tonight about The Congo but it seems a bit like a travelogue to me." He went on to explain a little about Moise Tshombe, the new President, who he thought was a really good person. He was very dedicated to the cause and the likelihood that the entire Congo could take lessons from him rather than trying to fight him. "The Katanga was like many African countries as they were about to leap into the 20th century. Colonial leaders are trying to hang on, but the Africans are excited about taking over, but at the same time, almost completely ill prepared to do so. All of this because the colonial leaders had not learned that independence was inevitable and already a fact in western Africa. Poorly prepared Africans could only expect to bring on external meddling, guarantee incompetence, and result in chaos." He explained that Elisabethville was a very modern city and if we were stationed there, our facilities would be very good except when were in the field. We would be integrated into native companies, about 30 westerners to 70 Katangese. "The entire idea is to make them self-sufficient in military matters, but keep commercial matters as a joint effort. Believe me, there is a long road to follow. Oh, yes.

The bugs and creatures. Remember this is the tropics and you will be arriving towards the end of the rainy season. Take your pills. Use your mosquito netting. Watch for leeches." Mike asked "How about cannibals?" The Steve turned and gave us a strange look. "I'll have more to say about that when we get to the range." We continued the drive in silence.

The biggest surprise when we got to the range and unloaded our gear was that I was to use an FAL. It was a short-barreled carbine but the same caliber and action as Mike's. It had no scope. Max said, "The reason for this is that you don't always win the sniper game. If you are attacked in close quarters, the Mauser bolt action will not be of much use. This is my decision because I believe that you two are familiar enough with firearms that you can handle the three guns. The disadvantage is weight, and the need to carry more ammo. Overall, I think this is the way to go. Along those lines is this: It is all well and good to be a good shot, and I think that you are very good at that, but the other issue is getting into position without being seen." He introduced us to the Ghilley suit, which was a strange netting that went over our uniforms that had some artificial vegetation stuck into it. Steve put one on, and it looked very awkward. "Yes, I know, they are a pain. But they may be your best friend if the enemy comes patrolling." The idea was to cut some native shrubs or limbs and stick this stuff into netting. Steve demonstrated. In about 5 minutes, he had pulled up weeds and brush that was growing around the station wagon and stuck this stuff into the netting. There was a small shrub nearby and he broke some limbs off and added them into the netting. He looked himself over and then laid down in the grass and the weeds. "Now you two walk out 20 yards and look back." Even though we knew exactly where he was, we could barely see him. "Wow!" said Mike, "You have made me a believer!" Steve looked stern. "You know, in your army, snipers will spend months disguising themselves and practicing this art. You have today."

We took it seriously and spent most of the day sticking twigs into netting. Then we shot a lot, mixing the sniper stuff with the FALs. Steve gave us some tips about defensive operations. We were an offensive team when we were in the sniper mode, and we would expect other members of our company would be nearby. But just in case we came to be alone, and the bad guys began swarming, it was FAL time. We spent an hour burning up ammo on full automatic. That led the discussion to the cannibals.

We sat down in the weeds as Steve pulled the twigs and grass out of his hair. "Mike, you asked about the cannibals while we were driving out here. So let us talk about that. The deal is, not every Baluba is trying to kill you. It varies, tribe-to-tribe, and area-to area. But they are all generally hostile because, rightly so, they will see you as an intruder. In fact, as Katanga secedes from the Congo, the Balubas are now trying to secede from Katanga! And to further complicate all of this, the U.N. has now created a 'peacemaking force' made up of Swedish and Irish soldiers and there is every reason to believe that Belgium troops, and you, could be fighting the Irish before long, rather than Balubas tribesmen and Congo troops. But I will leave that to the lecturers, and you should listen carefully. Having said that, I'd suggest that you continue to focus on military skills and leave the screwed up political situation to others." Mike and I were glazing over at the complexity of something we hardly understood at all. What we thought to be a straightforward issue of creating a new country actually seemed to be impossibly fucked.

Steve added advice. "If you are split from your group and they see your vulnerability they will try and capture or kill you. You will prefer the killing part. Do everything possible to avoid being an easy target. This is no place for individual heroes." I thought that Steve was beginning to sound like Mr. Falques back in Bakersfield. Jeez. Bakersfield. It seemed like years ago and it was less than a week that we had left LAX! He continued. "Ritual torture is part of their culture. They have many ways to disfigure a person and do unimaginable things to a live human being. Disembowelment, scooping eyes out, pulling living hearts out of a person's chest. Then eating them. Once captured, there is not a single survivor that I know of. We find the remains and they are beyond description. You men elected to bring side arms with you. That is a good idea. If you get are about to be captured, and I mean several feet from them taking you, my suggestion is to take your pistol out of its holster and shoot yourself. Capture is death. Why not do it painlessly? Better yet, just avoid capture."

Silence. Scared shitless. Why are we doing this for $300 a month? And so it went until Saturday evening. More target practice, more lectures, and more confusion about who was fighting whom. Some older guys who had been in Indo-China, Algeria and even WW2 looked like they took it all in stride. As we got to know them, they advised us to do our job, take our money and eventually go home. Leave all of the palace intrigue to others. Still. The idea of shooting at an Irish soldier was making my stomach churn. In fact, shooting anyone was beginning bug me. Why? What had they done to me? Mike and I kept our thoughts to ourselves, but once in our room, we talked about the overall mess. And we were about to become a part of the mess. I ventured "The thing that all of these lectures tell me is this: A hundred years ago the European countries carved up Africa for their own exploitation, and ignored thousands of years of tribal boundaries, customs, and traditions. Now, the natives want to adjust some of this and everyone in the West is fighting it. Who the fuck is on the right side? Why are these arbitrary boundaries so important? We talked about this in Bakersfield if you remember. I mean, if you look at a map of Africa most of the borders are straight lines for hundreds of miles. Yeah, some of them follow rivers, but even then, who says that a river divides a tribe or a culture?" Mike added "Yeah. And when you bring up questions about all of this in the lectures, they look at you as if we should mind our own business. Then why bring any of it up?"

That evening we saw a movie about The Katanga focusing on Moise Tshombe. The emphasis was on the powerful forces who oppose him even though The Katanga was probably the only province in the Congo that made any sense. Of course, they avoided any discussion about the Belgium role who joined other European powers in creating the Congo! After the movie, a Belgium Colonel stepped to the podium and announced "You will be shipping out Monday morning. You should work with your advisor and get your gear clean and packed."

Wow. We thought we would be here for at least another few days.

# Chapter 13

Sunday started just like the other days, but after our half-cooked bacon and runny eggs, we met with Steve. "Tell you what", he said "Let's go to your room for starters and I want to see you break down your guns, clean them, oil them, reassemble them, and pack them. This has to be an almost automatic thing. Practice this when you get to Elizabethville. Your rifles are your friends, and you will be operating in a hostile climate. The last thing you need is a mechanical problem." So, we spent three hours familiarizing ourselves with every tiny detail of the FALs and the Mauser. They had all worked perfectly but Steve reminded us that with an automatic, just a piece of crud or carbon in the wrong place would stop the gun from operating. He examined all of the magazines and was not happy with two of them. "Look at this," he said, "The lips on these magazines are a little rough and you can see where the phosphate finish is worn off after just a few days of shooting. Get to the quartermaster today and trade these. Oh yeah, also tell him to give you 100 rounds of .300 Winchester Magnum match cartridges. If he gives you any shit, tell him to see me. It's unlikely that you will find any of that ammo at the corner drug store in Elizabethville. And don't forget to get more 9mm. ammo for your pistols." We assumed that we knew all about the P.38 and the Browning, so he didn't bother checking them, but he did check the blades of our knives and was satisfied. He opened one of the emergency medical kits and explained the contents. He went over the concept of compression bandages, tourniquets and gave an imaginary lesson on how to give a morphine shot. He had us oil our boots and adjust our belts, made sure we had water purification pills, and a dozen other things. "On most maneuvers, you will have a medical guy with you but you can never be sure. You need to learn to be as self-sufficient as possible."

At lunch Campbell told us "You will all get on a bus at 0800 in the morning and head for the airport. The flight to Johannesburg will leave at 1200 hours. All of our gear will go in several crates, so have it ready on the dock by 0700 and make sure your name is on everything. Unless you have something special, everything should go into the canvas bags that were issued. We will take care of the tickets and travel papers at the airport. Questions?"

Later in the day our hosts fired up a barbecue and we had a great steak dinner, with a large supply of beer, and all of the fixings. When the food was gone and we were sufficiently softened with drink, all of the advisors stood and gave us their best wishes. For us, it was going to be difficult to leave Sargeant Piquart. He had taught us a lot. Still later, with our gear stowed at the foot of our beds, we lay there, stone sober, unable to sleep. We went over the entire program. Was this really better than Viet Nam? Was this breakaway province worth our lives? Was this actually the adventure we thought it would be? We looked at the ceiling, and laid still. Minutes later, Mike said "Tony?" "Yeah, what?" "It doesn't really matter. We're going to Africa."

The next morning, we were lined up on the dock in front of the barracks. We had stowed all of our gear in plastic crates. Except for the Mauser and Mike's optics. Sargeant Piquart had made a decision to treat these particular weapons systems with extra care and he intended to take them directly on to the Sabena airliner and assure careful handling. Actually, none of this was surprising. Sabena was Belgium's national airline and here we had three dozen young men in cammies flying to Africa. Everyone involved thought that they knew exactly where we were going and the cooperation was complete. Mr. Campbell walked down the line, and shook each of our hands and wished us luck. It was a serious moment for everyone. We broke ranks as two modern busses drove up. We entered he first bus while some of the base personnel loaded all of the supplies into the second.

Except for Mike's and my special gear. Sargeant Piquart brought those on board in the original special rifle case and a separate plastic box, and sat down across from us. "Hey!" I said. "Are you going?" "No, at least not for a few weeks. I'm here to make sure your supplies get loaded without a hitch. When you get to Johannesburg it will be your job to personally take them from this plane and hang on to them to wherever they take you for the night. The chartered plane on Monday to Elizabethville will not pose any problem. Just take them aboard." "So you might show up down there?" asked Mike. "It is very possible that I will accompany the next group of recruits. I kind of miss the place!" I thought that after all of the talk about Balubas he would stay as far away from The Katanga as possible. But from our perspective, we had made a bond with him and the possibility of him joining us it was great news. We said it together "Great" and Mike and I each gave him a bear hug. The other guys looked at that farewell with a strange look on their faces, but Mike said "Fuck 'em!"

We cleared a separate gate at the airport and were herded into a room reserved for our group. We watched T.V. and just generally killed time. Art sat down with us and he was nervous as a cat, despite having gone through several military experiences. At about 11:30 we were all herded into a special bus and taken out onto the tarmac where the shiny 707-320 sat. There was a front and a rear entrance to the plane, and we were told to take the rear stairs, and to sit in the back of the aircraft, all together. An airline person gave us each an I.D. as we started up the stairs saying, "Print your name on this and put it in your pocket." As we boarded the plane there was a gorgeous stewardess to meet us and she helped us stow the rifle and the plastic box.

About ten minutes later, the civilian passengers boarded through the front entrance. A few minutes later we were accelerating down the runway and lifted off at that amazing, so it seemed, 45-degree angle. In a minute, we were above the clouds in bright sunshine. The 707 banked and headed south. It was much too late for second guessing!

# Chapter 14

As we flew south, the day became clear and even at 33,000 feet, the world below seemed both immense and tiny. Crossing the Mediterranean took about 20 minutes, but the Sahara was endless. And as we flew into sub-Saharan Africa, it was endless green. We even got a look at Mount Kilimanjaro. When the European masters were carving up Africa, so the story goes, the Bismarck wanted a mountain in German East Africa, so today, if you look at the border between Kenya and Tanzania the map shows an arrow-straight border. Except for a jog around Mt. Kilimanjaro, just so the Bismarck could have his mountain! And that has lasted 100 years. Most African borders just make little sense, and I had to wonder, if indeed, borders were that fickle, what was the big deal about a province seceding and creating a separate country. A black country at that!

It soon got around to the front end of the plane that there were soldiers in the back, and every now and then, someone pushed the curtain aside dividing the aircraft and peered in. We even got a couple of 'thumbs up' even though these folks had no actual knowledge, but many suspicions about our destination. After all, The Congo was the only Belgium interest in Africa The stewardesses were more than accommodating in bringing us meals, drinks and seemingly whatever we asked for. Of course there were all kinds of marginal jokes and attempts to flirt but the crew stayed both accommodating and proper at the same time. Mike said, "I am going to get tired of this all-male arrangement very quickly!"

We ticked off some of the countries as we headed further south, skirting the Atlantic Ocean. Some of them like Benin were so tiny that that they went by in a blink. Even The Congo is very small at the confluence of the Congo River and the Atlantic but inland, it stretched beyond the horizon. Eventually both Mike and I tired of the geography lesson, put our seats back and took a nap. I thought of my dad who always said 'naps are good.' I had thought that applied to old geezers but he was correct, even at age 21.

When I awoke, I was surprised to see that we were over the Atlantic. But after looking at a map in the seat pocket magazine, I realized that Africa juts westward and then we would make a landfall over Angola and Namibia, then slice across South Africa to Johannesburg. But from the air, it all looked the same. We were descending now and I was getting excited! I nudged Mike and said, "Look! We're losing altitude and you can see villages and stuff." Mike rubbed his eyes and leaned across me to look out the window. "Look forward", he said, "I see skyscrapers ahead of us." Well, they were at least multi-story buildings, and neither of us expected that. We knew from our lectures that South Africa was the economic engine that dominated all of southern Africa so I do not know why we were surprised. However, we still had this image of Africa as a continent of mud huts and thatched roofs. "Looks like a modern city to me," said Mike. We were lower now and we could see neighborhoods and guess what? Thatched roofs! However, as we dropped low over the runway approach there were scores of industrial buildings and modern highways. We heard the 'clunk' of the landing gear dropping and within a couple of minutes, we were on the ground, the tires screeching on asphalt. Mike leaned over, said, "We're actually here," and shook my hand. The 707 taxied towards a fully modern, huge terminal, that had many aircraft, mostly propeller types, neatly parked around the buildings. I reminded myself that the 707 we were on was cutting edge stuff, common at LAX but not in Africa. The stewardess informed us that we would be deplaning out of the rear door, and a bus would take us to our destination. Here it was again, an apparent effort to disguise our presence. Odd thinking, I thought, because there were dozens of people looking through the terminal glass for their friends or relatives stepping out of the front door! Oh well, whatever. However, it did make me think that we were being treated like lepers or something.

Once the front of the plane was empty, we began deplaning down the portable steps, and there was the waiting bus. Mike had his plastic box and I had the Mauser case tucked under my arm. I was thinking that Sargeant Piquart would have my ass if anything happened to that rifle. As we entered the bus, I could see a large flatbed truck loading all of our gear. About twenty minutes later, we began driving around the perimeter of the airport winding in and out of maintenance facilities and war-weary old airplanes. P-51s, a lot of DC-4s and some Constellations. They looked functional and complete for the most part, but had peeling paint, insignias painted over, and other signs of deterioration. Some of them were being cannibalized, apparently for parts. I had heard that Africa was the last stopping place for old airplanes. Most of the countries were dirt poor, and war surplus aircraft were dirt cheap. Overall, I was amazed at the size of the airport, and the variety of the airplanes, new and old.

The bus and the trailing truck pulled up to a huge hangar with open doors. It was clearly a military facility but there were not any signs or indication of just what its purpose was. Then Mike pointed it out: "There are a couple of guys with assault rifles." There was no question about it. We were leaving the civilian world and entering the military one, ready or not. As we followed a uniformed person into the hangar, we saw rows of cots on one side of the building, and a kind of portable kitchen on the other side with steel tables and chairs scattered around. An officer stopped us and said "Welcome to South Africa! I am Lieutenant Tom Robles from the South African Air Force. You will be staying here tonight. Select a cot, and pick up your personal gear once the truck is unloaded. If anything is missing, contact me immediately. I will be over by the kitchen and I will have more information once you all settle in. There are cold drinks available behind my table right now." I made a head count of 36. Apparently the rehabilitated recruits were still with us.

A couple of laborers unloaded the truck in the middle of the building, and I was glad that Piquart had taken precautions with the Mauser and the optics package. It was not that they were careless; it was just that they were not particularly careful either. There were probably 100 cots and we wondered what they were preparing for. We located Art and decided to bunk in the corner of the building. Others were finding their buddies and reorganizing the cots into small groups. We piled our gear onto our cots and while we had no suspicions about theft, we also agreed that one of us would always be on guard. After all, these goods were now our personal responsibility and it would be a major event if someone lost an FAL. Losing a Mauser sniper rifle might be a capital offense!

After dinner, which consisted of a self-serve arrangement providing beans, sausages, runny eggs and toast, we settled in and lounged around, bullshitting with casual acquaintances we had met in Belgium. But the doors to the building were now closed and there was no way we were going anywhere. Later, Lt. Robles made a few cryptic remarks: "Breakfast will be at 0700, and you will move to your next destination at 0900. Your plane will be moved to this building during the night. Make certain that you have your gear ready to go. If you haven't already figured it out, there are heads and showers at the back of this building. We're now going to show a movie for those who are interested." A couple of guys were arranging folding chairs in front of a large screen and we decided 'What the hell? What else do we have to do?' However, we also honored our commitment to guard our stuff, and the three of us ended up watching the film from our cots. It turned out to be a B class western, with sweaty guys with six guns and women with a lot of cleavage hanging out in saloons. There were a couple of gun battles and quick draw artists. Not academy award stuff, but we enjoyed the cleavage!

The next morning the three of us were showered and ready for breakfast at 0600. Anxious, you might say. Breakfast consisted of exactly the same food we had for dinner. Leftovers, I guessed. During the night, it seemed like the eggs had dried out which was good.

# Chapter 15

After breakfast, a guard rolled back the sliding doors and what we saw was somewhat unsettling. Not particularly surprising but unsettling. This was no shiny 707. It was a Lockheed Constellation with peeling paint. It looked like it was an original WW2 MATS cargo plane, although the gorgeous lines of the triple-tailed Connie were still admired. A crew was already loading our gear, which was a small part of the load. We saw box after box of military stuff loaded onto pallets and being lifted into the front cargo hatch with a forklift. There were no guards or restrictions so Mike, Art and I walked around the four engine propeller craft. It was clear that several insignias had been painted over, which raised the question: where had this plane come from? There was a rudder number but that was it. Mike noticed hydraulic fluid leaking down the landing gear struts, and I pointed to a very large puddle of oil under the number four engine. Maybe we were just being spoiled with the new 707s, perfect rifles and other specialty stuff, but this old airplane was a definite step in the wrong direction. Still, these Belgium people knew what they were talking about up to this point, so it was probably just worry with no reason.

Old it may be, but a Constellation is a very large airplane, and the front landing gear placed the cabin about 20 feet off the ground. We could see a couple guys in the cabin, probably the crew doing their pre-flight. About 30 minutes later two workers pushed a rusty, wheeled set of stairs up against the rear door and a crewmember opened the hatch. There would be no pretty stewardesses to greet us on this flight, which would end in Elizabethville, some 600 miles to the north. No one was in any apparent rush but all of the recruits were outside now, looking at their surroundings and at the airplane.

I heard quite a few not-complimentary remarks. "Tacky old granny, huh?" "Suppose they have run out of money?" "Can we wait for the next flight?" Etcetera. The lieutenant from the hangar walked to the stairway and said, "You received a form when you left Brussels. Make sure that your names are printed in the space provided and hand them to me as you board." Of course, everyone had forgotten all about the form, but since we were still in the same clothes, all of us eventually came up with a crumpled piece of paper. We scrambled for some pens or pencils but eventually everyone had a completed form. "You may proceed to board." Mike, Art and I got together and began climbing the stairs as a whine came from the outboard engine on the opposite side of the plane. We could see the propeller turning over very slowly, then faster as the engine caught, and a huge cloud of blue smoke blew out of the exhausts. When we got to the top of the stairs, we looked in the fuselage and were more than surprised. There were about 60 seats in the rear of the plane and the cargo was tied down between the seats and the cockpit opening. The fuselage was raw aluminum, and airline seats looked like they were older than the plane. The floor was raw metal. It seemed clear that this Connie was making a living mainly by flying cargo, but could take passengers in a pinch. Mike had it all figured out: "You see, if the seats were in front, and we had a crash, we would be crushed by the cargo." I had a different take. "If we have a crash everyone will be crushed."

My Mauser and Mike's optic package were a little awkward in this situation, but we were damned if we were going to turn them over to some unknown clod who just might drop them onto the concrete. It took a little growling and a lot of nasty remarks, but all 36 of us settled in, leaving a lot of empty space. A khaki shirted guy emerged from the cockpit and walked around the cargo pallets just as the #2 inboard engine came to life in another huge cloud of blue smoke. "I am John Walters, and I am the flight engineer and the navigator. "Today we will fly north to Elizabethville at 12,000 feet. The weather is clear and we should have a smooth flight. We will enter Rhodesia to the north, and then across Nyasaland, and then through Northern Rhodesia and land in about three hours. The head is in the rear of the plane and there is a cold chest with drinks if you want anything. I'll give you a progress report from time to time." And then he disappeared into the cockpit. The plane began to move as the pilot started the #3 and then the #4 engines and we began our taxi to the runway. We followed a small light plane, and waited for him to take off. There seemed to be very little traffic for such a huge airport, but we learned later that we actually had left from an auxiliary runway that was seldom used. It looked like it with pavement cracks, pot holes and the like. In a few minutes, the engines revved and were on our way! "Jeez, Mike, this is actually happening." He nodded and just turned to look out the window. The Lockheed rolled on and on, slowly gaining speed and the difference between this and the 707 was very clear as the plane finally lifted off, after accelerating for 6000 feet. We left the ground in a slow climb and heard the landing gears retract with loud 'bumps'. Slowly we gained altitude, circled the outskirts of town and headed north.

I was also still amazed that all of this was actually happening. "Mike, I understand the purpose and all of that, but I keep thinking, why choose us? OK, so we make a good long range shooting team. So what? There must be thousands of people like us." At that, Art joined the conversation. "I don't think that you are grasping their needs for special contract employees. Yeah, there are many people who can do what you can do, but they are all in our Army, or France's army or Germany's army etcetera. In addition, by the time the people who do these things leave their Armies they are retiring, they are sick of military life, and besides that, their eyesight has begun to fade, and they can make much more money doing other things. You just do not go to the employment agency and hire snipers. So our employers do the next best thing and create their own. However, in this case, you two have done most of the work yourself. You already have those skills. Don't minimize them. And look around the plane. Except for you two, the rest of us *are* old and experienced!" I said, "You know, that makes some sense. So if we had just tried to sign up as regular troops and not mentioned the marksmanship angle, we would just have been bypassed." Mike came to life "Don't you remember? When that Falques guy spoke up, he asked us if we had any military experience, and when we said no, he asked us why are you applying?" That was exactly correct. "And when I said that I thought that you were looking for marksmen, that is when he perked up and flew to Bakersfield. Well, all I can say is that I hope we live up to their expectations!"

The plane droned on, hitting bumps because of the relatively low altitude and was encountering occasional clouds and rain showers. The 'upside' was that I was able to see small farms and villages below, but nowhere did I see a city or a paved road. Oh, there were a few larger buildings here and there, but for the most part, it was just very small farms, neatly divided by hedges, or what looked like paths. We learned that a native farmer might have started with an acre or two of land, but then had a family and the plot was then divided. One half acre per child. Then again. One fourth. Then one eighth. And when you arrived at one sixteenth, the yield was inadequate for even a small family, and starvation began. My observations were interrupted by an unusual 'bump' that was noticeably different from the air pockets. And as I looked out the window, I noticed that there was a thin wisp of blue smoke exiting the exhaust of the # 2 engine. From my involvement in the old car trade, I had run into mechanics at the airport who worked on radial engines, and I knew that there was a tendency, particularly when the engine had many hours on it, for small amounts of oil to gravitate down the pistons of the cylinders pointing downwards. That, and an imperfect gas/air mixture, was the reason that they barfed so much smoke when they were initially started. But I had not heard of an engine continuing to visibly burn oil, evidenced by the bluish-white smoke coming from the exhaust once the plane was airborne. However, there it was, coming out of the exhaust ports and the aluminum fairing around the engine. Then it happened. An actual flame shot from the exhaust port, accompanied by a very big 'kerflunk'. The pilot was obviously aware of this and immediately throttled back on that engine, and the rhythm of the four synchronized engines changed to a kind of raggedy feeling. It was like an engine with a couple of spark plugs disconnected. But we flew on. Something was wrong, but maybe it was a normal event flying a decrepit old airplane. A nice time to have four engines. I leaned back and forgot my concerns. Then there was more than just a bump and all of us on the left side of the plane looked out and saw hard parts crashing through part of the aluminum cowling. The cowling itself detached and flew by, banging into the fuselage, and I supposed, possibly hitting the tail section and the control surfaces. I'd heard of engines self- destructing but not flying completely apart! We all stayed glued to the windows as the pilot shut the engine down and feathered the prop, reducing the drag on the stationary propeller.

Then the guy in the khakis was in front of us, supported by a pallet tie-down, shouting above the noise of the engines "We're OK. We can easily fly on three engines. We will be landing very shortly so buckle up!" With that, he disappeared around the cargo and went into the cockpit. The Lockheed lost altitude very quickly, banking over the African landscape. It seemed to me that the remaining three engines revved to compensate for the lost 2200 horsepower, and we began an even more radical descent. I knew that ahead was our destination at Elisabethville in The Katanga, but where the hell were we now? Was there actually an airport or were we about to crash? The trip that began as an adventure was beginning to feel like a fiasco. It all seemed so well organized in Belgium, but once in Africa, it was a continual goat fuck, with obsolete equipment, hung over pilots, and weapons that might or might not be with us.

The Khaki guy flight engineer stuck his head out the cabin door and said, "Don't worry guys! We'll be OK. We're doing fine on three engines". The guy across from me hollered "Make it where? Where the fuck are we?" The engineer yelled back like we had a map or something. "Nyasaland. We will land in Blantyre, Nyasaland." Just about everyone looked puzzled at that. Where the fuck was Nyasaland?

Many of the old guys took the whole thing in stride. After all, we had six month contracts, and a day stalled in an old airport still counted as one of the days. However, my buddies and I figured that we were about to auger into a cornfield, which was getting larger by the second. We had signed up for military operations in the north, and it had all gone well on the way to Johannesburg in a brand new Boeing 707, complete with drinks and gorgeous stewardesses. But this was something else. Helpless in an old propeller airliner with a shaky-looking looking flight engineer telling that we were about to land in some unknown dirt bag airport in central Africa.

With most of the engine cowling now residing in the farmland below, I could clearly see the engine cylinders, and several of them were missing. Then there was a ragged bump, which turned out to be the landing gear being extended, and I thought there might be hope after all. At 21 years old, optimism was always ahead of realism. And in a few minutes, the old girl settled over a runway and the reassuring screech of rubber on asphalt told the story. The rundown was very long and ended at a farm at the end of the runway. While we could not see the pilot, I had to assume that he was breathing a sigh of relief as he turned the plane around and taxied past a small, marginally maintained terminal and then continued for about a quarter mile away to a rusty, old corrugated metal hangar where he shut the remaining engines down. "Shit! Fuck!" Were the words coming from the mouths of about 30 of us. But looking around the cabin I saw four or five grizzled looking old vets who had slept through the entire thing!

The silence was a beautiful thing, but the smell of vomit quickly permeated the plane as someone outside opened the double cargo doors and let some of the air in and the smell out. Outside, the air was thick with moisture, and at that very moment, the skies opened up and rain came down in sheets. Not buckets, but sheets! It was just thirty minutes ago that we had clear skies! We all gathered up our personal gear and Mike and I held on to our special goods and hustled down a ladder to the asphalt runway, and ran to the old hangar. At that moment, I wondered how much worse this could get: a broken old airliner in an emergency field, in some Godforsaken African town, pouring down rain. But this was the good news. Things were to get worse.

We were under a kind of veranda attached to the building, covered by a leaky roof. But in a few minutes the rain stopped just as quickly as it had started, and the heat immediately penetrated our uniforms. Sweaty and sticky. That was a condition we would encounter on many, many days, but never get used to. There was an airport laborer trying to open the door of the hangar, but while we waited, I wandered out under the Constellation and looked up at the broken engine. Wow, I thought, there were several cylinders that had actually blown off the engine block, with pushrods, rocker arms and cylinder heads just sort of hanging catty-whampus from wires and tubes. Then, looking around I saw a huge gash in one of the landing gear tires. Apparently when the engine and cowling let go, a piece of metal had penetrated the landing gear door and sliced through the tire. And the other companion tire was completely bald, with fabric reinforcing exposed. We were damn lucky, no matter what that flight crew said.

Looking back at the old Connie and into the now-opened hangar, I thought that the plane would never fly again. It would join that collection of old graveyard planes scattered across Africa. On the other hand, it had brought us down safely, despite the incompetent and underfunded maintenance under which it had lived its last years.

The hangar was empty except for a couple of small military helicopters. We sat down and leaned against the walls. And waited

# Chapter 16

After about 15 minutes of waiting, with some wandering outside to either take a leak or puke, the pilot, co-pilot, and flight engineer came through the door. The pilot spoke, in a cheerful voice. "Welcome to Nyasaland, chaps! I apologize for setting you down in this place but it's just one of those things! The tower informs me by radio that all of you should stay put right here and wait for a solution to all of this as soon as they come up with one. But one thing is certain, it will not include flying that airplane outside. Cheerio!" With that, he and his crew picked up their bags, went outside and began the trek to the terminal.

"Let's follow those guys! They must have a way out of here," said Mike. "Nyasaland? It sounds like a street at Disneyland," I countered. Art commented, "This is bullshit!" There was not much doubt in that. We didn't wander too far from the old building, but closer to the terminal we saw several olive drab helicopters and two old WW2 propeller fighter planes with flat tires. Across the runway was a C-47 that looked serviceable, and one that looked cannibalized to make the other one fly. It had insignia roundels that we did not recognize, but we assumed that they were Rhodesian.

About half an hour later, a jeep headed our way from the direction of the terminal, and pulled up under the wing of the Constellation. The fellow in the passenger seat got out and walked toward us. He was in proper military dress, although he was wearing short pants, and looked to be an officer. The other recruits stopped their wandering and gathered around the jeep. "Good afternoon! I am Lieutenant Tim Summers and I am with the Nyasaland defense force. We are connected with the Rhodesian Federation. I am definitely not a part of your operation, but I know where you are going and I will make every effort to get you on your way. But that is not going to happen today. We have talked to your folks in Elizabethville and they are making arrangements to bus you to your destination, hopefully by tomorrow morning. Questions?" That didn't take long. What do we eat? What do we do tonight? "Ah yes, good points all," he said. "There are no modern facilities here that can accommodate all of you. A hotel is under construction in Blantyre but is not yet ready. The rest of the facilities are primitive in nature and spread out over a broad area. Instead, I am having bedding from our Army stores brought over in a couple of hours along with some military meals and water." A guy in the back shouted out, "K rations?" "Well, I hope they are better than that, but you have the right idea. I think that you will just have to make do tonight. Some of you can sleep in the airplane and maybe some under the wings. There is no problem with being cold around here. You can also use the building here, but I know it is unsatisfactory. I'll also have some mosquito repellent brought over and I urge you to use it. Malaria is very prevalent. If you are on Quinine, continue to use it. Sorry to bring all of this bad news to you chaps, but your leaders up north hope to have you on your way tomorrow. One more thing. Just in case you are wondering, there is commercial air service here twice a day from Kenya but your travel status will not get you on a plane. So I think that means you are stuck here for the time being. Sorry for your inconvenience, but it's not unexpected in central Africa." With that, the driver started the jeep and off they went.

After an hour of grumbling, we started talking about what to do. We saw that a few guys were already climbing the stairs into the plane, and we decided to follow them. Sitting in an airliner for hours is bad enough, but sitting in one overnight, with virtually no ventilation in the tropical weather was like a sauna. With no alternatives, we ate the swill they called food, and the guys outside made some bedding with the blankets they had brought out and placed them under the wings of the plane. In the morning, a truck towed out a portable toilet, a container of hot tea and some pastries. Yeah, I thought, it was the shits being abandoned but that was not the fault of these locals, who did what they could to make us comfortable. The 36 of us were getting a little ripe, living in our clothes for two days in the heat and humidity, and wondered what lied ahead today. A German guy had a crumpled map of Africa in his bag and figured that it was probably 900 kilometers from where we were to Elizabethville if you followed the roads. In an African bus on roads where pavement was just a suggestion, that could take days to get there.

About Ten A.M. the Jeep with the proper Nyasaland military guy returned, and we were all ears. "Gather round, chaps, I have news." With that, he sat on the hood of the Jeep and we formed a semi-circle. "I have some good news for you…" and that met with cheers and clapping! "Here is the program: In about an hour there will be a bus here and….." Everyone groaned. "Where is the good news?" a guy asked. Nonplussed, the officer on the jeep went on. "Patience men, listen for a minute! The bus will take you to Lilongwe, which is about the middle of Nyasaland. Accompanying the bus will be a large truck, which will carry your gear. This is not a long trip. And you should be there in about three or four hours. Tonight you will be in a hotel, which I know to be very nice, with a swimming pool and all of the amenities. Actual beds! Tomorrow the Katanga chaps will send a transport plane to Lilongwe to pick you up, and you will be in Elizabethville by the afternoon. Now how is that for a treat?" He got a lot of thumbs up and 'good job' comments for that. He mingled with us for a short period and tried to respond to continuing questions about where the fuck we were.

"OK, newcomers. While we wait for the bus, gather around and I'll try and give you a short geography and political lesson on what is going on around here." Most of our group stayed right where we were, but some of the grizzled old veterans wandered away. They had been this way before, and these lectures were getting to be a little repetitive. On the other hand, each one added a little more knowledge, and what was the alternative? Sitting in a smelly, broken airplane?

"You chaps are coming into Africa at a very unsettled time. Right now, you are in the southern end of Nyasaland, which is a narrow north-south province about 500 miles long and maybe 125 miles wide. Adjacent to us is Rhodesia which has been, for practical purposes independent from the U.K since the 1950s. To the west and north, is Northern Rhodesia. These northernmost entities are still colonies, but also loosely gathered together in a federation with Rhodesia. It is our hope that they will form a permanent federation. To the north of northern Rhodesia is The Congo, and Katanga is a province of that country. That's where you're going. How all of this is going to work out is actually unknown. There is an independence movement going on all over Africa, started by Ghana over on the west coast. Our Federation is not at all popular with the indigenous population and they want their areas to be independent too. As you probably know, these areas are now largely run by white people. Nyasaland, where we are, would become Malawi. Northern Rhodesia would become Zambia, and The Congo would become Zaire. Rhodesia, my country, would be Zimbabwe. Now, the thing of interest to you is that while the federation transition would be from white to black, in your case, it is blacks trying to remove Katanga from other blacks. Generally speaking, at least as far as I understand this, is that your role is to help those blacks create their own country. By the way, if the various people in this area are successful in creating Malawi, Lilongwe will be their capitol, and that is where you will be staying tonight. I have business in Lilongwe and I'll be accompanying you today, so if you have questions along the way, just speak up!"

There were questions and mumbling but this generally was consistent with what we had been told, but it did place the regional questions in some perspective. Everyone was pleased that this officer was going to travel with us and be our tour guide. The discussion went on for about another 30 minutes when reasonably modern Volvo bus arrived.

# Chapter 17

The most notable part of the trip north were the crazy truck drivers. This was a reasonably well paved two lane road that followed the rolling terrain. The road would crest at a summit of one hill and then descend into a small valley and then up again to the crest of another hill. The problem was that when we were on the upside, large trucks coming in the opposite direction passed other vehicles with no ability to see what was heading their way. The officer who we now knew as Lt. Tim stood and said if you take a look into these small valleys or canyons you will see the result of passing with no sight distance. Sure enough, in almost every valley or canyon, there was a gruesomely bent and ruined truck that had met another of its kind at the top of a hill, and tumbled into the canyon. Occasionally the crash was a truck and a car, and the car was not usually recognizable as a car. It was a mouth-dropping scene, and one that could happen to us at any time. Summers could see our reaction, with our noses pressed against the windows and said, "There is no solution for this. It's like American cowboys and Indians. Just keep your fingers crossed!"

After about two hours the terrain levelled out and we all breathed a sigh of relief that we had survived our second African experience! Lieutenant Tim stood said "We're coming into the important town of Ncheu to get some bottled water for you all. Ncheu is a regional town, and politically, attached to the Lilongwe power base. You can expect to be surrounded by villagers trying to sell you food and I'd suggest that you pass on that opportunity. The natives here are harmless, but they will be pretty pushy trying to earn a Tambala or two."

Ncheu looked like I'd imagine hell. If this was some indication of where we were going, I planned on deserting. Mud huts, thatched roofs, runny mud, naked kids, stagnant pools of water providing an invitation to mosquitos, men urinating openly along the road, and oh yes, here came the vegetable sellers. Those people, men and women had clothes tattered beyond garage rags, and dirt to match. But here they were, holding up not only tomatoes and potatoes, but wood carvings and all kinds of junk. With pleading eyes, it was difficult to turn them down. The bus driver had disappeared around the corner and then re-appeared with an armful of quart-sized bottled water, which Mike, Art and I vowed not to drink a drop! A couple of guys bought wood carvings and that just concentrated all of the other salesmen and women around that particular window. Incredible. On the one hand I was happy to get out of there, but on the other hand, I felt very sorry for these people. An important regional town?

We arrived in Lilongwe an hour later. On the outskirts of town, it looked like Ncheu, and we saw women walking along the highway with impossible loads on their heads. But as we continued into the center of town, things got a little better. Women in colorful wraps walked around with an incredible amount of stuff on their heads, carrying a babies on their backs. We did not see men carrying anything. At a stop sign there was a crippled guy with shriveled legs sitting on a kind of frame with roller skates attached. He moved around very quickly by pushing with his hands against the pavement. I asked the Lt. Tim what that was all about and he said "Oh, yes, that is fairly common. They still have polio here." And on through the city center where there were political banners pasted everywhere, all about Dr.Kamuzu Hastings Banda who we eventually learned, had proclaimed himself 'President for Life' if and when independence was granted. So much for democracy. On the other side of town, there was a lot of construction of government buildings as someday, this was to be the national capitol, even though the British had constructed a provincial capitol in Zomba, to the south. That, presumably was because Banda was from Lilongwe. Apparently politics preceded independence. Banda, as we found out, was that single western educated African doctor in all of Nyasaland! But as we pulled up in front of the Capitol Hotel, I knew everything was going to be all right.

The next day, we boarded the bus for the airport. Our clothes had been washed, we had a swim in the pool, a good dinner and a bunch of Carlsberg beers. We quickly learned that there was a Carlsberg beer factory in town, and the only choice you had was a 'brown' (stiff) or a 'green' (light)' We just ordered round after round of greens. Or browns. And the beds. Real beds! Mosquito nets. A good breakfast. Life is good! The airport was about 10 miles north of town and it too was under construction. The bus dropped us at the temporary terminal and we saw the truck with our supplies arriving behind us. Of course, throughout all of this, Mike and I hung onto our special goods, never letting them out of our sight. Along the way we saw dozens of men cutting the lawns next to the roadway with machetes. Machetes! And every few hundred feet we saw little kids grouped in a circle only a few feet from the highway. I asked Lt. Tim what they were doing, and he said "Oh yes. The season for subterranean flying termites is on. These kids wait until a bug appears, grab him and pull the wings off, then put them in a bucket. Tonight they will be cooked in oil and become part of their protein intake. They will also be sold in the local market." I burped.

About an hour later we were standing along a chain link fence waiting for the plane. Lieutenant Simmons said his goodbyes and we all shook his hand. He had done a good job on the spur-of- the moment. To the east we saw a plane growing bigger, with its'landing gear down, and hoped that was our passport out of here. That would mean that in a couple of hours we would be at our destination as opposed to riding in that bus for two days through Northern Rhodesia. But then, as the plane dropped to the runway we had second thoughts. This time it was a two engine, surplus Curtiss C-46. The lettering on the fuselage said 'Ethiopian Airways'. Holy shit! Let's re-think the bus!

But despite our initial misgivings, the plane was clean, it had good seats, and seemed to be in good shape. The pilot and co- pilot even had uniforms, and they welcomed us at the top of the boarding ladder. It took another 30 minutes to load all of our stuff off of the truck, and after only a few minutes, the pilot fired up the engines, and taxied to the end of the runway. In short order, we accelerated and were airborne. Mike looked at me. "Ethiopian Fucking Airlines! I'll have something to tell my grandkids!" We laughed and laughed until Art poked us in the ribs, and we settled down.

An hour later we landed in Elizabethville, The Katanga. Or the Congo. Or Zaire. All depending on who won this struggle for independence.

# Chapter 18

What a change! There were airplanes everywhere. Several small British-made airliners, helicopters, and a scattering of various kinds of fighter planes, propeller driven as well as jets. The first thing that we noticed was the climate. At an almost a 4000-foot elevation, it was cool, with a soft breeze blowing. What a contrast to Lilongwe of a couple of hours ago, where the air would cling to us like a shower without a towel. At the gate there was what looked to be a welcoming committee of officials in uniforms, who were probably curious to see if we would ever arrive! But here we were, all 36 of us, anxious as hell to see what the next step in our adventure might be. At least that was how Mike and I saw it. About half of our group had played this game before, and while they were indeed curious, their heads did not look like swivels on a stick, looking up, down, and around like we were.

As we filed through the gate a Belgium Colonel (sun burned but white) and a Katanga General (black) shook each of our hands and welcomed us to the new Republic of The Katanga. When it was my turn I had to put the Mauser case down, and received a peculiar look in return. The case obviously held something other than golf clubs, and I suppose they must have wondered what was so special about this particular item when everything else taken from the plane's cargo hatch was being thrown around like potato bags.

As we entered the terminal several cute teenagers were serving cold drinks and cookies and welcoming us again. It sure didn't feel like a foreign country. The group meandered around the waiting area while mixing with the brass, but eventually we were directed to two large vans in the parking lot. A sargeant stood between them and said, "We'll take you for a quick tour of the town and then head out to our facility which is about two miles away." The tour was a real eye opener, at least to begin with. We were driven by the white colonnaded Palace of Justice, the Grand Hotel, a traditional looking cathedral made of bricks, and the University of Elisabethville which we learned was established just a few years ago. On the other hand, however grand this was, I figured that this tour must have been repeated hundreds of times before for all of the previous recruits. And, as we left town and hit the suburbs, everything started to change. The houses went from well-kept western type of houses with verandas and lawns, to older run-down dwellings with corrugated iron roofs, and then to mud houses with thatched roofs. Just like Lilongwe. Downtown Elisabethville was an island in the middle of Africa.

As the deteriorating human condition went by, we encountered the very worst. This was an area of about five acres surrounded by two layers of barbed wire. Inside, there were huts made of cardboard, packing boxes, and whatever could provide shelter. And a lot of shabby canvas tents. All of it planted right in the middle of a muddy pond, with naked kids running around, with men sitting on boxes drinking Chibuku. Chibuku, we learned, was fermented (alcoholic) yogurt in a wax-coated box. It was cheap. We tried it a couple of days later and vomited. On the other hand, this was the only apparent escape for these poor fuckers in the compound. If I was trapped there, I might acquire a taste for the stuff. From what I could see, this was much worse than Ncheu. At least those poor souls could walk away. I looked over at Mike and Art and they both had that 'What the fuck is this?' look.

Another twenty minutes or so and we came to a military facility with a guardhouse and a ten- foot high fence surrounding acreage as far as we could see. There were no trees, just short stubble. The guard examined some papers and we drove about 200 yards and parked at what looked like a reception or administration building. A platoon-sized group walked by in full camouflaged uniforms with FALs, apparently on their way to a training exercise, paying no attention to us as we got off the small busses. From the outside, the facility looked to be in good shape and well maintained, which was a stark contrast to the mud pond we had just passed.

We walked through a small reception area and an enlisted man pointed us to a large room with fold-up tables and chairs that would probably accommodate 150 people. It looked like a training room and that is what it turned out to be. An enlisted guy advised us to take a seat and proceeded to set up a small table and a couple of chairs in the front of the room. Shortly, a uniformed Katanganese Major and another white person in civilian clothes entered the room and took a seat at the table. In perfect English, the major said "Welcome to The Katanga! Welcome to Elizabethville." I am Major Chiluku and with me is Captain Jacque Phillipe." He added, "The captain is usually in more appropriate clothes", which brought a round of laughs. "This facility will be your home base and includes not only your quarters, but eating facilities, outside training fields and training lectures, which will usually be held in this room. Four hundred men are assigned to these quarters." That brought a buzz. This was a major installation and I realized that it was a lot larger than was initially thought. "However", said Philippe, "There will rarely be that many men in this facility because our field work takes throughout the country, usually in small groups."

Major Chiliuku gave us the expected pitch. We were free to select our roommates, four to a room; where the eating and bath facility were, and other logistics. He told us that we were free to settle in this afternoon and evening, sandwiches were available in the cafeteria, and we were expected to be in this training room at 0800 in the morning. Further, he added that "We do not have the luxury of a prolonged training period. You were selected because of skills that you already possess and we are going to tell you how you can put those skills to work." With that he asked that we stand and state our names and country of origin. We were surprised that there were only five Americans out of 36, with three of us, myself, Mike and Art from California. The bulk of the remainder were from Germany, France, England, and the rest scattered between other European countries. We felt very conspicuous because Mike and I were undoubtedly the youngest men there, and I could just imagine the thinking: 'I wonder what these kids have to offer?' On the other hand, they had all seen that 900-yard target with the hole in the guy's mouth, so maybe I was just self-conscious. We were told to sign up in groups at the back of the room and that our personal gear would be delivered before nightfall. Chiluku stated that the training and actual field instructions would be handled in English and French, and he understood that everyone had at least a speaking knowledge of one or both of those languages. He encouraged us to learn the Katanganese language, but the official language was French, so we had two languages to learn. We would be working with indigenous soldiers who, for the most part, spoke only their language, and we had better make sure we understood. That was it. "We'll see you ready to go at 0800, right here." As we broke up, Captain Phillipe came over and asked me "I am just curious. What is in that rifle case that you are lugging around?" And to Mike, "And the box?" We laughed at that and told him that our training sargeant in Brussels told us to "Hang on to these things, and not to check them as luggage or anything else or he would have our asses!" Phillipe chuckled and said "Well, I'll be interested in your unveiling these secrets tomorrow."

Mike and I managed assignment to the same room along with Art Stepan and a Georges Villier who had introduced himself as "France via Algeria." He was about 35 and looked like he had many stories to tell. We had a room with four bunks and a footlocker, and there were showers and toilets at the end of a very long hall. It looked like there were about 25 rooms along the hallway, and as I glanced out the windows, it appeared as if there were at least four more identical buildings.

During the evening we grabbed some sandwiches and brought them back to the room, and talked until, one at a time, we just fell onto our bunks and went to sleep, full of dreams and thoughts about whatever was ahead of us.

# Chapter 19

At exactly 0600, there was a loud knock at the door and a guy with a small wagon was there with our belongings. All neatly segregated, here was an extra set of cammies, our personal bags, our side arms, FALs all bagged in plastic with our names and numbers attached. Numbers. I was now # 01-265US. It was almost like Christmas and Mike and I immediately went for our automatic pistols to see if there was any damage. My P.38 looked unmolested and our FALs now had our I.D. numbers stenciled on the stocks. These guys ran a pretty crappy airline, but other than that they were very organized. They had even included 100 rounds of 9mm ammo for the pistols.

After another great breakfast of watery eggs and half-cooked bacon, a person in civvies stood at a portable podium, and identified himself as Jacques Poincare and that he was an advisor to the Prime Minister, Moise Tshombe. He started "I'd like to give you information on some logistics and what you can expect for the next several days." He went on about rooms and hygiene and other details but finally got to it. "This morning I am going to give you a talk on the situation here in The Katanga. As you probably have assumed, this is complicated business, and each of you need to understand who the players are in the political game going on all around us. It is a very fragile thing. A friend now could very well be an enemy tomorrow." This seemed to launch into still another familiar topic, but once again, these talks incrementally advanced our knowledge. He went on. "You need to fit into this business and even though, like many of us, dislike politics, you need to understand it for your own safety if nothing else. After lunch, we are going to the shooting range, which is adjacent to these barracks. You will receive instructions on breaking down your FAL, cleaning and reassembling it. These guns are your link with good health and you need to take this seriously. I know that you have been through this in Belgium, and we are going to see what you have learned." The business of our health brought a mild case of laughs. "There will be an NCO for each six recruits. We will be shooting mainly at targets at 100 to 300 yards, although a couple of you will be shooting at much longer ranges." Mike and I turned a little red, but by now, everyone knew what our purpose was.

"Tomorrow, most of you will go on patrol for an overnighter. We do not have the luxury of a formal training program, and you will learn 'on the job'. This will be a relatively safe operation, but it will help familiarize you with conditions and the terrain. So be sure to get some sleep tonight night because you will be humping it tomorrow."

For two hours, Mr. Poincare went on about the reason for all of this friction, the secession, the various players and generally held us all spellbound for two hours. He was very good at what he was doing. "I know that you have been given a briefing in Brussels last week but I am going to give you a more detailed account to a very complex issue."

"The first item is The Congo generally. Along with Independence last year came a Prime Minister in the form of Patrice Lumumba, 'democratically' elected, who was outspokenly a supporter of full socialism. He was also a Moscow protégé, so almost anything pertaining to the Congo was immediately thrust into an international issue. But in order for socialism to have any chance, there has to be some form of wealth to distribute. In the Congo, about 60% of the readily available wealth is located in Katanga province." I whispered to Mike that I wished that someone could consolidate all of this, but in all of our time in The Katanga, these kinds of briefings/propaganda/status meetings continued. It was not that they were not informative, but for two twenty-one year olds, we just wanted to get on with it.

"Lumumba is a charismatic leader, but his attachment to Moscow lead the U.S.to initiating fighting a proxy political war with Russia, which has been a common feature of the entire world following World War Two. The western world regards the export of communism as a threat, and while the west did not openly oppose Lumumba neither was there support. The stage was set for conflict. That came last year, just the day after independence when Katanga province seceded from the Congo and started their new country under Moise Tshombe. The west interpreted this as an internal issue and fought African protests including Lumumba's appeal for the United Nations action to reunite the Congo and throw out Belgium interests. Eventually, the U.N. sent what they call 'peacekeepers' to Katanga late last year, but they were ordered to not enter into the fray between Lumumba and Tshombe, which, of course, brings into question the entire purpose of these troops. Today, both Swedish and Irish uniformed troops are in The Katanga and in fact, Mr. O'Brien, the U.N. representative has an office right here in Elizabethville. You will see these troops, around town, and in some of the surrounding cities towns such as Jadotville. Your job is to get along with these people. At least for now, they pose no threat to us."

Poincare went on. "But back to Lumumba. The day after the independence proclamation, he stated that he would keep the Belgium officer corps in charge of the army. Two days later the army mutinied and went on a rampage in Leopoldville. It was full-scaled violence against any westerner. Congolese troops ravaged western homes and then waited in line to rape the women. It was a hideous event and two days later Lumumba backed down and ordered all Belgium troops out of the Congo, about 5000 in number. He then took the initiative and appointed politically connected people to run the army, and the first major decision was to send his army to reverse the secession. However, at least for now, he is not a real-world threat. They have a trip of thousands of miles in rag-tag old Soviet vehicles and obsolete weaponry. We get reports of the progress, which is apparently not a happy sight. Undisciplined troops, rapes, pillaging and abuse make us wonder if they will ever get here, let alone kick us out. That being said, they are approaching our border and before long, we will go to meet them. If necessary, we will fight them. None of this seems to have a scintilla of impact on the U.N. or separate countries. Their objective is total independence, and anything that stands in the way is to be crushed." I looked over at Mike and just shook my head. Poincare continued, "Then there are the Balubas who are an indigenous people spread throughout The Katanga. These people have existed since antiquity, and live in small villages and are only loosely federated under different chiefs. But they all have a common culture: they do not like white people, or any intruder, and they practice ritual torture if you are unfortunate enough to be caught. This is why we try and travel with a reasonably large group. Small groups are very vulnerable, and if caught, you face an almost certain horrible death. This is not an idle concern. Late month one our contract employees, a chap named Simon Donaldson wandered away from camp to take a leak or whatever, and was taken by the Balubas. They ate him. We found the small parts several days later. A severed foot was discovered near a fire pit, and doctors determined that the foot had been hacked off while Donaldson was still alive." The reaction was palpable. 'Holy shit' erupted several times. Those that were getting bored came to attention. Mike and I had heard about these guys in Brussels and we were happy to have our side arms with at least one bullet for ourselves. In fact, we kept hearing the same story over and over so it made a major impression.

"To our north, we have Hutu and Tutsi populations in Rwanda . There are major internal hostilities there, including massacres and from time to time, the fighting crosses our borders and we have to occasionally guard against that. They seem to be fully occupied killing each other rather than bothering us. We do get reports from the area, and last week we learned that literally thousands of bodies were floating in Lake Victoria, pleasing the alligator population. However, you may encounter refugees spilling over the border and we expect them to be treated in a humanitarian manner."

"Oh yes, one other thing. Mr. Lumumba is the Prime Minister of the Congo but he too has his adversaries. Mr. Joseph Mobutu is jousting for power and who knows? The only silver lining here is that if Lumumba and Mobutu are fighting each other, there will be less pressure on The Katanga. Mobutu might have a chance at success. He was educated at Catholic missions in the Congo and in Brussels as well. How this turns out is anyone's guess. Finally, I need to explain our resources. After Belgium troops were sent home, 300 advisors were left in The Katanga. We have about 500 contract soldiers in addition to this group. There is now pressure to send home those 300 Belgium advisors and all mercenaries, as they call you. But the ultimate intent here is to train a 5000-person army of Katanganese, and in most of our maneuvers you will be a part of a mixed group. But remember this: The ranking Katanganese will almost always be in command. There will be exceptions to this and a captain or a major from our contract group will many times accompany a maneuver or patrol, but the Katanganese will always be in official command. You need to understand, respect and accept that arrangement. As the indigenous army is developed, we will have fewer and fewer contract troops."

Poincaire continued, "We have a tiny air force of about ten planes, a mixture of jets and prop planes that can offer a degree of ground support when necessary. We have several light planes that can act as surveillance for ground troops and can advise our guys of possible surprises in the area. Now then, I am sure there must be questions." There were dozens of those and the session continued right up until lunch. Mike asked "When we came into town we saw a refugee camp or something like that. Who are these people and what are they doing here?" Mr. Poincare cleared his throat, thought about that for a moment and said, "These people are Balubas from the tribe that ate Simon Donaldson. We don't know what to do about them. We will probably truck them back to their area and let them go."

# Chapter 20

After the lectures, a group of NCOs assembled the group on the dock and a lead man said, "The first thing we are going to do is understand our FALs. Most of you know all about these weapons but you will go through this exercise anyway. We will divide into groups of six and our staff member will lead each group. Just spread out on the dock. There are a stack of mats and rags here to help you, as well as cleaning materials. This is for FALs only. When we are done here, we will shoot at 100 to 300 yards, then clean the guns again." Mike and I had our special equipment on the dock but they stayed in their cases until we were through with the FALs.

The disassembly went very easy. We had all read the manuals and many had a close familiarity with the FAL. We removed the magazines, the bolts, disassembled the bolts and cleaned the gas pistons that allowed the gun to operated semi or full automatic, cleaned the bores and reassembled the rifles. About four times. The staff looked very closely at what we were doing and in several cases, they took a rifle, disassembled it, scrambled the parts, laid them on a mat and said "Put it back together." When they were satisfied that everyone could handle this chore, we were told to each grab a bandoleer of loaded magazines and follow the staff to the range, about a mile away.

The range was well organized with 10 shooting stations and each of us had ear protection. With 30 guys all shooting in close formation, the earmuffs were a welcome asset. A pulley system allowed retrieval of the targets without interrupting other shooters. The targets were initially spaced at 100 yards and then 200 and lastly at 300 yards. We shot standing, at a seated bench and in a prone in-the-weeds position. At 100 yards we adjusted the sights as necessary and proceeded to fire three rounds in each position at 100, 200, and 300 yards. Mike and I did fine, placing all of the bullets in the black bull's eyes. Not perfect but pretty good. At 300 yards we knew there was a tiny ballistic drop and we roughly compensated for that. The .308 NATO round was well-suited for a 300 to 400-yard range and the FALs all worked flawlessly. Some of the guys had to keep working at it, but after about 90 minutes, everyone had passed muster, even though it was clear that a few guys needed some practice.

Our NCO, Alex Bartlet called a halt to the shooting and gave the shooters a choice. They could go back to their quarters and get ready for tomorrow or stay where they were and witness a long range shooting demonstration. That gave us the jitters, because we knew that meant us. I thought that some of the NCOs were a little suspicious of us youngsters doing anything beyond normal shooting and about half of them hung around. This was a different arrangement. Mike's original spotting scope had been replaced with a newer version that actually digitized the number of yards to the target, a technology that had been developed by land surveyors. In its prototype status, it was still an amazing, if clumsy piece of equipment. The concept was for a beam of light to bounce off a solid object and translate the time it took to hit that object and bounce back. Time is then translated to distance. The system had its limitations. A wooden post was placed next to each target to establish that 'solid object'. The assumption was that while a man would constitute a solid object, things such as bushes or, in this case, paper targets might not. Bartly explained that if you could travel around the earth at the speed of light, you could make about 7.5 complete trips in one second, so for our purposes, "We should accept that the calculation is instantaneous." I looked over at Mike who said "I think I can accept that!" Later, we learned that far more compact setups were being planned, and radio waves and other such physics were being developed, all beyond my understanding. For now, all I cared about was if this system worked.

The range had been reconfigured to targets at 300 yards and then in odd increments all the way to 1000 yards. Bartly knew exactly the distance to each target but it was up to us to figure that out. Determining the distances should not be difficult, given Mike's range finder. Still, it was disconcerting to Mike to rely on an electronic box rather than cross hairs vs. scope magnification and simple experience that he was used to. The targets themselves were man-sized torsos and heads rather than the bulls eye targets that we had been using. I opened the Mauser case and everyone there had to take a close look. They were all obviously jealous, having never seen anything quite this beautiful. They were all interested, but still, most were skeptics, especially considering the finger-nailed size of the almost invisible 1000-yard targets. But technically, it seemed simple. Mike calls out the distance, and having memorized the .300 Winchester Magnum ballistics chart, I knew how much a bullet would drop at any given distance. Duck soup. Except: A slight breeze could screw everything up. A slip off the trigger could as well. Or a tiny difference in bullet weight, one bullet to another. Or a gun battle going on all around, distracting the shooter. But if everything was perfect, I should hit that guy's head at 1000 yards.

After setting up, I shot a round at 300 yards, wheeled in the target and Mike and I examined it. The hole was exactly at the bridge of the nose, but just slightly off to the left. Nearly at the corner of the eye. Of course, the Mauser had bounced around in its case for several thousand miles and a slight adjustment was to be expected. I made a very slight horizontal correction and fired again. The hole was exactly between the eyes, right where the nose met the forehead. I chambered another round, used the set trigger, going off at one pound. Just a touch was all that it took. We reeled the target in and there was the same hole. I heard guffawing behind me until Bartly correctly said that the second bullet had travelled through the hole made by the first bullet! I told Mike to reel out the target to the second post and give me a distance. In an instant, he called out 423 yards. Wow! The bullet drop would be minimal at this distance. I fired and Mike reeled the target in. It was the exact same hole, maybe just a little fuzzed up on one side. Mike taped over the holes and reeled the target out to the next post and said "670 yards." This was getting serious but I felt confident. The result was a new hole right at the tip of the nose. Now the audience was at full attention. "Mike, take it out to the last post." Mike reeled the target out. "Distance?" "1047 yards, no wind." Round chambered. Trigger set. I adjusted for a considerable bullet drop at this distance. The round should still have well over 1000 foot pounds of energy left, but it would be running out of steam, but still plenty to easily take out a man. We were at about ¾ of a mile, or nine city blocks away. Fire. Reel in the target. Now we had a new hole, between the upper lip and the nose. Not bad. I heard clapping in the background and Bartly said "Very nice shooting guys." Mike and I got up and turned around, and got as few some slaps on the back. There were no skeptics left. Of course, Mike and I knew that it wouldn't be that easy. Men move around and posts do not. Still, you just could not fault the Mauser.

That evening our bosses brought out the barbecue and we had another great dinner of steaks and Belgium beer. It was wonderful! Mike and I also sensed a little more of the comradery exhibited by the more 'mature' people in our group. Clearly the word had been passed around once again about our shooting and we now seemed to be a more equal part of the group. They seemed to be saying "Why fight them at 100 yards if we can kill them at 1000 yards!" Or something like that.

Later, Mike and I were laying on our bunks and I said "You know, we've never killed anything bigger than a jack rabbit. Those paper targets really don't seem like opponents." Mike was quiet for awhile and then said, "But think about that Donaldson guy. They fucking ate him! Do you think you could do it? They hacked his foot off when he was still alive!" I thought about that for a minute. "Yeah," I said, "I think I can do it."

# Chapter 21

The next morning it was back to the watery breakfast routine, but there was no bitching that I could hear. This was the day we were finally going into the real world. Even the veterans were quiet, waiting for orders. They came soon enough. Our Sergeant Bartly stood before the podium with a blackboard behind him that identified a 20-person platoon with I.D. numbers on it. Before he said anything we noted that our numbers were on the list.

"At 0900 we will assemble by the dock and we'll get your kit sorted out. Bring your undies, spare socks and your rifles and we will supply the rest. We'll be gone three days and two nights. The numbers on the Board behind me will go today. The others will go on a similar trek tomorrow in a different direction. I hope your boots are well broken in because we're going to do some humping. I expect we will cover about 60 miles in the three days, a comfortable hike! We'll be bivouacking at two farms along the way. The entire purpose here is to get you acquainted with the terrain and your equipment, and show the flag to our rural citizens. We do not expect any action on this particular exercise but you just never know around here. You need to be alert and have your arms ready to use."

The first thing that registered was that our 20-person group was made up of an equal number of whites and blacks. We learned later that the Katanganese troops had gone through four weeks of training but this was their first real exercise. The group was led by a Major Mkandawire, and a Captain Hagen, which was a little rich for a very small platoon. Maybe it was more like a squad. But on the other hand, the situation here was new to everyone and it seemed smart to start off with as much guidance as possible. Mkandawire walked through the group shaking hands and he immediately noticed my holstered P.38. "Ah, another Walther fan I see", pointing to his own P.38 in a shoulder holster. That was very cool. This person really knew his Walthers, because when the pistol was in my holster, all he could see was the holster itself, which fit tightly over the pistol with a leather flap, and the bottom plate of the magazine. I still cannot figure out how he did that, and finally assumed that someone had tipped him off. "What vintage is it?" he asked. "My dad brought it home from the war and it's an ac 42." That stood for a Walther made pistol manufactured in 1942. "Ah, very nice. Mine is a byf 43, made by Mauser." The reason that these 'ac' and 'byf' codes were used by the Germans was to confuse the allies as to where the guns were built. If it simply said 'Mauser' they would know exactly where to bomb. Anyway, he un-holstered it and handed it to me butt first and I commented that it was a very good example. We shook hands a second time and then he continued down the row of recruits. He didn't comment on Mike's Belgian Browning which pissed Mike off.

Several NCOs were adjusting backpacks for each of us, which had been filled previously with emergency first aid gear, an extra uniform, a gun cleaning kit and emergency food that looked to be 20 years old. We each also received bandoleers with five extra 20 round magazines for our FALs. We also received a folding shovel that strapped to our back packs, and a 6" holstered knife that hooked onto our belts. Hagen said "I hope that you notice how all of this stuff is packed because this is the last time we'll be doing it for you." About that time two jeeps pulled up pulling small trailers stocked with ammo cans, tents and bedrolls. When the NCO got to me, he knew all about our special equipment. He gave me a flexible cover for the Mauser, another box of 9mm ammo for the P.38, and said "We're going to pack you and your friend Mr. Genard here a little lighter because of the extra gear you will be carrying. I realized that I'd be packing both the 12 pound Mauser as well as the FAL. There was a kind of jerry-built canvas bag for Mike's optic stuff, and of course he had to carry his own FAL. And then there were our Ghilley suits all rolled into a neat ball

The way they had the march arranged was that three recruits plus an NCO led off, followed by a jeep and a trailer. The jeep had a .50 caliber machine gun mounted where the jeep's rear seat used to be. Mkandawire rode in the passenger seat. Then there were groups of four that followed, each of them spread out somewhat, walking the shoulders and where possible, outside of the graded roadway. Just before the final four was the other jeep also with a .50 caliber machine gun, with Captain Hagen riding in the passenger seat. A final four lagged some distance behind, sometimes marching backwards, covering our rear. Mike, Art and I were sandwiched in the middle of the group. The pace was not fast, and the jeeps simply idled along stirring up dust as we left town when the paved road turned to dirt. We stopped about every hour for a quick break, then were on our way again. The vegetation was a mixed bag. At times, growth extended right to the edge of the road, which made us a little edgy because there was no visibility into a stunted forest. At other times the roadside growth didn't amount to much at all, with brush and grasses allowing visibility for over a thousand yards. As we walked down into canyons, the growth turned almost to jungle, with vines growing between trees, with visibility nil. That bothered me. You cannot hit what you cannot see. What would be the utility of a 900 yard shot in a jungle? At the second stop, about eight miles from town, we stopped and Mkandawire dismounted and asked us to gather around. The weather was warm, about 90 degrees but not too humid. "What I want you to do is to look over to your left. Do you see a slight wisp of smoke several miles away?" Most of us nodded but we had not noticed anything until he brought it up. "Most likely that is a Baluba village. These chaps often times build a village made of mud huts with thatched roofs, and it may be there for a year or two, and then it's abandoned and they move on and build another, almost identical village. This village, if that is what it is, was not there two weeks ago. No one actually knows why they move around like this. It could be the availability of game or water, or possibly a feud with another tribe. The point for you is, always be alert to a new village. You might have been by here a week ago and an old village was apparently thriving. Then it is abandoned and they move on a few miles and start over. You never actually know where these guys are. Always be alert. You might have noticed a small aircraft at a high altitude. That is a Piper Cub reconnaissance plane, and we have radio communication with the pilot. When he reaches his range limit he will return to Elizabethville, but until that time, we have eyes in the sky." The plane was flying so high and so slow that I could not hear the engine.

At noon we stopped by a tiny village that had a general store, and we were all treated to cold drinks while we ate some of our rations. In my case it was crackers with peanut butter. We rested about 45 minutes and then moved on. As we disappeared around a corner, I thought of that guy, either French or Belgium, running that store. How vulnerable was he? He didn't have any machine guns or Jeeps. He probably did have an FAL. He was just a settler, like in the old West, but with a radio set to contact the nearest military camp.

About half way through the afternoon the lead jeep came to an abrupt stop, and Captain Hagen ran past us to talk to Mkandawire. They walked up the road and looked down at a seemingly flat surface. We were all called forward to take a look. One of the NCOs reached down and pulled at what looked like a woven mat and pulled it aside. It was a cleverly camouflaged pit. If a person unknowingly walked over the mat, he would fall down into the pit which was about 6' deep. At the bottom were sharpened sticks pointing upward, covered with some sort of goo, which we were told was probably human feces. Hagen spoke. "This is what the Balubas call an elephant trap. This one is too small for an elephant or even a Jeep, but a man might die here. Most likely its purpose is to trap game wandering along the road, because the camouflage was not done too well. But these things can actually be made to trap an elephant. You need to be constantly alert. The Balubas will always be more at home in the bush than we will ever be." Four guys were appointed to fill in the hole, and we proceeded in a northerly direction. By 1700 we walked into a farmer's field who came out of his house with a wife and a couple of kids and gave us a warm welcome. It wasn't just the Balubas that they had to contend with, but also the threat of the Lumumba army, bumbling their way across the Congo, having perfected the art of pillage and rape. And the United Nation pests who also patrolled these roads as they 'kept the peace' but whose real agenda was to kick the Tshombe regime out of Africa. And if Tshombe left or was kicked out, The Katanga would look just like the shambles that existed in the rest of the Congo. Our soldiers were their salvation and every white, black or brown farmer, settler or store owner and they heaped food and praise upon us.

The bivouac was an open field next to the farm house that had been deliberately left level so that the farmer had a good field of fire if he suddenly came under attack. The jeeps were pulled into the flat area and we began to learn how to set up the tents, dig latrines, set up our pickets and activate our field kitchen. It was kind of a goat fuck, with people stumbling over each other, using unfamiliar gear and all of that, but we also knew that this was actually elementary stuff, and after a few nights, it should be duck soup.

After dinner some of us spent a little time rubbing our feet and working some gun oil into our boots. If we raised and popped an actual foot blister, the next 40 miles was going to be torture. But by the time it was dark, we were in our bedrolls and happy that we had not been on the guard duty list.

And so it went. Visiting farms and villages, showing the flag, giving reassurance to the population and prepared to fight if that need came our way. Another benefit was getting to know the rest of the patrol. The Katanganese seemed to have mellow personalities and had a free and happy way about them. There were some obvious cultural problems the NCOs had to deal with, because our western organized way of life was not the life of a native. But they were coming along well, and were frequently complimented, even if there were some corrective measures sometimes taken. They were basically competent and dedicated, and interestingly, we visibly saw that there was no reason why whites and blacks could not co-exist in an African country. What a concept! It was really too bad the Belgium rulers had not thought about that 100 years ago. Today, across the Congo, it might very well be too late. Mike, Art and I enjoyed the three-day March. It was good to do something besides sitting in broken airplanes, attending lectures and just worrying. We stretched our muscles and saw at least 60 miles of the country. Still, when we marched through Elizabethville, we looked forward to a hot meal and a bed that had a mattress.

# Chapter 22

After dinner we returned to our room and found that we had some mail, scattered across my bed. It was all good until I read the letter from my mother. Andy Schmidt, the guy who lived on Sunset Ave. in Bakersfield…. yes, the guy who was called to take his physical and all ..yes, the guy who convinced us that there might be better alternatives than Viet Nam…remember? Well, according to Mom, rather than wait a week or two to be drafted, he went to the army recruiting office down at the Post Office and…get this: he joined up and he was going to Germany! Germany! Where the beer is strong and the girls are all blonde! And no war! I yelled at Mike and Art looked at me without understanding…"Can you believe this?" Mike sat with his mouth open but finally said "Yeah, but he's still only making $88 bucks a month!"

Folded in a separate manila envelope were our passports. So much had gone on since that trip to the Post Office. Our routines became uneventful as we settled in to Elisabethville. We went on one epic seven-day jaunt that tested our ability to live in the bush and also showed the flag in several villages. Even though this was the 'dry' season, we had a tropical downpour outside of Jadotville that was unbelievable. Crackling lightning strikes just a couple of hundred yards away followed by almost simultaneous thunder that sounded like bombs going off. And then the rain. It was like being submerged. Constant sheets of water made us wonder how we could get any oxygen! None of those wimpy California rains, this was a deluge that went on for over two hours. Our tents struggled to stay put, but generally speaking, if they were erected properly, they kept us dry. But the most unbelievable part was the next morning. We expected all kinds of post-rain disasters, but the sun came up and everything looked completely normal, like nothing had happened. That was just the way it was. Eight inches of rain through the night and everything was normal the next day. In Bakersfield, it would have been a county disaster. The day turned out to be more humid than most, but other than that, it was just another warm day in The Katanga.

We also did several overnighters that included a two-hundred-mile C-47 trip to the west where some very troubled settlers treated us like royalty. Between our ventures into the bush we spent time target shooting, practicing with our Ghilley suits and improving communications during our maneuvers. One issue that just never went away for me was carrying the weight of two rifles. The staff tried to compensate by reducing other stuff I was carrying but that had its limits too. We needed ammo, food and water and the rest of the stuff didn't weigh much. This was particularly true if we were actually deployed as a sniper team, because we might be isolated for 24 hours or more, remote from the rest of the group.

On Sundays, we were free to walk into town although it was suggested that we stay in a group of at least three, and wear civvies. So Mike, Art and I went on a weekly sojourn into town. We went to the movies, hung out around a bar, and did our best to hook up with some girls. There was promise, but no immediate results. Once you adjusted to the city and accepted that the ratio of Blacks to Whites was about 15:1, it was much the same as any mid-sized city. Of course, we realized that blacks in America had the same situation. There was bus service, a museum, a university (where the girls hung out), a major hospital and small smoke-belching cars everywhere. The military presence was always there, but definitely in the background. The U.N. 'peacekeepers' were much more visible than we were, despite our much larger numbers. They marched around town in the blue caps, looking a little embarrassed and people giggled a little as they walked by. What was their purpose?

Behind the scenes, the political problems The Katanga faced were heating up. On Mondays we were briefed on the latest, which this week included a bunch of third world nations demanding that the U.N take an active role in ousting Tshombe and his 'Rogue Government.' As far as we could tell, The Katanga was about the only thing in the Congo (now re-named Zaire) that actually worked. A major issue was the white influence. Whites were just not accepted, even though the complaining black countries expected to be fully accepted in the white countries, and especially at the U.N. Of course, it was much more complex than we made it out to be, but then we were 21 years old and definitely not politicians.

The latest problem was on two fronts. First, the Lumumba government troops were on the move again, and were approaching our border. Farmers and shop-keepers in outlying areas had radio communications with Elisabethville and the volume of the contacts was very high. We were briefed on an almost a certain engagement and this would not be practice. Our leaders were confident that we could handle the situation because intelligence reports suggested that all the government troops were interested in was pillaging, getting drunk and rape. Of course, this panicked the ordinary people in Elisabethville and over in Jadotville, about 70 miles away, and absolutely brought a feeling of growing hysteria to those living in remote villages and farms.

The other threat, with far greater consequences, were talks going on in Leopoldville (now re-named Kinshasa) between Tshombe and the Lumumba government. On the face of it, this was good news. But behind the scenes, our officers and civilian bosses told us that this was a complete sham. That these 'talks' were limited to getting Tshombe out of Africa and dissolving The Katanga. For a brief period, there was talk about Tshombe assuming control and ousting Lumumba. But that fizzled out and Tshombe left the talks to return home.

About then, the shit hit the fan. At the political level at least. Joseph Kasa-Vubu took theoretic control of the Congo as president, but Lumumba was appointed as Prime Minister and continued in effective charge, which by now was largely *out* of control. When Kasa-Vubu edged towards the U.S and the west, open political conflict took place between he and Lumumba, when Joseph Mobutu, a Congolese army officer staged a successful coup. Initially, our information was that Mobutu would be an effective leader until we heard about the fate of Lumumba. In full public view, he was handcuffed and was forced to actually eat his last political speech, then brutally beaten. He was then reported to have been bundled into a C-47, flown to the remote village of Tshiltembo in The Katanga and was never seen again. Months later, it was reported that he had been shot, cut into pieces and dissolved in a barrel of acid. The Balubas had no corner on the torture market. Within a few days, pictures leaked to us showing Lumumba being beaten, and eating the speech. All of this raised a huge storm at the U.N., anxious to blame all ills on The Katanga and Moise Tshombe, the criticism coming especially from all of the newly minted African countries and the Russians. However, there has never been proof that Tshombe was responsible or involved in Lumumba's death. It was just another way of discrediting The Katanga.

We talked a lot about the possibility of the U.N troops actually becoming a fighting force. The idea of shooting Swedish and Irish troops was still not attractive. We were all mercenaries, but all except the most grizzled were disgruntled at that prospect. It was not a racial issue, at least for us as we were limited to intercepting marauding, torturing tribes. But for the time being, we had an appointment with the Congolese army near the border and issues having to do with the U.N. slipped into the background.

# Chapter 23

We were in the sack at 2200 hours, but there was not much sleep. Tomorrow would be the real thing. No more training. To Mike and I, this was a huge deal. All of the planning, the classes, the shooting and just hanging out with a bunch of mercenaries was a very cool thing. Plus, we were in the employ of a country that hardly existed. But now, we're talking about killing people. True, it sounded like these people needed killing, but my God! Targeting a human being and placing a .300 Winchester Magnum hole in a guy's skull was very heavy duty. Troubled, we both slept a little but the dreams were not pleasant.

We were called to get up at 0430. The heads of this operation staggered the get-up time so everyone would get fed in a relatively small room which was designed for about 150. It was the usual stuff. Watery eggs and half cooked bacon. However, I assumed that however bad it was, it was better than what we would be getting on the road.

The good news was that we met up with Sargeant Piquart! He had arrived with a newly recruited group following ours, and we greeted each other with a lot of handshakes and hugs. Better yet, the upper echelon recognized Piquart's involvement in our sniper education and he was made a part of the group we were attached to. With no conflicting orders, we followed him like ducklings follow their mother. Mike, Art, and I had all of our stuff and found that our four trucks were first in line. With not much to do except pop anti-acids and speculate, we talked with the Sargeant, and, other guys in our group gathered around and asked questions and tried to understand what we were facing without listening to a guy behind a podium. Most of the group had not met Piquart but he had this sense of stability and knowledge that attracted people. Even the old guys wanted to pick his brain.

By 0600 we were on the road. The lead truck pulled a trailer loaded with food supplies, tools, ammo, tents, and whatever. In front of us was a Jeep with a .50 caliber machine gun. There was about a quarter mile gap between our trucks and the next group, so the entire procession covered a mile or so. The general idea was that each group of four trucks would be self-sufficient, and where appropriate, deployed in that manner. Steve, as we knew him, was in the shotgun seat in the cab, and all of us peons sat on hard wooden benches along the sides of the truck. There was a canvas covering but we tied it back to the cab, because even at this hour it was hot and very humid. I wasn't sure if the sweat was the weather or my nerves.

Our first day destination was an army facility in Jadotville, an easy 70 miles away. It was explained that in the afternoon we would get an up-to-date intelligence report, along with a final briefing. As we left Elisabethville, the asphalt turned to dirt and the dirt turned to pot holes. These were off-road four-wheel drive trucks and felt every imperfection in the road, and there were millions of them, jolting our spines, our butts and anything else prone to discomfort. After about 25 miles we stopped at a farmhouse for a break and doused our heads under a hand-pumped well. The farmer, his wife and kids all came out and offered us cookies and thanked us for our help. I had thought about these people who were incredibly exposed to all kinds of dangers, yet they struggled on, growing crops and hoping for better times. Better times seemed to me to be a crap shoot. Everyone was talking about the Lumumba assassination, but no one had very much actual news.

Jadotville, now named Likasi according to Mobutu, was a town of about 35,000 that was intensely pro-Tshombe. It was reported that every resident had arms, black and white, and they had an organized militia. They loved us but they were not relying on anyone. We drove right through the town and then on to a run-down army facility about three miles further on. Our group set up tents and camped outside but others rounded up some brooms and swept the place out and laid their bedrolls inside. We had field rations for dinner although a huge pot of beans was prepared. We ate beans and biscuits.

We set off at 0700 hrs. for Kamina, about 175 miles away, enduring increasingly poor roads. We had learned to sit on the floor with our backs to the wall of the truck so that we could brace ourselves from the next pot-hole shock. It was all day torture but we arrived intact at about 1500 hrs. We had gone through some tiny villages and had a chance to stretch and get cold drinks, so it actually wasn't all that bad a trip. The alternative was to walk, and I thought about those Congolese army guys walking over a thousand miles. Kamina, which is very close to the Katanga border, reminded me of an old west town. It even had some false front buildings and all of the necessities for farmers. There was a welding shop, a feed store, a vet, grocery store, a bank, a marginal looking café and a bunch of other businesses along those lines. There were no must-see cultural stopping places in Kamina. The people were the same, eager to see us and shake our hands. They had set up a kind of barbecue on the main street and we were treated to great food, cold beer and even some cute farm girls waiting on us. Everyone was talking about the coup, but the rumors were wild, ranging from good-guy Mobutu to Mobutu the butcher.

But there was a definite downside in play. Refugees were beginning to show up from the north, keeping ahead of the Congolese Army. If those guys got to farms before we stopped them, the refugees expected very little left if they ever returned. About 100 miles to the north, some did not get out soon enough, and at least a dozen families were reported missing. If they were not in Kamina they were assumed to be hiding in the brush or dead. Stories abounded via the radio system of people signing off and heading south on tractors, old cars, or on horseback. One enterprising bachelor locked his house and placed all of his liquor supply by the roadside, thinking that if the troops became drunk enough, they might just pass out. Steve said that was wishful thinking because once they got drunk, the pillaging began. In any case, at 0700 the next morning we were headed north, this time on foot.

Our leaders had studied maps and were undecided on whether to set up a surprise defense or just march until we encountered them. The latter seemed to be the favored approach, and with 750 well trained, sober men, they figured that we could make short work of the rag-tag army. That may be true, but it didn't calm my nerves at all. By the time we had hiked 20 miles, we assumed that there could be an encounter around the next bend. The officers stopped and had a conference of sorts, then passed that information down to our Lieutenant Edward Lambrette, who told the NCOs including our Sargeant Steve, who then passed the strategy on to us. An advanced patrol of about 15 men would start off and stay off the road wherever possible. We were warned that this could be very slow going as half the rest of our group, about 40 men, would follow after about 45 minutes, and keep a good distance from the lead patrol until contact was made. The idea was that the lead group would stay as invisible as possible until it was clear what the situation was. Sergeant Steve told Mike and I that we would be in the second group and for us to check out our sniper equipment now, especially the range finder. Art was included in the initial patrol and we wished him well. He seemed relaxed and anxious to finally do something worthwhile.

Mike and I broke out our gear and replaced the battery in the range finder and we checked it against a steel culvert 500 yards away. We then paced the distance and were satisfied that the equipment was working OK. After a brief break, the 15-man patrol set out and the remainder gathered in a small hollow in thick vegetation. We were now at the 4600' elevation and at least the weather was cool and dry. But the vegetation was much thicker and visibility was very limited. The NCOs had radio contact with the Lieutenant and in our case, Steve gave us a kind of satellite ear plug that transmitted one way. The purpose of this one-way communication was very limited. But when he said "Take the shot," we knew what to do.

As the patrol left, there was an eerie quietness that came over us as our trucks turned around and parked about a mile away. We heard a very slight sound and looking up, we saw a light plane, the Piper Cub that must have been 6,000' above us, circling through cumulus clouds. We assumed the pilot was attempting to locate our enemies at a distance. It didn't take long.

The first evidence that we were very close was an increase in refugees. This was not just white farmers and merchants but native Katanganese, who were every bit as vulnerable to drugged and liquored up troops as we were. They were in a hurry, carrying suitcases, backpacks and small children. These were the people of Katanga, technically running away from their own army, and running into the arms of the bad guys, which technically was us. About an hour later, the advance group radioed that they had made contact. Their report was short and unusual. They had not run into a large group, but a lot of smaller units, maybe 200 or so each, but these groups seemed to be spread over a large front. They did not have an estimate of the total number of troops, but there were apparently fires in dispersed areas. Steve briefed us on all of that and told us to prepare to move. We looked towards the hills beyond us and saw wisps of smoke across several miles, suggesting that these guys were not just marching down the road, but advancing through the forest, probably burning property as they came towards us. Or maybe they were through and camped for the day. Steve said to "saddle up" and we followed him in four man groups off the roadway and into the brush and semi-forest. We stopped after about 30 minutes and the Sargeant appointed a point man for each four-man group and told us when we made visual contact to stop and not engage. Clearly, Steve wanted to get a feeling for what was ahead before some hot shot started shooting. He was heading our small group and was constantly on the radio, and we assumed that other similar patrol groups were advancing as we were.

The terrain was not too difficult and the vegetation, while dense, did not require any clearing to make our way forward. The problem was limited visibility. I could just imagine passing by a tree and coming face to face with one of these guys. Thinking about that, I paused and pulled my Walther from the holster and checked to make sure I had a round in the chamber. Mike did the same, he with his Browning and we looked at each other like 'that was pretty stupid' or, 'why hadn't we checked that?'

We smelled fire before we saw anyone and Steve held his hand up and told Mike and I to get our Ghilley suits on. That took a while with two rifles, a back pack and other gear. But in a few minutes there we were, looking like something from the black lagoon. Steve pulled some vegetation from bushes and planted them in our head gear while the rest of our squad looked on. He spoke in whispers. "I want you guys to move ahead as quietly as you can. When you believe you might be detected get down on the ground and crawl forward as far as you can. I will be very close behind you but the rest of the group will stay further back. Let's get this thing started right because once the shooting starts, all hell will break loose. He gave Mike a very small transmitter and told him it was only good for about 40 yards.

We moved, hunched over and trying to be quiet. After a few minutes Mike held his hand out and we stopped. Ahead there were about ten guys, around 500 yards ahead, gathered around a fire, laughing and clearly not paying any attention to a possible threat. It was quite a distance away, and it was difficult to understand their focus. Whatever it was, we heard laughter, even at this distance. We reported to the Sargeant and dropped to the ground and continued on our bellies. This was pretty frightening because we knew that somewhere in these woods there was anywhere from 500 to 2000 troops and we could only see 10 of them. Where were the rest? We came to a halt behind a large boulder and I slipped the Mauser out of its soft case, unfolded the bipod and took a look. Mike unpacked his optic gear and I asked him to get a range on the fire. "625 yards" and I admonished myself for being so far off in my estimate. Surprisingly, I was calm, but unsure of the next step. Then Mike used his spotting scope and found the reason for all of the laughing. They had a native guy tied to a post and they were beating him with their belts. His chest was covered with blood but he didn't seem to be making a sound. I reported back to Steve. He slipped in behind us and said "I'm going to fire a warning shot and see what they will do. If they fire back, take a shot at whoever you think the leader is. I am responsible for this. You just focus on the shot." I made sure Mike and I were on the same page. "Mike, I'm looking for the leader and whoever is in on this. If I make the shot, guide me right to the next shot."

A few seconds later Steve fired a single .308 into the brush hanging over the fire pit and a branch and some leaves fell, scattering around the troops. Instead of scattering, most of them picked up their AK-47s and started firing on full automatic, in all directions, bullets flying everywhere but nowhere near us. The guy actually holding the belt just stood there looking around. It was time. And it was an easy shot. I slipped the Mauser off safety, adjusted a small amount for elevation, set the trigger and then squeezed. The Mauser bumped my shoulder and I brought the scope down to the target in time to see that not only had I hit the guy in the head, but half of his head disappeared in a fog of pink mist and jelly. He actually stood there for a half second and then toppled into the fire. By then Mike called out "four right." I moved the barrel an inch and there was another guy without a shirt, obviously stunned and looking around when the second bullet hit him in the forehead, the back of his skull bouncing into the air, accompanied by solid fragments and another pink cloud. He dropped instantly. All of this had taken maybe two seconds and the other eight guys came to life, instantly sober, their AKs held in one hand and looking around, unsure where this instant death came from. But they didn't wonder long. They turned around and ran in the opposite direction, leaving the guy tied to the post.

Steve was there a second later and said "I think this was their advance group, so when they show up in their rear, we can expect all hell to break loose. Oh, by the way, good shots!" It dawned on me that I had just killed two human beings, but after looking at the guy tied up to the post, it didn't bother me. Why all of the torture? What the fuck had this guy done? Their form of entertainment? Surely he would be dead in an hour or two had we not shown up. There was no doubt about the torturers. They looked normal from the shoulders down, but their heads were not recognizable. Just bone and mush. Everyone looked and two of them vomited. Art gave us each a hug! Steve was busy on the radio and apparently the other groups were making contact, and the adjacent squad wanted to borrow us. So, we hiked to the left about 800 yards and ran into another squad of about 12 of our guys. We still had our Ghilley suits on and the squad looked at us like we had come from Mars. This sargeant said they had a serious problem. He said that ahead in a clearing some kind of mayhem was taking place because he could hear a woman screaming. The Congolese troops had a perimeter staked out and had heard our shots but stayed in place. He guessed that these guys must of thought that the noise was just random fun and games. "We need you to get as close as you can to this and see what you can do. It's fairly open and anything we do has the potential resulting in the person screaming getting the worst of it."

We nodded and knew what to do this time. The 'see what you can do' statement was accepted that we were free to shoot if we could nail the bad guys. I pulled the bolt back and inserted two more rounds into the Mauser magazine. I heard a horrible scream, but it was a very long way away. I slung my FAL on my back, and with the Mauser in one hand, Mike and I moved slowly forward. After a couple of minutes, the lack of vegetation caused us to drop to the ground and we continued ahead, very slowly. Ahead five yards. Stop. Ahead another five yards, stop. After about 30 minutes we could see some people gathered and I imagined that they were looking at us. But that was imagination. We looked like the stubble, and besides, these guys were about the size of my thumbnail at this range. We continued ahead. After about 45 minutes we could see the group. We eased up to a slight dirt berm and settled in. This was as close as we were going to get and it was not very close. I extended the bipod and Mike unloaded his optics. Before I was even set up, I called out "Range." Mike whispered back "1275 yards". "Shit," I said. "This ain't going to be easy." Mike responded, "Looks like a 4 mph breeze from left to right judging by the smoke." That was cool. We were getting ready to kill some guys and Mike delivered a weather report like he was in an office!

We adjusted our scopes and I instantly saw the problem ahead. There were about twenty guys in a semi-circle, wearing something that resembled camouflaged uniforms and they had two hostages strung up to a tree. Their arms were held to branches above their heads and their feet were barely touching the ground. Then I realized that one was a woman, a brunette and very thin, her clothes stripped off. The other one was a man, I assumed her husband, also tied up with no clothes. Every few seconds someone would walk up to the man and belt him one on the stomach and kick his genitals. He was in extreme agony, and then I saw the third person. This was a kid about eight years old, and he was tied to another tree, apparently being forced to watch all of this. He too got an occasional slap and when that happened, the woman screamed. Every second or two, someone would walk by her and fondle her, and there was not much doubt what was in store for her if we failed. "Fuck," I said and then to myself, I wondered why these people didn't get out when they could.

Mike looked over and said "What do you think?" I looked back and said "I think that we need to get those two guys nearest to the hostages, then maybe light the place up with our FALs and see if we can't make them run. We need to get these people cut down. I used the little transmitter and said "You better get a medic ready. And once I fire the Mauser, we plan on lighting the place up so we can use some help." Steve simply said "Check." Steve? Apparently he had followed us to the new location

I settled in. This had to be perfect or it would fuck everything up. Mike looked through his scope and said "I think they have one of his eyes gouged out, and the woman is going nuts and they are slapping the shit out of her." The .300 Winchester Magnum had plenty of power at this range. The problem was accuracy due to the bullet drop. Now there was also the wind. Over 1200 yards, wind, and these guys were moving around. I tried to block the screaming out of my mind and chambered a round. Off safety. God, it looked like a torture chamber and now to the left I saw the small boy, apparently unconscious. No time to analyze any further. "Wind drift," I asked again. "I'd up it to 6 miles per hour." Set trigger, take a deep breath and squeeze. The guy closest to the woman dropped like a bag of potatoes but I could not see where I hit him. The next round chambered. Mike called out 4 feet right. Set trigger. Deep breath. Squeeze. This time I saw what had happened. I was a little high and the entire top of the guys's head came off. The rest of the troops were stunned, looking at these dead guys and staring at each other. I decided to take one more shot. This guy was moving toward the woman. "Guy next to the woman." "Five feet right" Mike responded. "Wind kicking up." Round chambered. Adjust for wind. Deep breath. Set trigger. Squeeze. This wasn't such a good shot. The guy had stood on a rock on his way to the woman and the round caught him directly in the crotch. I looked at Mike. "The woman doesn't have to worry about that fucker."

Meanwhile the rest of the squad advanced and we followed them, FALs blazing away. We had to get within shooting range and so a few got away. But by the time we got to the torture scene there were 12 troops sprawled around, dead, or about to become dead. What I had not expected was the way my long range shot paralyzed these guys. They actually froze in place for a second or two, allowing a second and third shot. And then the rest ran.

# Chapter 24

The entire invading force, however many there were, all retreated into the forest. A picket line was immediately set up and a bunch of tin cans and other stuff was set up across a wide area along the border to help warn of any new incursion. Not hi-tech, but then neither was the opposing force. Troops dug in behind the noise-makers and waited. It was moving towards dusk and I suppose the thinking was that chasing them involved more risk than benefit. We were also very close, or perhaps even across the border, and we had no authority to move much further. The bulk of the troops hiked back, and formed another defensive line. And behind that a medic station was set up and that is when we saw the victims at close range.

What a fucking mess. The woman was wrapped in a blanket and did not seem to be physically injured, but was crazy with fear. From time to time she screamed and asked for her son, and hugged him so closely I thought he might become injured. The medic gave her a shot of something and she quieted down, sobbing and slowly moving between consciousness and unconsciousness. The boy seemed completely stunned and neither wept nor said anything.

The man was another matter. His right eye was hanging by a tendon or nerve material about an inch out of the socket. His testicles were bleeding and swollen, and here we were again, his ear being sliced off. But he was conscious and actually talking. We were not part of the medical team, but could hear what was going on. The medic seemed to be unable to do anything with the eye except cradle it in soft, moist material. His head was heavily bandaged and the medic gave him a couple of shots. I could hear him saying, almost shouting, "I've been at my farm for 20 years in this country and never hurt a soul. These motherfuckers are savages" Then, he would drift off but come back and say, "Get those savages!" We helped move the injured towards the rear and just the sight of them was heartbreaking. Meanwhile, a crew dug a mass grave and dumped what was left of the soldiers into the hole. We didn't want a tell-tale flock of crows giving our position away.

We assembled in the rear and had a short de-briefing with Sargeant Steve and the Lieutenant. We agreed that the sniper effort had some unintended benefits, stunning the troops for enough time to disrupt them and take charge. Plus, the guys who deserved to die were dead. That night we cleaned our equipment and slept on mats. Steve came over and congratulated us on our effort, and brought us up to date on the overall exercise. As far as could be determined, the Congolese troops had retreated about two miles before settling down. For now, the idea was to keep them at a distance. Art came over from another squad and we all talked late into the night, looking at the stars and wondering what tomorrow would bring. One of the medics dropped by and told us that the victims were doing as well as could be expected and were being trucked to Jadotville, where a doctor had been imported. His concern was that except for the eye, they would all recover, but the woman was so mentally disturbed, he wasn't sure what would happen to her.

But, there's a little humor that can be found whatever the situation, and when we got to Jadotville we ran into the doctor who treated the family and I asked about the guys' eye. The doctor looked at me, hunched his shoulders like 'why are you asking' and said, "Oh, that was no problem. I just pushed it back into the socket and it looks OK. The muscles that control the eye movement need a little time, but as long as the optic nerve was undamaged, the eye will probably be OK." I just never thought of an eye being like a shoulder dislocation, but there you are. I had to ask him one more question: "Well, when the eye was essentially looking down towards the ground, was it still seeing?" "Well, of course. It was just seeing the ground!"

The next morning, we got unexpected news. The supposed execution of Patrice Lumumba had moved the U.N into action and the blue hats were now authorized to use force to get all Belgium soldiers out of the Congo. It was not proven, nor years later was it proven that Belgium soldiers had anything to do with executing Lumumba, but his death simply gave the U.N. fuel and justification to reinforce what they had already started. This created quite a buzz, and we started to dissect what constituted a Belgium soldier. All of the Belgium Army in Leopoldville had already moved back to Europe, which of course, created a vacuum for the Russians to make their mischief. And, most of the soldiers in The Katanga had gone, being gradually replaced by a far more limited number of 'advisors', plus the contract employees such as ourselves, with the ultimate goal of an all Katanganese army. But that would take time. What the U.N. seemed to want was the existing Congolese army to be the only force. The same guys ravaging the country and torturing civilians. The thing that was a mystery was how illogical all of this was. Tshombe was an alternative to Lumumba and had a new country where law and order prevailed. He was black. Why the obsession to get rid of him? The only explanation seemed to be to preserve the territorial integrity of the Congo. What integrity? Something that a despotic Belgium king created in the last century? And who would actually rule after Lumumba?

Of course, all of this was above our tiny pay grade, but that didn't stop the speculation. One thing we could count on was that the gang we had sent packing yesterday was not going anywhere. They had hiked halfway across the continent and while they were undoubtedly licking their wounds, we expected more action. Most probably, they would soon hear about the U.N.decision, which could fit perfectly into their needs. That is, let the blue hats do the fighting and the U.N. handle the political issues, and they could just walk into Elizabethville and have their way with the civilians.

Later that day, Mike and I were part of a patrol that explored the border but the entire area was quiet. We saw our Piper Cub circling the area and when we returned to our base camp, we heard that the Congo gang was about three miles beyond the border, and appeared to number about a thousand, grouped in four separate encampments. To us, it seemed that they would be on the move again before very long. More disturbing was rumors that an Irish Company were going to occupy Jadotville. Some of our guys had actually socialized with the Irish troops despite the opposing roles. We learned a lot from those relationships but up to now, nothing threatened us. There was nothing official about any of this, and the Lieutenant told us that everything was calm in Elisabethville. Maybe it was just a scare tactic, but based on our popularity with the Katanga population, and especially the population in Jadotville, these Irish guys had their work cut out for themselves.

We waited a couple of days when another group rotated into position, and we started our trek back to Elizabethville. This time, we had the benefit of doing all of the travel by truck and we all shook hands with the incoming group about five miles from the border. There was plenty of to talk about our situation: we now had Congo troops in front of us and U.N. troops behind.

# Chapter 25

The rotation of our troops was a little peculiar. We had only been in contact with the enemy for a little over a week, and while we looked forward to a mattress and showers, we expected to be in the field for a much longer period. Later, it was explained to us that this was not the initial plan. The second group was inserted as a means to reinforce our group, but when the Congolese troops retreated, and now were seemingly re-grouping, the thinking was to utilize the transport and give us a short rest. Our patrols reported that Congolese were busy sacking the farms they had walked through a few days ago. And, just for the hell of it, according to the Piper Cub pilot, once they had collected everything of value, they torched the farm houses and barns. We guessed there was also a strategic reason: there was no incentive for the farmers to return.

It turned out that there was another reason for our return to Elizabethville. The new policy for the blue hats raised a huge question for The Katanga. These U.N. troops, mostly Irish and now Swedish, with a scattering of African nations, had always been well behaved, and there was an amicable relationship between Mr. O'brien, their chief in Elizabethville and our troops. It seemed naïve, at least to us, that their announced job was to 'keep the peace' when there was no fighting! What was the point? Well, the point was that while the lesser powers in the U.N wanted to summarily kick any white person out of the Congo, they could not muster either the troops or the political power to do so. At least until this Lumumba execution prodded them into a more aggressive stance. A few days after our arrival back in Elizabethville, the U.N. had actually used our own airport to bring in three armored cars using C-113 flying Boxcars. It was also rumored that other heavy equipment was being landed in Ndola, right across the North Rhodesian border. That action, if true, hit a raw nerve because Rhodesia had been on our side.

To add to the complexity of the political moving target, when we got back to our headquarters, we learned that at least 200 Congolese troops under a white flag, had surrendered to The Katanga, stating that they wanted to change sides! That was a mind blower to us. So, if you stepped back and looked at the whole mess, we had a major defection of Congolese troops to fight *with* us, which placed them on the opposite side of the U.N., who wanted these same guys to kill us!

The next morning, we met in the training room and were told that the administration was recalibrating our position. As they said, we were completely unprepared to fight an actual war with an armored vehicle opposition. Particularly if the majority of nations in the U.N. were against us. Even so, the relationship with the local U.N. office continued excellent, and there were no reports of more troops massing. If the intent was to provide better leadership to the now-stalled Congolese army, that strategy seemed completely unlikely, given defections and our own successes. O'brien had his information sources as well, and the U.N. position seemed unrealistic unless the plan was war.

From our point of view, as the chiefs made their calculations, we had a respite and we made plans to spend a day in the city. We hopped on the shuttle into town wearing civvies, and had two plans: one was to have a couple beers and see what the female situation was, and two, to check how our banking arrangement had worked out. By now, we should have several months of money deposited. The beer was great but the female situation scored a zero. We were not quite to the point of connecting with barflies and prostitutes, which usually had the simple effect of spending everything we had without any secondary 'benefits.' Our next step was the bank, and that worked out as advertised. We each withdrew $100 in The Katanga money, and an additional $200 in U.S. Dollars, and placed the rest in a savings account. We reasoned that if all hell broke loose and we ended up on the run, Katanga money would be worthless. Hedging our bet, I think it is called. We wandered around town for awhile, and walked by the U.N. office just out of curiosity. Behind the building were two large Ford armored cars with turrets on top of them and two carryalls that had all kinds of custom work such as metal windows with slits for visibility. These were serious looking vehicles and we would have liked to examine them further, but a dozen or so blue hats were milling around and who knew? How long would the goodwill last?

So, we started back to the bus stop and saw a sign over a small store "Katanga Hardware." Why not? A hardware store was the next best thing to a gun store! We walked in to an old building with high ceilings and half a dozen fans circulating air. This was a very old fashioned store with bins of products of every size and purpose. Wrenches, hammers, rope, seeds, nails, nuts and bolts…the whole deal. There were even some Winchester lever action rifles hanging on the wall. So, we just walked around picking stuff up and putting it down and continuing to the next aisle. There was a pack of special gunsmithing screwdrivers for the equivalent of $4 and I picked them up and walked over to the checkout register. That is when I saw her. A tall willowy blonde with stunning looks, studying some sort of catalog. "Good morning" I offered, and she looked up with a dazzling smile and returned the greeting. I made the transaction but I just could not go. She said, "Let me put those in a bag," which I took as an opening to have a conversation, but she started. "You have a different accent. Where are you guys from?" The plural reminded me that Mike was still in the store, hanging back a little and just observing this little dance. I gilded the lily a little and said "Southern California" which was technically true, but not quite the beaches and Hollywood the response implied. Bakersfield was not Malibu! "Oh how interesting! And what brings you chaps to central Africa?" "Well, Mike and I are working out at the base. I'm Tony Ward, and this guy behind me is Mike Genard." "My name is Anne Scott and my dad and his dad have owned this place since 1920." "And you work here I see." "Well,"

Anne said, "only for a day or two. I am a nurse at the hospital down by the roundabout. I fill in here when the regular staff is out." Wow, I thought, she talks in a very sophisticated manner, and now I figured that she must be a little older than Mike and I. I said "It sure is good to meet you after seeing nothing but army guys for weeks!" She laughed and we began a three- way conversation about life in Elizabethville. Ann was a great and funny conversationalist and well above in class than my dates in Bakersfield! We were interrupted a couple of times by customers, but she always came back to resume talking so I decided to chance it. "I see that there is a movie theatre in town. Any chance you could go to an afternoon flick when you are not working?" She paused for just a moment, but then smiled and said "I would enjoy that if you could do it the day after tomorrow." Could? At that point I'd go AWOL if I had to! "For sure I'll be here...even if I have to walk from the base." She burst into a kind of infectious laugh and then looked over at Mike and said, "Mike, I have a friend who works at the newspaper. Would it be alright if I invited her?" Mike was beginning to feel like a fifth wheel and said "Oh yes! I'd really appreciate that. Camouflaged clothes and mud are getting me down." We all laughed at that and agreed to a time to meet. Ann reached out with a slender hand and held my hand for just a second more than necessary for a greeting. I was floating!

As we left, we turned and began walking, and all we could do is celebrate our great luck! "Wow," I said, "You can just never go wrong in a hardware store! She is knock-em dead beautiful!" Mike responded, "Yeah, but I wonder if my date will be a dud. You know, of course, that her willingness to have a date was that it was in the middle of the afternoon with a friend along." I said, "Well, it could take place in the middle of a church ceremony and I'd still be fine with it."

We kept walking until Mike said "Hey, are we walking all the way to the base? We're going the wrong way if we're going to get the bus!" We laughed as we turned around and I said "Love is more powerful than logic!" Wow! Money in our pockets and dates in just 48 hours. A Baluba couldn't remove the smiles on our faces.

# Chapter 26

The next morning Mike and I were summoned to a small meeting with a lot of brass, plus Sargeant Steve. We became very nervous but Steve motioned that all was OK, and that settled us down. Colonel Mkandawire, apparently just promoted, stood, startling us with a statement congratulating us, stating that we had stopped the action by the border with our surprise sniper skills. He then took a paper out of an envelope and read:

*"In August 1961 Anthony Ward and Michael Genard surprised the opposition during field operations near the northern border so that a hostage rescue was made possible, which was duplicated the next day. Countless lives were saved due to their calm command of long-range rifle fire. Therefore, the President's Medal for significant duty beyond expectations is awarded. This document is signed by Moise Tshombe"*

With that, the Colonel stepped forward and pinned an impressive medal and ribbon on our collars, and then shook our hands. A one mile per hour breeze could have knocked us over. But then, he went on to say, in a less formal manner, "I cannot actually award you a rank since you are contract employees, but your pay level will be advanced to the Sargeant level, effective immediately." Our faces reddened as we saw Piquart give us a thumbs- up and the dozen or so officials all gave us a 'Here Here', along with a round of applause.

Mkandawire asked us to take a seat and said "This is more than an award ceremony. We have a serious problem which we are going to discuss, and I believe that you two will play a critical part in the solution." All I could do was to finger the medal and wonder what surprise could be next. A Colonel Simpson and Mkandawire sat down behind a table and everyone else sat before them in a largely empty room. Simpson started by stating "There are three significant Baluba uprisings to the north of us. We are not certain how this got started, but we suspect that the setback of the Congo Army has something to do with it. I believe that a strategy has developed that would place the Congo forces in front of us, and Balubas behind us, and who knows where the U.N. will be. Some of us think the U.N is orchestrating this because they are still very cautious about an open fight, but they are surely capable of behind-the-scenes planning. Or mischief. As you know, the Balubas are disorganized, but they come together when the subject of ejecting white people comes up. And, they are attracted to extreme violence, something the U.N. has no stomach for.

Simpson unrolled a large map of The Katanga, which had been marked with the troubled areas. "What we want to do is to nip this rebellion in the bud, and in part, use the skills of our sniper team to help that effort along." I felt a need to head for the head when I heard that. What was this shit? Give us a $5 medal and then turn us loose in Baluba territory? But he went on. "Much to our surprise, the sniper fire of Ward and Genard had an amazing effect on these people. The Congo troops could not see where the death came from but their people were dropping like flies. We think that this impact will have an even more effect with native tribes. We expect to travel very light with the sniper squad but have a large backup contingent available if our assumptions are wrong." Yeah, I thought, we'll be 700 yards from the butchers and the contingent troops will be forty miles away. I was feeling like dog meat about now.

"Here's the strategy. We are going to try the sniper effort in a totally different manner. If our assumption is correct, a very long range kill of a tribal leader will confuse a tribe's actions without the need for broad military action. The intent here is to convince them that they should quiet down because now they are up against almost supernatural powers. We definitely have no intention or even thinking about getting rid of the Balubas. There are almost a million of them, and if they ever got their act together, there is no way that we could prevail." Simpson went on. "Now we do not know if this will work but it's worth a try. Also, keep in mind that the Balubas mistrust the U.N. troops as much as they mistrust us. If the U.N is not actually fomenting the Balubas, it's possible that we could be on the same side. Keep in mind that the U.N now has about 15,000 troops in the Congo, but they are spread over a huge area, and they are experiencing losses due to these tribesmen. Thinking that we could be on the same side is a long shot, but still a possibility."

"As a specific issue, we are going to upgrade Ward and Genard's equipment and I will dismiss them and Sgt. Piquart to attend to those issues."

"Wow",was all I could say as I looked at Mike, who had a semi-glazed look in his eyes. We got up and walked toward the door with Steve and I said "Did I hear this right? We're chosen to make some very long range shots that are supposed to convince the Balubas that they have no chance?" Steve responded, "I think you heard it right. Their theory is to take out a few leaders which is a more economical arrangement than a full scale action, and, it fits into the fifteenth century mentality of these tribes. The idea is that they will see this as magical and calm down." Mike said, "Maybe we have been too successful. It sounds to me that we're headed for an experiment where we're outnumbered by the thousands." We stopped at the Quartermaster's shop and he referred us to the armorer, who was in the next building. But as the three of us walked in, he said "So you are the chaps who are going to work a miracle."

The armorer, a bearded Dutch guy about 60, sat at a work bench in a room that looked like it had every machine tool ever manufactured. About 200 different kinds of screwdrivers hung on the wall, three lathes that we could see, hundreds of little bottles filled with screws, nuts and bolts, several vises and well, you get the idea. He had two large cardboard boxes in front of him and said "Welcome to the skunk works." We knew that he was referring to a few miracle workers at the Lockheed factory in Burbank, California who had developed incredible aircraft. Everyone who was into military affairs knew about them, including, of all places, The Katanga. If we were to be armed with that kind of quality, maybe this was worth a shot.

He introduced himself as Andrew van Zandt and said that his job was to upgrade our equipment. "Jeez'" I said, "I thought it was perfect!" "Well", he went on, "please fetch your stuff and I'll explain what we are going to do."

Mike and I were coming out of our daze as we went to our room and gathered the Mauser, our FALs, pistols, and all of Mike's optics, range finders etc. When we returned, the armorer had the new boxes open and some really amazing stuff was laid out on a table. We sat down on some folding chairs and he said "All of this equipment is from Zeiss in Germany. It is the best." First, he picked up the giant scope and explained, "This is an experimental, non-variable 50 power scope and my job is to replace the scope you have and calibrate this one to initial 800 yard crosshairs." I said, "Isn't the non-variable part a step back? I thought that the variable part gave us a lot of flexibility." The old guy leaned back, lit a cigarette and said, "Can I call you Anthony?" "Make it Tony." "OK, Tony, I know that you are taking out targets that range from 200 to 1200 yards. But we are not interested in the shorter range that this new strategy envisions. If we cannot make an 800 yard or better shot, and if I understand our direction, we will not make any shot at all. After all, keep in mind that the entire idea is to spook these guys into thinking this is magic. People dropping, heads exploding, and there are no visible troops around." I said, "Tell us more."

"What makes this possible is that we know exactly the cartridge you will use, and we have improved on it. We have 300 rounds of new ammunition with a slightly hotter load than you are used to, and, the bullets have been individually machined to Rolex standards. We know exactly the 'drop' of this ammunition from your Mauser barrel at 100 yard intervals, all the way to 1700 yards. Therefore, the crosshairs start at 800 yards and then there is another crosshair for each interval to 1700, and an offset hairline for each 50 yards after 1200 yards. We also have an advanced range finder for Mike which relies on radio waves and emits no light. That covers every issue except wind. That will still have to be estimated by Mike. It is still not perfect because obviously there are continuous drops at extreme ranges and the scope only calibrates every 50 yards. Still, it is much better than what you have, and still allows for your interpolation between cross hairs. And, we're talking a mile away. To the naked eye, you will not be able to even see the target, which leaves it to Mike to locate it, first from his 10 power scope that has a relatively wide field of vision, and then moving to an identical 50 power scope similar to the one on your Mauser. The round itself is fully capable of a kill at 1700 yards."

So I asked, "There are always downsides. What are they?" Van Zandt did not pause. "Most of the downside has nothing to do with the capabilities of the rifle, or you, the shooter. All of this assumes that there is a clear bullet path from the rifle to the target and if not, you have to either get closer, a risky proposition, or abandon the hunt." He made it sound like we were going deer hunting. "And there is the obvious issue of finding a target you cannot see. I understand that we will have air cover which will try to detect attractive locations, and then leave to avoid detection themselves. The Balubas have this odd habit of having fires going 24 hours a day to either cook or to torture, and the smoke will be your first clue. The second will be from Mike's spotting scope. I'm sure that you know the biggest problem of all: if this strategy is to work, you have to locate a leader, and kill him with a single shot. There is no second chance. A ricocheting bullet will reveal the whole works, and then, it is time for you to either hope your Ghilley suit does what it is supposed to do or get the hell out of there. I'll have the scope set up in the morning and I urge you to get out to the range and begin practice. Oh yes, there is one more thing. The downside is that this is one more item you have to lug around", as he reached into the box and came up with a huge set of binoculars. These will give Mike a 50x magnification with a better field of vision than the scope. There is a lot riding on your success." Mike said "Gee, thanks, just what we needed for our mental health!" We all laughed at that and I suppose it was our youth and the accompanying feeling of invincibility that allowed us to see the lighter side. But we were learning.

# Chapter 27

After dinner it was understood that we would be on the range all day and we were told that the team was leaving the day after. Mike said "What about our date?" "Oh shit."

This was the time for us to use a few blue chips, given that we had medals and all of that. We looked up Steve and found him in his room studying ballistic charts! This guy was 100% business. "Hi guys, what brings you here?" "We have a problem Sarge. Not much of a problem to you but a huge one for us." Piquart had a questioning look but said "Go on." "Well, here it is. Mike and I had dates planned for tomorrow afternoon and it is now obvious that cannot happen. We are wondering if you could let the driver take us into town, for no longer than an hour so we can at least say 'sorry'?" "My, my, blokes, this is a new one on me. You know we are supposed to stay on base after dinner and all of that." "Yes" I said, "but it will only be for a short time and the driver will be waiting to bring us back. We'll only go to her parent's house, who own the hardware store in town." "Yes, I know that family. They have been here for generations. It is Mr. Scott." "Yes, that's the one. Anne Scott!" "And what about you, Mike. Do you have a date too?" I could see that the Sarge was softening. "Well, sort of. Miss Scott promised to bring a friend to the afternoon movie. She is a reporter at the newspaper. Her name is Rene Stolz." "Oh! Rene. I know her from an interview she did for us. Kind of a recruiting effort. She is a true knockout!" That made Mike's face go white and I said "Please Sarge, we will not make a habit of this and I promise we'll be back in an hour."

Minutes later, having cleaned up a little, we hopped into the van and were on our way. The driver had been told of the arrangement and the address of the Scott home and we just hoped she was there. In about 10 minutes we pulled up in front of a very nice house with a wrap-around porch and stopped. "OK chaps, you have 30 minutes. No more. If I go back empty you are in a shitload of trouble!" For me, this was more pressure than the Balubas or the U.N. could ever apply!

We walked through a garden to the front door and knocked. Mike smoothed out his hair. I knocked again, and a small window in the door opened, and there was a middle aged guy, presumably Anne's father who said "Yes?" I stumbled but said "I am Anthony Ward and with me is Mike Genard . We met Anne at the hardware store and we wondered if we could talk to her for just a few minutes. We're both part of the military contingent out at the base." The door opened and he said "Come on in. We're always friendly with our boys in uniform." Which reminded me that we were still in uniform, complete with our new medals! He introduced himself as Robert Scott and gave us each a firm handshake. "Vivian, come over here and meet these boys." An attractive fifty-ish woman who looked for all the world like a beautiful, yet mature Anne, stepped into the foyer where we were introduced. So I just blurted it out: "Mr. Scott, we only have a few minutes and there is a car outside ready to take us back to the base, and we wondered if we could have just a few minutes with Anne?" Mrs. Scott said "Well, of course. You are in luck because she usually works this shift at the hospital. Come on into the sitting room and I will get her."

We nervously remained standing and in a minute she came back with Anne trailing behind her, who had another woman with her. "Anne, these gentlemen are here from the base to see......" But Anne, beautiful in cut-offs and a tee shirt put her hand to her mouth and said "Tony! And Mike! Oh….and let me introduce you to Rene! We were just talking about the movies tomorrow!" Anne softly took my hand and brought Rene alongside. Mike was stunned. Here was another gorgeous woman who shook his hand but stood aside slightly. She had long almost black hair and a delicate complexion that was truly stunning. Over my shoulder I saw that that Mr. and Mrs. Scott must of thought everything was under control and they moved into another room. Anne said "Come in, come in and sit down! What a surprise!" I sat next to Anne on a divan and Mike and Rene sat in two easy chairs across from us.

"So what brings you here so un-expectantly? And you two all in your uniforms and so on!" "We apologize, Anne. We have been looking forward to that movie ever since we saw you, and in fact, thought that 'Breakfast at Tiffany's' would be a good flick. But our Bosses have other ideas and we have to go on field maneuvers for at least two weeks and we will not be able to make it. We just wanted to tell you that we are very disappointed and didn't want to do this with a note or a phone call. Can we have a rain check?"

"Oh", said Anne, looking over at Rene, "We are disappointed as well. And the movie you picked would be our first choice." Rene looked at Mike and said "Do you really think you'll be back in two weeks? A date sounds like fun!" A date! I had not quite had the courage to say that word but these gals had been talking! Anne spoke, "Yes, life in Elisabethville can be pretty boring. Especially with all of the security precautions. But we will have our own guards!" Everyone laughed at that and Mrs. Scott entered the room with a teapot and some cookies on a tray and placed them on the coffee table. Anne poured the tea and we all seemed to enjoy looking at each other. Rene broke the ice. "Anne tells me that you live in Southern California where all of the movie stars are. And the beach!" Mike looked at me as if to say 'you dumb shit'. "Well, I stumbled, we do live in Southern California but I have to admit, I was more interested in trying to impress Anne than being totally accurate. I apologize for that. The beach is about 120 miles away!" The women looked at each other a little questioning but Anne said, "Oh that is alright. I'm sure that there is plenty to do anywhere in California." I thought to myself. Yes, like shooting jackrabbits.

So we talked, and most importantly Anne placed her hand on

mine and talked about her job at the hospital and some of the casualties she was caring for. She knew about the poor guy that had his eye hanging by a shred and we asked about him. "Well, he recovered very nicely. The doctors managed to re-set his eye but we're not so sure it will be very useful. Time will tell. But his wife is another story. She was seriously traumatized and just sits in a trance most of the day. Hopefully she will show some progress over time. The boy seems fine." Rene talked about her job at the newspaper and how that all spilled over into the confused political scene. She was not wedded to Elisabethville as was Anne, and said she was considering moving to South Africa. Mike bravely said "Well maybe we can talk you out of that!" and everyone had a good laugh.

But time was moving. Mike touched his wristwatch and I got the message. Anne caught that and said "I do not want you to get into any trouble but I so wish you could stay longer." My heart just swelled at that and I held her hand. But time prevailed. We stood up and poked our heads into the next room, and said our goodbyes to the Scotts and then walked towards the front door. I saw that Mike was holding hands with Rene, so he was doing just fine. He and Rene paused at the front door and Anne walked me out to the van. She said "I am so impressed that you came over just to tell us the date wouldn't work. I'll plan something really nice for two weeks away!" With that, she stood on her toes and kissed me softly on the lips and whispered "Be safe."

I almost fainted. Rene and Mike walked towards the van, still holding hands, and I thought, what a spectacular visit! We got into the van and waved our goodbyes and the driver started the engine and started down the street. We turned and waved and there they were, waving back. "You chaps cut it mighty thin. We'll have to hurry or we'll all be in hot water." And away we went, from heaven back to the prison.

# Chapter 28

Mike and I spent the next two hours reconstructing our 30-minute visit with Anne and Rene until Art-from-Bishop said "You guys should be thinking about this strange patrol we're getting ready for. How about knocking it off?" And, we finally drifted off to sleep.

After breakfast we met with the Sarge and walked over to the armorer to see if the gunsmith had finished his work. He was at his workbench, cleaning up the excess parts and placing them in a box. He turned and said "All done. I'll go with you to the range to make sure about final adjustments. But let me point out a few things. First are the cartridges. As I said yesterday, these are hand loads with specially machined bullets. I urge you to forget the magazine and insert a single cartridge into the chamber by hand and then close the bolt. Even a tiny scratch resulting from injecting a round from the magazine could change the ballistics of the bullet and remember, you're only going to have a single shot. So forget the magazine. Here are the 300 rounds and as you can see, they are packed in special ten round boxes." He opened a box and showed us that each cartridge had a special compartment. "I've also added a flash suppressor. We want you to be a stealthy as possible." Steve said "A lot of attention has been given to this. Thanks for all of your expert work." Van Zandt just beamed.

Van Zandt went on to explain the nuances of the new spotting scope, together with how the range finder worked. All of Mike's gear was much lighter than the equipment he had, which was greatly appreciated. One day, years ahead, this device would fit into your hand. But not now. I said, "Hey Mike, with all of the weight saving maybe you can lug my FAL!" Steve put that idea to rest. "One downside to all of this, is that you could be in position for many hours waiting for that shot. That requires rations, water, and don't forget your pistols. I have to remind you what they are for." Van Zandt chimed in. "We have a short indoor range around the corner and I've serviced the P.38 and the Browning and they both work flawlessly." With that, we gathered up all of this iron and headed for the long distance range.

It was different this time. There was a small dirt berm which we positioned ourselves behind. We were going to shoot in the prone position. Steve gave us the lecture. "You must be invisible. If you can, dig a hole if you can do that without raising suspicion. You can use either the built in bipod or the small shot bags in your kit. The point is an absolute sound foundation for your rifle and Mike's optics. At the distance you will be shooting from, a one sixty-fourth of an inch shift with your rifle means a miss."

We sat up as Piquart went on. Van Zandt was mesmerized. Putting the rifle together was sort of an abstraction to him. Now he was listening to how this operation was going to work. "You will be accompanied by 16 troops. Their entire objective is to assure that you are not outflanked, and *if* you are discovered, they will offer firepower. We could send 200 guys with you but that would defeat the entire theory behind this. We will travel by Jeep until we see some evidence of trouble. "Trouble" means a large Baluba gathering, and any sign of hostage taking, Drunkenness will be an almost sure sign that they are up to no good. But, on the other hand, remember that we are responding to reports of uprisings and violence, and we do not want to be the ones who are creating the problems. Once again, if we have this figured out correctly, if you can nail a crazed tribal chief from 1400 yards, the entire village will be so mesmerized that their party will stop right there and then." I looked at Mike and we nodded, realizing that Steve thought about 1400 yards as a given. Chip shot. Eight tenths of a mile. Nine and one half blocks. Target size? Without a scope, about an eighth of an inch. For a big man.

So we settled in and took aim at 800 yards, the target being a full size Baluba Chief with a carton of Chibuku in one hand. Excellent art-work by someone. This was the minimum distance we anticipated. Anything less would probably be discovered and be virtual suicide. Mike set up his rangefinder, which was still somewhat clumsy, and I loaded a single round into the Mauser and closed the bolt, and set the initial trigger setting. "Range" I asked. "809 yards" responded Mike. We were not taking anything for granted but nine yards was too small a difference to be consequential. Mike said "Shoot when ready" "Ready" was an emotional and a scientific term. I started by taking a couple of deep breaths and then heavily exhaling, which in turn reduced my heart rate and concentrated the mind. I adjusted the scope for sharpness, settled in, and pulled the trigger. I didn't notice any change in the kick back. Mike called out "Two inches to the right. Elevation right on." This imperfection was to be expected when a person changed a scope. An armorer could do only so much at a work bench. I had hit the target two inches to the right of his forehead over his left eye, and the imperfection would not have been noticed by this particular Baluba chief, who would have had half of his skull cascading across the gathering. Still, 800 yards was just a starting point and at twice the distance, I might have only blasted the guy's ear off, whereupon all hell would break loose. Van Zandt walked over and I handed him the rifle. He made a small adjustment to the scope with tiny clicks and handed the rifle back to me. I loaded another round. I almost felt I should polish these bullets but I just shoved it into the chamber and closed the bolt. I set the trigger and settled in with the same target. Focus. Shoot. "Great shot," Mike said. You drilled that fucker on the bridge of the nose, between the eyes.

Steve had seen this kind of thing before, and van Zandt's job was to make these shots possible. Still, they just looked open-mouthed. "Amazing", said the armorer.So, we then ratcheted up the distance. With the scope adjusted perfectly the only variable was wind and bullet drop. Theoretically, the ballistics chart for this specific round, which showed the drop in 50 yard increments all the way to 2000 yards, translated by the crosshairs in the scope. Wind was still a dark science with Mike in charge. The range master changed the targets. This one looked like Hitler. Same routine. 1100 yards. Adjust for drop. No wind. Fire. The hole was precisely between his eyes. Try again. 1400 yards. This time it was some North Korean asshole. I fucked up on this one. The hole was in the middle of his nose. But one less Great Leader. Everyone was congratulating Mike and I and I said "Just for the hell of it, why don't we try 2000 yards?" Steve brought us down to earth. "We've run out of range."

It was Steve again who said "Good job, guys. Get some chow and meet the group you will be travelling with after lunch. Some dignitaries are going to lay the plan out and give you the latest update on our political problems. Listen carefully. Tomorrow is going to be a busy day."

We thought that some kind of political lecture was going to be boring, but in minutes we were riveted to everything the speaker said. The speaker. I should say 'speakers' because the head of the Katanganese Army was with Colonel Mkandawire, the same duo who spoke to us upon arrival. The general didn't say much except to urge us to listen carefully to the Colonel. He said "The Katanga is at a crossroads. We have opposition in many places. Your success tomorrow will keep a little light at the end of the tunnel, but the situation is now critical. Listen carefully." With that, he bid us farewell and left.

The Colonel started, stating "I will not mince words. Our future is very shaky." All eighteen of us were very attentive at this point. Shaky? Of course, we had heard about the UN and the fallout from Lumumba's death, but no one had suggested that The Katanga was at risk. We actually still had limited social relations with some of the UN troops in town. The Colonel continued. "Opinion at the UN is quickly turning against us. Behind the scenes, President Eisenhower had previously been on our side. Now, there has been an election in America and one of the top conversations is the western powers meddling in The Congo's affairs. The pressure has settled on Belgium and they have agreed to move all of their troops out of the country. Including advisors. We are of course fighting that. All of the regular army is already gone, so we do not know why they are making that an issue." There was a buzz in the room. What the fuck, I thought. The Katanganese troops were coming around but were far from being self-sufficient.

"For the time being, this will not affect contract employees like some of you. And, some of the regular Belgium troops are planning to resign from the army and sign contracts. Still, we will have no more than 500 contract employees all together. However, while our defense is diminishing, the opposition forces are being greatly increased. World opinion is that the Congo should be one country, and that includes The Katanga. The Irish and Swedish troops are being increased, and we now have word that Ethiopian troops are gathering near Rwanda and seem dedicated to neutralizing us as a separate power."

'Neutralizing' had a particular Hitleresque tone to it and Mike and I looked at each other as if to say 'what will we be once we are neutralized'? The Colonel was not through. "All of this has an almost fictitious ring to it for us, because in all of The Congo, The Katanga is the only province where law and order is being maintained. Ever since independence was declared the rest of the country has been in chaos as you found out on your trek to Kamina. The problem has only been worsened by Mobutu's coup. After a short respite, he has gone into high gear and seems intent on outdoing Lumumba. For an example: we are no longer Elisabethville. We are now Lumumbashi. Leopoldville is now Kinshasha. Politics has clearly trumped common sense. We are convinced that we are the answer, but everyone else sees us as the enemy! Now we hear the rumors about Jadotville. We may be in a direct fight with the U.N.by the time you return."

The Colonel stopped to take a drink of water and we noticed that he was almost red-faced with anger, despite his black skin. I caught most of the implications of what he was saying, but on the other hand, Mike and I had not signed up to battle the UN. "Now I'd like to talk a little about your mission tomorrow. It is part of a bigger picture, as I hope you now realize. One part of this are the Balubas. It should come as no surprise that they would like to have every single white person out of here. We have tried to manage the problem and have had some success, but they too hear about how the world is changing and it has emboldened them. So in addition to the foreign threat, we now have the Balubas stirred up. And, with respect to the Congo's army, it is difficult to distinguish between them and the various tribes. In any case, we believe that if we can calm them down, we can focus more effectively with the external threat, which could easily swamp us based on sheer numbers. So this is a crucial effort that this group will launch. Your platoon leaders will be Lieutenant Laurent, who raised his hand, and Sargeant Piquart to his left. This is a very unconventional effort. Our theory is that we will move into Baluba country with a soft footprint. Sixteen of you. You will be on the road for quite some time, looking for signs of violence, atrocities, and efforts to disrupt our economy. You will be in a mining area, and much of these products are the foundation of our finances. Where we find these conditions, if we can take out the leaders we will do so. The plan is to use a small group who will protect the snipers whose job it will be to take very long shots at those creating the problems. It will be done with stealth and very selectively. If the tribes discover that every time they create a problem their leader is killed by a mysterious bullet from nowhere, they will quiet down. Success remains to be seen, but this is one alternative to taking on all of the threatening foreign troops. By the way, this is one place where we are on the same side with the U.N. The Balubas make no distinction over their enemies. If you are from outside of the Congo, you are the enemy. If you are white you are worse. UN troops quietly hope we are successful. They have lost over a dozen men to these savages."

"So there you are with the big picture. Your Lieutenant and Sergeant will now brief you on specifics. We'll have a steak barbecue tonight at seven, recognizing that for quite some time you may be eating rations and less appetizing fare! Thank you and Godspeed"'

# Chapter 29

We were on the road the next day at 0700. Five jeeps and eighteen of us. A change had been made and it was Katanganese Lieutenant Mainala inserted into the chain of command along with our buddy, Sargeant Piquart. There were eight Katanganese troops and eight contract guys. With the news about sending all of the Belgium soldiers home, it seemed to us that panic might be setting in, and more reliance was being placed on the indigenous troops. We had every confidence in the troops, but the motivation to change bothered us. The overall numbers also bothered us. Even though we were training more and more native troops, with 700 Belgium men leaving, the net effect was negative.

It was clear from the start that this was going to be an entirely different effort. At breakfast it was explained that there would be surveillance from the air, and any sign of Balubas would result in stopping the convoy and sending carefully camouflaged troops ahead to try and pinpoint them. These would be the Katanganese, and they would travel through the bush, away from any road if at all possible. While they were handling the reconnaissance, our job was to be quiet and out of sight. The Balubas could also be wising up and have scouts, and if they discovered six Jeeps, we might become the hunted rather than the hunters. We stopped several times during the day while the advance troops moved ahead for a couple of hours. Each time they returned exhausted, having found nothing. A few miles later, a second patrol was sent out, but again, nothing was found. Both patrols had located some small Baluba encampments but nothing of an aggressive nature was discovered. Piquart kept reminding us that the purpose here was not to just shoot Balubas, but when we found some kind of atrocity taking place, we would go into action. It was a delicate balance because we knew that every Baluba settlement could change from peacefulness to war-like in almost on moment's notice. As dusk set in, we had covered only about 30 miles and camped at a small copper mining operation, staffed by a few dozen Katanganese workers and two Belgium engineers. These guys were well organized, and they reported no recent difficulties. If an uprising occurred, their strategy was to retreat into the mine, which had provisions for several weeks. All of their workers were armed with old AK47s and the engineers had modern FALs. We admired these guys, operating miles from any help, prepared to defend themselves and having no apparent desire to leave their operation. Still, like the farmers, they were always happy to see us and shared all of their delicacies with us. Like cold beer.

The next morning Piquart opened up a package, which turned out to be a dozen new Ghilley blankets! Mike and I were each provided with one, and the scout guys were each given one. The idea here was that we might be stuck overnight in some location and we wanted as much camouflage as possible. The nights were also getting cold and we began thinking about living a day or two in a hole. We began to figure that while the support troops gave us some confidence, if we found targets, we would be way out in front of any help. Mike said "Ever think about old Andy Schimdt sacked up in a feather bed with a blonde German?"

The day went along without any reports from the surveillance plane or the scouts, who had one false alarm. We travelled at good speed, despite the terrible road conditions and ended up in an open field where we set up camp. We circled the Jeeps, set up a couple of pickets, and dined on dry rations. One thing the army had recently picked up from the French was wine beyond the confines of our base. Now, it was available in the field. This was some kind of semi-concentrated stuff that you added water to and voila! Red wine.

The third day out we were all pretty grubby but became alert when we got the pilot's report that there was a large fire burning in an encampment about 12 miles ahead. We forgot about hygiene and quickly checked our gear. After about three miles we came upon a very small country store which had been thoroughly ransacked. We set up a perimeter and went into the owner's living quarters. There was blood everywhere. On the walls and on the floor, trailing off into the yard. I said "Oh shit, looks like we're on top of our targets." But the targets had been here and gone, and so we kept looking for the storeowner. Or the remains of the storeowner. We saw broken pictures of a family on the floor, and we didn't know if we were looking for one person or four. The first grim reality was in the back garden area. There was an entire leg hacked off with some kind of dull object and a few yards later, a hand. The rest was found in a muddy ditch and we could only wonder what horrible death this guy suffered. We buried him near his store and Lieutenant Mainala said a short prayer and a few words. "Here is an innocent grocer, hurting no one and just living a simple life. Lord, help us find these savages and put an end to this craziness. Amen."

I do not think anyone slept that night. I had my FAL by my bedroll and my P.38 in my hand. I was scared as hell and I think most of the other guys were as well. We had heard that Balubas gave special attention to Katanganese soldiers, who they regarded as traitors. But all of us thought about that poor grocer, buried in pieces for no logical or civilized purpose.

The next morning the pilot radioed that all hell seemed to be underway about 9 or 10 miles ahead, off the road about a mile. We ate our rations, gathered our kit, checked our weapons and proceed on foot with the two patrol guys walking about a half mile ahead. As best as we could, we walked a few yards from the roadway, wading across streams staying as quiet and careful as possible. The weight of my FAL and the Mauser, plus all of our gear was difficult. But I wouldn't have left any of it behind. In a couple of hours, we stopped for a break and the patrol returned. The news was as bad as it could be. They had found a woman, probably the wife of the grocer, covered with blood and dead with a crushing blow to her head. They explained that they thought she had been raped due to the massive blood flow on her legs and when they were through, they simply crushed her skull. We approached the scene with caution, thinking we might be walking into a trap, but all we found was this woman, doubled into a fetal position, fruitlessly trying to protect herself in death. We placed her in a shallow grave under a tree with a marker, thinking that if we got through this we would take her body to be with her husband. I repeatedly vomited and many others did as well. To imagine the pain and incredible degradation this woman had suffered not only made us sick, it angered us to the point where we were not thinking too clearly. Sargeant Piquart brought us back to earth. "Save it, men, we'll have our day this afternoon." We continued safety on, cartridge in the chamber, finger on the trigger.

About three miles ahead we stopped and Mainala gathered us together in a brushy area. "OK men, here is where we break up. A fresh two-man patrol will move ahead and Ward and Genard will follow a couple hundred yards behind. The objective is to find these guys, and then find a safe spot for the snipers to operate. The rest of you will follow in three groups of four. When the snipers leave the road, one group will follow to the right, one to the left, and one behind. You are specifically there in case things get out of control. If you start up your own war, our experiment will be lost and we risk a lot of men. Check your weapons and be ready but keep your cool." It was the first time that I heard we were an experiment.

As we moved ahead the existing advance patrol returned. These were Katanganese troops but their faces looked absolutely ashen. Obviously shaken, one of them pointed back and with tears in his eyes, he said "…..the children….."The grocer had indeed had a family. Not just a wife, but a small girl and a boy. The sight was so sickening that even the most hardened ex-Stalingrad warrior reacted with anger and sorrow. This kind of thing in 1961? The little girl's blonde head was placed beside her hacked off neck. We couldn't find the boy's head but his body looked like it had been crushed by a truck. It was unbelievably sick, and everyone was in favor of storming their camp and killing the lot. Lieutenant Mainala, with tears in his eyes said "No men. Stay with the program." He appointed a burial detail and the rest of us moved, unaware of the hell that was ahead.

It was mid-afternoon now and we headed off the road towards the smoke. Just Mike and I and the two-man patrol who were spread out on either side of us. The rest of the patrol followed quite a ways back and when we turned, we could not see them. Ahead was a strange landscape of sandy soil, bushes about five feet high, and an occasional stunted tree. We had to get closer to have a shot but remain far enough away to survive. Eight hundred yards was our objective, consistent with our training. But this wasn't a target range. We moved laterally, back and forth as we advanced, looking for a place to set up our position.

The vegetation gave us security, but not a clear shot. We continued and could hardly make out the guys on either side, winding in and out of low bushes. Then we saw the camp. Still about 1200 yards away. Like nine city blocks. We could see miniature figures running around, but to the naked eye they looked like tiny toys. But there was a lot of them and my stomach tightened. Mike whispered "If you look ahead, the brush clears out and we'll have no way to set up without being detected." He was right. It was like a dry riverbed all the way to the camp and this was as far as we were going to get. There was a possibility of circling the camp and see if there was a better site but we decided against that. We might end up shooting at our own guys if we moved to the opposite side. Mike pointed to a small rock outcrop and that is where we crouched in the sand. We had no idea where our escorts and support were, but we had our program and this was where it would be carried out. We laid down and began the arduous chore of putting on our Ghilley suits, and getting our gear unpacked. Did these guys have pickets or guards? Who knew? We generally thought that after the massacre at the general store they would be liquored up and looking forward to a night of partying. Of course, they understood that someone would eventually stumble by the general store and call for help, but they had no idea that the help was only 1200 yards away. In other words, they believed that they were secure.

We used small folding spades and carefully deepened the sand behind the rock outcrop to about eighteen inches and set up the equipment. I whispered to Mike that "We have to find the main guy. The leader. It will do no good to kill some lackey." I carefully took the Mauser out and unfolded the bipod. Mike was quicker, having already searched the area through his binoculars and optics setup. "Hey Mike", I said, "Lets cover up with those blankets. That should make us just about invisible. As we were doing that, and keeping as low a profile as possible, a small stone dropped right my left hand. Startling the shit out of me! I grabbed the P.38 and looked over to my left and there was one of our support guys, just thirty feet away. That was good news. He had set up shop and we were completely unaware of it. I removed the cartridges wrapped in the small linen-lined box, and removed one and examined it. I have no idea what I was looking for, but it was perfect, polished and ready. I placed it in the chamber and closed the bolt. Mike was only two feet away and said "I am picking up some targets but give me a minute or two." I asked: "Range?" "1245 yards." That was doable but certainly no cinch. I looked at the smoke trailing from the camp and there was no apparent wind at all.

The problem with my scope was that with the increase in magnification, the field of vision was very narrow, and it was nearly impossible to search for a target. Mike, on the other hand used two scopes, one with a wider view, and the binoculars. "OK", he said, "There is a very large tree right behind the fire. Find the tree and then focus immediately to the right and I think you have your guy." I moved the rifle only about an inch but that was a huge change with the scope, and I immediately saw what Mike was talking about. This guy was covered with animal skins, and was facing something, probably a group of people. I could see that he was waving his arms around. He clearly was the leader of the group and I focused on him. "Range"? "1248 yards." "Wind?" I knew there was little or no wind but that was part of our routine. "Nil." Now it was up to me. If I could drill this guy the theory was that they would be stunned at this bullet from nowhere, and head for safety. This in turn would stop their killing spree. At least that was the theory. Kill the head guy almost superstitiously rather than have a big scale battle. I began my breathing exercise. Deep breath, fully exhale, wait a moment and focus. Set trigger, make tiny interpolations with the scope, touch the trigger and feel the comforting kick. One second later Mike said "Great shot! The bullet went into his left ear and came out with half of his head in a cloud of grey slush and a pink cloud." Mike went on "Hey, you ought to see this! He just stood there for a second without half of his head and then collapsed. There is no one moving in the camp." I was on to something else. I accidentally picked up another target just behind the guy I had killed. He was sitting on some kind of stool behind a table and on the table were all kinds of instruments and appliances. I couldn't really tell about the detail. But just to his left was a human head. Blonde hair. Small. It had to be from the grocer's son. And I lost my cool. "Range behind the target." Mike was already clearing his stuff up but said "No Mike, one shot that's it" I said "Look at the guy behind the table." He was swiveling his head, back and forth, trying to sort out what had just happened. "Holy shit.....1247 yards...nail the fucker." Same routine. This time I couldn't focus on his head because he was moving around too much. I went for his crotch, under the table. The bullet blew the guy off the stool and a cloud of bone and guts followed. He was on the ground, twitching when a fountain of blood shot upwards and this fucker was dead. I said "Let's just stay here for a few minutes." And we did, watching through the scopes, with the people beginning to mill around, this way and that, but then walking into the bush. Maybe they thought they would get the next bullet. One guy came our way not because of anything in particular but just confusion taking over. When he got very near, we saw one of our patrol guys step behind him and slit his throat, dropping him into the sand with no more noise than a gurgle.

As the camp was abandoned, we began to retrieve all of our stuff, take off our Ghilley shit and began the walk back to the road. Lieutenant Mainala and Sargeant Piquat ran over to us and we told them what had happened. "Why the second shot?" "Because the guy had that little boys head in front of him and I just had to do it," That seemed to be enough for them. A lot of backslapping followed and the Lieutenant gathered the team behind some large rocks beside the road and gave an update. Justice at some level had been done and while we couldn't bring the family back, at least those two fuckers would never do that to another family.

# Chapter 30

We ended the day at a large copper mining enterprise about 30 miles past the killing. We had buried the family in a common grave behind their store and one of the Katanganese carved a small cross with the inscription 'Be with God'. We left the Balubas for the crows.

The mining facility was first class and huge. After sending a radio message to the Elisabethville facility, we met with the management staff to make them aware of what was going on in their neighborhood. They knew the grocer, who was from South Africa. He had fought for the allies in the World War and wanted to retire in a quiet rural setting. It worked out all right for a few years, but ended in tragedy. The officials at the mine were not worried about their own safety. They had a barbed wire fence around the entire facility, about 25 German Shepherds and more guards than there were in our patrol. The Balubas were smart enough to leave them alone. The problem came into play when they would convoy their product to Elisabethville in trucks. Once a truck had broken down, and the rest of the convoy moved ahead, having radioed back to the base about the stranded truck. But before the repair mechanics arrived, the Balubas had been there and gone. The truck had been burnt with the two- man crew inside.

The manager explained that this particular facility had been in operation for over 12 years and the Balubas had never been a real problem. A nuisance at times, stealing things that were left out and assorted mischief. But these engineers were very well connected, and in a talk session after dinner they gave us their take on political affairs.

"When Independence came all hell began to break out. For a

few days, all was quiet, until Lumumba announced that the Belgium officers would continue to be in charge of the army. For two weeks the army mutinied, tore up Leopoldville, sacked many civilian Belgium homes, raped women and had a full scale revolt going when Lumumba backed down and sent the Belgium force home. But that solved nothing. The army was free-wheeling now not just in Leopoldville but cities in other provinces. In fact, the Katanga secession, announced just one day after independence was the only calm city in the entire Congo. As for the Balubas, it was just too confusing to digest. But having the Belgium troops gone emboldened them. And later, when they learned through their jungle telegraph that the United Nations was sending more troops to stop The Katanga from seceding, many of the tribes thought that was their free pass to behave as they had since before colonization. In fact, for the last 1000 years." A lot of this was the same kind of reporting we had from officials in Elisabethville, but we patiently listened. But then there was more.

The head engineer passed the discussion to another engineer, who we later learned was a University of Southern California graduate. He went on. "Lumumba, the great hope for the Congo, had thought he was in charge. But actually, everything turned against him. He went against his Russian sponsors and turned to the U.S. He actually travelled to the U.S., seeking support and almost unbelievably, asked the Unites States to provide a staffed C-47 for his use. He could not arrange a head of state encounter, and the airplane was out of the question. Still, he went to Washington and was housed at Blair House, the traditional government facility in Washington for foreign dignitaries. Lower level officials did meet with him and he was consistently arrogant about his status and importance. The buzz at the mining facility was that Lumumba requested a blonde prostitute for his use, and in fact, the CIA acquired one. However, the administrator at Blair House, a prim woman of about 60, refused the woman's entrance to the facility, and reinforced the view that Lumumba was entirely over his head. And he never would adjust. Just two weeks later he was murdered under very strange circumstances. Repeating the story about being forced to eat his last political speech. Pages and pages of paper. Then he was tortured and shot, supposedly with Belgium personnel in attendance. And again, the rumors that he was dismembered, thrown into a barrel of acid until there was nothing left. As we had learned before, this had enraged the entire international community, independent of who supported what.

That evening, we were provided with a very nice dinner in a classy dining room. But neither Mike nor I could eat and that seemed to be the same with most of the rest of our crew. Beheadings and acid barrels did not mix with a pleasant dinner. But we drank a lot of beer, had a modern shower, and finally crashed on cots set up in a gymnasium.

We were on our way again the next morning, all riding in Jeeps, keeping alert to any sign of a gathering. The Piper Cub had also found us and circled ahead at a very high altitude. And so it went for two weeks. Dusty roads, stopping at settlements, showing the flag and hearing rumors, rumors, and more rumors. Is the Belgium Army all gone? Yes, except for advisors. Is it true that thousands of troops are coming into the Congo from many countries? Yes, that was true. Why? Two reasons: One, to quell the lawlessness in the Congo as a whole, and two, to stop the secession of the Katanga. And so it went. One question led to another and it became clear that one, The Katanga had a very poor means to communicate with the rural part of the country, and two, the obvious: how was The Katanga to ever cope with this influx of troops from the Ireland, Sweden, Ethiopia, India, Rwanda, and who knows where else? That last question had no answer. How indeed? It seemed completely hopeless. Here we were on a tiny mission of trying to control the Balubas while the entire country was going down the tubes. The only hopeful thing was that to date, none of these troops had yet taken up arms against us. Apparently, at least for the time being, they were occupied in the rest of the Congo, and in fact, some came to The Katanga to enjoy a little R and R.

THE KATANGA

As we slowly moved along, we picked up information and shared what we knew. It was almost too confusing to digest. The political fixation at the U.N. in New York was The Katanga, but the actual problem within the Congo was the successor to Lumumba, Joseph Mobutu. Mobutu was a self-appointed Prime Minister yet seemed to have strong backing, offering something more rational than Lumumba. He was also rumored to have participated in the murder of Lumumba. Then there was the larger political issue: Lumumba, for the most part, had ben oriented to Soviet Russia, and Mobutu was friendly with the United States and the western world. But power had apparently gone to his head. After he had re-named all of the cities and placed his cronies in positions of power in each province, these guys were rumored to be completely out-of-control. Previously, we had been told that Mobutu had been educated in Catholic Schools in Africa, and then in Belgium, which gave people some confidence that an enlightened ruler might take charge. But as the saying goes, 'Power corrupts, and absolute power corrupts absolutely.' And, we were the bad guys. World opinion supported Mobutu, which must mean that any opposition to him must be wrong. Or it seemed like that to us. In our trek, mining officials would try and explain all of this since they were wired into the world economic scene. Actually they didn't give a shit who was in charge if they could be left alone to pursue their business affairs. However, even to we field soldiers, it was stupid to imagine the Balubas, the Congo Army, the egocentric Prime Minister and the U.N itself all against The Katanga. We were wrong about that. Long after we had left The Katanga, Mobutu stayed in power as Mobutu Seso Seke, a true mad man, who allowed the mining concerns to function so long as they paid their ransom to him. It was the only productive source of wealth in the Congo for many years. And the U.N. bought into all of this. It was as if the black people were good and the white people were bad, yet in many respects, they were equally bad.

# Chapter 31

The terrain became more forested, and it reminded us that the 'long range sniper strategy' had its limits. We tested the possibilities, but unless we just happened into an open area, about 300 yards was as far as we could count on. We didn't need all of this sophisticated equipment for 300 yards. The other issue was contained in digesting the overall threat to The Katanga. Mainala became more conservative, even without new orders. When we encountered drugged and liquored up Balubas, if they posed no specific threat, we just passed them by. Killing a handful of Balubas was not going to change the international situation. If our Katanganese scouts saw no evidence of mayhem, killing or torture, we just went on our way.

That all changed about a week later. We were getting damn tired, having been on the road for weeks. We had stopped at a mining facility that had a subordinate setup about 20 miles away. There was a small writing room at the headquarters building and I dashed off a letter to Ann about our whereabouts. To show my state of mind, the letter went something like this:

*Ms. Ann Scott, R.N.*
*% Elisabethville General Hospital*
*Elisabethville, The Katanga*

*Dear Anne:*

*Just a short note to tell you that I have not forgotten about taking you to that movie, and hope that you have not forgotten the promise. I also hope that you and your family are safe and in good spirits. We hear a lot about*

*growing troop movements around Elisabethville and I hope you are secure.*
*Our trek around the country was exciting at first but it is becoming much*
*longer than we thought, very tiring and usually, but not always, boring. I*
*think we will be back in about two week or three weeks and I hope that we*
*can get together again. I miss you.*

*Love,*
*Tony Ward*

I wondered about the 'love' business but figured, what the hell?
I really did want to see her again, and why not be honest about how
I felt? There was no regular mail service as such, but semi regular
convoys from commercial establishments had worked out a system for
delivering packages, records and personal messages that couldn't be
handled by radio communications. So, I dropped the envelope in the
mail pouch and hoped for the best.

The next morning, we were on the road again, and this turned
out to be a day to be remembered. About 12 miles from where we
had stayed, we saw a small red car up ahead that seemed to be stalled.
We were immediately alerted, as it was highly unusual to see a single
civilian car out in the bush. When we were about a quarter mile away,
our jeeps stopped and I got the Mauser and Mike grabbed our FALs
and optics stuff, then joined a group of eight Katanganese troops and
we began walking towards the car. It didn't take long to figure what
was wrong, and that sent a chill up out spines. A ditch had been cut
across the road, which obviously stopped the car. There were papers
everywhere, the driver's door opened, and worst of all, the engine
was still running! Whatever happened here, happened a very short
time ago. On one side of the road there was a cliff, so Mainala decided
we should hunt on the other side, which was bordered by heavy brush
and then trees a few hundred yards away. Then one of the troops found
a woman's purse in a bush and brought it forward. It was open and
nothing was in it but we realized the worst: A single woman, driving

without any guards in the heart of Baluba country? Impossible, but it looked like it might be true. It was total insanity to allow such a thing to happen.

Mainala gathered us together and told us his assumptions. One, this was country not suitable for snipers and besides, we had no time to set up the equipment. Two, we were only minutes behind some abductors, and three, he instructed four of our guys to guard the convoy equipment, and the rest of us to make sure we had extra magazines, and to fan out, about 15 feet apart. "We might make a rescue here, so be careful if you take a shot. We don't want to shoot the person we're trying to rescue and we don't need any friendly accidents either. Keep you heads and let's go."

We had only walked about 300 yards, dodging trees and rocks looking around, back and forth but making good time. Mainala held up his hand and we stopped as he pointed towards a spiral of smoke. We progressed a few more yards and we saw what we didn't want to see. A Baluba chief of some kind, wearing a bunch of animal skins was frog marching a blonds haired woman ahead to a gathering of about thirty tribesmen. By now she was clearly visible, and the Balubas were focused on her, not our approach. This guy was jerking her around by the hair and she started screaming. Before we could take any action she pushed away from the guy, and reached into her dress, and pulled a very small pistol out, shoved it up against the Baluba's chin and fired. He immediately crumpled and then she turned the gun and put in her mouth and fired. Transfixed for a second or two, we were aghast as the entire tribe attacked the woman, who was surely dead, and started hacking and cutting. What followed was carnage on a large scale. We usually saw the aftermath, but this time the entire episode unwound right before us. Mainala said "Move" as he leveled his FAL and fired on full automatic at the pile of savages. And then we all started firing, fourteen of us. Flesh and blood was flying everywhere, heads exploding as we dropped empty magazines and started all over again until there were several piles of dead Balubas. Well, not quite.

One guy lifted his arm and four FALs immediately dismembered him. The damage to a human being by fourteen FALs is hard to describe. Skulls opened with blue-grey matter falling into pools of blood, hunks of flesh and bone everywhere, and then total quiet. We pulled the dead Baluba's bodies off of the woman who was clearly dead as well. Her little two barreled .41-caliber two shot derringer had done its job in a way unexpected for such a tiny gun. And the Balubas, in only a few seconds, had already managed to almost chop one of her legs off. The apparent leader she had killed was equally dead, the bullet travelling through his mouth and out the top of his skull. At least this time, all of the hi-tech stuff had no place whatsoever.

We stood there, breathless, thinking about the terror the woman must have felt, and what might have been if we had arrived only seconds before. Could we have saved her? Probably not, but who really knew? Our anger quickly turned to the shithead who had allowed her to be out on the open road by herself. Mainala said. "Let's head back to the mine and have a talk with those assholes."

We turned the vehicles around and one of the scouts drove the small red car. We placed the woman as gently as we could into the back of one of the Jeeps, covered her with a blanket and headed back to the mine. We honored our usual policy and left the Balubas for the crows and other assorted animals and bugs in the forest.

What followed was something we did not witness, but we heard that Piquart and Mainala crashed right into a meeting, both with blood on their hands and uniforms, and shouted "I want to see the chicken-shit asshole who allowed a woman in a small car out onto the highway by herself. And if you doubt the consequences of your incompetence, come out to the front of the building and you will see her, shot through the head and dismembered! You fuckers should pay for this!"

Mainala turned and headed for the door and Piquart informed us later, followed, shouting as he went "Assholes!" Stunned, the staff stumbled out of the building and surrounded the Jeep, looking down at this poor woman who killed a person who was pushing her toward certain death, then almost beyond brave, turned her gun on herself, avoiding an inevitable torture session. The mining executives were appalled, some turning away from the woman, others crying and choking. One guy turned and vomited against the side of the Jeep. We found out later that a nerdy little staff guy had sent the lady on her final trip because he wanted a package 'expedited.' The next morning this little piece of shit showed up with a massive black and purple eye and a couple of broken teeth. He was handcuffed and thrown into a closet for the time being. The manager of the place, clearly outraged said "I'll expedite this little fucker all the way back to Belgium and make sure he'll never find another job."

This had been Brenda Halloran, age 27, who had been at this station for only four months, having come from Scotland to experience a little excitement in Africa. She was reported to have been a happy person, competent, and a hard worker. She deserved much, much better.

That afternoon, we all attended her burial, with many of us having tears running down our faces.

# Chapter 32

The next day we were on the road again, and we saw little evidence of any Baluba activity. Once again, our secondary purpose was to show the flag, and comforting people in outlying communities and farms. Everyone had radio communications and they were fully aware of not only the Baluba issue, but moreover, the growing spectacle of foreign troops marching on The Katanga. Thousands were already in the country and they represented the combined force of the United Nations. In fact, President Kennedy had initially (and quietly) supported the Katanga independence move. Unlike other efforts to expel European powers, the Belgium government was already gone, and he reasoned that this was a matter for the Congo to sort out. He saw things in a different light. But he was quickly embroiled in our role in Indochina, and a confrontation with the Soviet Union was brewing over the Russian intentions in Cuba, which was leading to the Bay of Pigs failure. He had his hands full and Africa seemed to be a remote problem for the U.S. As a practical matter, it was convenient to just go along with the U.N. This ended up being the final nail in The Katanga coffin, although at the time, we were still trying to think positive.

Two weeks after the Brenda Halloran outrage, we were encamped outside a farm, and towards the evening, all eighteen of us were gathered around the dinner wagon, in one of our 'down' moods, talking about the hopelessness of it all. Mainala tried to put a good face on it but he finally admitted that he was discouraged and saw no positive outcome. True, our little effort was having the intended effect of suppressing the Balubas. The 'jungle telegraph' was working well and these guys were clearly keeping a low profile. Intelligence indicated that our 'bullet from nowhere' terrified them and chiefs had little interest in having their heads blown apart from completely unknown sources. Their superstition worked to our advantage.

However, the overall problem was not the Balubas, but the well-armed soldiers who seemed to be on the verge of an out-and-out invasion. We could take care of the natives, and probably the inept Congo national army, but with all of the Belgium soldiers gone, and only 500 'advisers' and a half-trained Katanga army, we were so outnumbered that it was almost laughable. Our actions were a very small pin- prick when compared with the massive forces staging against us. There were already troops from Ireland and Sweden in Elisabethville and while they were not taking any overt action, at least for now, it was clear that political forces were pushing them to do so. And, we were victims of the many rumors we picked up at way stations. We were now over two hundred miles from Elisabethville and how were we to know what was actually going on? My thoughts came back to Anne. I thought that she should get out of the country. Rene had a family in South Africa and Mike and I agreed that we should suggest them moving south, at least until we knew how all of this was going to end. I had not heard from Ann but that night Mike and I addressed a letter to both Rene and Ann, care of the hospital. The letter would take at least a week to reach her, but we both felt better that we had at least made a suggestion about their safety.

And so the sojourn through The Katanga continued. A couple of days later, we came upon a small, remote farm burned and ransacked, and a single butchered man hanging from a tree. But there were no signs of the savages that committed the crime, and all we could do was to once again preside over a burial, and report the details via radio the next day. The constant in these discoveries was that we never discovered a single bottle of beer or liquor. And some of the places were stores. We cynically concluded that to a Baluba, the drunken result of consuming a bottle of whisky was sufficient justification to torture and murder a resident.

We all thought that we had reached the point of diminishing returns, and had been on the road for over two months and were simply tired. Mainala made radio contact the next day and apparently provided a suggestion for relief, because by the end of the day, he had new orders. We were going to speed up the return to Elisabethville, and if we found problems we would deal with them, but the estimate was that we would be home in a week.

The other issue was our contract. Both Piquart and Mainala lobbied us to 're-up', but re-up to what? Would the country even exist in six months?

# Chapter 33

M ike and I had grown up a lot since coming to Africa. What began as a diversion from a potential trip to Vietnam, and maybe an adventure of sorts, had morphed into a true fiasco. We had gained an appreciation of the confusion and incompetence in diplomatic circles, witnessing atrocities, actually killing other human beings and wondering what lay ahead for us. We agreed that if we had to do it all over again, maybe Vietnam would have been the better choice. As it was, eight months after leaving the U.S., there *still* had not been any draftees sent to Vietnam. Maybe we would have received a sweetheart deal in Germany like Andy Schmidt. But here was our own personal reality in The Katanga. Even though we understood the origins of Africa's basic problem…that of crude colonial exploitation, looking ahead it seemed like events were pushing Africa into still another abyss. From what we could tell, the rush to independence all across the continent was a fall out from World War 2. On many occasions, including our endless lectures, we heard that the United States was on a mission, taking the position that a world war had not been fought in part so that colonial powers could simply resume their control over other races and geography. The African countries, of course, had railed against colonialism for decades, but had little power to create change. But now, the United Nations took up their cause. Even the crummy third world countries had a vote. It was beyond logic that given basic realities, no one could stop the train.

We listened to businessmen at the mining facilities that we visited, as well as farmers and community leaders scattered across the country. We remembered one Belgium executive who said "Whatever the injustices of the past, plunging Africa into overnight independence was a recipe for an entirely new kind of chaos. The fact is, no African country was ready to govern itself in a complex world environment, however abstract judgments based on moral issues sought to justify the massive change. Just look at what is happening: Russia now meddling and making mischief wherever they can. The superpowers beginning to make Africa the next international crisis."

We thought about that a lot. But from our tiny perspective, we thought that if one country could succeed, it would be The Katanga. But they were opposed by practically every nation. Here we had a black president, respected by the people, a growing economy, a banking system, solid backing by the previous powers, but opposed by world opinion. So what if The Katanga failed? It seemed obvious to us that the result would be to dissolve the province into the general chaos of the Congo. What kind of a solution was that? We talked about this stuff endlessly, but we still had only one decision. To stay or go home.

Elisabethville looked very different from the bucolic place we had left. There were foreign soldiers everywhere, who were behaving themselves, but they were obviously not there for a picnic either.

Some of the smaller stores were boarded up, and the place had taken on a defeated look. As we passed through the city, we were amazed that the Baluba compound was empty! Where the hell had they gone? Still, as we pulled into our barracks facility it was like coming home, even though it also had a kind of hang-dog look, very different from the crisp, well maintained facility that we had left. We helped unload the jeeps and took our gear into the building. One chore the next day would be to clean the weapons and make sure everything was working for the next adventure. There was our small room, with all of our stuff safe and secure. Art Stepan was off on some other maneuver, so we had the place to ourselves. Art was a really good guy, but there were things that Mike and I shared that we just couldn't discuss with him. We took a shower, got some clean clothes on and wandered down to the canteen and picked up some sandwiches. Then we crashed for ten hours.

# Chapter 34

The next day changed everything. We had dressed early out of habit I suppose, and we were actually pleased to see the runny eggs and half-cooked bacon still on the menu. But there was a lot of confusion in the room and it was announced that there would be an emergency meeting at 0900. We just decided to hang around and wait for the meeting, kibitzing with some of the guys we hadn't seen in eight weeks.

The room quickly filled and a little after nine, Colonel Mkandawire came into the room and prepared to address the group. This must be something special. And it was. He started "The United Nation office in Elisabethville has sent Irish troops to occupy Jadotville. We have very little information on this, but our intention is to confront and remove them. We have tolerated their presence in the city for months, but this is an armed takeover and it will not be tolerated." He continued, "Apparently the Irish troops had come from Kamina, near the border where we had been months before to repel the Congo Army. Our leadership immediately sought information from the U.N. What was going on? Why was this action taking place? The information we received was that the action was taken to 'protect the citizens.' That raised a lot of buzz in the room because we had been heroes in Jadotville just three months ago and there was outright hatred towards the U.N. presence.

The meeting was short and sweet because it was apparent that the army had been caught with its' pants down and didn't know what to do. We were all ordered to be back at 1500 hours and there would be more information. The colonel also advised that we should all concentrate on cleaning our weapons and getting our kit in order.

Mike said "Shit. We have only been back for half a day!" The halls were alive with rumors and theories. Was this the beginning of what we all feared? Foreign troop takeover? We had no idea of the number of troops in Jadotville but there were thousands of foreign army contingents in and near Elisabethville and it looked like this was the beginning of an effort to reclaim The Katanga.

In our case, there was nothing to do with our weapons. Mike and I cleaned them daily and we wished that there was some kind of surprise inspection just so we could be smug. Most of our small group of 18 understood that if we could not depend on our rifles, we were dead men.

Back in our room, we started talking about Rene and Ann. We needed to see them and make sure that they were not vulnerable with all of the chaos unfolding around us. We also agreed that we needed to pay a visit to the bank and get more of our money. If everything went to hell in a hand basket, we needed cash. According to our calculations, we would each have almost $4000, which would buy a lot of transportation in Africa. We changed into our civvies and caught the shuttle into town. This wouldn't be much of a social event as we had to be back by 1700 hrs, but we were very nervous about the women.

# Chapter 35

Our first stop was the hardware store, which sent a chill through us. It was completely boarded up. There was a sign on the door that said 'Gone on vacation. Armed Guard on the Premises.' Shit. That was just code for 'We're gone and we hope no one robs the place'. So we looked at each other and decided to drop by the bank then head for Ann's house. The bank was a zoo. Lines of people drawing money out of their accounts, obviously thinking that we would all be a part of a lawless Congo before long, where Katanga money would have no value. We patiently worked our way in line and drew out everything but $100. Our office had a peculiar way of compensating us because we had far more money than we figured. We asked for a statement and understood that for the last eight weeks we had 'combat pay'. All together, we would each have $5500 rolled up in our pockets. We talked a little about the 're-up' option which brought another bonus with it. Even though we were damn nervous about the rumors in Jadotville and what that might lead to, we could always leave. Who would stop us? After all, the intent of the U.N: to get rid of us!

We hopped a cab to the Scott residence and asked the driver to wait, but we were shaken by the appearance of the house, which had been carefully manicured when we left. More importantly, there were plywood sheets covering the windows. It looked deserted. It looked like the Scott family had gone. We hustled back to the cab and directed the driver to the hospital. The hospital didn't look much better than the bank. Refugees were beginning to leave rural areas and come to the city looking for protection from a threat they did not fully understand. But it was obvious that many of them came with their valuables in case they could not return to their homes. It wasn't a huge number of people but quite a difference from eight weeks ago when the lobby had a receptionist and polished marble floors. It was the usual assortment of ailments: kids with sore throats, the flu, or whatever, but their parent's ability to care for these problems had been left behind. Sometimes 200 miles behind.

Rather than get in line to see the screening nurse, we walked over to a guard and asked him if he could tell us where Anne Scott worked. He looked at a directory and said "Oh yes, Anne. She is in the surgery section, floor 2. You can go through this door and walk up the stairs." Well, that was encouraging. We went up the stairs and found a reception area and asked the nurse if we could speak to Anne. She looked at us and asked if we were friends, and she accepted our explanation. The Katanganese army was very popular in Elisabethville. However, she said, "Ann isn't on duty today. You can find her at her home." "But we were just there and the place was boarded up." "Oh, I think she is in there. Her parents have gone to South Africa and they wanted to make sure she was safe. You go on out there and bang on the door. She has worked double shifts so it might take a while to wake her up!"

We caught another cab and Mike said "How about stopping by the newspaper? I want to see about Rene." That made everything more mysterious. The newspaper was a small operation with a tiny reception area. We walked in and Mike asked the receptionist "I'd like to see Rene." The receptionist blinked a couple of times and asked "Would you happen to be Mike Genard?" "Well yes, that's me, but what about Rene?" The woman reached into a drawer and handed Mike an envelope. "Rene isn't working here anymore, but she left this for you," and handed the envelope to Mike. Mike muttered "Thanks" and turned around and tore open the envelope. We walked over to a corner of the room and Mike read:

*"Dear Mike. Thank you so much for the letter you wrote and I am happy that you are OK. I asked about you out at your base and they said you were*

*on duty and they couldn't tell me when you might return. With all of the rumors and stress around this town, I decided to leave and I now have a job in Capetown, South Africa and I work at the local newspaper. By now, you must have some vacation time and I am wondering if you could plan a visit down here. The weather is gorgeous and the beaches are perfect. You can reach me at Cape Times, Telex 23-771.*

*Love, Rene.*

Mike's face flushed and said "Lets desert right now! Let's get out of this shithole!" I said "Before we get crazy and go AWOL, can we try and find Anne?" Mike looked at me with a kind of blank face and didn't say anything for a second or two, but then "Sure buddy. I'll give you an hour!"

We flagged another cab and headed back to the Scott residence. It was now 1300 hrs. and we didn't have a lot of time. When we got to the front door I knocked. Loud. I waited a minute and nothing. I knocked again. Then I shouted "Anne"! In a few seconds I heard a weak "Who is it?" "It's Tony! Are you alright?" I heard a rattling of chains and a couple of cross bolts moving and the door opened a crack, and then opened completely as she saw it was really me. She practically came out on the porch and threw her arms around me and said "I am so glad that you are alright." She squeezed me so tightly I almost lost my breath! "Oh," she said, I am such a mess, which was partially true. I held her in my arms and then pushed her away from me and I said "Just let me have a look. Hmm. I pronounce you the most beautiful woman in Elisabethville!" Her blonde hair was all messed up but that twinkle in her blue eyes and that dazzling smile just lifted me off my feet! She pushed away and I saw that she had on some kind of a bathrobe and she obviously was not expecting visitors. "No, I was wrong. You are the most beautiful woman on the planet." She said "Come in, come in. There is so much happening!" Then she saw Mike and said "Mike! Come in!" Mike looked at me and said, "No, I'll just sit on the porch for awhile but it is great to see you!" She didn't argue and pulled me inside and planted a perfect kiss on me. I pulled back for an instant and then returned the favor. Then we just locked together and held each other. Anne seemed to have lost a lot of weight but that didn't bother the kissing! We were about out of breath when I said "Tell me what is going on! Everything here has changed." "That is right," as she held my hand, "Everything. My parents are now in Brussels and I doubt if they will ever come back. The foreign troops hassled them so much at the store, stealing things and messing around, being extremely rude that they just gave up. The local police had no power to do anything and the army didn't want to be involved. It is an impossible situation for businesses." I changed the subject and said "Let's try another kiss" and that one was the best one yet. Her robe slipped open and she wore nothing beneath. There was the most beautiful body I had ever seen. She couldn't ignore my looking and waited a second before she closed the robe. "My God, you are so beautiful!" She looked at me and said, "Not now. We have serious stuff to discuss! I was so happy to hear from you and know that you were safe. The rumors we get from the refugees makes it sound like the entire country is out of control. You know, I knew Brenda Halloran." Now that brought me out of my passion and recalled her hacked off leg, the derringer in her mouth and Baluba brains and flesh flying everywhere. "Good Lord", I said, "You probably know what is going on in the bush more than I!" "Well, probably not, but the stories these people tell are horrifying and now it seems to be happening right here! Have you heard about the U.N. taking over Jadotville?" I thought, the news travelled fast. "Yes, I know, and in fact I have to be in a meeting at 1500 hrs. to see what we're going to do about it. But I just had to see if you were OK." She held my hands and that wonderful robe fell open again. She was like soft porcelain, smooth and perfect. She quickly dropped my hand and closed the robe and all I could do is say "Oh my." She just smiled at me and gave me a hug. I was in heaven! She said, "How much time do we have?" I looked at my watch and realized we had no time at all. "I guess none. But can I return?" "You better, or I'll come to that base and fetch you! Besides, we actually do have serious things to discuss. Did you know Rene has left?" "Yes, and that is something we need to talk about. Getting you out of this place." I began to think a little more rationally, and remembered Mike out on the front porch! Anne said, "There is so much to do at the hospital and I have been placed in charge of the nurses in the surgery ward. So many nurses have left that we are seriously understaffed and it obviously is getting worse. There are actually families on the steps of the hospital waiting to be seen! Who would have imagined?" Now she had tears in her eyes and I brushed them aside as tenderly as I could. "Anne, it's time to think clearly and concentrate on your safety. You're not going to be helping anyone if these U.N. Troops overrun the country. They will stay awhile and go home and you know who will take over. Do you know who will stay? The rogue Congo army that is as bad as the Balubas. There may be a future here, but it is beginning to be a long shot." "Yes, I know, but I have been here all my life and I love the place so. Please get some time for us and lets' make a plan. Does that sound too serious?" She just amazed me. "No, not at all. That is what we need to do. After this afternoon I will know how I fit into this mess." With that, I stood and pulled her up to me and I said "I love you. Keep locked in and I'll be back as soon as I can." We kissed and I said goodbye and we went to the door, holding her hand. Anne said "Please don't forget." "How could I possibly forget?"

The door shut behind me and I looked over at Mike who nodded in a knowing way, then at the cab. We were going to have a very healthy fare. By 14:30 we were back at the base, in an entirely different world.

# Chapter 36

W e dressed in our uniforms and headed for the training room. The entire place had an electric feel to it, with people running back and forth with papers and reports and more brass than I ever remembered. I said to Mike "It's a good time to be a peon!" True, but I was still drifting back to Anne's living room!

The room was packed with over 200 men. There were guys out in the hall and they set up a speaker so they could hear as well. For the first time we saw Major Mike Hoare, a legendary soldier of fortune who actually commanded an independent mercenary group on our side. This is the first time our paths had crossed and it caused me to wonder about all of the many things that I had no knowledge of. A member of Moise Tshombe's cabinet opened the meeting with an ominous statement. He said that the purpose of the meeting was to brief us on the latest change in the U.N.'s position on The Katanga, and moreover, to adopt a strategy on dealing with the issue…very quickly. The room was completely silent, which usually occurs when life is in the balance.

The first speaker was a person who ran one of the biggest copper mines in the country, a Mr. Roland Schuman. His purpose was to explain the world situation as it related to The Katanga, which he said should make the current events much more understandable. These businessmen were always on the front lines of anything that might affect their billion dollar investments. And this guy wouldn't be here to talk to a bunch of soldiers if it wasn't important. He started with "I want to explain the new dynamic in The Katanga and the relatively small control we have over any of these events. There are powerful forces that will affect us, and we may be in a position of reacting to them rather than attempting change." This Schuman guy was a smooth speaker and didn't seem to be interested in mincing words. The problem was, they turned out to be the same words. The same speech. "The overall problem we face is the world–wide rejection of colonialism. It is like a tidal wave and while the overall trend towards self-government is the correct one, there are all kinds of anomalies that crop up. All countries are not the same and some of the world powers are switching positions as we speak here today. Of course you know that the Congo is already self-governing albeit in a cruel and savage way. In our situation, Mr. Tshombe has developed a functioning government and broke away from the Congo. This is not a colonial issue. Mr. Tshombe is an African and if he ran the Congo, there might be no reason to have The Katanga! But that is not the case. Mr. Mobutu has developed into a narcissistic ego-maniac following the Lumumba execution and is destroying anything good in the Congo, just so long as it benefits his bank account and those of his cronies. By the way, in world capitals, you might be interested to know that Lumumba's death is being blamed on The Katanga. But we know as a matter of fact that his murder was all orchestrated by Mobutu. The Congo is in a tailspin, its' currency moving towards almost nothing and skilled people are leaving in droves."

Schuman proceeded to give the oft-heard story about the excellence of The Katanga, the incompetence of Mobutu now reaching criminal levels and the U.N seemingly content to just implement the wishes of third world countries, and doing it in their own form of incompetence. It seemed to many that there was so many problems in the growing cold war, that the major powers simply didn't want to bother with a decent solution for Africa. These were reasonable and decent men (with the exception of Mobutu) making unreasonable decisions, mainly out of default. Nevertheless, as I listened to Schuman droning on, I realized that short of a miracle, The Katanga was washed up. Still, we were respectful but the words had been heard so many times, I thought that I could write the script.

Finally, a half hour later, there was a call for a break. The next speaker was none other than our Colonel Mkandawire for whom we had a high level of respect. He started: "Gentlemen, first of all, let me express my thank you for the service you have rendered, and our President Tshombe wants to add those thanks. My talk is much less lofty than Mr. Schuman's", which raised a little laughter from the audience, mostly in relief. We were mostly in the nitty gritty bunch who mostly accepted what Schuman had said, but our nuts and bolts question was what are we going to do? We all supposed that there was some utility in understanding how the world had arranged events against our tiny effort, but so what? "As you have no doubt heard, the U.N. has sent Irish troops into Jadotville, and claim to occupy that city in order 'to protect the citizens.' Of course that is a laughable claim because the U.N. has no known support in that city. But just as important is how they have occupied the city. As near as we can tell, one company of about 150 of the Irish army are involved in this 'takeover.' This is epic incompetence. What the U.N has managed to do is place these 150 men in a situation where they are surrounded by enemies! Some have disparaged the Irish troops because they have not been in an armed conflict since 1917. Well, I reject that argument. There is no reason to cast doubts as to the Irish competence or bravery, but as I said, the incompetence in placing this handful of men in this situation is truly enormous. This cannot stand, however stupidly this act was handled." This brought scattered applause, but when combined with Schuman's briefing, it was damn scary.

Two aides placed a large map of Jadotville on an easel and Mkandawire pointed out exactly where the U.N. troops were located. Quickly we could all see the craziness of this. Mkandawire pointed out that at the border with the Congo we still had 1000 men guarding against the Congo army incursion. Then there was Jadotville itself, where the citizens were armed to the teeth and were intensely opposed to the U.N. In fact, Mkandawire said, "It is actually a surprise that the militias in Jadotville haven't taken the law into their hands and run these guys out of town." He then pointed out where the Irish were, fanned out around the entrance to the city, pointed towards Elisabethville and according to local radio reports they were thoroughly dug in.

"Now here is what we plan to do." We were all ears. "We will move two full companies within two miles of Jadotville. We will demand that the U.N. cancel their action, and guarantee safe passage to the Irish back to their base. Further, and as you know, we are entering the hot season, and the City of Jadotville is prepared to shut down the entire water system in the city. We will make that request as soon as this meeting is adjourned. Within three days, these troops will be suffering a lot. The citizens are used to crisis, and they are prepared for this one. Our troops will be armed with normal rifles, along with a few mortars. If necessary, we can use our two Fouget Magistrar jets to do some flyovers and possibly strafe the opposition positions. I want to emphasize that our primary strategy will be to convince the U.N. that this is a foolish thing they have done and give them a chance to return to their bases."

"On the wall over here are the names of the platoons making up our forces. If your name is on these lists, you are advised to be ready to move out at 0600 tomorrow. There will be transport all the way to Jadotville and you could be engaged by noon. Get your kit together and make sure your weapons are in perfect condition. If you have a problem with any of your gear, see the quartermaster immediately. Thank you men and thank you for your service."

Of course, that prompted a mass movement to the lists of people on the wall, including Mike and I. It was arranged in Platoon order so we looked for Sargeant Piquart's name and it was not there. So, we scanned every individual name on the list but we were simply not included. Maybe it was because we had just returned from an eight-week deployment, but we didn't know. Eventually we located Piquart and he had no reason why certain groups were chosen. However, he said "Don't think you are off the hook. I'd make sure your weapons are ready."

Back in our room, I said, "You know, I am not too excited about blowing away Irish troops who have been placed in this situation by total idiots. Remember a few weeks ago we were having a beer with a couple of these guys at the pub in town." But it was a wake-up call regarding who the actual enemy was. We wondered if the U.N. was so fucked up that it set up these Irish troops in a way that could cause an international incident. Sacrificial lambs? It was hard to believe that their leader, a Commander Quinlan could not see through such a thing but then the multi-headed U.N. didn't manage things in conventional terms. We also wondered if our leaders could handle this in a professional way and not over react. The troops were still only about half-trained, which seemed to be OK in small groups with close supervision, but 300 soldiers is no small group.

We laid on our cots and talked about every scenario we could imagine, but by 2200hrs. we had run out of scenarios. We planned on being on the loading dock in the morning to see the guys off, but then shifted gears to our own situation, and that discussion went on until midnight.

There were two parts to this: How to guarantee safety for Anne, and, what to do about our status. Rene had done the sensible thing and simply left. But Anne thought of Katanga as her country. Why should she be forced to leave by a bunch of political hacks? We were surprised that her parents had left her behind, but then she had a career to pursue, and was now 22 years old. We could just imagine the arguments that went on in the Scott home before her parents finally left.

We drifted on to our situation. If things went bad at Jadotville, a conventional departure might be impossible, particularly if we waited too long. As it was, the only commercial airline heading south was Air Ethiopia, which we understood had traded their C-46 in for a British Tri-Star jet. There were various chartered planes coming in and out but these were primarily for military needs, and a contract employee might very well find himself in an awkward position asking for permission to leave. Which brought up still another issue. The Katanga army had stopped asking for re-ups and merely said that there would be a $1000 bonus for those staying beyond their contract, paid in two stages: $500 now and $500 when the following six months was complete. We talked a little about the wad of $100 bills wadded up in our pockets, but we were unwilling to even consider allowing a third party to care for our assets.

Which brought us back to Anne. How could we calibrate the military situation so closely that Anne could just keep working indefinitely? We could imagine a scenario where we might have to walk overland to Northern Rhodesia in order to get out. How did Anne fit into that kind of a goat fuck? It all came down to getting her out. After all, a registered nurse could find work just about anywhere. And, if by some miracle things would settle down here, she could always come back. That became our position. All we had to do was convince Anne!

So there we were, sandwiched between Schuman's lofty worldwide scenario and our small army helpless to alter worldwide opinion. It all came down to extracting ourselves somehow.

We talked a little about this Mike Hoare guy. The rumor was that he intended to continue a guerilla war, no matter what the U.N. did or did not do. Even if Tshombe gave up and surrendered. We agreed that we should talk to him or his captains and see just what this was all about. Then exhausted, we slept.

# Chapter 37

The commotion in the hallway woke us up about 0500 hrs.
Dozens of men were tromping up and down the hallway, hauling
their gear to the loading dock. There was also confusion down the
hallway at the bathroom area where nervous guys were getting sick
over their nerves. The smell of sick men is not a great way to start
a day. We dressed quickly, chucked down our runny eggs and half-
cooked bacon and went outside. Things were better organized here,
with squads lining up and Sargeants checking gear, ammo supplies,
canteens and all of the other stuff a nervous recruit might forget. All
in all, it looked like a dicey operation, and revealed how unprepared
the young country was for an actual military fight.

The troops were loaded up into trucks with benches along the
sides, and I did not envy the rough ride they would have to Jadotville.
Just to add a little to the confusion, the U.N. was now calling the city
Likasi, in keeping with Mobutu's obsession with removing any hint of
Belgium rule. The trucks began to depart in close formation, turning
on to the main highway and were soon gone. We would just have to
hope that things went well, but we wouldn't know anything until the
day was over.

My attention shifted to Anne. Sargeant Steve caught up with us
and reminded us that we were still on call, and we ought to have our
gear ready "Just in case." I told Steve about my reservations regarding
shooting Irish troops. "Shooting someone who is torturing a family is
one thing, but shooting a guy just because some asshole placed him in
an impossible situation was quite another." Steve sidestepped the issue
and said "Just have your shit ready to go." I told him that I had some
business to take care of in town and asked permission to leave the base

until dinner time. Of course I wanted to see Anne and try and talk her into leaving the country. My plan was to go by her house, and if she wasn't there, to go to the hospital and see if she could go to lunch. I had been told that there was a decent Italian Restaurant behind the hospital and I would see if she could get a couple of hours off. What I really wanted to do was hide with her in the Scott house for a few hours but that seemed out of the question today. I could not get that open robe out of my mind. I explained to Steve the three places I would be, and I planned to be back on base by 1600 hrs. That seemed to be OK with him and he left saying "Just don't disappear."

Mike and I talked for awhile and his intention was to spend most of the day writing a letter to Rene, not only to see where she thought their relationship was but also to get some ideas from her about how Anne and myself might fit into some kind of plan. I also asked him to visit the armorer and see if he could get the cartridge box of .300 Winchester Magnums filled up.

I caught a cab and headed to town in my civvies, which were the same clothes I had left Bakersfield with. So, I stopped by a general store and bought a polo shirt and a pair of denims and threw the old clothes in the trash. I wanted to look presentable. I took another cab over to the Scott house and figured she wouldn't be there, so I asked the cabbie to wait, and walked to the porch hoping for the best. But despite prolonged banging on the door, it was clear that no one was home. Then I noticed a piece of paper on the floor, by the door. It read *"Tony: Sorry I missed you. I am at the hospital. Maybe I can get off for a few minutes if you can stop by. Sorry about last night. Love, Anne."* Wow. Sorry? It had been the highlight of my life! A person like Anne attracted to a jackrabbit shooter-college-dropout from Bakersfield? I got back in the cab and said "The main hospital and don't spare the horses." The driver had no clue about 'the horses' but he got his worn out Peugeot there in record time!

I knew the routine now. I got a pass to the second floor and looked for the nurse's station. And as I looked left, there was Anne coming out of a patient's room, looking gorgeous! There was no stringy hair or worn-out robe (although I loved that robe), but she was in a bright white, starched uniform, with her blond hair tied up above her head, under her nurse's hat. She was simply the prettiest thing I had ever seen. She put her hand to her mouth and came quickly over to me, giving me a hug. "Tony! I am so glad that you could get by!" I saw the other nurses giggling at their work stations as we held hands. She said "Oh Tony, we are so busy right now. This place is an absolute zoo. We have refugees from all over Katanga and we're very short handed." I said "Well, do you think that you could get away for lunch? I hear that there is nice restaurant across the street." "I think I can. I probably can get away at noon, but I'll have to watch my time." It wasn't what I hoped for, but I said "Tell you what. I'll go over there and get table after 11:00 and just wait. How is that?" "Perfect," she said," Then, couple of orderlies rushed came to her side and pointed to some kind of crisis down the hall and she said "I have to run but I'll try to make lunch!"

I was a little dejected, but what was I to expect? After all, she had a job and, she said she would try to make lunch. I walked down the stairs to the lobby and immediately noticed all of the people crowding the walls and the floor. There were families, with little kids running around, all with some kind of medical problem. The same situation was on the steps of the building, and I sort of selfishly resented these people who might keep Anne away from me! I kicked myself in the ass and suggested that I be a little more understanding. I thought that Anne was doing the same job as I was, me shooting the bad guys, and she patching up those who got caught in the fight. Or some rationalization like that. It just seemed like I could never shoot all of the bad guys and she lacked the resources to fix all of these poor people.

# Chapter 38

I wandered around the area and noticed that the movie house was 'Closed for Repairs'. In fact, in a four block area there were quite a few businesses closed, just like the hardware store. I wondered how many of these storekeepers were still in the country.

I bought a newspaper, and walked over to the restaurant, hoping it was still in business. Geez, I didn't want to have lunch with Anne in the hospital cafeteria. This was pretty little place with tables inside and on the sidewalk. I asked the waiter if I could have a quiet table inside and since it was early, he showed me the choices I had. Of course. The one sheltered by a plastic vine making the booth semi-dark. It was only 1030hrs. so I had some time to kill. I ordered a coffee and a pastry and said that I would be meeting someone at noon. That seemed OK with the waiter, and I assumed that given all of the circumstances in town, he was not overwhelmed with business. So, I read the paper, drank coffee and waited.

It was after 1215 hrs. and Anne hadn't shown up. Very depressing. Meanwhile a couple of tables away, three soldiers came in and ordered beers. They were from some eastern African country, probably Ethiopia. They were about my age and their uniforms looked starched and new. I thought, 'Just wait you fuckers, you won't look like that after eight weeks in the dirt'. I let my mind wander and theorized how they would look in the crosshairs of my scope. One thing was sure: they were not on our side. I had ordered a beer and I was just taking a sip when I saw Anne crossing the street. She had a shawl around her shoulders and her hair was down around her shoulders, looking far less official than she had this morning. She was just beautiful, a point not missed by the Ethiopians. She saw me, waved and came over to our table, taking my hand and giving me a quick kiss on my cheek. Heaven! Anne looked at my beer but said she couldn't drink when she was working, so I ordered a couple of ice teas. It was little awkward because I wasn't sure how she remembered last night. But she took care of that. "Tony, I have to apologize again about last night." "Apologize? For what? It was wonderful." "Yes, but I was too forward. I was just so scared of what was happening here and what might have happened to you that I had to cling to you." I said "Look Anne, maybe you haven't noticed, but I love you. I think about you every day. Please don't apologize again. Just say it was great." She squeezed my hand and said "It was great!" We laughed and I ordered salads and spaghetti. "Tony, I have to be back by about 13:00. Can we eat all of that stuff? I said "Well, to tell you the truth, I would forego lunch if we could just be at your house on the couch!" She laughed and blushed but didn't say anything. We had found each-others feet under the table and her legs against mine was sexy as hell.

The food came but we just nibbled a little and talked. She talked about her workload but I changed the subject and reminded her that The Katanga was in a very delicate and probably a fatal situation, and I thought that maybe she wasn't facing reality. "Oh, in my heart, I know. How can you ignore our lobby at the hospital? You are correct, I need to make some plans." "Well, I'm glad that we got that settled. So what do you think the plan should be?" She said "I've thought a lot about this. I know it will not happen, but it is possible that this thing will work out, so I could take a leave of absence rather than just resigning. I could go to Brussels and be with my parents, but I have also been corresponding with Rene. We can communicate using the Telex between the hospital and her newspaper. She says there would be no trouble getting a nurse's job in Capetown." "Wow!" I said. "You have been busy," as I touched her knee under the table. Every now and then I saw these Ethiopian guys ogling Anne, which pissed me off, but on the other hand, if I were an Ethiopian, I'd be ogling her too!

I thought that we were making good progress when a black Land

Rover skidded to a stop at the front door of the restaurants. Out piled Mike and Sargeant Piquart! They spotted me and walked very quickly through the restaurant to our table. Oh Christ, I thought, what could bring *this* on? Of course, I had told them where I would be, but what could cause this kind of hustle? Sargeant Steve touched his head towards Anne and apologized for the interruption, but said to me "Tony, we have an emergency in Jadotville we need you. Now!" "Steve, what do you want me to do? Here I am in civvies. What do you want me to do?" "Tony, we have your uniform in the car and all of your equipment. You can change on the way. We can be there in an hour." "What the hell is going on? What is the emergency?" Steve said "We apparently did some stupid things at Jadotville. We lost control of our own troops and they attacked the dug-in Irish. They had no protection of any kind and I suppose they thought that they could just scare the Irish guys to give up. But it didn't work and we have almost a third of the company down. 30 guys have been shot, and we think that out of that, and at least 12 are fatalities. We're formulating a reaction, and one of them involves Mike and you. You need to come with me immediately. My apologies again, Ms. Scott, but you might alert your hospital that many injured soldiers are on their way to your facility! Lets' go, Tony". Anne and I stood and kissed, and I said I'd be back as soon as I could. "Please be safe Tony, I love you."

Mike led Anne to the sidewalk and she started across the street while I left some bills on the table and walked behind Steve. When we approached the Ethiopians one of them gave me a thumbs up and said 'nice'. In turn, I kicked the chair out from under him and he landed on his ass. He got up and his buddies stood, ready to confront me but Steve stepped towards them and said "You start something here and you better be ready to go to that hospital!" They all sat down. We ran to the car and were gone in a puff of burnt rubber.

"Well, you guys sure fucked up a great lunch." Steve ignored the remark and said "All of your stuff is here. Get changed and we'll talk about the situation." So, I stripped down as we headed out of town at 70 mph, and put on my uniform. I asked Mike if all of our stuff was in order and he said "Yep. FALs, Mauser, optics, and a cartridge refill." The driver was some kind of professional who went with the Land Rover, which belonged to a high ranking officer, and seemed to be unaware that the vehicle had only one pedal. The throttle. "OK, I said, what do you guys have in mind?"

Steve turned and said "This is serious shit. Our guys actually started this by charging the Irish. But they either misunderstood their orders or had none. They just reacted to the foreign troops on our soil and away they went. They were just mowed down. I don't think they hit a single opposition soldier, but the Irish let go with their entire company and our guys were in an open area and had no protection. It was a stupid thing for us to do but there you are: a dozen dead guys and the militias in Jadotville want blood. We have to defuse that and come up with a solution or we'll have an international fiasco on our hands." "OK", I said, "What are your ideas?" Mike explained that the original idea was to cut off their water and they would give up. That happened a couple of days ago. "It'll be 104 degrees in Jadotville today and they have had no water for three days. They can't last in this weather. This probably would have worked except for the stupidity of our troops and several hundred militia members lining up behind the Irish. It could be a massacre and we'll end up being the bad guys. Then your reputation came up and we thought that if we took out their commander, they would give up. There's no decision on that, just an option." I said, "I've got to say for the third time, I'm not too anxious to start shooting Irish troops who are only there because some asshole sent them to an impossible situation. It was just about as stupid as what our own troops did." We stopped talking for awhile and all we heard was the whine of the engine and the tires thumping into potholes. We were now going over 80mph, and I thought we'll be there before we know what to do! We began to see a procession of ambulances and trucks going the other way, and I figured that Anne's day was finished too. I spoke up and said "Do the Irish have any water re-supply capability?" Steve said "Not from anyone in that city. They are ready to shoot and emotions are running very high. The U.N. does have a large Sikorsky helicopter who might be able to bring supplies, but those militias might shoot the fucker down!" I said, "Let me think."

I was weighing the scant number of options and an idea germinated. "How about this: let these guys go through tomorrow with no water. That will be four days of dehydration, and it'll give us time to share a strategy with the locals." "Yes" Steve interrupted, "And then what?" "Well, it seems to me that the Irish must know that they are now in an impossible situation but they want to save face. You know the old macho deal. They haven't fought a battle since 1917 and now they fuck this one up. How's that going to play in Dublin?" "OK," said Steve, "But what is the strategy?" "Try this: we put on a shooting exhibition. We clear out of the area and set up 700 yards or so from their foxholes. We find a visible target near their Commander and shoot a hole through that target. And another one through the first hole. Then another. And another. Then we stop. I guess we have a bullhorn but maybe that isn't necessary. It should be crystal clear that if we can shoot a hole in a hole in a hole in a hole, it would be very easy to shoot the first blue helmet that pops up. That ought to appeal to the militias, and together with no water for four days, they might raise the white flag. How does that sound?" Steve thought for a minute and said "And what if they don't give up?" I was ready for that. "We start shooting blue helmets. If these fuckers are that dense, then they deserve a bullet." Mike said "I like it!" Steve said "I think I like it too, but we need to sell it to those militia guys and our bosses. But the main point I see is that there is no risk. No downside."

We rolled to a stop in the outskirts of Jadotville about a half hour later. Some recruits were setting up a tent and our old buddy Colonel Mkandawire was there. I'd never seen him looking so distant, and we could see that he was listening to some subordinates. To us, that meant that he had not arrived at a solution. During the trip, we had been so preoccupied with the problem that I had forgotten to ask who had ordered us to be there on an emergency basis. Someone above Steve had to have provided that Land Rover and ordered us there as an emergency. It had to have something to do with our sniper skills because that was the only skill we had that was not shared by everyone else. He noticed us and asked us to sit in on a strategy session. That is pretty unusual, a sargeant and two corporals being asked to participate in a planning session with a colonel. A circle of about ten folding chairs were set up under a tree, and Mkandawire asked the three of us to sit. "If you want to know why you are here, it's because I do not like the options being presented that will root out these Irish troops. Right now, we have no solution except perhaps to just kill them all. And, after losing most of a company, I can understand that viewpoint. That is what everyone seems to want to do. Just drop a dozen mortars into their trenches and that would take care of them! I am looking beyond that. There's no doubt that we can wipe out these men but how will that play in the bigger picture? Katanga troops slaughter a small group of Irish troops? Our president has asked me to come up with something less aggressive than that! Why should we be the aggressor? I think that we are the victims!" So, I thought, Tshombe was personally involved. Mkandawire went on "We have already passed a note to Quinlan that we would offer safe passage back to Elisabethville but they would be under our supervision. They refused. Given their situation, they seem very stubborn, which makes some of us concerned about the possibility of more of their resources coming our way." One of the captains stood and said "How can there be any doubt? They are the ones doing the slaughtering! We should act now!" Mkandaweri thanked the captain, but said "Remember captain, earlier today we effectively lost an entire company because emotions and a lack of discipline has killed a dozen of our troops. He looked toward Steve and calmly said "I know that you have been thrown into this difficult situation, but I know that you have two men here who have exceptional skills and I'd like to hear about any ideas you have." The captain sat down, mumbling about talking instead of acting.

"Well, actually we do have a concept that we put together on the drive up here." He asked me to explain and I walked him through the idea. "One of the unknowns to us is the terrain. We would need some place to set up somewhere between 600 and 1100 yards from their positions to make this work, and from what we can see, there is a lot of open ground between these troops and that distance." Mkandaweri asked an aid to bring some topographical maps in order to get an idea on terrain, and then asked for questions. There were a lot of them. The best answer was Steve's point. What was the downside? If this failed, you could always kill them! They wanted to know about our track record, and why this would cause the Irish to give up. Steve explained how some of our exploits had calmed down the Balubas.

The aide with the maps came over and pointed out a rock outcropping that might work, but it looked like it was over 1100 yards from the trenches. "OK" said Mkandaweri, "Here is what I want to do. Sargeant, you take your men to this area and examine the distance and see if it is adequate for your success. I appreciate the creativeness of your idea and it is worth a try. We always have the option of an assault if it doesn't work out, but if it does, we will be the ones who have valued human life, not the Irish. After you examine the terrain, I want to circle around the city and consult with the militia leaders. I need them to sit aside until we try this out. The last thing I need right now is for a bunch of rogue shooters taking charge simply because we haven't communicated our plan. Get with it, sargeant, and we'll meet right here, in two hours. Oh, yes, sargeant, if all of this falls into place, when do you propose to initiate action?" Steve responded. "We have talked about that and we should let them suffer one more day. Let them cook. If they haven't voluntarily surrendered by the morning of the fifth day, we start at 0800, about when they are eating whatever they have to eat. "I like that" said the Colonel. "There's always the chance that they will just give up. OK, we'll firm this up in two hours and work out the details." Mkandaweri left in a group of three Jeeps and we went to work.

It was quickly ascertained that the outcropping of rocks shown on the map was as good as we were going to get. But we had to know the exact distance and be very critical about our chances of success. There was a lot hanging on this, and we had to get it right. Mike dug out his optics package and we all hiked towards the spot on the map. We could see the rocks but from our starting point, it looked pretty meager. Particularly if the Irish started shooting back. We approached the rocks from the back side, trying to keep as invisible as we could, although at this distance, we would be very tiny images if they could see us at all. What we found was a lump of rocks, about 25 feet in length, with an elevation slightly above the Irish position. It looked like the entrance to an old abandoned mine. That part was ideal. We could do a little digging and have some protection and invisibility. The distance was another thing. Mike set up his range finder and by now, the shadows were deepening and it was difficult to get an accurate fix. '1276 yards" Shit, I thought. About 3825 feet. Three quarters of a mile. Nine city blocks. Possible but not easy. We also had to find a target that would make our point. By now, the shadows were deepening and Mike and I crouched low and settled in behind the rocks. Mike noticed something and called me over. "Look at this, Tony. There is a blue U.N flag flying about in the middle of the trenches. It looks like it is attached to a wooden pole. What if we just shot the pole and brought down the flag?" "Good idea, Mike. And if they get stubborn and nail the thing together we'll shoot it again. If we can do that four times, they ought to get the message!"

When Mkandaweri returned, we got back together, remaining very unusual, corporals talking directly to colonels as equals. But he accepted that our skill was something that we had, and the chain-of-command really had nothing to do with it. Another time, another issue, and we were sure that we would be immediately demoted. In any case, Mkandawire reported that the militias had agreed to sit tight till the evening of day number five. He said it was a tough sell and that they disagreed with all of this pussy-footing around. On the other time, what was the danger of waiting?

That evening, Mkandiweri had a big steak cook-out a mile from the Irish, hoping that the great charcoal smells would waft over the Irish.

# Chapter 39

After breakfast the next morning Mike and I hiked back to our new position by the rocks. Mike grumbled about being out on an eight-week deployment, sleeping in a bed one night, and then back on the ground again in Jadotville. Working out the kinks was made a little easier by the guarantee of a very hot day. By 1000hrs. it was an easy ninety degrees, and by 1400 hours it would be well over one hundred. Those Irish troops, with little or no water, were going to suffer. I thought that they must be yearning for Ireland, where everything is green and it rains every day. Or something like that. Mike and I dug around the apparent entrance to the cave and found some ancient equipment and an actual passage-way that looked like it was blocked about thirty feet from the entrance. Youthful curiosity suggested that we should explore, until Mike brought me back to the present. "C'mon, Tony, we've got some shooting to plan for."

About an hour later we heard the thumpety-thumpety-thumpety sounds of a helicopter, and it was coming our way. Quickly, a very large Sikorsky came into view, and it had something hanging below it on a cable. It looked like a large black bladder, and we realized that it must be water for the beleaguered Irish. Unprotected, it was flying very fast, but then slowed and hovered over the trenches and dropped the bladder, which caused the copter to immediately pop up in elevation and fly on. But not for long. The engine began to miss, and I said "Oh shit, some cowboy just shot the thing and there goes our humanitarian strategy." But that wasn't the case. As we later discovered, it was just another crapped out piece of machinery in Africa with zero maintenance and the engine blew some oil lines all by itself which in turn caused a bearing to burn out and the pilot had to shut the engine down. We could see the copter wind-milling down about two miles away, landing hard on a hilltop. A Jeep with four of our soldiers immediately headed in that direction, and we supposed that Mkandaweri wanted to secure the crew in case they had clever rescue plans.

Our attention turned back to the black bladder and Mike had his scope on it. Two Irish soldiers, clearly not the brightest in the group, headed towards the bladder, in full view. An easy shot, but apparently they were thinking about a huge supply of cool water and not about .300 Winchester Magnums. Mike followed their actions and we talked about just blasting a few holes in the container. We needn't have worried. One of the soldiers undid a cap and cupped his hands to test the water, and immediately blew it out, looking like he was choking or something of the sort. The other guy tried too, with the same result. Unbelievably, the water was undrinkable. "Those guys are the world's stupidest! I'll bet that they loaded water into an empty fuel bladder and didn't bother to check it." "No matter", said Mike, "Now they still have no water and they lost a helicopter in the process!"

That evening we reverted to rations, and afterwards, fine- tuned our planned operation. Mkandawire invited us over to his tent and we met three militia leaders. They were there because they were curious. What equipment could do such accurate work? Especially in Africa! After all, the Irish couldn't even keep a helicopter flying for a few miles and apparently could not tell the difference between water and gas! We were introduced and I could see that they were not impressed with our age. They must have been imagining some survivor of Leningrad or wherever. A Paul Merkle was the head person and he politely asked if he and his partners could see our equipment. Mkandawire nodded OK, so I said "It's over at the NCO encampment and there's quite a bit of stuff. Would you mind walking over with us?" No problem. All of a sudden they were enthusiastic. These guys lived and breathed guns.

We had set up a portable plastic table as we planned on a good cleaning session, so the equipment was already on the table but still in their cases. Mkandaweri came with them and we had a group of about seven guys, which included a couple of our captains. The first thing Mike did was un-wrap his optics package, which required some explanation. He explained, "We have four basic pieces of equipment: a set of binoculars, a medium ranged, Zeiss 10x40 scope, a huge 20x80 Zeiss scope and most importantly, a rangefinder, powered by battery." The huge scope and the rangefinder were something new to them. Mike assembled the whole package into a wire rack and explained "I need to move between a scope that has a wide field of vision to one that sacrifices the field to distance. The rangefinder will tell me exactly the distance to the target to an accuracy of about 12 inches at 1500 yards. Of course we know exactly what the drop of the bullet is at a given range so we can know exactly how to interpret the scope crosshairs on the rifle." Merkle was just wowed by this and they hadn't even seen the rifle. Mike went on. "You see, I have to be able to move from one piece of equipment very quickly without fooling around and communicate all of this to Tony here." Everyone gathered around was impressed and looked over the equipment but Mike made sure no one touched any of it. He was very possessive about this stuff. Finally, Merkle said "What about the rifle?" So I went to the black case and unlocked it and pulled out the Mauser, still in a flannel cover. I removed the cover and pulled the rifle out. They all moved closer, and cooed their appreciation. "Look at the heavy fluted barrel, and the polished action." Another militia guy appreciated the oiled stock which while in my possession had acquired a mellow sheen. One guy asked about the bolt action. "Couldn't you use a semi- automatic FAL with a special barrel? I just wonder about having only five shots." I said, "Well, the work we have been doing with the Balubas was all based on a single shot, taking out the chief. Actually we usually load only a single round. If we need a lot of shots, our basic surprise strategy goes away, and probably would eliminate any chance of a hostage rescue. So, we thought that the same basic idea might work here. As far as the bolt action rifle question, both the Belgium Army and the Mauser people believe the bolt action is marginally more accurate than a customized FAL. Our armorer told us that the fewer moving parts the better." Most of the group nodded their understanding. Still another person mentioned the custom recoil pad and asked about the caliber. ".308?" he asked. "No", I said, ".300 Winchester Magnum." Merkel chimed in, and asked if that was a military round. "Only for snipers in the U.S. and in Germany." He asked what my best shot was. Steve gave the answer which I appreciated as I didn't want to be bragging. He said "Tony blew the head off a Baluba chieftan at 1700 yards." "Shit, one of them said. A fucking mile!" It was clear that they were all sold.

I brought up a separate issue. "We plan to take action between about 0900 and 1000 in the morning. As you know, this is a shooting exhibition and we're not trying to kill anyone. We're actually trying to show them that opposition would be futile. But it doesn't always work out that way. Who knows, some crazy guy might start shooting and their entire company might charge. So our advice is to place our troops about 2000 yards back from the Irish and try to avoid a shooting situation. If our strategy does not work, there should be time to set up a proper assault." Mkandiweri said, "I agree with pulling the troops slightly to the rear. In fact, if all fails, we and the militias have a strategy worked out, but I want to at least try this out." I added, no doubt unnecessarily, "Please just tell the guys to keep their fingers off of their triggers until we see how this goes. One shot from them will ruin all of this." The colonel looked at me like he didn't really need that advice, but shook his head in the affirmative. As the group walked away, Mike said "Shit, I hope we can live up to the sales pitch!"

# Chapter 40

The next morning came with a very hot sun, rising with brilliant reds and oranges, like a ball of fire. Under different circumstances it would have been beautiful. I was polishing some cartridges and Mike said, "It will be best to get this underway as soon as possible. By 1000 hrs. the heat waves could begin to distort the target image." After having a couple of beers the night before and drinking water several times during the night, I thought of those poor Irish guys 1200 yards away. They must be suffering terribly.

So we did what we were paid to do. We had some cereal and coffee for breakfast, then humped over to the rocks, coming in from the back way, just in case someone was scoping the territory this far away.

By now, all of this was a mechanical exercise, and we had to keep reminding ourselves not to get too cocky. But it all went together well, and by 0830 we were about ready. Steve crept up behind us and said "I have a transmitter. When do you want to do this? I need to alert Mkandawire." I said, "I'm thinking about 0900." Steve sent a message and I assumed everything was a go.

Mike started scoping and there was the blue U.N. Flag, hanging in the windless air. He said "I think it would be a good idea to target the post about two feet below the lowest point on the flag. Otherwise, they will not get the full impact of fracturing the post and watching the flag fall." "OK, Let's get started."

I positioned the rifle on some bean bags, and looked through the scope and adjusting it for clarity and bullet drop, based on the range Mike had called out yesterday, and said "OK, I have the flagpole in view, and there are blue helmets walking around. They are completely vulnerable from here." I plucked a cartridge from the felt-line box and looked it over, even though I knew it would be perfect. I inserted it into the chamber and closed the bolt. I looked through the scope and had the pole in my cross-hairs about two feet below the flag, as Mike had suggested. "Range?" "1276 yards." "Wind?" "Nil". I fine-tuned the scope adjustment and said "Ready. Tell Steve." Set the trigger. Safety off. Deep breath, exhale and hold. Caress the trigger and received that comfortable push against my shoulder. I actually heard the round hit the wood, and Mike called out "Flag down!" I looked through the rifle scope and some guys were looking around their position to see where the shot came from, but in the process, it should have occurred to them that I could have just as easily have shot them. I saw someone pick up the flag and the stub of the flagpole and walk into a dug-out position. "Great shot, Tony" said Mike. Steve said "Good one." "Thanks", I said, "but now we need to see what they will do. We're assuming these stubborn fucks will fix the pole and have it up again."

We didn't have to wait long. Within fifteen minutes the pole was up, with a wooden stake taped to the broken pole, doing a fair job of reinforcement. I said, OK, lets' try again. I am going to aim at the same place and try to hit the stake at that point. "I took another cartridge out of the box and inserted it into the chamber and closed the bolt. "Wind?" "Nil." Safety off. Set trigger. Caress the trigger. Mike couldn't contain himself. "Exactly right on Tony. The bullet penetrated the stake at exactly the same spot and went right through the fractured pole! Flag down!"

This time, there were about six blue helmets swiveling their heads this way and that? Their reaction was what we had hoped for. The first shot might have come from some lucky yahoo, but two shots in exactly the same spot? And from where? They clearly did not know because they kept looking this way and then that. We assumed that they ignored our position because they probably couldn't imagine a rifle being accurate at our range. We timed the repair at 20 minutes, and the flag was up again. Through the scope I could see that this time, the reinforcement was more robust, with a stake on each side and a whole lot of tape binding it all together. You had to give it to these guys. They didn't have flag pole equipment available, and if nothing else, they were being loyal

"OK guys, one more." I took another cartridge out of the box, checked and unbelievably, it had a nick in the copper jacket. I couldn't imagine how that happened, but I set it aside and selected another. Perfect. I inserted it into the chamber, closed the bolt and set the trigger. I took one last look through the scope and touched the trigger. Mike said calmly "Flag down." Steve, Mike and I all had a good, but quiet laugh. Looking through the scope I saw some high level guy, probably Quinlan, examining the broken off pole with the flag hanging between his legs. I said, "Boy, would that make a great shot!" Mike said. "Mkandawire says to hold off because he's going to try the loud speaker. He adds his congratulations!"

A few minutes later, in clear, precise English, the message said "Walk forward and deposit your arms in front of your position and walk to our flag at the top of the hill. You will be treated humanely. We have water and food for you. I do not want any more bloodshed." And with that, a Katanga flag was raised behind a jeep. Now it was wait and see.

After about five minutes, a pole with a white flag appeared, and a minute later an officer stepped from the Irish position to the field. He advanced across the open field and stopped about half way to our main position. He cupped his hands and shouted 'Parlay.' "Wow!" said Mike. "This guy isn't in a great position to bargain!" But Colonel Mkandawire walked out to meet him. They talked for a couple of minutes and the Irish officer turned and returned to his position, and Mkandawire did as well. Later, we learned that the officer wanted reassurance that his troops would be treated according to the Geneva Convention, which was to say 'humanely'. He asked for medical treatment to several men and all to be released to the U.N. Mkandawire was OK with the medical treatment but said the Irish would be quarantined in Elisabethville until arrangements could be made to trade for twelve Katanganese troops who had been imprisoned in Kamina for unknown reasons. Quinlan, the Irish officer, stated that he would make every effort to arrange that release. Then, in a display of European chutzpah, he also asked to keep his pistol, which was OK with Mkandawire. It was like keeping a battle sword in the 1800s. A few minutes later, the Irish company appeared, deposited their rifles, and began walking to the Katanga position. Two men were on stretchers and we understood later that this was from severe dehydration rather than any battle wounds.

We walked over to the area where the troops were being received and saw them given water and an area to rest. Interestingly, two of the Irish troops nodded to Mike and I as they walked through a line. Mike nodded back and said to me "Those guys had a beer with us back in Elisabethville". We thought that justice had been served when the first decent meal provided to the Irish was runny eggs and half cooked bacon!

# Chapter 41

After a two-day rest, the Irish troops began a supervised march back to Elisabethville. It was clear from the start that there was going to be no problems with the Irish and they ate the same food as ours and were treated with respect. The two troops who were on stretchers recovered satisfactorily but were placed on trucks for the entire trip. In fact, once most the Katanga guys were back at Elisabethville the trucks turned around and trucked the Irish troops back to the city. There was no doubt that they had suffered a lot from a lack of proper food and almost no water, but we considered that the real villain was the idiot who had placed these guys in the middle of an armed camp of militias. If they had wanted to conquer Jadotville, they should have sent at least a regiment, maybe more.

But the real surprise was that when we returned to our barracks, we found that The Irish were going to be housed in the adjacent building! How that would work out remained to be seen. In later years, what stuck in our craws was the myth of 'the brave Irish, outnumbered and without water, holding their ground against a superior force.' The bravery of the Irish was not the issue, but the competence of the U.N. leadership certainly was. And, when considering that we had lost a dozen men made us gag at all of the revisionist history. Not one Irish soldier was maimed, killed or mistreated.

Once everything was figured out and the trek back to Elisabethville began, our militia friends came by to invite us to dinner. They reassured Mkandawire that they would get us back to Elisabethville the next day, and the public relations aspect of the offer was something the Colonel couldn't resist. So we stayed over and what a feed these locals put on. They were still mesmerized by the shooting exhibition but the cold beer soon made the conversation move to more pleasant subjects. About 150 people attended the dinner which was held in a gymnasium. There were steaks and goodies and even a small band. The local girls asked us to dance and how could we say no? It was a sensational response to our efforts, which no doubt avoided another bloodbath. We slept in real beds in a small hotel and while we slept, someone had taken our uniforms and washed and pressed them during the night. After warm showers and a huge breakfast, we were ready to call Jadotville 'home.'

About noon Mr. Merkle told us he was going to drive us back to Elisabethville and what do you think? He parked a shiny Mercedes at the front door to the hotel and ushered us into the cushy leather back seat! But it all had limits. After about 40 miles we caught up with our troops and there was no way Mike or I were going to pass them in a Mercedes! So against Merkel's protests we shook hands and offered each other thanks and we climbed into a truck with our gear. This was no doubt the high point in our residence in The Katanga. Then, I began to think about Anne, and how to deal with her safety.

# Chapter 42

By the time we got to the barracks we were dead tired, and a little hung over from the Jadotville evening. The next morning, we left our gear with the armorer to check, had our usual breakfast and started to arrange a trip into town. But we were delayed when Mkandawire summoned us to his office where there was a representative of Tshombe's staff. When faced with this huge difference of authority we always wondered if we had done good or bad! On the other hand, we had developed a good relationship with Mkandawire, so we felt reasonably secure. We needn't have worried. The official from Tshombe's office stated that he wanted to express the president's thanks for handling the problem in Jadotville with competence and creativity. Then he gave us each an envelope and invited us to open it. In the envelope was a check in the amount of $2000 for each of us! Wow! What followed were a lot of hand shaking and a photog came in and took our pictures. What a great way to start a day!

The downside of this was that Mike and I had been carrying around a wad of $100 bills for several weeks on the assumption that overall, conditions were getting worse and we might need that cash on a minute's notice. This would just add to the wad. The notion that 'things were getting worse' was illustrated by the fact that the Irish troops could occupy the adjacent buildings was that many contract employees had left. There were fewer men at breakfast, and all of the Belgium soldiers were gone, completing an exodus that started months before. We estimated that there were now about 70 contract employees left, and plans for future operations oftentimes were accompanied by the word 'suicide.' Then there was this Mike Hoare guy who seemed to operate separately from our chain-of-command.

He controlled around 100 plus mercenaries, seemed well respected and we agreed that we should again look him up. Despite being treated well by our superiors it was time to begin making some concrete plans for ourselves. The Katanganese army was slowly developing but there was no way that they could sustain a battle with the combined U.N. forces who were reported to be growing every day. A good example of the army's immaturity was the assault at Jadotville. What actually occurred was an undisciplined attack on the Irish, which ended in tragedy. Justified or not, The Katanga had become a pariah in international affairs, in favor of a totally dysfunctional Congolese Army that spread death everywhere they went. What would happen when all of the U.N. troops eventually left? Most people envisioned chaos. Chaos already existed in all other location in the Congo except The Katanga. Why couldn't the U.N. see this? We talked about all of this palace intrigue but at our pay level, there were more tangible things to consider. No one was interested in our take on world affairs! Our focus was not if we should get out, but when. And how.

We took the shuttle into town, and headed to the clothing store. During that emergency trip to Jadotville, I had changed clothes in the car, and my civvies had disappeared somewhere. However, the store where I had bought my clothes was now boarded up, an increasingly common sight in Elisabethville. Another change was the absence of the squared away Swedish troops walking around town in groups of fours. In their place were Congolese troops wandering around town, both singularly or in unorganized bands of six or eight. These were not an organized military force, but seemingly, just soldiers drifting into the city. We assumed that the main army was somewhere out there but that seemed to be a mystery. Maybe our bosses had just given up on the idea of a fight, given the vast gap in manpower and equipment. These men typically gathered at the front of a bar or a store selling liquor. There were laws against drinking on the streets, but there was no realistic way to enforce such a measure, with several dozen cops vs. thousands of soldiers. So there they were, bottles in brown paper bags, some of them outright drunk and some just a little tipsy. It must be a real mess after sundown.

Mike and I finally found a used clothing store and bought some duds that were in surprisingly good condition. We bundled up our cammies and when we went to the register to pay, the owner did a double take when we pulled out our roll of hundred dollar bills, which were now in the $8,000 range. Then, we headed to the bank to cash our newest bonus check and talked a little about the stupidity of getting mugged by these roving bands of undisciplined soldiers, making this entire adventure a disaster. I gave some thought about carrying my P.38 just for defense. At the bank, conditions were worse. We waited in line for over an hour, and when we finally got to a teller, we were told that we could only get $1000 in U.S. dollars, and the rest in Katanganese bills, which were essentially worthless on the international market. It was clear that the entire governmental apparatus was collapsing around us, and we felt more vulnerable in Elisabethville than we did in the bush!

My next objective was Anne, and Mike went his own way as I headed for the hospital. It was very disorienting seeing the deterioration of the town as I walked away from the main street. About 50% of the small stores and apartments were boarded up and I wondered why an owner would bother spending money on the plywood. Things were not going to get any better unless some miracle occurred. But the worst scene was the steps to the hospital. Families were living on the broad entrance to the facility, in sleeping bags, portable tents and cardboard boxes. Apparently there was no place to house hundreds of refugees and security must be horrible. These poor people who had lost almost everything were no doubt easy pickings for bandits and soldiers on-the-take. I worked my way to the entrance where three burly armed guards blocked the doors. I told a Sargeant that I was here to visit nurse Anne Scott and he looked through a hospital roster, asked me my name and dialed a number on an intercom. After a minute or two he nodded to me, and opened the door.

If the steps to the hospital were grim, the lobby was beyond belief. There were people on gurneys, cots and laying on sleeping bags. All either had serious sickness or had what looked like bullet wounds. As I walked towards the elevators, I glimpsed a familiar person. It was Art! Art Stepan from Bishop who intermittently had been our roommate. I walked to him and his rheumy eyes tried to focus on me and he made a forced, weak smile. "Tony! What are you doing here?" I said "The better question is what are you doing here?" He pulled a sheet back to his waist and there was a bloody bandage that started at his left elbow and continues across his shoulder to his neck. "Jesus," I said, "what in the fuck happened?" He said he was part of an ill-advised maneuver over in Jadotville and he was one of the lucky ones. "Twelve of our guys are dead and I hear that two more might not make it." "Holy shit!" I said, "Mike and I were just up there." I told him about capturing the Irish troops and he said that was the only good news he had heard. "Well what in the world are you doing here? Isn't there a room? Is anyone taking care of you?" Art responded with the obvious. "Look around. This place is packed and the doctors and nurses are leaving as the patient load increases! There are guys a lot worse off than me. The food is sporadic and medical treatment is worse. I mean, the employees are working night and day but my bandages haven't been changed in two days and it smells like shit." I just shook my head. "Has anyone been here from the barracks? Has anyone contacted you?" "Well, I've been sort of in and out of it for a couple of days. The strategy seems to be to just conk you out so you don't cause any trouble! I have no idea what is going on!"

"Look, Art, I have some friends here in the hospital. I was just going upstairs to see them and I'll try and find out what they are doing for you and if something better can be arranged." Art said "Thanks, mate, anything you can do will be appreciated, but look at all of these people!" I asked about the nature of the wound and he said "A large caliber bullet, probably a .308, entered my arm just above the elbow and exited through my shoulder. I don't know if anything is broken or not because no x-rays have been taken! I get lots of pain pills but I have no idea about the injury." I looked around the room and thought, what the fuck are all of those Irish guys doing at our barracks, three meals a day, and clean beds? "This fucking sucks! Let me see what I can do." I gave his good arm a squeeze and he dropped back on his sheet and shut his eyes. He murmured 'thanks' and I headed for the elevators. Bad idea. There was a note on the door that said 'Out of order.' I took the stairs two at a time to Anne's ward.

This was worse. The real basket cases were already clogging the rooms and the hallways. It was a mix of refugees and the wounded from Jadotville, plus the usual illnesses and accidents that happened in The Katanga before the world went to hell. I walked by the nurse's station and one of them said hello and simply pointed down the hall. As I approached a room Anne turned and placed her hand over her mouth. "Tony!" she said and dropped some bandages on the floor and came to me and we hugged closely. "Tony! I just have to look at you," as she pushed away and then gave me another hug. "It is absolutely wonderful to have you back." I took her hand and pulled her into a utility room and gave her a great, wet kiss which she readily returned. We hugged and I pushed her away just to get a look at her and I was shocked. Her uniform was spattered with blood or some kind of fluid and she looked like she was bone tired. She had deep circles around her eyes and looked exhausted. "Anne, you look very tired. Do you get any sleep?" She bowed her head and said "Oh I am so sorry I look a mess. The work here is so overwhelming that it just never seems to stop." I said "From what I have seen in the lobby and around here it's not just overwhelming, it's impossible!" Tears welled up in her eyes and she nodded, then pulled towards me.

"When can you get out of here?" She shook her head almost hopelessly and said, "Maybe about 6:00 P.M. We're working 12 to 14 hour shifts, and every day it gets worse because there are more and more patients and we keep losing staff. People are leaving The Katanga in droves." I nodded and she brightened up a little and said,

"Tony, you have become famous around here! You have been shooting flags instead of people and stopped a big battle!" Embarrassed, I just shook my head and said "Overstated. Now when can I see you?" She thought for a minute and said "I can be at the house after 6:00 P.M." That sounded like heaven. "How do you get there? The streets are awash with thugs and they have guns." She nodded and said "Oh they drive us to our homes. No one is allowed to just go walking around. We have three rape cases right here in my ward to prove the point." I just shook my head as she rummaged around in her pockets and came up with a key. "Why don't you just go over there and I'll be along when I can. Can you get off work?" I said, "An atomic explosion couldn't keep me away!" She laughed and began to turn back to her patients. "Anne, I know that you are overworked and things look very tough here, but I have a friend laying on a blanket down in the lobby. He has been shot and has been seen by a doctor but his wound is festering and he's drugged up for the pain but I don't think anyone is tending to him. Is there a chance that someone could take a look? If he can be treated I can get him out to the base and there's one less customer. His name is Art Stepan. Anne looked baffled. With all of this chaos, she seemed a little angry that I had asked for more. "I'll try" she said, and wrote Art's name on the palm of her hand with a ball point pen. "Now I have to go. I'll see you this evening." I said "Great! I'll have dinner waiting for you!" She laughed and gave me that dazzling smile, turned and left.

On the way out I found Art in the maze of bodies in the lobby and shook him awake. I said "Art, someone will be down here and fix you up. I'll try and get you back to the base." He cried through the obvious pain and said "Thanks, bud, I might not make it." "Oh you're going to make it all right. I will personally see that you get some runny eggs and half-cooked bacon as soon as you get back." He managed a short laugh and laid back down, obviously in a mental fog.

I caught a shuttle back to the base and found Mike napping in our room. I told him that any luck, I'd see him in the morning. "Lucky shit" he said. I looked up Sargeant Steve and got informal permission to be off base for a few hours. I cleaned up and hopped another shuttle to Anne's. Along the way, I stopped at a grocery store and bought a pile of food. I was going to play cook!

# Chapter 43

What impressed me once again was the boarded up street where Anne lived. Weeds, trash, and wrappers had replaced trimmed lawns, flowers, and well-kept homes. I had to develop a strategy to get Anne out of here. Anne? How about me? I picked up some newspapers on the front porch and opened the front door. The place smelled a little musty, no doubt due to Anne keeping the place locked up. So, I left the door ajar and opened the side door. The electricity was on, and the inside of the house looked orderly but very gloomy due to the plywood covering the windows. I shuddered to think of Anne. I set the groceries down and had a walk through the house. It was easy to find Ann's bedroom because it still had little-girl purple and pink colors and a bedspread with cartoon characters. Those must have been happy times for her, and she was no doubt reluctant to let them go. Something caught my eye near the bed and I could see that it was a pistol. I picked it up, and looked it over. A Smith and Wesson Model 28 .357 magnum. Aha! I thought. Anne may still have a bedroom that was furnished for a 12-year old, but a .357 Magnum was all adult. Obviously no one was going to take advantage of this woman without a fight!

I went back to the kitchen and started to sort out the groceries. I decided on a salad, spaghetti and red wine. I hadn't done much cooking in months...in fact hardly any at all given an Italian mother, but I figured spaghetti would be easy. There was cold beer in the fridge, so I opened one and walked out to the front porch and sat down on the swing. I still could not get it through my head that this perfect place could be so ravaged by ideological politicians and ignorant soldiers. Every now and then a couple of Congolese soldiers would walk by and they looked over at me and then walked on. Maybe there were easier pickings down the street.

I fussed with the dinner preparation for a while but figured that Anne wouldn't be home for a couple of hours so I just settled in on the couch and took a nap. Broken glass woke me up and I was instantly alert and ran to the door, which was still open. That was a stupid thing to do after worrying about Anne. But when I got to the porch all that was there was a broken wine bottle. Whoever threw it had made a fast getaway. A warning? To Anne? I swept up the mess and went back into the house, locked the side door, picked up the .357 and went back on the front porch. I opened the cylinder on the pistol and pulled out a cartridge. Hollow points. This girl was not kidding! Then I waited.

By 1830 I was getting worried but about 30 minutes later a van pulled up, a guard stepped out and Anne was behind him. There were others in the vehicle and I was relieved that these people were at least being realistic about the threat on the streets. The guard saw me and walked up the sidewalk with Anne, his pistol in his hand. Anne turned, and must have told him it was OK and he turned back to the van, presumably to deliver more exhausted hospital workers. She had removed her nurse's hat and her blonde hair tumbled down around her shoulders. I jumped down the steps and we gave each other a big hug. And a kiss. And a hug. Then we stepped on the porch and into the house and repeated the hugs and kisses. Anne said "That food smells good Tony! I was beginning to get used to the moldy odor! What are you cooking?" "Surprise! Just sit down and get off your feet and I'll bring you a glass of wine. How's that for service?" She settled down into an easy chair that looked a little like my dad's TV-watching chair and said "That would be super." I went into the kitchen, poured the wine and cut up some cheese, but by the time I got back to the living room, Anne's head was leaning to one side, sound asleep! I just sat down in another chair and looked at her sleeping. That was better than dinner, although I did drink her wine!

About an hour later she woke up, shook her head a little and said "Oh! I am so sorry! I just drifted off." I gave her a kiss on the forehead asked her if she was ready for dinner. Anne looked down at her dress and said "Yes, but I need to get cleaned up. I've been in this outfit for about 15 hours!" She got up and walked down the hallway. I put the spaghetti sauce back on the stove.

I set the table and got the salad out of the fridge when she came back into the kitchen. She looked like a new person in shorts, a frilly kind of blouse and barefoot. I held her shoulders and looked at her. "Fabulous" I said. Her hair was still damp from a shower and she looked like a new woman. Not that there was anything wrong with the old one!

What happened next is something of a wonderful fog. We finished our salad when she got out of the chair, came over to me and sat in my lap, her arms around my neck. She said "Come with me," and lead me to her bedroom. At times like these, I remembered that exhaustion and hunger didn't count. I'm not sure who was the quickest, her unbuttoning me or me unbuttoning her. But it all came off and we ascended into heaven for a long, long time. It was a little clumsy at first, but heaven trumps clumsy every time. I woke up a couple of hours later to the smell of something burning and found the spaghetti sauce burning to a crisp, turned off the stove then I went back to the bedroom. She was awake, so I hopped in and asked her if she was hungry. She said "Only for you", and the night light went out and heaven was there once again. I awoke about sunup and found the bed empty, but there were smells coming from the hallway. I walked into the kitchen, and there she was in her old robe, cooking breakfast. She playfully came to me, embraced and said, laughing, "I've had enough of you. Now we need to have some breakfast!" We sat across from each other playing around with some scrambled eggs, looking at each other with goo-goo eyes.

After breakfast Anne said "Now I really have to get ready. The van will be here between 8:45 and 9:00 and I need be at the front door. She walked towards her bedroom and I asked "Mind if I come along?" "Only if you behave yourself!" A few minutes later she came out of the next-door shower with a towel around her. I was sitting on a tiny make-up chair when she dropped the towel. The touch of her in bed at night was only exceeded by her looks in broad daylight. I just sat there in awe as she reached into a drawer, and pulled on a pair of frilly panties. She turned towards me, made a coquettish pose, which nearly caused me to fall off the chair, and then fastened her bra. I said "I cannot believe that I am this lucky! I have had you on my mind ever since that day in the hardware store!" "Well", she said, "It took me a little longer but I'm right there with you!"

She reached into her closet and came out with fresh starched nurse's uniform, and slipped it on over her head, asking me to button her up in the back. I started, but slipped my hand around to her breast and she uttered a little gasp but then pushed me away and said, "Twelve hours from now and have the spaghetti ready!" Then I got serious. "Anne, we need to have a serious discussion about your safety. I know you are dedicated to helping people, but 200 Annes cannot help The Katanga. You just need to face reality." She said "I know that you are right but how about you? You are not only in the same country but you are shooting guns. And soon people will be shooting guns at you." "Well, I know that and I need to leave. Mike and I are looking at a plan, and I'd like for you to be a part of it. Would you be willing to join Rene in South Africa until something more permanent was arranged?" She looked at me a little sternly like 'I can take care of myself' but said "I'll think about it. I'll wire Rene today and see what her situation is." That was about as far as I could go. "Oh yes. Where is my revolver?" Here I was, yakking about safety and I had moved her only safety device. "Sorry. It's by the front door and I'll put it back on your night stand."

Anne disappeared into the bathroom and came back with her makeup on, and her hair bundled up in a bun. I said "I'll bet that every man in that hospital is in love with you!" She gave me a little pinch through my shorts and said "I'll see you after work."

The van was right on time and off she went. I cleaned up the kitchen and flagged down a shuttle to the base, thinking about how I could get another pass. As we headed toward the base the driver said "Big storm coming in this afternoon. It's all across central Africa and so you need to expect flooding. The shuttle may not run." I thanked him but I thought I would just swim. Little did I know that something far more serious than a rainstorm was on its way.

# Chapter 44

I got a little kidding from Steve and Mike but I could see that they were desperately jealous. We were sitting around the cafeteria and Mike saw that I was only having coffee. "Why aren't you eating?" I looked at him like he was a dunce and said "I've already had mine." Steve changed the subject. "Earlier we got a note from the hospital and they said Art Stepan can be released to us. They examined him and found that he only had a bad infection so they cleaned him up and he's ready to go. They said it was a miracle that no bones were involved, but that the muscle tissue loss was a real mess and he'd need therapy somewhere besides this fucked up town. Anyway, they will load him up with penicillin, give him a bunch of pain pills and we can pick him up around noon. If he can travel, I think that we'll get him on a plane to Lilongwe or Johannesburg. His soldiering days are definitely over." "So you are asking me if I'd like to go over to the hospital and get Art?" "Correct." I thought Steve could be pretty lame at times. And then I thought what a wonderful person Anne was, to have sorted through that mess at the hospital and had Art treated.

We talked awhile about this business of sending Art home. So I just asked "Look Steve, it is very clear that this place is going to hell in a hand-basket. What about all of us? What is the plan?" He said, "There is a lot of talk about this but for now, we're still hoping things will work out here. In fact, I understand that the top guy at the U.N. was going to meet with Tshombe and Mobutu soon to see if something sane can be arranged. The higher ups are placing a lot of importance on this."

Outside, the storm clouds boiled up and lightning could be seen in the distance, and the rain began. Big, single drops at first turning to walls of water. I thought about what the van driver said, 'expect floods.' I looked outside and said "We had better get going if we expect to get Art today." Steve had a lot of pull and rather than screwing around with a shuttle he said "I can have a Jeep at the front door in fifteen minutes. I want to get that guy back here." So we all decided to go. Steve wanted to see the mess at the hospital first hand, and I thought that maybe I could see Anne for a minute or two.

The streets were indeed flooding and the windshield wipers on the Jeep had hardly any effect at all. The canvas tops on Jeeps are not exactly waterproof either, and by the time we pulled up to the hospital we were soaked. And the situation there was immeasurably worse. The rain had forced the sick and injured people into the already packed lobby and dozens were huddled under the covered entryway. It was pathetic. Little kids running around, people on stretchers, not only without treatment, but with no shelter either. We parked at the curb and ran inside the packed lobby and over in a corner we saw Art, in a wheel chair, he was overjoyed to see us and said "Jeez, Tony, you really helped. Who do you know, the head doctor?" "Almost," I said. His arm and shoulder were heavily bandaged and some kind of contraption held his arm away from his body. He handed me a folder of papers and said "These are my discharge papers. No one has any time for formalities and they just said wait for your friends from the base. These papers will explain my medical condition. So, here I am!"

There was no way we could wheel Art through the lobby so the three of us picked up the wheelchair, with Art in it, and made our way to the front door. I thought about detouring to see Anne, but that was out of the question. It was pouring outside and we asked Art if he could make it to the Jeep. He said "I can run the 100-yard dash if you can just get me the fuck out of here." So that is what we did, with my arm around his waist and Art's good arm around Steve's neck. Back at the barracks we had a medic check Art out, making sure he knew about his pills and all of that. We tucked him into a clean bed and he was immediately asleep. For some reason I looked at Art's calendar on the wall, with a picture of Bishop, California. The page was on December, 1961. I'll not soon forget that month.

# Chapter 45

That afternoon it was still raining and the barracks were surrounded by lakes. My dream of getting back to Anne's was fading quickly unless a rowboat was available. I assumed that she would probably have to stay at the hospital, which was a grim way to spend a night. After breakfast we noticed a lot of activity down the hall where the offices were for officers and other brass. It got almost humorous with people running back and forth and so we peons began to guess what the hell this was all about. We didn't have to wait long. The loudspeaker system came on and provided the message "Alert! Alert! All personnel will report to the cafeteria at 0900. This means all personnel. Alert! Alert!" Since we were already there, we just moved our chairs against the wall and waited. A janitor opened up a sliding door, making the room larger and began setting up chairs. Another guy was setting up a lectern and a PA system, and we began to get nervous. Despite all of the alerts, we had not seen this kind of activity before.

Support employees, half-dressed troops and specialty personnel began to flood into the room and find chairs. The armorer saw us and came over to sit with us. A medic helped Art into a chair across the room. I noticed that the wire contraption holding his arm out from his body was gone and he now had a more conventional sling. He noticed us and flashed a 'V' sign. The room was soon buzzing with whispers, with everyone wondering what this was all about.

The brass came in together, including Colonel Mkandawire, but there were also military men above his pay grade that we had never seen before, and a couple of civilians in suits. Mr. Poincare from one of the big mines who had talked to us before, introduced himself as representing the Foreign Affairs Office. Obviously, there was very little space between the mining industry and the government. But what he had to say unhinged all of us.

"As some of you know, and others have heard rumors, Dag Hammerskjold, the Secretary General of the United Nations, was scheduled to hold peace talks today with Presidents Tshombe and Mobutu in Ndola. The same storm we are suffering from is affecting Ndola, in Northern Rhodesia, about 130 air miles to the south. His DC-6 crashed on approach to the Ndola airport in a violent storm and Mr. Hammerskjold is among the many fatalities. Mr Hammerskjold was considered by The Katanga to be an objective, fair diplomat and we held high hopes for these talks." Of course, this set of a huge buzz in the room as Mr. Poincare seemed to be saying this might have been our last chance.

He went on. "Already, there are international conspiracy theories taking place, and most of them place The Katanga as being responsible. It is a continuation of diplomats in New York despising The Katanga, our president and everything we stand for. And now this. For the time being I want you to know that everyone is confined to this base until we sort this out. Our presence in town could set off a huge protest by foreign troops and we cannot allow that. There were several survivors of the crash and the U.N. is already trying to determine what might have happened. There are rumors of missiles and struggles on the plane itself, plus the clear possibility that this storm is the only culprit. We are in a very fragile situation here, and I pledge that we will provide every scrap of information that we receive. Finally, there is the possibility that we will have to evacuate this facility on a moment's notice. I repeat, a possibility. But all of you should get your gear together and be ready to leave on very short notice. I will be back here at 1400 hours and pass on any further information that we have."

It only took 30 minute to get our gear in order. The firearms were always cleaned, and our personal belongings were just about non-existent. My concern was for Anne. If the army evacuated, what would the civilians face? We had an administrative guy in the facility who had a lot of information about travel and could book flights in The Katanga and we walked to his office. We were not the only ones with concerns but we thought of it first and there was a growing line behind us. He was helpful but very nervous about the dozen or so troops lined up along the hallway. He said "What can I do for you?" "OK," I said, "I want to know what the travel options are for travel to Ndola, Mzuzu, Lilongwe, Blantyre, Capetown and Johannesburg." "For how many?" I said, "Right at this moment, only one." He looked at some papers and telexes and said "Travel from Lilongwe, Blantyre, Harare and Blantyre to either Johannesburg or Capetown is unaffected by our problems here. There are daily flights to all of those cities by Air Ethiopia, Air Kenya, and a variety of airlines to South Africa. The problem is getting out of here to Ndola." I asked if I could get a ticket from Ndola to Lilongwe the most efficient way possible, but leaving the dates open for now. He said "That is not a problem." He looked up some more data and gave me a price of 400 U.S. dollars which seemed astronomical, but I said "Write the ticket in the name of Anne Scott". As he dealt with the multi-carbon copy ticket blank I reached into my pocket and peeled off $400. As he worked, I asked about the connection to Ndola. "That is the big problem. It is only a little over 125 miles away but it seems like the different countries have all of the commercial airlines locked up. There is a daily bus, but you must be prepared for interruption due to road problems, and violence is also reported along the way." He finished up with the ticket and I gave him the cash. I looked at the ticket and it said 'Lumumbashi' with no flights listed. I asked "Why Lumumbashi?" He said Lumumbashi is actually your starting point but we have no schedule yet to Ndola. You knew that the airlines now accept the name change from Elisabethville to Lumumbashi, didn't you?" I just stuttered. We were now officially in fucking Lumumbashi! He said "I would not wait too long to reserve a seat. Things are changing hourly and right now there are only a few of seats left during the next few days." I wondered why I hadn't done this a few days ago before the shit hit the fan, but then I doubt if Anne would have gone anyway. I picked up some travel brochures and said 'thanks' and we turned back to the cafeteria. The travel guy was in for a busy day.

Back in the assembly room Mike said "Wow! You really did that in a hurry! Do you think she will go? "I am sure going to push it. This place is going to hell in a big hurry." Mike asked "Why Lilongwe?" I said "Remember that new hotel? The pool? The air conditioned rooms? The food? Got any more questions?" "Actually, yes. You are in The Katanga and she will be in Nyasaland." Well of course he was right but I responded, "I'm thinking about getting out of here too. What does the future hold around here? What do you think?" Mike thought for a minute or two and said "You are right. I suppose that it will get to the point where we can't get out. Then what?" I nodded and said, "That's why I bought the ticket."

We went back to our room and talked a little about our options and, saw a mail package for us. It was addressed to both of us and it was nice to see something from Bakersfield. Nice, calm Bakersfield. We tore into the package and got news from home. We also got a box of crumbling cookies, but the thought was nice. But there was a smaller envelope to both of us from my dad. The note said "The local draft board is asking about your current whereabouts and when you will get home. Let me know. They are very insistent." Mike said "Well, fuck me. Here we are trekking around Africa killing the bad guys and those real estate assholes want us back? Do you suppose that they could help getting us back?" I thought about that and said, "Fuck 'em"

We wandered back into the cafeteria, grabbed a sandwich and found Art. He was actually doing very well. He had managed a shower and was trying to figure how to get out of Elisabethville. "Join the crowd", I said. Soon, Poincare came back in the room and he had lost his buttoned down appearance. His hair was mussed and his shirttail hung out. He went to the lectern and shuffled some papers. The loudspeaker went off again, 'Alert, Alert, all personnel to the assembly room'. This time the people moved quickly.

At exactly 1400 hrs. Poincare spoke. "I have new information on the plane crash. We now find out that only one passenger is still alive, and he maintains that as the plane went down, he saw Hammerskjold laying on the floor with a bullet hole in his forehead! So, gentlemen, if you thought I had bad news this morning, this is much, much worse. We expect that the third world countries at the U.N will go bezerk and want blood. Our blood. They just assume that it was we who shot him and brought down the plane and there is no one...no one to stand up for us. The world is polarized against us. Our leadership will meet this evening and come up with some options for us as a group and for you individually. The local U.N. guy is already asking for our surrender and the Congolese Colonel says "Surrender or die."

"Now here is something you need to listen to. If any contract employee wishes to surrender, we will not find you in a contractual conflict. We understand that when you came here, the international plight we are in was not anticipated. The Congolese government in Kinshasha, formerly Leopoldville, is allowing two days to give up all arms, and surrender. Their promise is to fly you to Kinshasha and repatriate you to your home country. But our concern is that promises do not always work out when you are dealing with the Congolese government. The Force Publique, which once numbered about 23,000 men, was formerly a function of the Belgium government, but those that are left are now effectively a part of the Congolese government. Do not regard these uniformed police as friendly, and they are now spreading out around the country. There have been many, many outrages in the capitol as Belgium citizens left. Some were imprisoned. Some were tortured. And raped. We would be hopeful that with all of the international attention being given to this conflict, that these kinds of things would not occur. But there are no guarantees. Once you leave for the airport you are in their hands. Whoever decides to surrender will leave their arms here, and be at the Opera House at 1400 hrs., two days from now."

"So you will want to examine the alternatives. Working against you is the reality that no reliable transportation is available out of the country. Ndola, in Northern Rhodesia, is close by, and if you can figure out how to get there, airline and bus service exists, but it is severely overloaded due to huge numbers of people leaving The Katanga. If you go, try and go in a convoy. Incidentally, many major countries have consulate or embassies in Rhodesia. We will beef up the travel office down the hallway in case you want specifics on your personal travel."

"Then there is, of course, the option of staying. We will do everything possible to protect you, but you must know that the odds against us are very large. We now have troops from seven countries in The Katanga. One other item. There is a force being assembled called Force Katangaise. This group is mainly made up of Katanga citizens who refuse to recognize the superiority of the massive U.N. forces and intend to take the fight forward. They are well funded and have units emerging all over The Katanga. Included in this group are 'Soldiers of Fortune'. Major Mike Hoare is a part of this organization but the actual leadership is still emerging. It would appear that they envision some kind of guerilla warfare. Among their assumptions is that eventually the U.N. troops will leave, and the remaining Congolese army will be overcome, and The Katanga, or some version of it can be resurrected. Their military and financial bases include the dozens of mining installations around the county, who themselves have substantial defense staffs. All of this is in its formative stages but for those of you who were at Jadotville, you know that these people are well connected, well organized and are heavily armed. Part of their group is only a mile away and are currently housed in a High School gymnasium. You might want to contact them yourselves."

# Chapter 46

It was a bombshell announcement. We wondered what all of these troops and organizations would eventually do, and now they had done it! We decided that we needed to get into high gear.

The first thing we did was talk to Art and get him to the travel guy and buy a ticket. I told him if he was short on cash we would loan him some. His thinking was to get to Ndola somehow and then travel to Europe and then home. He wanted out of Africa and the sooner the better. So he wheeled down the hall in his wheelchair and we thought of the next step. Mike said "Let's find this Hoare guy." Hoare was something of a mystery man and it was not a simple thing to just make an appointment. Once again, Sargeant Steve helped out not just to be nice, but because he wanted to be in on the same conversation. As it turned out, an informal meeting was arranged for late afternoon, and by the time we were ready to go, 15 others had joined. The water levels had gone down quite a bit and a truck and two Jeeps made it down the road for the meeting.

The gymnasium looked like a very quick housing arrangement for troops. There were rows of cots and neatly rolled sleeping bags that could accommodate around 50 men. There was a food line in one corner, and a row of seats for briefings in another. Right away we noticed that the lowest paid personnel were mixed up with the officers and there seemed to be no consideration given to rank. Sitting in a folding chair, we found Major Hoare, who was in a tee shirt, cleaning a Browning Hi Power. Mike and I had never been inculcated with the stiff rules of the military so we thought it was pretty cool watching one of the leaders cleaning his own weapons. Having expected us, as our group approached him he stood and said, "Welcome to Force

Katangaise. Why not grab a beer or a cup of coffee and I'll tell you about our operation."

A couple of his lieutenants joined him and walked around introducing themselves. Wherever we looked, the men seemed very fit, yet cordial and informal. There was a wide range of ages, and we figured that a 40 year- old had probably seen action in WW2. I thought about that. We had signed up for an adventure, not a career. For whatever reason, it looked like war was the only thing many of these guys knew.

Hoare was not a big man but he exuded an air of authority, and it seemed like he had a high degree of respect. He began "First of all, it seems to many of us that The Katanga, at least in its current form, is doomed. The entire world is organizing against us. But that does not mean that we intend to give up." I thought, we're doomed but not willing to give up? That sounds like suicide. He went on: "I want you to know that I am a part of our operation but I am not in charge of it. I just happened to be here to talk to you. Right now, we are small. We intend to take action against invading forces in a guerrilla fashion. We are well organized and we are well trained. We intend to grow. We do not believe that the foreign powers are willing to maintain their armed forces here indefinitely. The thrust here is to take action where we can and outlast them. Hopefully common sense will eventually prevail and the world will see that our model is more apt to succeed than those of the Leopoldville thugs. That's about it." But he went on "Our first maneuver will be to leave Elisabethville. Oh! Pardon! That would now be Lumumbashi. If we don't get out of here now we will never get out. The first stop will be a reservoir about 12 miles from here, and there in the bush we will talk specifics. How we start small and grow. We are well funded and have friends across the country. Now, more specifically, what I have here is a map of a variety of trails that can be used to get to the reservoir. The reason for the variables is that if we begin by tromping through the bush, we'll surely be found before we even begin. We'll start tomorrow and continue during the next two days, leaving from this location. If you choose, be here with your kit, including your arms, if you can get away with them. There is not a fixed schedule. Just be here during tomorrow or the next day. I am going to stay here and answer your questions but just let me say a few more things. Your options are lessening by the hour. I warn you not to take the offer to surrender. Our guess is that if you do, you'll end up in a Leopoldville oops!.Kinshasa jail. And, these jails are very primitive, with primitive men guarding them. If you choose not to join us, then my advice is to get out. Very soon. Northern Rhodesia is not far away and that is one of two or three countries that support us. Do not expect any rescue parties. And I take you at your personal honor that you will not talk to others about what you have learned today. In 48 hours we will be gone. I know that you will want to know about your specific situation and we want to know more about each of you. So stay as long as you can, and we'll talk about pay, transport and the like."

We stayed for another hour and learned quite a bit. Breaking into small groups, we learned that every effort would be taken to continue our compensation. That if we started but decided that this was not the life we could continue, then we could leave. There are no desertions in this guerilla force.

Then, they wanted to know about our skills. As soon as they understood what Mike and I had been doing, we were shuttled off to a small cubicle and a couple of captains were transfixed when they heard what we had accomplished. One of them, a Captain Jules Perry said "I have heard about you chaps and I am honored to meet anyone who has made a head shot on a Baluba at 1200 yards!" The other captain asked us to explain the flagpole incident in Jadotville. We talked about it for awhile and Mike said "The idea was to win without killing" That stopped them. Winning without killing? Hmmm.

Sargeant Steve had a different experience. The Hoare group were interested in his leadership skills and his experience in The Katanga and he quickly began a discussion that ultimately placed us on separate paths. That was a very nervous moment, thinking of us going our separate ways.

In any case, no decisions were made, but it was very clear that they wanted us. On the way back to the base, I asked to be dropped off at the Scott residence which brought a look from Mike. "You are thinking about love when all of this shit is coming down on us?" "No", I said, "I'm talking about getting Ms. Scott out of this country." They stopped in front of the house and I saw a light on, so I told them that I'd find a way back to the base. And I walked up the sidewalk to the front door and knocked as the Jeep drove off.

# Chapter 47

I t took a couple of minutes until I saw a shadow walking past a crack in the plywood covering a window. Then I heard the unmistaken sound of a hammer being cocked. Oh shit, I thought. The .357. "Who is there?" Anne asked? "It's Tony." Chains rattled and the door came open. Anne was still in her nurse's outfit, which was spattered with all kinds of unknown fluids, the .357 hanging in her right hand. Anne looked exhausted even though she flew through the air and hugged me. At that exact moment, I thought that life was very good. "Don't shoot, don't shoot" I whispered into her ear. She managed a laugh and pulled me inside. She re-locked all of the chains and set the bolts, and I said "I think I'll just come in through a window next time." She laughed and we went into the living room. A business card couldn't have fit between us.

"Anne, I have some serious business to talk about." We held hands and I began to talk about the hopelessness of our situation in The Katanga. How our own organization was now advising us to either surrender, join a bunch of mercenaries, or leave. There was a total collapse in the defense organization and I explained that within a day or two we would probably be arrested. "How can your hospital be safe if the army itself was imploding?" She looked at me, very sadly, and cried. "I know, I know", she said, "I just don't know what to do. We have hundreds of patients and only two doctors. The nurses sometimes come to work and sometimes they just disappear. Tell me. What should I do?" I said, "Well I am glad that I dropped by because I have the answer!" She laughed and I began.

I pulled an envelope out of my cargo pants and handed it to her. "This is not perfect but it is an open Air Ethiopian ticket from Ndola to Lilongwe. We would have to get you to Ndola as there is no reliable source out of this city, but I have a plan for that. There are American and Belgium consulates in Ndola which would be safe until a Lilongwe flight is scheduled. Do you have a passport?" "Oh yes as she pulled it out of her pocket. I have been thinking about leaving too!" That relieved me. I thought that there would be a fight over that. "Do you have any money? And I'm not talking about Katanga money which is now worthless." She said "That is a problem. I have a bank account but I cannot get any foreign exchange funds. The bank says they are frozen." I said, "Yeah, it's more likely that the money is simply gone." I reached into my pocket again and pulled out my wad of U.S. money and peeled off 20 $100 dollar bills as Anne's eyes widened. "Here's $2000. Keep it with your passport in a safe place. Like your bra." She laughed at that and we fussed about the gift, but she finally had to admit there was no other way. "I'll do what you say" and tucked the bills at her collar neckline and into her bra. That unsettled me and I began to forget about travel. But just for a few seconds. I was determined to get this settled.

"Here is my plan. You remember the guy with the arm injury that you helped out? He is much, much better, thanks to you, but he is in no condition to stay here, and there is no conventional way out. If he surrenders, we believe he'll end up in jail. So here's the deal. Mike and I are going to borrow a Jeep tomorrow to drive him to Ndola. I want you to go too. We can pick you up at around 0800 and be on our way if you can pack a bag and be ready. If you need to, we can stop by the hospital and give them your goodbyes. It is only about a three-hour trip and we can get you to a safe place, and then return the vehicle here." "Wow, you have it all worked out! Why can't you go too?" I said "I don't think I will be far behind. But there is of course the matter of stealing a vehicle, plus, there are some other possibilities Mike and I are looking in to." "Why Lilongwe?" I said "On the way up here from South Africa, we encountered just about everything bad that is imaginable. That is, until we got to Lilongwe, and came across this beautiful, brand new hotel with a swimming pool, a good restaurant, nice rooms and crisp, clean sheets. It seems like a great place for a week's worth of R&R before we face reality again." "It sounds super!" So that was the plan.

We walked into the kitchen, and I poured glasses of wine and we sat across the breakfast table holding hands. That mellowed us out a little and then Anne always surprising me, asked, "Would you like to take a shower with me?" I was so stunned that I knocked the wine glass over but quickly recovered. In a flash we were on our way down the hallway. This time, we were even more efficient with the unbuttoning process and in less than 30 seconds. Anne was alert enough to place her passport and money on a table, and I ushered her into the shower. With the warm water on, we did more hugging, touching and kissing than soaping, but it was both refreshing and passionate at the same time. We were again in heaven but the warm water finally ran out and we headed for the towels. And then the bed. I remember the wonderful times, but I cannot find words to express the love.

About 0400 I woke with a start and knew that I had a grueling day ahead. I had to get back to the base and figure out a way to borrow a Jeep that would get the four of us to Ndola and back to Elisabethville by day's end, and there were no guarantees about any of that. My first priority was to get Anne on that airplane and I felt a real responsibility to Art who was still in a lot of pain and would need a doctor's attention. Anne was sleeping like a rock, and I dressed in the dark. I gave her a little caress and she opened her eyes and saw me fully dressed. "What is going on? Where are you going?" So I reminded her of our agreement that I would pick her up between eight and nine, to pack her bag and wear suitable clothes. Like denims, boots and work clothes. Nothing flashy. As close to drab as was possible. I knew that she could never look drab, but she understood the message. She got up and made a pot of coffee and she said "I really need to go by the hospital, if only for a minute. I cannot just disappear." I nodded and said we would sure make the effort but with roving bands of men carrying guns, nothing could be guaranteed. Perhaps by eight o'clock the worst of these guys would still be sleeping it off and we could slip out of town. We had some toast and I said I had to run but to expect me before nine A.M. "Yes, you don't need to remind me. I'll be ready." There were tears in her eyes and it settled in that her life here was over. She said "You know, I was born in the same hospital that I work in, and it just seems wrong being kicked out of my home and my country." What could I say? I just nodded, thinking how she cared for all of those sick people and had dedicated her life to helping the helpless, despite the overwhelming odds. I dried her tears with my collar and we kissed. "I'll see you in a couple of hours. I love you." With that, I shut the front door and walked down the sidewalk, wondering how I was going to get to the base.

# Chapter 48

As it turned out, there was a local policeman patrolling the residential area and seeing that I wore Katanga cammies, he gave me a lift. He also chastised me for walking around at this time of the morning. He said "Are you armed?" I said "No, I hadn't expected to be out this late." "Well, you better get used to protecting yourself because the city is unravelling." I nodded and wondered what he would think if he knew I shot people at 1700 yards.

By the time I got to our room it was past 0500 and things were beginning to stir. The usual routines were interrupted, but some things just never change. I woke Mike up and said "Let's get our asses in gear. We need to get our stuff together and a few clothes because we don't actually know that we will be coming back." Mike rubbed his eyes and then went back to sleep. "Hey asshole!" I shook him and pulled the blankets off of his bed. "We have shit to do!" So, he struggled awake and I went next door to get Art awake. Art was unaware of our plan, but once I got him awake and explained it, he was all ready to go. He knew the end was near and was scared that he would be left for the U.N. guys, or worse, the Congolese. Despite the pills, he was in a lot of pain and his wound was beginning to smell. So, we all hustled to the showers and tried to get an early start on the morning rush. It took a while to get Art cleaned up but by 6:00 A.M., we were dressed, had our gear packed and headed for the cafeteria for some runny eggs. We talked about what we actually needed for the trip, and of course, Art needed all of his clothes, and whatever personal things he had collected. Mike and I, on the other hand, needed our weapons. If all went well, we would be back by about 1800 or 1900 hrs. Mike had his Browning and FAL, and I decided to take the Mauser and my P.38. There was just no way I was leaving that Mauser behind. Art said he wanted his FAL even if we had to bring it back this evening. "I might not be much of a shot one-handed, but I can still spray a magazine of bullets." Why not? I figured that Anne would have a fully packed suitcase. After breakfast we found Steve and told him our plan. What we needed from him was a 'loaner' Jeep for the day, along with some jerry cans of extra gas. A little shocked, he said "I'll never see you guys again. Why not just go out to the motor pool and steal a vehicle?" But we persevered and pleaded that we fully intended to return so we could check out the Hoare fellow. Mike sweetened the argument by returning to our room and brought back a fifth of Johnny Walker Double Black Scotch Whiskey. "OK guys, as a matter of providing security to this bottle, I'll go talk to the motor pool guy. But if you don't return, I'll hunt you bastards down." Of course, Steve was so connected to the Katanga exercise, he had probably lost touch with reality. By tonight, the motor pool might not even exist. But he was very sympathetic to Art, and he felt very strongly that anyone who surrendered would end up in jail. We didn't mention Anne. And, he had his own personal negotiation going with those guys in the gymnasium, so he was inclined to stretch the rules to their elastic limit. Still, it was odd how a military outfit could even still be concerned by rules when we were about to be captured or overrun.

Our next stop was the travel guy, who was just getting to work. Cutting to the chase, I said "We need a ticket from Ndola to Johannesburg." "I have no communication with any ticketing agents so the best I can do is give you an open ticket, and maybe you can book the flight at the airport." "OK," I said "How much?" He looked through a folder and said "$650." I peeled off $600 and a stack of Katanganese money and he looked at the local money, shook his head, but finally said "OK" and wrote out the ticket. I handed the ticket to Art and said "Pay me back when you can. Maybe in Bishop!" He was very grateful and said "Yes!. And steaks too! I was stupid for not changing any of my money when I could. You'll get every penny!" I said "Don't sweat it."

There was a commotion visible through the windows and we saw the Irish troops that we had been boarding next door walking towards some trucks. So here it was: we didn't even have the power to keep our prisoners. Obviously, they were being released back to their own encampment, and probably to their own country. Despite our cynicism, we walked outside to see just how a prisoner release worked, and a couple of sargeants who recognized us from the flagpole shooting exercise walked over. "Best to you mates! Getting out of that fix with nothing more than a flagpole was a great thing to do! If you're ever in Ireland, look our guys up in Dublin at the Pig and the Goose pub! My da owns the place and the drinks are on me!" We shook hands all around, and as he walked toward the trucks he said "And the arsehole who put us in that situation will not be around!" We all laughed as they began to drive away. It really was not their fault that they had an incompetent captain. On the other hand, we still had Art in a cast and 12 dead and counting. But still, it was getting to be more and more difficult to separate the good guys from the bad guys.

This was also the day that we were supposed to surrender in front of the Opera House and I wondered how that was going, and it was clear that there were fewer contract guys in the building and we wondered if we should have just hung up our jocks and left with them. But then we had to think about Sargeant Steve's admonition: You surrender and you will be in jail.

At 0815, we loaded Art into a Jeep, checked the fuel and the extra 5 -gallon jerry cans, dumped all of our stuff into the vehicle and drove through the base gate. Mike said "This is going to be a very crowded jeep, especially with Anne's female stuff." Art said "Female stuff? Anne?" So we told him the rest of the story on the way to Anne's house.

# Chapter 49

When we pulled up in front of Anne's house, there she was, sitting on a chair on the porch with her bag beside her. She looked like a poor waif dressed in jeans, a sweatshirt and a baseball cap. Yes, she was beautiful!

I jumped out and walked to the porch and gave her a hug and a kiss. I picked up the bag and said "What have you got in here? Rocks?" "Well," she said, "I have a very brief bikini swim suit, a nice evening dress and some frilly under wear." I said "Well, that is great but what is creating all of the weight?" "I have my medical books, ammo, and my Smith and Wesson." I just laughed and I got her into the Jeep next to Art and cobbled a place on the rear bumper, and with the help of a few bungee cords, secured the baggage. As we started down the street, she looked back and was wiping her nose and crying. This had been her home for her entire life. I asked "Did you lock it up?" "Why? It will be trashed by sundown. I left the front door open."

I drove to the hospital and it was a shambles. Jerry-built enclosures, lines of people and the little kids just broke your heart. No home, no hope. Anne ran to the door and after a little spat with the guard, she went in. It looked to me like he did not believe this was Anne Scott, but when she took off her baseball hat and her blonde hair came rolling down over her shoulders he apparently saw his mistake, and let her inside. The three of us just sat in the Jeep, examined occasionally by tough looking guys walking the streets. I mentioned to Art that there was an American consulate in Ndola, and if he couldn't get on a flight today, I was sure that they could help him with a room for a night or two. I doubted that there were many Americans in Northern Rhodesia. In about ten minutes out came Anne, her hands to her eyes, crying. I tried to comfort her but she jumped into the jeep and said "Just go."

Our route out of town passed the Opera House and there were about 30 of our guys being roughly herded into the back of a truck. I concentrated on just being anonymous and driving but Mike yelled "They have them handcuffed!" I said "Those lying sonuvabitches. Steve was right! They are probably going to the Leopoldville jail!" We pulled over for a minute and these U.N. troops began scanning the street for more of our friends, then focused on us. Finally, one of our handcuffed guys yelled "Get out! Get Out!" And we did.

# Chapter 50

Anne had her head bowed as we got to the suburbs. The combination of losing her home, saying good bye to the hospital and having a close call with the U.N. had left her almost paralyzed. As I drove I reached back and held her hand but she wanted to be by herself. As in most African cities, the middle class homes eventually gave way to the slums and the crunching poverty. But now, the middle class homes were there for the taking and this was the result. Broken doors, clothes littering the lawns, furniture broken or being hauled away, and in some cases, just burnt out hulks. How burning the town down was going to help anyone was a mystery to me, but then I hadn't lived in cardboard boxes either. I wondered if this could happen in Bakersfield.

Leaving the city, the pavement was occasionally paved, but more typically dirt. In fact, it would have been smoother if the asphalt was removed, because the broken pavement created pot holes, and we dodged them as best we could. Sometimes I just drove at the edge of the road, but that was hindered by many refugees walking along the shoulder, carrying their belongings on sticks, in kid's wagons or just on their backs. It all looked hopeless.

Further along, we occasionally saw small groups of soldiers, stopping the refugees. It looked like they were rifling through their belongings, looking for valuables or money. These were the same guys who the international press thought were sent to The Katanga to 'protect' the citizens. All of this awakened Anne, who shook her fist at these marauders. But, we were making good time and figured that we could be at the border in about two hours. The refugees on the road became denser and when we were on level ground, I sometimes ventured off the road.

We came to a small village and I made a mistake by slowing for a road block. It was just two guys beside a saw horse, and there was a pile of belongings beside them, no doubt stuff that they robbed from powerless people on foot. This guy held up his hand and Art said "Veer towards him and then floor it! Don't stop!" I saw that if I did stop we might be in a fight that we were not ready for, so I turned toward these guys and they jumped back, one of them dropping his AK 47 and I floored it. By the time they collected their wits, we were around a corner and out of town.

We continued to make good time and I thought that we might cross the border by about 11:30 hrs. but that idea was quickly squelched about 30 miles from the border crossing. We ran into some very well organized signs, unlike anything I had seen in Africa. 'Slow ahead; flagman ahead; inspection station; police' and stuff like that. As all of this came into view, I couldn't figure what they were trying to do. We were leaving the country, not entering it. I pulled over and asked "What do you think?" Mike said "We sure can't run through that gauntlet. I think we should try and go around them into the bush." There was no dissent, so I turned onto what looked like a dirt trail. There were quite a few refugees with back packs and whatever who had the same idea. A person just had to make the assumption that any road block should be avoided. After about four miles, we figured we were about even with the road block but well out of view, probably over a mile to the west. Then things changed. The refugees began to clump together and stopped along the roadside. There was no forward motion at all and we wondered what this was all about. We stopped the Jeep and started talking to the group of about 30 men and they said "There are some armed crazies up ahead, not a part of the organized group along the road. But look over there. Do you see the smoke? Some people would not cooperate and now they are beating them and they are completely out of control. Can you help us? We have no arms." Mike looked over at me and said "Looks like old times, doesn't it? I wonder if they are Balubas or Congolese just taking advantage of the situation. I can't believe the Swedes, Irish or whoever would be beating these people." I shook my head and said, "No matter. We have to do something about it. Anne, get out and stretch your legs but stay right here beside the Jeep. Mike, let's get the stuff out. Art, stay in the Jeep. We don't need to fuck up your arm." Anne looked very scared and said "I want my gun." That made me laugh but I dug around in her suitcase and came up with the gun and handed it to her. "Tony, please be careful!" I wondered if she knew how to use the revolver, but on the other hand, having some protection seemed like a good idea. I gave her a hug and said "No problem. We won't take on more than we can chew. Just be ready for a mad dash to the border!"

I gave Art's FAL to him and Mike pulled his out of the pile of supplies in the Jeep. I said to Mike "Give me the Mauser." The Mauser was well protected in its' case, and I pulled 10 rounds of the match ammunition from the special wooden box. Mike did not have his optics package so we were just going to have to rely on a small pair of binoculars I had. By this time, people were closing in on the Jeep asking "What are you going to do? Can we help?" I said, "We're going to try and get the assholes to calm down, and hope no one is hurt. Just take a rest and we'll see what we can do."

With that, I loaded the Mauser and we headed towards the smoke. It wasn't long before we saw what the problem was. Through the binoculars we saw about ten guys whipping several men who were tied to a huge tree. There were also several women and some kids sitting in the dirt and it looked like they might be handcuffed. Beside them was a stack of household goods, probably all that they owned, strewn about on the ground. We couldn't hear them but by their looks both the torturers and the tortured were yelling and screaming. Several of the assholes, whoever they represented, were holding AK 47s. We moved ahead and took up residence behind some scattered boulders, over 1000 yards from the problem. Mike was looking through the binoculars as I set up the Mauser and said "This is more of a problem than we thought. Those men are bleeding and one guy is starting to drag a woman round. They are all handcuffed." I looked through the scope and searched for the head guys. "Mike, I see the women and kids." "OK, just about 10 yards to the right." "Got 'em". Mike went on, "It looks like those two guys with the red bandanas are the leaders. What are you going to do?" "What am I going to do? I'm going to waste the fuckers. These are just simple, drunken outlaws! What do you figure the range?" Mike was better than I about distance even without all of his paraphernalia and responded, "I'd say 1300 yards."

"Tell you what Mike, when I let off a shot, spray a magazine on full automatic and maybe they will think that there's a lot of us." Mike nodded and we got down to business. I sighted in on the guy who seemed to be doing the most damage. He was moving around a lot but every few seconds he would stop, and looked like he was taunting his victims. I had the crosshairs on his head but the range was not exactly correct, so I squeezed the trigger and blew out his chest and spinal cord. He crumpled like a wet doll, and Mike opened up with twenty rounds of .308, shoved in another magazine and shot in other directions and they quickly gave up. From my left, another couple of rounds went off and I thought 'what the fuck was that?' and turned to see Anne with her Smith and Wesson pointed to the gang. Anne?? "Hey Anne, cease fire!" She had a grim look on her face and I suppose that after losing her home, her career and her country, she had had enough. She was on the offense. Meanwhile, 1300 yards away, a white flag emerged from the bush and the gang, now apparently sober, came towards us. When they came within shouting distance, Mike yelled "Throw your guns down and come single file." Guns, knives and hatchets were immediately dropped and on they came. "Sit," said Art and piled out of the jeep with his FAL. I advanced and said, "Where are the keys to those hand cuffs?" One of them said, "No keys, they are plastic." Mike and Art guarded the gang numbering nine, now that the tenth was just about torn apart. Then, I looked to my left and here was Anne, her .357

pointing at the group. I smiled to myself and thought, man, that woman has balls. No, retract that thought! I continued towards the clearing and picked up a couple of discarded knives along the way. Several women, a couple of men and kids struggled to their feet and ran towards me, and three other woman ran to their husbands tending to them as best they could. I was getting hugged so much I thought I would end up on the ground but I started cutting the hand cuffs and the hugging started all over again. It was a good time to have a nurse along, and Anne got the three guys untied and used some of their pile of clothes to start cleaning their injuries and bound up their wounds. Two of them were deeply cut by the whip, but they were not life threatening. They seemed so relieved to be cut down, it seemed as though they had no pain at all.

In the encampment, I found a sack of hand cuffs and walked back to the men sitting on the ground, and began handcuffing them They offered no resistance and Art looked like he was planning payback for his shoulder wound, but settled down when he saw them all cuffed. Mike found a section of rope in the jeep and ran it through the handcuffs so we had nine guys, cuffed and roped together. We ordered them to stand, and walked them over to the Jeep and tied the rope to the rear bumper. Five women ran over to Mike and I, and gave each of us a big hug and a kiss. Anne sidled up to me, her revolver tucked into her sash and said, "I'm not sure I approve of that!" I smiled and said "Hey trooper, I am glad that you are on our side." The action apparently rid Anne of her depression and she smiled for the first time today.

So we got organized and began to move, leaving the dead guy for the crows. This must have been the most bizarre procession ever. Starting were the hostages, a mixed bag of men, women and children, then came the Jeep with the two most seriously injured men on the front fenders, then Mike and I in the front seats, And Anne and Art in the back seat, looking back at the prisoners. The tied-together prisoners started bad mouthing Art, realizing that they had been captured by two men, a woman and a cripple, but Art took care of that with a couple of rounds about two inches above their heads. They quickly settled down. Anne had her .357 also pointed at them and she seemed to be looking for an excuse to shoot.

We were idling along at walking speed and it became clear that we were going to have to cut back to the highway because of rock outcroppings directly ahead. We only had gone about a half mile when we saw a large encampment of U.N. soldiers, this time Swedish. Behind them was a professional looking roadblock, and I thought we would have fared better if we had just stayed on the highway. On the other hand, there would be several dead refuges by now, not to mention molested women. Who knew how that would have ended. Two guards saw us coming and immediately called for their Captain. All we hoped for was not to be turned back. Instead this tall, blonde Swede with 'Hanna' stenciled on his pocket, walked up and asked "What in the world do we have here?" I said "We were headed for the border and found these guys behind us torturing the refugees ahead of us. So here we are, trying to find someone to take these assholes off our hands and take care of several injured hostages." He had a serious look on his face, no doubt wondering what could come next in this screwed up country, but he said "I think that we can solve your problem." He yelled over to a group of soldiers staring at this spectacle and two soldiers, one with a submachine gun and the other with a knife, cut the rope from the Jeep. He gave some kind of order to the bandits that they seemed to understand, as he led them across the encampment like a master leading a dog on a walk. The second soldier followed but paused where Anne and Art were sitting and said in broken English "I think it safe for you to put your guns down!" We all laughed except for Anne, who said, "I am keeping my pistol right in my lap until we cross the border!" The soldier said to Mike and I "You have some special woman there!" We nodded and smiled, and we also managed to get a grin out of Anne. But the .357 stayed right in her lap.

A couple of medics came up and lead the hostages away, one on a stretcher. They walked away but they all turned and said 'Thank you, love and kisses, etc'. We sure could have won a popularity contest at that point!

We had loaded their weapons in the back of the Jeep and I got up and dropped them in a pile on the ground. Then the big Swede came over and said "What are we to do with you?" So we explained that three of us were Americans and Anne was a Belgium citizen who had worked in the hospital in Elisabethville. We were trying to get our wounded friend and Anne across the border to safety. They both had flights out of Ndola. "And what about you two?" "Well, let me be honest. Obviously we have combat clothes on and we work for what is left of The Katanga government. We need to deliver these people and come back this evening to return the Jeep and wind up our affairs. We plan on leaving in a few days." He responded "That was decent of you to tell me the truth. What I want to know is, how did you arrange the capture of those vultures? We have lost several good soldiers to people like those. As he asked, a small crowd of Swedish soldiers gathered around. They wanted to hear too. So I repeated the story, the 1300 yard shot that stunned them as Art sprayed .308 ammo all over the place. I guess that between their leader and all of those rounds being fired, there believed there must be a dozen or so guys so they just gave up." The Swede nodded and said "I think I might have heard about you guys. Just how did you manage a 1300 yard shot?" So I explained. "I have a special rifle and Mike and I had spent a year in The Katanga killing terrorist Baluba leaders and scaring their tribesmen. We have rescued many people, black and white, and done it in a way that minimized killing. For instance, they only casualty around here can be found about a mile back. Right under where the crows are circling." They all laughed at that and he said "Mind if we see this special weapon of yours?" I said "I'll show it to you but I'll have to fight if you try and take it!" "No, no, I just want to see it. By the way, are you the chaps who were over in Jadotville who saved the

Irish platoon?" Mike said "That was us. We didn't know if our strategy would work but it was worth a try." The Swede laughed and said "So it was really a shooting exhibition?" I said, "Why risk the certainty of getting get shot if they could see us shooting flagpoles at 1400 yards?" I got out of the Jeep and turned to pick up the Mauser case. "Yep, that was us and we were glad it worked!" I undid the clasps and opened the case, taking the rifle out. A crowd quickly gathered and wanted to hold the Mauser but I drew the line at that. But the compliments were unending. The double set triggers, the huge scope, the machined (but not polished) bolt, the fluted heavy barrel and everything else. The captain said "Very, very nice. And thank you for saving these people. I wish there were more of you who preferred brains to massacres. Now, what can I do for you?" That was a dream question.

"Well, if you could just expedite our trip to the border that would be terrific. We need to get back to our base and I'd like to get there before dark." I suppose that Captain Hanna knew that he was violating every rule and order, but he yelled out for an administrative guy and said, "Fix some passes for these four people, and two with a return trip. These should get you across the border with no problems, but I'll ice the cake a little as well. "What a relief! If he had of jailed us I wouldn't have been too surprised. I looked back at Anne who was both crying and smiling!

A medic came over and took Art's bandage off, and he and Anne examined the wound. He had a kit with him and cleaned the injury and asked if he was taking any Penicillin. Art said yes, but he had neglected to take the pills since yesterday evening. I said "You mean to tell me that we are risking our ass and you can't even take your pills?" Art looked apologetic but the medic had a better suggestion. He pulled out a hypodermic needle and said "This will get into your blood stream quicker. And are you in pain?" Art nodded, "Oh yes, it hurts like bloody hell!" So the medic reached into his kit and pulled out another hypodermic and said "This is a mild shot of morphine. You'll be pain-free for a few hours. But take your pills!"

Then the Swedish Captain did the impossible. "You proceed to the border and we will follow with an armored car. Here are your passes and I wish you all would stay on the other side of the border." With handshakes all around, we drove ahead onto the highway with the armored car behind us and made quick work of the remaining trip at 50 miles per hour. We showed our passports at the border and were out of The Katanga .

# Chapter 51

About a half mile past the border there was a tent city being erected for those managing to get across. People were unloading their paltry household goods into their assigned tents. I said "Just look at this. These people were living in nice homes and owned businesses or had jobs just a week ago. Now they are probably penniless, living in a tent. All because the U.N believes that the outlaw Congo army is a better bet than The Katanga authorities. It just makes me want to puke!" That set Anne crying again and I turned and apologized. What was the point of stating the obvious?

We pulled up to four Rhodesian soldiers who were directing traffic and were told that we should drive through town and there would be a sign to turn right to the airport. Ndola was a much smaller town than Elisabethville and it also appeared to be more primitive. The side roads were all dirt. But all of the normal stuff was there, including a general store, a market, a very small hospital and even a movie theatre. But the main difference was that there was no war going on. We continued on to the airport, figuring that if we were lucky, we could get Anne and Art on a plane today. That was a long shot but worth a try.

The airport consisted of a parking lot and a small terminal and customs office. But the runway was capable of handling large aircraft and based on the crowd of people in front of the terminal, there was a lot of business. And a grim reminder. We circled the terminal to find a place to park and just to the west of the runway we saw the unmistaken rudder of Dag Hammerskjold's United Nations DC-6 sticking up out of a pile of blackened rubble. We parked and I said, "You guys stay in the Jeep, and I'll take Anne and Art's passports and tickets and see what we can do to get you on a flight. Don't wander off. I'll be back as soon as I can."

The terminal was packed, but most of the people there were using the building for shelter, awaiting a flight. The lines at the small counter were reasonably light. There were signs for Air Ethiopia, Air Egypt, and Kenya Airlines. I got in line for Ethiopia. Every time I thought about actually getting on a plane from Ethiopia I had indigestion, but I remembered that the incoming plane a year ago was clean and seemed to be competently managed and piloted. Months later, we learned that Air Ethiopia planes were maintained by Pan American Airways, who had a contract for training pilots and other staff personnel. It would have been comforting to know that at the time!

When I worked my way to the front of the line I was greeted by a beautiful Ethiopian clerk who seemed misplaced in the chaos of Ndola. I stated my business: I had two friends in the parking lot, one going to Lilongwe and one to Johannesburg. I added that one was seriously injured and needed to get to a proper hospital as soon as possible. I gave her the tickets and passports. She looked over the documents and a telex listing of flight times and reservations, and said "You are lucky. I have a reservation for the Johannesburg gentleman on a plane leaving in about two hours. The Lilongwe flight is a bit of a problem. There is a flight scheduled for three days a week, and the next plane out is tomorrow at 2:00 P.M. Do you want a reservation?" I thought about that as other people began pushing me in line, and everyone had a short fuse. I asked, "What are the chances of one of the other airlines having something today?" She looked at the flight schedules and said "Kenya Air doesn't fly to Lilongwe, and Air Malawi isn't flying until the day after tomorrow." "OK," I said. "Book the Ethiopian flight for tomorrow." She did some paperwork involving many carbon copies and finally gave me the tickets back, and said "I suggest that Mr. Stepan get in line at the gate as soon as possible. We can get a wheelchair if he is unable to stand." So I thanked her, gathered up all of the paperwork and shook her hand. My, was she beautiful. Just as I learned much later about Pan American Airways, I learned that virtually every Ethiopian woman was beautiful! No matter, I was committed to one even more beautiful, and besides, she had a .357!

I found a tattered wheel chair on the way back to the car and I said "Art, you need to hustle. Get your stuff together because you are leaving on a plane to Johannesburg in about an hour and you need to get in line. This isn't LAX and if you are not there you might just have to stay." That was a convincing statement and Art struggled out of the Jeep, picked up his overnight bag and I said "You need to leave the FAL!" I reached into my pocket and got my roll of bills out and peeled off $1000. When you get to Joburg, try to get a flight to the U.S. If you cannot, get a cab to the U.S. Consulate and ask for their help and advice. Sorry, but you are on your own from here, and I'll collect the steak dinner in Bishop!" By now, Art was crying, saying "You don't know how I appreciate all of this. I'd still be in that hospital lobby but for you. What great friends. And Anne, thanks for the doctoring and help. You are the best!" By now we were all crying, and Mike jumped out and wheeled Art into the terminal. Anne looked up and said "What about me?" "It's not so simple. I have you on a flight tomorrow afternoon but we need to find you a safe place to be until then. Do you think the Belgium consulate can help?" She said "I don't know but let's give them a try." Mike came back and jumped into the Jeep and I asked a guard at the parking lot entrance where the consulate was, and off we went. The Belgium flag flew over a nondescript building a couple of blocks over, but the crowd surrounding the place was anything but nondescript. Here was the end point for hundreds of Belgium citizens fleeing The Katanga and they circled the block. "Shit" Mike said, "We should have brought our sleeping bags." I stopped for a few minutes, considering what to do next. One idea was to just head south in the Jeep and drive to Lilongwe. But then there was the moral thing. We gave Sargeant Steve a promise and I aimed to keep it. I asked a guard about the American consulate and headed that way. The American facility was a little more substantial, but the main difference was that there were virtually no Americans in this part of Africa. So I parked the Jeep and asked Mike to guard the guns, and Anne and I hopped out and headed for the front door.

# Chapter 52

I had heard that formally attired U.S. Marines guarded these kinds of facilities, but not in this backwater. There was an old guy with a cigar hanging from his mouth, who was a little more alert than he looked. "You'll have to check that handgun here before you enter." So I handed the P.38 over and thought about Anne's .357. She winked at me and I realized that she had in in her purse. There was just no way anyone was going to separate that revolver from her. Inside, there was an African receptionist and an empty lobby. I showed her my passport and explained that we had a special problem and asked to speak to an agent. So we sat down on folding chairs, and I said "Anne, if we cannot get you a proper place here, I'll just stay overnight. But if there is a safe and clean place, I think I need to get back to Elisabethville to return the vehicle and wind up my responsibilities. They also owe me a lot of money and that could help us. If it is hopeless, I'll be along in a couple of days. If not, here is some more cash and I think that you should either get to Capetown and stay with Rene for awhile, or, book a flight back to Brussels. No matter where you are, I'll catch up." She was reluctant. "After all we have done for that place I think you should come with me." She was probably right. Clean sheets and a swimming pool in Lilongwe sounded like paradise!

A very informal fellow opened the door to a hallway and introduced himself as Counselor Officer Vinson. He didn't actually look like an officer, but then this was Ndola, Northern Rhodesia. We followed him back to his office, a small cubicle with stacks of paper all over his desk, and he asked what he could do for us. So we introduced ourselves and I told him our story. What we needed was a safe place for Anne to stay tonight and transportation to the airport tomorrow afternoon. "Well, that seems simple enough but it is a bit irregular for me, making arrangements for a Belgium citizen." So we pumped a little. "Ms. Scott here is a registered nurse and just saved the life of an American citizen in Elisabethville. Is this asking for too much? We can pay for any lodging but I cannot leave her in some motel." Vinson leaned back in his chair, revealing leather patches on the sleeves of his sweater. "Hmmm", he said, "Let me think about this." I thought that he looked like a history teacher, and a kind of detached one at that. I looked at Anne, and I could see that she was holding her .357 through her purse. Jesus, what was she planning to do? I just smiled at her and shook my head. She winked.

We spent the next five minutes watching Vinson stare at the ceiling, his hands clasped. He didn't look like the number one candidate for the next ambassador to Great Britain. But then we were surprised. He turned and said "I might have a solution." We perked up and he said, "What if I registered Ms. Scott as your wife? That would clear up the Visa issue." I looked at Anne and said, "I am now proposing. Will you marry me?" Surprised, Vinson looked at her and she said "I had actually thought of something a little more romantic, ..but...the answer is yes!" So I gave Anne a quick kiss, and while the actual marriage had not taken place, Vinson seemed satisfied. There was a box of cigars on Vinson's desk, and I picked one up, removed the paper ring, and placed it on Anne's finger. Then we all had a good laugh!

Vinson said, "Congratulations! Here is the deal. "We have several rooms in this building that we use for visiting staff from the State Department, who show up once a year for inspections, meetings, etcetera. Let's go down the hall and see what you think." All of a sudden he had come to life, happy to have solved a problem without a bureaucrat looking over his shoulder He unlocked a door off the hallway and we went in. The room was clean, there was a real bathroom, and a double bed. It looked about equivalent to a Motel 6 at home but in this city, it looked like the Biltmore. It also had three deadbolts on the door and wire mesh on the window. Anne said "I'll take it!" Vinson, now proud of his decision to erase the citizenship issue said "There is a small restaurant right around the corner. Would you join me for a celebration and lunch?" We quickly agreed, and headed down the hallway towards the front door. But I had forgotten all about Mike! I corrected that with Mike and said to Vinson "I forgot about my friend. OK if he goes to lunch too?" "The more the merrier," he said. I suggested that we go in the jeep because it contained all of our valuables. So we jumped into the vehicle and drove about a block to the restaurant. I looked at Mike and said "I'm glad that you could come to the reception." "Reception?" "Yes," I said, "Anne and I were just married." A look of incomprehension came over Mike's face, but he slowly nodded. Counselor Vinson turned out to be a really good guy. The restaurant defined a 'hole-in-the-wall', but it was clean and a waitress/cook/bottle cleaner took us to a table at the back of the room. Vinson was clearly on good terms with this waitress, and we soon figured that there was something going on besides waitressing. No matter, he ordered beer and asked for the 'special', which turned out to be roast beef sandwiches and a salad, strange for a restaurant billed for 'Mexican Food.' The conversation was easy and friendly, I proudly showed Anne's elegant ring to Mike and he said "But this is actually just an engagement ring. Where will the real wedding ring come from? A Cracker Jack box?" We all had a good laugh, but time was moving. I said to Vinson "I truly appreciate all that you are doing for us, but I have one more request". Vinson gestured with his hand to go ahead. "Could you use your Telex machine and wire the Capitol Hotel in Lilongwe and get a reservation for...Ms. Ward? For two weeks? Near the pool in a nice room? I would be forever grateful if you could do that." But he merely waved his hand and said 'no problem' and ordered four more beers.

All of this had taken a couple of hours and Mike gestured to his wristwatch. "I think we need to be going." Vinson didn't seem to be in any hurry and I thought about mentioning his working hours, but then again, why risk a problem? I said "We need to be in Elisabethville before nightfall." So we loaded into the Jeep and headed around the corner to the consulate. Anne got her 70-pound suitcase and I carried it into the building. She had her arm around me and was holding tight. Vinson got the key to the room and handed it to Anne and said "It's all yours. There is a small cafeteria here for snacks and all, at the end of your hallway." So we went to the room, unloaded her stuff and held each other. I said "I expect to meet you at that hotel in a few days, so please just try and relax and enjoy the place. But please stay there. No exploring. This is still Africa." Anne smiled and said "Just because you're now my husband, don't think that you can order me around! Remember, I still have a gun!" We kissed and hugged, and then I pushed towards the door, saying "I have to run, love. I'll see you in a few days." With tears flowing she shut the door and I heard multiple locks being turned. She was going to be just fine here.

On the way out, I thanked Vinson again and said "I'm proud to be an American." We shook hands and I retrieved my P.38 at the desk and headed towards the Jeep. Mike had the engine running and he said "Let's get out of here."

There were no problems getting back to Elisabethville. The crowd was leaving the Katanga, not entering. Our passes from Captain Hanna worked like a charm both at the border and at a check point about 70 miles further on. We were beat by the time we got back to the barracks and were shocked to see the disarray.

# Chapter 53

I had to remind myself that we had only left Elisabethville that morning. But with the 250 mile round trip to Ndola, taking time out to kill a guy and rescue a bunch of refugees, getting Art onto a flight, proposing to Anne and having lunch with Counselor Officer Vinson, it was 1930 hrs. when we drove through the gate. Usually at this hour, the various soldiers and contract employees were inside, nursing a beer, reading a book, cleaning their weapons or just bullshitting. Emphasis on the bullshitting. But now, there were guys outside, sitting on the loading dock, talking and whispering in small groups. There was an electric feeling in the air, like something was about to happen, but no one actually knew what it was. We knew the 'happen' part was eventually going to be leaving this place, but it was difficult in the short term to understand the urgency.

Some officers came out into the night and Sargeant Steve was among them. He came over to us and I dug around in my pocket, grabbed the keys to the Jeep and plopped them into his hand. "Great to see you guys back, but it might have been smarter to just steal the Jeep and be safe." I looked at him and said "What *is* going on here? Why are these guys out here wandering around?" As Mike and I started to gather up our stuff from the Jeep he said "Mkandawire and that guy from the Foreign Ministry are going to talk to all of us in about a half hour and I think these guys out here are speculating what they will say. But at the top of the list are those troops who surrendered this morning." Mike asked "What about them?" Steve responded, "You guys must be the only people on the planet that don't know. We got this information from a radio contact about 3 hours ago. When that plane got to Leopoldville, 29 of our guys, who were promised repatriation, were put in ankle chains, and handcuffed and marched to the central jail. You have to learn about that jail. It has been there since the 1880s and is actually a torture chamber, rat infested and the most miserable place on earth. It is very surprising when someone is actually released. The point is, you can't believe what the U.N. guys say. Once the Congo Army takes control, the U.N. has a hands-off policy. After all, they reason that it is their country." Mike just said "Sonuvabitch! We even talked about getting on that plane!" Steve shook his head and said, "It gets worse. We have contact with the Swedish command here in town, and these guys are very professional. Problem is, this crisis is a political one, and they have very little control over military activities. However, they report that by the day after tomorrow, there will be a demand for our full surrender, and if that doesn't happen, they will take military action. You know what that will mean. It will be like your Texans at the Alamo. We will be brave and fight hard, but in the end, we will lose. So what I understand is, Mkandawire and this other guy are going to outline our options."

We told Steve about our adventure, capturing the rogue troops, rescuing hostages, killing the leader, and getting a pass from Hanna. He was very pleased that we got Art on a plane, but his jaw dropped when I explained my marriage. What he actually said was "You're shitting me!"

Steve helped us get our gear into our room and then we went to the assembly room, found a seat, and waited. Minutes clicked off, and every now and then someone would come to the front of the room and announce a delay, and then as a complete surprise, a kitchen worker wheeled in an actual refrigerator full of beer! "Help yourself!" That took the edge off and about twenty minutes later, Mkandawire and Poincare walked in and took a seat at the front of the room. Mkandawire spoke first. "Good evening. I want to bring you all up-to-date on the political and the military situation. But first I want to thank all of you for your loyalty, professionalism and hard work." I wondered. Was this it? He went on. "I will not sugar coat any of this.

The Katanga is finished. Only a miracle can save our country and there are no miracles in sight. Our President, Moise Tshombe and his family have left The Katanga in two light planes from a small field outside of town. His intent is to board a transport plane in Rhodesia and fly to Spain, where he will live in exile." That started a buzz and hands going up, people standing and blurting out questions but Mkandawire raised his hand and asked for quiet. "We have a lot of ground to cover. Yes, we are devastated about Tshombe's exodus, but it is a fact. Unfortunately, world opinion is that rather than have a successful economy for both whites and blacks, it is preferable to simply hop on a rush to destruction and support criminals and incompetents. And the lies. Just ask those men who sit in a primitive jail in Leopoldville what a U.N. promise is worth. There is no one more disappointed and devastated about this than I. All of that being said, we must move on."

The room quieted slowly and then Mkandawire continued. "One of the main things that we want to get across here is that you have a few alternatives and you will have to decide which one you will take by tomorrow by about noon or the U.N. will make it for you. You might be OK until the day after tomorrow but I would not push it. Whatever option you take will most likely require funds. Money buys a lot. At the conclusion of this meeting, please form a line at the table to my left and receive an envelope containing U.S. Dollars. The local money is worthless. The amount that you will receive will relate to your time here and the duties you have performed. No one will get less than $1500. If you choose to leave the area, this should get you to some kind of reasonable transportation, or help you in the alternative you choose. Also in the envelope package will be the money we owe you for your regular service since last payday. We sincerely wish we could do more, but the situation we are in precludes that." Surprisingly, that led to a smattering of applause, and then the audience began to rise and the clapping continued for a minute or two. I thought about Anne, and how fortunate we had been to get her out of this place.

Makandawire raised his hand again for quiet. "I want to raise one more military issue before Mr. Poincare provides you with your options. You are free to take all of your military gear with you. If you do not, they will end up in the hands of those outside of the gate. The quartermaster's area will be open all night. You are free to get extra magazines, rations, canteens and any other equipment that you believe would be helpful to you. But don't get bogged down so that you cannot be mobile. Take what you need. Now, Mr. Poincare is going to explain the few options available to you. Listen carefully. These are going to be personal decisions and you had better evaluate them carefully."

Poincare stood up and began. "None of these options are good, but all of them are better than waiting for the U.N. to take you away in a day or two. First, you are all aware of the various mining concessions in The Katanga. The larger ones are very secure and have facilities for many people. It may not be a permanent solution but far better than staying here. I have a stack of maps here that give you the locations of the most logical installations. The entire economy of The Congo depends largely on keeping these commercial enterprises working. It would be the ultimate stupidity for the invading troops to shut them down. But then we see many stupid things going on. Number two, there are well staffed militias all over The Katanga especially in the Jadotville area. I am not sure what kind of reaction they will take when they digest the facts of our collapse. I doubt if they will just roll over, but that is a real wild card. The third and final option I am aware of is the group currently housed in the high school gym right up the road from here. They have some big-name mercenaries in the group, are very well funded and intend to fight a guerilla war. The thinking here is that once all of the U.N. troops leave, maybe in less than a year, they will only have to contend with the Congo Army, with their aim being to overthrow the system they intend to install here. They expect to swell their ranks, now about 90, to over 400 men."

"The problem with all of these options is that you place yourself in extreme danger with very little in the way of backup. Medical facilities, transportation, and arms will all be on the primitive side. On the other hand, these options might be an interim solution. That is, if things go badly, the most likely direction to safety is overland to Northern Rhodesia. At least for the time being, there is a sympathetic government but even there, an independence movement is underway to create the State of Zambia. And guess what? The U.N. supports that. But for now, this seems like most likely way out. There is still air and bus traffic at Ndola, traveling south to Rhodesia, Nyasaland and South Africa."

"Once again, everyone in The Katanga thanks you for your service. If there are further questions we will stay here informally until detailed questions are answered, but there will be no further general direction. Please line up and get your pay envelope. This meeting is now adjourned."

From the look on everyone's faces, there were still hundreds of questions. A few Germans, who had gone through years of prison in Russia only to find their family and homes destroyed when they finally crossed their border sat silent along the wall. They had undergone hardships that were almost unimaginable and now it was happening to them again. I figured that at their age, the only thing they knew was war, and they would probably go with those options.

We lined up and collected our envelope along with everyone else, all simultaneously opening them and examining the contents. Mike and I each received $2000 but there was another, smaller envelope. We opened them and it simply read "Please report to Mkandawire in his office immediately." So we did.

# Chapter 54

There were two other guys that we had seen before in the anti-room to Mkandawire's office and we introduced ourselves and learned that they had operated in a different part of The Katanga than we had. Mkandawire appeared in the doorway and ushered us in. His statement was brief. "I asked the four of you to visit me privately because your contribution has been beyond any of our expectations. I could give you a medal but I thought a cash bonus would be more in keeping with your needs. Each of these envelopes contains $5000, and I hope that it allows you to seek a safe way home and will help establish a satisfactory life. And also for you, Mr. Ward, a special gift. I remember that when you got off the plane a year ago we exhibited good taste and we admired our P.38s. I now pass along my P.38 to you and I hope that it finds a safe and permanent home."

I couldn't believe it. But Mike and the other two guys shook my and Mkandawire's hand and then, in a spontaneous un-military fashion, Mkandawire treated me to a bear hug! We stayed for a couple of minutes while the others admired my new pistol, and Mkandawire said he had some other things pending and he disappeared into an inner office. We stayed and talked about the decency of these people. We agreed that Mkandawire and other brass could just as easily pirated the cash out of the country to start their own life. And, perhaps they did some of that, but they thought of us too. They were not leaving us high and dry.

We joined Steve sitting in a corner and began considering the alternatives. Steve said "I guess that we can forget about surrendering." Mike said "Yes, unless you would like a constant diet of cockroaches." I got serious. "I doubt if those poor bastards in Leopoldville are joking. It seems to me that those guys at the gym are pretty well organized but what is the point? What we couldn't do with 5000 troops we're now going to do with 500? Then what? We get a bunch of guys killed and the U.N. sends in some fuckers from Thailand or wherever and eventually they win. It's just so one-sided that the only motive could be money." Steve nodded and said, "You are probably correct. The end result is defeat. You would not be fighting for a cause." Mike chimed in. "I don't mind fighting for money as just another job, but lets' face it. Tony and I are pretty specialized. Killing people at long range. Who will we be killing? I didn't mind killing those Balubas who were torturing people and we had a chance on winning. But this is different. We would be fighting troops who are only here because their country sent them, and after all of that, we have no chance of winning. Money isn't that important to me." Both Steve and I nodded at that but it was a lot easier knowing that we each had over $10,000 rolled up in our pants pockets.

We were silent for a minute or two and looked around the room at all of the other guys, most of them clustered with their friends, probably having the same conversation. Finally, I said "I think that we should go to that gym and see if we could hook up with one of the big mines. Surely they are recruiting. I doubt if there is any long range solution there, but at least the Congo government is unlikely to shut these golden geese down. We would have a little time to get the lay of the land and at least be safe for a week or two." Steve said "In other words, take advantage of them." "Well maybe. But maybe we can do something productive while we figure out how to get out of this mess. I'm wishing right now that we had kept the Jeep in Ndola. Shit, we were home free!" But Mike cut in. "Don't forget the bonus for coming back. And your P.38!"

And so it was, going back and forth, trying to make some sense out of all of this. Steve finally stood and said "Why don't we take a break and visit the quartermaster. He may have some goodies that we could use." So, we hiked down the hall to a semi-mob scene. People were coming the other way with huge loads of supplies that they could never carry for any distance. We settled for some bandoliers of loaded FAL magazines and a couple of extra canteens. The armorer recognized Mike and I and took us to the corner of the room. "Do you need any of that special ammo?" Of course he was talking about that hand loaded .300 Winchester Magnum stuff and of course I said yes. I probably had plenty, but where would I ever get any more in case I ran out? So I wound up with another fifty rounds, all packed neatly in a leather pouch. We said out good byes to the armorer and he said, "I have heard about your good shooting. Please go safely." We shook hands and headed down the hallway. I wondered about all of these support employees. They were behaving like this was just another day at the office.

I suggested that we go to our room and get packed. I asked Steve to come by when he was ready and said "We need to come up with a strategy. I'd like to get out of here before dawn." And so we went to our room for the last time, and began packing our stuff. There was not likely to be any re-supply so we were very careful. Extra socks, foot powder, underwear, water purifier tablets, malaria pills, military emergency rations, and much more. Then the military stuff which we could pack in our sleep. We left some stuff behind. Like bayonets for the FALs. They had never been out of their sheaths, and I said, "If we get close enough to a Baluba to use a bayonet, it's over anyway." I examined Mkandawire's pistol and it was a beauty. Something to treasure. My dad had brought mine home from WW2 and now I could bring one home from Africa. Assuming we got home. I packed it in a wool sock and placed it in my backpack. I lifted the pack and was certain that I exceeded 75 pounds with my FAL and the Mauser, but I could think of nothing to leave behind.

Steve knocked and we all sat on the beds and I advanced my idea. Take a nap until about 4 A.M. and then head for the gymnasium. We can sort it out there, but my notion was to hear them out but actually look for a mining concern to hook up with. Maybe these things overlapped, but I was not interested in signing up for an extended guerilla war. To me, that was hopeless. We looked at each other, and

Steve and Mike nodded 'OK'. A bad plan, but there was nothing any better. Mike and I crapped out immediately. It had been a very long and stressful day. I don't know what Steve did, but at 03:45 he was knocking on our door.

# Chapter 55

S teve started the day with the worst possible news. During the night Colonel Mkandawire had committed suicide! This was a first class officer who was always in the field where the action was. He was understanding with the troops who came from so many different backgrounds that there were conflicts in cultures that he seemed to take in stride. He had supported Mike and I from the first day we got off the C-46 in Elisabethville, and was almost a father figure. He had left a note behind stating, in part that *"My hopes and dreams were all focused on the success of The Katanga. You may not know, but I have no family and when our new country failed, there was nothing left for me. My hope is that each of you will succeed in your lives and not be reluctant to take on controversial and ideological challenges. If I have contributed only a tiny amount towards that goal, then my life has been a success. May God keep you safe and God bless The Katanga."*

All of this left a hollow pit in our stomachs. Even the most hardened mercenaries were silent when they heard. What could you say? A person so selflessly dedicated to an honorable cause simply gave up and killed himself. It was never revealed how he committed the act, and no one really cared. He was gone.

We cycled silently through the grieving, but time was not on our side. We grabbed a cold roll in the cafeteria, gathered our kit together and walked out across the rifle range and out a back gate. That part of our lives was over, but it would never be forgotten.

We looked back at our barracks from the summit of a small hill. The entrance that was usually used was blocked by a line of vehicles, and they were are coming in, not leaving. "Look at that," Steve said, "I think they have something in mind when it becomes light. And you can assume that all of those guys in the gymnasium will be next." We continued on and Mike said "You know, I'm not sure we know what the fuck we're doing. We have no defense against armored cars and large caliber guns and mortars." We kept on walking and I said "I think the idea is not to hit them head-on. These guys cannot live in their armored cars." The gym was part of a now-closed high school facility and we looked down at it from a slight ridge. It was lit up like a Christmas Tree with men scrambling around like ants. The biggest surprise was a couple of helicopters parked in an open field next to the gym. "Wow, that is some expensive machinery down there," I said.

We walked down the ridgeline and came up on a line of heavily armed guards who checked us out pretty thoroughly before allowing us to a path that led to the entrance to the building. Compared to our previous visit, there was much more activity and it looked like a lot of the men were getting ready to leave. That seemed like an excellent idea with a row of armored cars just three miles away! We looked around to get our bearings and saw a large group around Mike Hoare. He was handing out maps on paths out of town that would eventually lead to the reservoir outside of town. On the other side of the room we were surprised to see the mining guy who had briefed us back at the barracks. He was sitting and talking to a couple of civilians and they all appeared to be relaxed and unconcerned about the obvious threat nearby. We had decided that the mine installations seemed to provide at least temporary safety, so we wandered over to the table. I was surprised when Poincare rose from his chair and came over to see us. "You are the long range shooters, correct"? I said, "Well, I didn't know we had that kind of reputation but yes, that is what we do." We all sloughed off our backpacks and rifles and shook hands with him and two of his associates. Surprisingly, he asked "Have you hooked up with anyone yet? Time is getting very short." Steve responded, saying "The only actual decision we have made is that guerilla warfare is probably a losing proposition. The idea of being with a mining operation looks attractive, mainly because you seem organized and have good connections." I added "To tell you the truth, we are not long time Katanga residents if we can help it. We're just not sure that our skills have a fit."

Poincare shook his head and said "Not so. In fact, we had been talking about what you guys have accomplished. We are concerned that we have no capability to keep the opposition troops at a distance. We have talked about some kind of longer range capability just to keep them honest and not near our front gate. You guys have any interest?" I said "One of our problems is how to get out of this place. I suppose we could buy into a very short term arrangement to train a couple of your guys if you could help us into Rhodesia. But I'm thinking of about a week." Poincare rubbed his chin and turned to his team. "What do you think guys?" One his men asked "What about equipment? The rumor is that you have the best stuff available. We can buy more but given the circumstances right now, that could take a week or so, and I am not sure that we know what to buy." I broke in "Well, I don't know about Steve and Mike, but if we can actually get out, sniper rifles and all of the other stuff will not be of any use to us, other than the fact that we are emotionally attached!" That brought a big laugh. Mike said "Not to press, but I think that we need to get something nailed down. If this Hoare guy is leaving and nothing else gels, we need to get moving on our own. It's about a 175- mile hike to the border and I'm not looking forward to that." Poincare said "Understood. Can we see your equipment?" And so we unpacked Mike's optics package, which mystified them, but they also understood its' purpose. Mike said "Good for range finding out to 2500 yards." That brought some knowing smiles. Then I opened the Mauser case and a group of guys suddenly gathered around us. "This rifle shoots .300 Winchester Magnums. Our longest kill is 1750 yards. That is slightly over one mile." The mining folks paid close attention to the rifle and I said "It has fewer than 50 rounds through it." The Hoare guys had admired the equipment but probably thought that a bolt action rifle was a little outdated. The mining guys had more specific ideas and grouped together for about five minutes, gesturing, arguing a little but ended with nodding heads. I began repacking the stuff and Poincare asked me to join their group. "How long do you think it would take to train a couple of guys?" I said, "We work as a two- man team and have had good luck. So I'm assuming you would need four men who are very good with an FAL. They would need to be patient, have perfect eyesight, and of course, know how to care for precision equipment. If we have the right men and a blank check, I'd guess that we could have them up and running in a week. Ideally, it would take a couple of months but no one has that kind of time. And obviously, you would have all of our stuff but only one complete setup, until you can import more."

Poincare turned to caucus with his team. They nodded and he turned to the three of us. "Here is what we can do. We are both in a bind. You want to leave and we need your capabilities so training may be our best option. But what we need specifically are the skills offered by Mr.Ward and Mr. Genard. Frankly I believe that Sargeant Piquart's background more closely fits Hoare's outfit. I suggest that you try and make a deal with him. His shortcoming is leading a conglomeration of men who have never worked together, and you obviously could fill that need. What do you think?"

Steve nodded as though he had already switched his mind about signing up with a guerilla outfit, and since everyone seemed to be funded by the same sources, our paths wouldn't necessarily end here. He said "I think I agree and I'll go over there and try to make a deal. I'll regret losing my American friends for awhile, but this is probably the best solution." It sunk in that we were going to be playing the role that Steve had in Brussels. All of a sudden, I felt unprepared. Still, time was short and we had to get on with this. Mike and I walked a few feet away and exchanged personal feelings, vowing to stay in touch in some way. A couple of bear hugs ensued and Steve headed across the room. We watched with a lot of uncertainty, then turned and walked back to Poincare.

Poincare didn't delay. "I know that you men did not want to be separated, but I have to make some hard decisions, and I think that both the Sargeant and you men will better fit into this arrangement. So let's get to it. We can pay you a total of $12,000, including your equipment, and provide a way out of the country after a week. That actually is no problem. We have helicopters. Where do you want to go?" I blinked. $12,000? "At least to the Ndola Airport, but ideally to Lilongwe."

Poincare said, "We need to be going. But I want to be clear on what our problem is, because for a week, you are going to be right in the middle of it. Our base is actually a mining facility but it is almost the size of a small city. The reason that we are not leaving is that billions of dollars have been invested, and the taxes and commissions for the products from this, and other mines will keep the Congo afloat. So it is in their best interests to leave us alone, as long as they get their cut. However, as you know, the Congo is a sort of fiction in itself. Troops from around the world, some operating not as soldiers but as bandits, corruption on a gigantic scale, and then, of course we have the Balubas who have no allegiance to anyone. The point is, the overall picture seems rosy, but in the real world, we are constantly under some kind of armed threat. Things may work out in the long run, but we have to live today." I looked at Mike who seemed to be taking it all in. I thought that after living in and around Elisabethville for the last two months, all of this seemed obvious. The only difference was that this guy seemed to have positive hopes. He continued "We have a competent small militia or police force, but their arms are limited to rifles, hand grenades, pistols etc. We had not planned for war! We need to be able to keep the rogue raiders away from us and we think that you folks are the answer. People getting shot a mile away should slow them down. Are you OK with all of this?" "We have shorter term objectives. We can do anything for a week!" He said, "OK, let's get going. We have several other recruits so we'll take the two copters to our facility which, by the way, is about 110 miles from the Northern Rhodesian border. Poincare got up and gathered his papers, and we re-packed our gear and backpacks. "We'll get a proper contract signed when we get to the base. Let's go." So we followed to a side entrance and Mike nudged me and said "You now, our equipment is probably worth $5,000, so it isn't quite as good a deal as it seems." I looked at Mike and said "Have you forgotten that our cost is zero? And we're also 40 miles closer to the border?" Mike nodded. There was no way we were going to carry a sniper rifle and all of Mike's optics all the way through Rhodesia to Nyasaland. And what then? What would we do with them?

As we left the building I looked over towards Steve, who was surrounded. I could see that he was going to be just fine. Nevertheless, he had a huge impact on our success and we hoped that out paths would cross. We followed Poincare and his team across a sports field to a couple of fresh looking helicopters that had a decidedly military look to them even if they were painted light blue. We learned that these were Bell UH-1 machines, identical to what was being shipped to Vietnam. I said "These guys must have real clout, or money, or both to grab a couple of these things." Mike, still wondering about the meager $12,000 pay for a week said "Yeah. Emphasis on money. We could have got more." "Mike, $12,000 is about what my dad makes in two years!"

Poincare pointed us and two other recruits to the second helicopter and he and his helpers headed for the lead machine, which already had its' rotors spinning. Clearly, they sensed an immediate security problem. The interior of the helicopter was sparse, with webbed seats and no windows. So we climbed aboard, nervous because we had never been in a helicopter and shook hands with the other two guys, and within a minute the engine was running and seconds later we lifted off. We could look past the pilots and through the windscreen and see the blinking lights from the lead copter, but otherwise, it was a black, featureless night. It was also noisy. We gave up on talking and just settled in for the ride.

# Chapter 56

The trip took only about 45 minutes as we began our descent. The copter circled but we could see nothing. It was like being in a very noisy blacked out closet that was moving vertically downward. A very unsettling feeling, but actually uneventful, and we touched down with just a slight bump. The engine shut down and the pilot supervised our getting out and gathering all of our stuff. The other two guys climbed out as well, grinning, and I suspect it was their first ride in a helicopter. We all gathered into a group and followed Poincare to a one- story building. The building turned out to be a huge installation, larger than the barracks we had been living in. Poincare introduced us to an aid, a Mr. McKenzie and told us that he would show us around, but also, he would be our contact and decision-maker for the mining company. The first stop was our own room where we dropped our loads and briefly looked around. It was kind of another Motel 6 arrangement, with two beds, a shower and all of the basics, and it looked clean and new. Not bad, considering the alternative was walking to a reservoir and sleeping on the ground. We then went on a guided tour with the other new guys who turned out to be ex-French Foreign Legion. We were shown an assembly room, a cafeteria, a hallway with private offices, and a separate wing, which housed laboratories to test ore samples. And then down another short hallway where we could look through large windows into an infirmary. There were about 15 beds, with three of them occupied by young guys me who clearly had been badly injured. I asked "What happened to them." McKenzie looked at me and said sharply, "Bullet wounds." That was our first wake up call. McKenzie said he wanted to start early, that we could grab a sandwich in the cafeteria but suggested that we then get some rest in our room. It was clear that this McKenzie guy was going to be more than a tour leader. Sleep sounded good to us, and we stripped and were asleep in twenty minutes.

The wake-up call came over a speaker in the ceiling. It let us know 'Breakfast in 30 minutes'. I looked at my watch. 0430. I pulled the covers off of Mike and said "Looks like they want their money's worth!" We showered, dressed in our spare Katanga uniforms and headed down the hallway. The first thing we noticed was that our very own cook at the government barracks was hunched over a grill, and Mike said "Looks like we get world's worst breakfast cook." He was right. Runny eggs and half-cooked bacon. We lose a good friend in Sargeant Steve and get a bad cook.

After breakfast, we found the assembly room, but on the way, we went by a room with a 'Communications Center' sign over the door. I could see a clerk through the door, and I said to Mike "Lets's check this out. I'd like to send a telex to Anne. How about you and Rene?" Mike nodded and we went into the room. The clerk looked up and I said "Hi. I am Tony Ward and this is Mike Genard. We signed on in Elisabethville last night and I wondered if we could send a short message to our family". She stacked some papers and said "Sure, but it'll have to be very short because the machine is really cooking today. Is it in Africa?" I nodded and she gave me a couple of blank forms to fill out, along with a pamphlet listing the telex numbers of most installations in Southern Africa. "See if you can find the numbers, and fill out the forms and I'll get the message out in an hour or so." It all seemed very organized, with machines humming and a couple of clerks coming in and out of the room with papers and what looked like personal mail. Mike and I went over to an empty table, and I quickly found the telex number for the Capitol Hotel in Lilongwe. I thought for a minute about what to say, and finally settled in on "Anne Scott-Ward STOP Safe here STOP Expect arrival Lilongwe in a week STOP Stay safe love Tony." I handed the form back to the clerk and she looked it over and said "OK" and handed it over to the machine operator. Mike was having a hard time finding the number for Rene's newspaper so we went through hundreds of Capetown numbers but finally found the number for the Cape News. He thought for a minute and jotted down a message which I saw over his shoulder and wrote "Rene" and then stopped, red faced. "Hey Mike, do you remember Rene's last name?" "You dumb shit. You're in love and you don't even know her name? It's Stolz!" Embarrassed, he filled out the form. "Rene Stolz, % of Capetown  Cape News STOP Arrive in Lilongwe Nyasaland in about a week. Can you join Tony and Anne and me for a week vacation? STOP Please? STOP. Love Mike STOP". I said "Sounds like a reunion!" Mike nodded and said "Yeah, I just thought of that when I was filling out the form. Any problem?" "No," I said, "But I may be holed up in our room for a day or two." "Well, I can hope too!" Mike laughed. "You are a little more advanced than I but I'll work hard to catch up!" He handed the form to the clerk and we turned to leave when the clerk called me back, laughing, "Mr. Ward, you have a response. Your addressee must have been sitting on the Telex machine! "My heart almost stopped as she handed me the message. It read "Hurry Tony STOP Safe STOP Presents await. STOP I like my new name. STOP Love STOP Ms. Scott-Ward STOP. I just froze there for a minute savoring the note. Presents await! I thought about that a second or two as my privates responded to an embarrassing level. Then we turned and headed for the assembly room. It was 0600.

There were not a lot of uniforms in the room as this was a civilian operation. McKenzie, in khakis, a work shirt and boots quickly found us. After all, we were the only men in Katanga Army uniforms. He re-introduced himself as Bill McKenzie and asked us to follow him to a small conference room. There were eight military-looking guys sitting around the table and we proceeded to introduce ourselves. We would get to know some of them but for now, McKenzie got right down to business. "You men have expressed in interest in joining two new sniper teams. Mr. Ward and Mr. Genard will be with us for a week. We have very little time. These men will provide training to you and whittle the eight of you down to four. These men have had amazing success with the Katanganese, with kills out to 1500 yards." That set off a buzz around the table. A mile? McKenzie continued. "The idea here is to keep some of our opponents as far away from out facility as possible. We're not particularly interested in killing anyone but that is always a possibility. You have been chosen from about 20 men because you have superior eyesight, a solid record, patience, and a mathematical bent. We are purchasing duplicate equipment that Mr. Ward and Mr. Genard have brought with them, and hope to have it all here in two days, direct from Germany. These men will provide training including a short orientation, but concentrating on field operations, and this will begin after lunch in this room. That will give your instructors time to put their program together." Everyone laughed a little and it was obvious that we had been caught by surprise. I said "Surprise. That's right. I didn't know that we would be school teachers!" It was a good exchange and everything settled down. McKenzie said "OK. You two have it. Good luck."

Tony and I tried to collect our wits and I said, "Tell you what. We'll meet here after lunch and go over the equipment we have. We'll explain our purpose and some of our operations and then we'll do some shooting. We'll start with iron sight FALs, and move on from there. My instructions are to reduce this group to four men in a time frame that usually takes a couple of months. We went through this in Belgium and there is a lot to learn. Unfortunately, most of it will be after we leave. But we'll work on the basics. Questions?"

A very fit looking guy around 30 asked "It sounds interesting but I'm not sure just what we will be shooting at. Can you help with that?" I said "That is a very good question. Our experience has been mainly with Balubas who are raising hell with kidnappings, rape, burning out settlers etc. So we were very mobile, and in the bush for weeks at a time. We learned that if we could find some atrocity about to take place or underway and managed to take out their leader at long range…and when they didn't know where the shot came from, they scattered due to fright, some kind of supernatural fear or whatever. It slowed them down a lot." Mike continued "You have a different situation here. You have a fixed base, yet are being harassed by various troops. Maybe even some Balubas. So we'll try to quiet some of these guys down. We might take a trip into the bush too. There is a hell of a lot to learn." There was a lot of head nodding and a show of respect for us. But no more questions. I said "OK, we'll see you right here at 1300 hours and we'll get started." They filed out of the room, some giving us a handshake as they left.

I stood there looking at Mike. "Fuck. Are we supposed to have a syllabus or what?" Mike just shook his head and said "We should have gotten more money!"

So we returned to our room and unpacked all of our stuff. The Mauser, the optics, special cartridges, the Ghilley suits and tried to remember all of the training Sargeant Steve had given us. We made some notes about some of our exploits. By the time we had our thoughts together, there was a knock on the door and a clerk handed Mike a Telex. "Oh shit, I hope this is good news!" He read it out loud. "Mike Genard. STOP. Can you come to Cape Town? STOP. Have new job difficult to leave STOP. Also have new apartment STOP. Looking forward to your visit STOP Love, Rene STOP. Mike had a huge grin on his face. "A new apartment? Does that mean I could stay there?" I said "Mike, you are so dense. I think she wants to start a relationship." "Wait for me. I want to send a quick telex." I said "I'll meet you in the cafeteria. We need to grab a quick sandwich." A bout ten minutes later Mike sat down at a table with a sandwich. "I told her I would check airlines." Mike had this glazed look on his face and I said "We've got to teach these guys how to be snipers in one week so we better concentrate." Mike obviously had other ideas but we gulped the sandwiches down and headed for the conference room.

# Chapter 57

It dawned on me that everything had been dark when we had arrived, and now I began to appreciate the enormity of the installation. Just looking out the window, I could see activity beyond my sight limits. Heavy equipment, roadways, and satellite buildings into the distance. And the size of the main building we were in. There were signs at hallway intersections leading to International Affairs, Corporate Offices, Executive Offices, Military Affairs etc. There must be hundreds of people working here, all seemingly oblivious to the chaos 100 miles away in Elizabethville. How could they be this secure?

We unloaded our gear and set up the rifle and the optics on the conference table and got semi-organized when the first recruits filed in. But after a minute I realized that there were only six of them. An older guy said "I think that the information about being in the bush for a couple of months discouraged them. Most military types here think that their job exists only within the fences."

This was a bad way to start, but I said "Let's get started. Please write your name and country on the blackboard and how long your contract goes." That knocked out one more guy who had only three months to go. "So unless you plan on re-upping, I guess that you are excused. Sorry about that." I saw no point in training a guy who was about to leave. The others signed onto the blackboard and the mix was two Germans, one Pole, one Belgium, and a Kantanganese, who stated that his contract was 'forever!' I laughed and said "That's great, Andrew, you own the longevity award!"

So we began. The focus was on the Mauser and even though it was basically an antique bolt action design dating to about 1905, they could all see that it was a very special piece. The flash suppressor, the set triggers, the fluted barrel, the huge 50x scope, a folding bipod and all of that, none of which existed in 1905. I explained that it was chambered for a .300 Winchester Magnum caliber, with an effective range of 2000 yards. That really opened their eyes. Well over a mile! I explained the bullet could travel at killing velocity further than we could effectively see a target, but that we had results at 1700 yards. "You killed someone at 1700 yards?" I looked at him and said, "That is what we do. We would prefer to shoot at shorter ranges, but we take what is served."

We demonstrated the Ghilley suits which were completely out of place in a conference room. Mike looked like a beggar or a tramp. But the point was made. Mike also explained the complex optics setup and gave a short talk on the amazing new equipment now being developed, that would eventually reduce all of this stuff to a hand-held device. But for now, what we had was the best in Africa. There were a lot of questions, and we hoped that we had provided an incentive to continue, especially after having three dropouts.

About 1500 hours, I called a break and asked the 'students' to return with their FALs, a couple of loaded magazines and whatever field equipment they had. They left, chattering away at this new adventure. Mike and I looked up McKenzie and we found him in a private office down the hall. He greeted us and asked about the training, but he had already heard about two of the dropouts. Mike said "Yeah, I guess they didn't know that we killed people!"

I asked for information on where we could shoot on the premises, and McKenzie told us that they had a 400-yard range set up on the far end of the property. He had secured a couple of station wagons and permission to use the facility along with an employee who would help us with the logistics, targets etc. I was asked when we wanted to do this and said "In about a half hour." "Wow" McKenzie said, you guys don't waste any time." Mike responded, "Well, you know we only have a week." McKenzie nodded, but by his look, I could see that he was thinking that maybe our term could be extended.

I said, "The bigger issue is a longer range. That is a very strong requirement" "How long?" I said "About 1800 yards." "And when?" I said "Tomorrow morning." He looked worried, and I could not figure out why. After all, we were recruited to train long range snipers and 400 yards didn't even come close. I went on to explain that we needed targets at 200 yard intervals from 600, to 1800 yards. And, the need for a couple of workers to replace targets between shooters and quickly label them so we could tally all of the results in the evening. He simply said "OK," got on the phone, gave some quick instructions and hung up. This guy was all business

I said "Sorry to place all of these requests on you, but there is one other requirement." Interestingly, he said "Shoot." I laughed a little at that and then McKenzie smiled and said "An unfortunate response!" I went on "My understanding is that we are primarily a defensive operation. To protect the installation and your employees. We may go outside the gates if we have to but that is not the usual mission." "That is correct." So I continued. "That being the case, it seems to me that we need a well prepared shooting base. That is, a field of fire up to 2000 yards, ideally free of trees, boulders, etc. A base that is about 4x4 meters with protection, maybe with sandbags, about one- meter high. If we come under attack, the enclosure would have to be well stocked with water, food, ammo etc. So I guess the question is, do we have a vantage point where we could create such a firebase?" He thought for a minute while rubbing his chin, which I learned was his way of activating his creative thought process. At least it seemed that way. Then he said, "I think we have such a place. Right on top of this building. That would put you about 30' above ground level." My eyes widened and I said "That sounds great! When could we have such a place operational? And what about the field of fire?"

McKenzie said, "Let me give you a little background here. When we built this place we knew there was a safety problem. We have been lucky for many years, but that is mainly because the Balubas take on the easy pickings. They knew that it would be a losing battle for them here. But now we have a different situation. I really don't know how it will play out with some troops well-disciplined and others no better than the Balubas. We'll just have to be prepared and see what happens. One thing is clear: It is not in the best interests of the Congo to ruin this facility because a huge amount of their funds come directly from mining companies. We definitely need to work out the Rules of Engagement in the next day or two. My fear is that some of the free-wheeling troops, for instance, from Rwanda or Leopoldville may be out-of-control and overrunning a base like this, just for hatred reasoning, and that is a real possibility."

"But back to your need for an adequate field of fire, you need to take a jeep and cover the ground out there. There are no obstacles out to 2000 yards from this structure. Nothing. We moved a jungle and huge trees to make it this way. It is a good thing that we had the foresight to clear the land, even though it has never been an issue until now. And, you are not aware of the size of this building. We have four floors below ground level, and over 500 people work here. Anyway, I'll have your rooftop facility up and running tomorrow and I'll make sure that only a few lanes of vehicle traffic are allowed from the field installations to this building. We don't want to be shooting our own people! I also want you to take your chosen team up in one of the Hueys so that you can appreciate the surrounding terrain. Maybe we can handle that tomorrow."

The cooperation was dead serious and it was clear that the puny $12,000 we were being paid was a mere drop in the bucket in comparison to the other expenditures McKenzie was willing to make. We thanked him and moved on to the conference room where our students awaited.

When we re-convened, there were piles of equipment on the conference room floor and I said "We have a couple of cars outside to take us to the 'short range', so I want you to just bring your FALs, two loaded mags, and if you have handguns, bring them along. We'll deal with this other stuff later. The Mauser was still on the table so I locked the door as we left the room. Mike and I took our own FALs. The drivers took us a couple of miles away from the building, beyond the perimeter fencing and into a small, remote canyon. This was the short range where the normal guards did their target practicing. Some small rough tables and benches were set up and we gathered around the largest table and set our gear down.

As the five guys stared wide-eyed, Mike went down the row and field stripped the FALs. Then he said "reassemble them." This was a standard test for anyone responsible for guns, but something the five candidates were not ready for. We figured that if these guys knew what they were doing, they could easily have them back together in less than 15 seconds. The clock ticked and the rifles began the assembly. In about 8 seconds, an older German guy, Rolf Richter, handed his FAL to Mike, who looked it over, made sure the magazine was out, pulled the bolt back to make sure the gun was unloaded, let the bolt spring forward, and dry fired the gun. "Good job," he said and handed it back to Richter, who nodded but had a look like he had merely brushed his teeth. Three others guns rotated through Mike, a little slower but all reasonable, considering nerves and all. The last guy, Lew Lewandowski, a Pole, looked confused and embarrassed. Mike took the receiver and showed him how to properly insert the bolt and bingo, all was well." Lewandowski said "I assure you that this will never happen again." Mike said "Well, we'll see how the shooting goes, but you better get this down pat or you'll be off the team." He nodded and said, "Yes sir."

We started the shooting in the order the guns had been reassembled, with Richter first, Lewandowski last. I explained "You have 20 rounds in your magazine. You will use only six of them. You will shoot at 100 yards, 300 yards, and 400 yards, two shots at each distance. Do not rush the shots, but move along at a reasonable rate. When the first guy is through, the range man will pick up the targets and place fresh ones. At the end of the exercise we'll collect the targets and see how you did. These are full size, feet to the head targets and I want you to aim for the center of the heads. OK, Mr. Richter, take your shots. Two per target"

The shooting went very well with no delays. I watched Lewandowski very carefully, and while he seemed nervous, he sighted the rifle well, shot with no visible jerking, and by the time he went for the last target, had a slight smile on his face. The range man gathered all of the targets, rolled them up and delivered them to Mike. I said, "Mike and I will evaluate the targets and we'll meet you after dinner in the conference room and we'll discuss the results."

We loaded into the vehicle and headed back to the base. As we left the canyon, one of the guys groused a little bit about having to wait to see the results but that was about the only discussion. But as we approached the headquarters building we saw a crane alongside of the structure, and several guys on the roof. As we neared the entrance I said "Hey those guys are lifting sandbags! These people move quickly." Mike explained that this was to be our defensive position, and everyone pressed their noses against the glass. We pulled up to a loading dock and I said "Conference room, seven P.M." And with that, the five candidates gathered up their gear and headed into the building.

Mike and I were as curious as the men were about the results, so we headed for the conference room and had a big surprise. There on the table was some fresh boxes, opened at the top, and in them was a Mauser sniper rifle exactly like mine, and a set of optical gear that looked to be a little more condensed than Mike's. There was a small metal ammo box and in it was 500 rounds of .300 Win Mag match ammunition, and two huge Leica binoculars. Mike said it first "Not only are these guys efficient, they are dead-fucking serious!" I said "Yes, and you know, those binoculars are something we really missed. You can sweep through a huge initial view of the landscape." So we carefully set the gear in a corner of the room and began studying the targets. They were numbered #1, # 2, #3 etc. The target for Richter was outstanding, but we sort of expected it. At 300 yards, he had one hole in the paper target at about the guy's forehead, and the other just above his mouth, pretty much obliterating the nose. The surprise was Lewandowski, who scored one shot in the mouth at 400 yards, and another in the neck, in an exact vertical alignment. Mike said, "He might have scored right up there with Richter but he didn't quite consistently correct for the tiny bullet drop." The rest of the targets were fine, and the lowest shot was in the lower chest area. But we kept in mind that they were shooting with iron sights, and who actually knew what shape the FALs were in? "I'd say we pass all five for the next step and have an extra guy on board in case of attrition." Mike agreed but hedged on the sniper rifle. "Lets' see how they handle it. After all, that is what this is all about." We rolled up the targets and went to the cafeteria. Mike gulped his food down and said "I'll be back in a minute," and headed down the hallway. About 10 minutes later he was back with a big smile. "I got tickets to Capetown for next week and I sent a Telex to Rene!" I had no idea where he wangled the tickets but I reminded him "There's still the small matter of getting to the Ndola airport". "Shit, I'll walk if I have to!"

We reassembled the group at 7:00 P.M. and told them that the winners were Richter and Lewandowski but they were all very good shots and we had decided to keep all five pending the sniper trial, and told them that we would start at 8:00 A.M. right here. They all filed out with smiles on their faces and we shook hands with each of them. A team was beginning to form. As Richter walked by I asked him to stay and so he took a seat and I asked "What did you do in the German army?" He looked unemotionally at me, just like the he did since I first met him and said "I was a sniper at Stalingrad." I was stunned. Mike came over and sat, while I began doing the mental math. Stalingrad fell in 1943, and here we were in 1961. Even if he was very young in the army, say 19, that would put him at 37 years old. He just looked at us, and I asked "What have you been doing since then?" So he told his story. He was drafted at age 17 and after training he was selected for sniper school and sent to the eastern front. When Stalingrad fell, he was captured and spent the next 12 years in a Siberian camp. He said "I was lucky to survive, because they detested snipers, and I was one of the last Germans to go free." He went on to explain that when the Reds let him out, all they did was to open the gate. "It was up to me to find my way back to Germany, begging and doing minor jobs until I finally got home two years later. But the problems was, when I got to Berlin, there was no home. My family's house was a parking lot in the Red zone, and no one could tell me what had happened to my mother or father. The nearest I got was 'a bomb.' I broke in, "So after spending 12 years in a Russian camp here you were back in Berlin and the Russians were in charge?" "That is correct. Every time I saw one of those mother-fuckers I wanted to strangle him. I could have worked for the East German police but the Reds were actually in charge. And so I went west, into the French zone and hooked up with the French Foreign legion. Algeria, Indo China, West Africa. I was released six months ago and came here under a 'guard 'contract." Mike said "So you have been at war your entire adult life?" He responded, "It is all I know how to do."

We tracked down McKenzie to give him an update and to try and understand how the hell he got a new Mauser sniper rifle. He looked up from some papers he was working on and said "Money, jet airplanes and helicopters. And more money." With that he laughed a little and received our report. He also told us that our long range course would be in place by morning and we would be shooting from the rooftop. He warned us to follow the course carefully as he didn't want to shut down the entire facility for our target practice. We laughed a little at that! He also explained that the Huey had discovered a large group of troops a few miles from the mining facility and it was unknown what they intended. However, he had begun to mobilize his guard force just in case they had aggressive intentions. "You guys might be in business before you know it. Ordinarily, I'd say that there should be no incentive to overrun this base. But on the other hand, with the mish-mash of countries involved around here, who knows? I'll send the Huey up this morning and let you know what we discover. Oh yes, for your information, your course will be set up in the opposite direction of these unknown troops.

# Chapter 58

At nine A.M. we assembled in the conference room and gathered up the Mausers and the rest of the equipment. As it turned out, there was a message in the new Mauser case from a gunsmith in the Mauser factory in Germany stating that the rifle had been sighted in and was 'ready to go.' Jeez, I thought, these guys think of everything.

I had noticed that all five of the trainees had breakfast together, and I was beginning to feel more comfortable about the team. All five trainees were eager to use the sniper rifles, but pretty shaky when I told them that the targets extended out to 1800 yards. Mike gave a little speech about the relatively narrow shooting range we had to operate on, and the need to be very careful. He also set up the spotting apparatus and explained its' use. I then set our 'old' Mauser on its bipod and explained its function, with emphasis on the set triggers. "We'll decide who the shooters are and who the spotters are when we get through with today."

It was about 10:00 A.M. when we assembled on the roof. The workers had arranged a very nice sandbagged enclosure that looked like a circle within a circle. They probably thought that we needed a separate area to store all of our gear, and it was well thought out. We set up the rifles in notches through the sandbags and I was about to demonstrate a 500 yard shot when a guy came running up the stairs, out of breath, waving a paper. The paper was a note from McKenzie, saying "I do not know what these guys are doing, but they are coming closer. Keep a close eye on them." So I told the group what was going on and had Mike turn the long range scopes around and began looking.

Then we began the target shooting. The targets were arranged beginning at 500 yards, and then extending at odd intervals out to about 1800 yards, where the target was invisible to the naked eye. The recruits were very focused and watched my every move as I took them through the steps. "In this first shot, we know the target is 500 yards away, and the bullet drop is negligible. Maybe an inch." I inserted five rounds into the magazine and closed the bolt. "Now watch. I will set the left hand trigger. It will take less than a pound of pressure to fire the right hand trigger." I sighted through the scope and added a tiny compensation for the bullet drop, disengaged the safety and fired. The target was a black human sized silhouette on white paper. I asked Lewandowski to look for the hole. He fooled around with the scope adjustment and it took a minute, but he said "I am not sure, but I think I see light through the guy's forehead." That got a brief hand-clapping but I said "Look guys, this is a chip shot. Nothing more."

And so it went. Each guy got two shots out to 1200 yards. We had the range guys hustling around gathering and resetting targets at each range, labelling them, and then going on to the next shot. It was a little complex, because each guy had a shot at a slightly different range in order to use the optics, so we were developing a stack of targets. We alternated between rifles, and I couldn't actually tell the difference between the two. And so it went until I took a shot at 1375 yards and then at 1700 yards. At this point we had a small radio set to communicate with the range guys so they knew who was shooting. The recruits made their shots as well, and it was early afternoon before we were done. About the time we were wrapping up, McKenzie showed up and asked how things were going and made a little small talk with the recruits. Mike supervised the transfer of equipment down to the conference room and I said "We have some analysis to work on, so get some rest, have dinner and we'll see you at 7:00 P.M". Obviously they would just have to wait for the results. McKenzie and I were left alone and he said "I do not know what the fuck is going on, but those troops out there are very aggressive and are challenging our guards who are stationed outside of the gates. You may have to use some of those skills before you expected." I said "Just remember, we are not magic. We might get something done out to about 2000 yards, but that is about it." "Well, that is about where they are. Maybe 3000 yards. We'll do a couple of overflights and let's talk about this when you're through with your guys this evening. I think we need a 'what if' strategy and we need it soon."

Mike and I tabulated the results and we were favorably impressed. Not surprising, at 1350 yards the #1 ranking was Rolf, and somewhat surprising was Lew in #2, followed by Andrew who scored two, Georges and Roberto with one each. It wasn't perfect but they were unfamiliar with the equipment and had virtually no practice. 1350 yards is a helluva long shot. When they filed in after dinner, we tried to be as upbeat as possible and explained that everyone was still on the team.

I then brought up the issue of side arms, the Baluba issue and 'last stands.' Rolf had a small Mauser .380 but the others had no pistols. The real problem was that no one had considered any action beyond the safety of the facility. When I brought up that possibility, Andrew was visibly shaken. He said "I didn't sign up for soldiering outside of the fence. Is that what you are proposing?" "I am proposing nothing, but I have explained that a huge number of troops of various origins seem to be pressing towards us. It could be that we will be called upon to go outside of the walls and try to scare them off. I don't know. But remember this: We are all in this together and if this facility falls, we all fall." Andrew wasn't buying it, but I couldn't change it. What did he think when he hired on?

I made it worse when I explained what some of the Balubas who were now being recruited into the national army. "If one of these groups gets you, the only thing separating life and death is torture. That is the reason for the side arm. For yourself." They were all pretty pale when we finished discussing it, but after kicking it around for an hour, they all settled down. I explained that they could acquire a personal pistol at the commissary in the basement, and I suspect that is where they all headed at around 9:00P.M.

Despite the hour, Mike and I tracked down McKenzie in his office, now dressed in a tee shirt and jogging shorts. We explained the success on the range and the unpopular reaction to possible operating outside of the fence. "That is what I want to talk to you about. On the last Huey flight at about 5:00 P.M. the copter was targeted by a rocket of some kind, maybe a bazooka, as well as small arms fire. There are actually two bullet holes in the tail section. We had a special photographer on board and we got some close ups of who the leaders are and about where their encampments are." He pulled about ten 8x10 pictures out of an envelope and while they were grainy, we could make out several command figures. The encampments were about 2000 yards apart, and one was clearly non-military and had all of the appearances of a Baluba gathering. Fires, dancing and a pole right in the middle that made me wonder who they intended to string up. The other was definitely military and two white officers could be identified surrounded by black troops who we assumed were Congolese, although they could be from any surrounding country. They were all obviously hostile.

McKenzie said "I think that these guys are possible Russians leading the Congolese, because all other troops are a function of the U.N. and under a lot better control. Not perfect, but better. I am very nervous about this. If these guys manage to breach our defenses the facility could be overrun. We have hundreds of civilian workers here and while we have a couple hundred armed guards, we were never set up to stop an army." I said "And we were not brought on board to stop an army either." With about four days left on my contract, I was not about to get involved in some impossible venture. On the other hand, McKenzie's fate was our fate. Like it or not, we were stuck here. The end result of encountering thousands of out-of-control troops was not attractive.

McKenzie said "I've been reading the reports about Mike and your exploits with the Balubas, and the Irish in Jadotville. With respect to the Balubas, from what I can determine, your strategy was to take out the leaders of the uprising and the rest of them ran away. Who wants to be next with an exploding brain?" "Well, that is true. However, we always had a group of trained Katanganese soldiers backing us up, helping us to identify targets, medical support etcetera. Plus, these encampments in the pictures have a semi-permanent look to them. We are not anywhere near in range of them."

McKenzie pushed an intercom button and said "Come on in here." A couple of seconds later, two uniformed guards came in and took a seat. We were introduced and McKenzie said "I want to explore a strategy." Mike spoke for the first time. "If we're going to talk about an offensive operation, I want Rolf Richter here. He is a very big asset and he will probably be your head shooter. Plus, he's probably been in more problem situations than we can count." McKenzie had a short laugh and said "Ah! So you have identified Mr. Richter's skills. That didn't take long." He pushed the intercom button and told an aide to "Track down Rolf Richter and escort him to my office immediately." McKenzie had some coffee and pastries brought in while we waited and I could see that this was going to be a long evening.

When Richter arrived, he didn't know if he was in trouble or what. But McKenzie quickly settled that problem and was told that he was there because Mike and I valued his experience and talent. Richter nodded but didn't otherwise react. So McKenzie went over the whole issue again. He explained that if we waited for an attack we could put up a fight but we were ultimately doomed. Hundreds of us. We needed a plan. I said "Maybe these guys are just trying to provoke you." McKenzie shook his head, No, Tony, Balubas and the Congolese troops are not into subtleties. They are sitting out there a couple of miles away figuring out how to defeat this facility, and the only ones doing any thinking are those two white guys and maybe the Baluba chiefs. The rest of them are thinking about burning, raping, and killing." Mike and I nodded. It all sent a chill up our spines. McKenzie said, "Be here with your crew at 0900. It will be a busy day."

When Mike and I got back to the room I had a Telex envelope on the bed. My heart fluttered as I opened it: Tony Ward STOP When? STOP Love, Ms. Ward-Scott STOP. I dropped the message on the table and flopped down on the bed. When indeed? This one-week thing was looking uncertain. As I undressed I pulled the wad of $100 dollar bills out of my cargo pants and did a count. $14,000. Mike did the same and came up with about $12,000. Some of his bills were so crushed, rolled, and sweat-soaked that it would awhile to flatten them all out. But it was a pile of money, and more was coming from the current arrangement. I said "We need to be very careful tomorrow and make sure we don't get drawn into this mess more than a day or two. We didn't bargain for combat." Mike rolled over, already half asleep. "My air tickets are only good for another week and there's no way I will miss that plane." "Well," I said, "Again, there is the small matter of getting you to the plane!" But he wasn't in a talking mood and rolled over. I assumed that he wasn't in a combat mood either.

# Chapter 59

The next morning, we gathered an expanded team in a large conference room. McKenzie was now dressed in a suit and looked a little spooked. Our five guys plus Mike and I were there, and four ex-Katanganse NCOs were present. Also included was the chief pilot for the Hueys. McKenzie began. "By now, you all must be aware of the threat outside of our boundaries. It's serious and we have to deal with it or talk about an open fire fight. It is obvious that these guys are not going to pack up and go home. And there is no way we can prevail over 2 or 3,000 troops. We're very vulnerable here with women, technicians, truck drivers and all, none of them equipped or trained to fight a war. We might begin evacuating the most vulnerable today but that will be a very small group. I have a plan to discourage these guys and make them think twice before they start shooting."

"Most of you know that Tony and Mike here are snipers. Not just your everyday sniper but 1800 yard snipers." That statement was a jaw dropper for those who were not acquainted with our skills or purpose. "For several days they have been training two sniper teams from our staff who are here with us, and in this very short time, they are just about ready to perform." "Perform what?" said the pilot. "Let me explain."

"All of this will take place tomorrow. The entire operation will be on lockdown. The only operational activity will be you in this room. Everyone else will be confined to these quarters or in the mines themselves. All staff will be informed of this by 1700 hours. Now to the plan. As near as we can determine, there are two groups. One is led by Russian officers and consists mainly of Congolese army troops. These are the same guys who took over a year to get from

Leopoldville to Elisabethville and they left a path of rape, robbery and mayhem behind them. They are undisciplined and a poor excuse for an army, but there are a lot of them. These Russian guys seem to keep them in line, but they will not sit still for long. The other group, roughly 3000 yards to the north are an odd collection of Balubas, led by some kind of super-chief who are looking for their usual targets. In this case, that is no doubt us, but the Russians have at least some kind of temporary control over their group." McKenzie went on to explain that these leaders held huge mega meetings during the early morning hours that seem to be a matter of getting these guys all torqued up to do some kind of operation. The Russian guy who wore the uniform of a major, actually has a sound system and seems good at raising the emotions. The Balubas, on the other hand didn't need an excuse to fight.

McKenzie elaborated. "What I want is your cooperation to launch an operation tomorrow morning at 0300. I want our two sniper teams to slip out through the gate and after about a mile, split into separate locations, one pointed at the Russian guy and one towards the Balubas. You should expect no opposition because our thinking is that the last thing they can imagine is us attacking them!" You will need to find your hides while it is still dark. You can meet with our pilots and see what they have sketched out from their aerial surveys. Clearly, the idea is silence and stealth. We could send more men but that would only increase the chance of detection. Tony Ward will be in charge of the operation once you leave the gate. You have today to scope out the details. But the strategy itself is for each sniper team to detect the opposition leaders I have described and be ready to shoot them at exactly 0900." That brought out a lot of mumbling and whispering and head shaking. One of the Katanga NCOs stood and said "Sir, won't that just stir up a couple thousand armed men? And how will we get back?" McKenzie had this well thought out. "Based on facts regarding long range sniper attacks against the Balubas is that these shots come from nowhere. The bullet arrives before the noise.

They are superstitious in the extreme and in prior situations, they simply panic and head into the bush. In this case, hopefully they will head for their individual home area, as far away as possible." The NCO stood again and said "Are these men the ones who carried out the attacks on behalf of the Katanga army?" McKenzie said "Yes. Right here. Tony Ward and Mike Genard." The NCO said "I've heard all about these men. What you say is true. It has been like magic. Kill the leader and the rest run. I feel much better about the plan if these guys are doing the shooting!" Mike and I nodded a thank you, and McKenzie said "Part of the shooting. The other part will be done by Rolf Richter sitting over there in the corner. For your information, he was formerly a sniper in the German army." That brought a little head-shaking because this was essentially a Belgium operation and the German army had over run Belgium in the first two weeks of two separate world wars. Richter just looked ahead, expressionless. "Mr. Lewandowski will be his spotter. The remaining members of the sniper team will be kept in reserve"

"That is the general plan. I want you to follow Mr. Ward and spend the day getting your equipment together and working out the details. If all goes well you should be back through the gate by 1100 hours and the threat should be over. At least for now. One more thing: the entire plan rests on killing these key people. One or two shots maximum. If anyone gets gung-ho and starts shooting off magazines, you will not have a chance. Kill and retreat. The NCOs are experienced men and are there to provide.at least a small perimeter in case someone wanders on to your site. They will have FALs. They will also have knives and they know how to use them. I will be working with staff to create a defensive position on the facility if all hell breaks loose. We have secure facilities in the mines, but they are also a trap. So take my word for it: this is the best of very few options. The alternative is to just wait for a wave of troops to take this place and the chaos that will follow. You will actually be in a safer place on this operation than if you stayed behind and we cancelled. Oh yes. One final word.

I am fully aware that this is an action unintended in your contract. I understand this and you will be generously compensated."

With that, the men followed me out to the front of the building where some folding chairs had been set up. I looked over at Mike and said, "A little over a year ago we were shooting jackrabbits. How the fuck did we get into this?"

I needed a little time to think this through. "OK men, I want you to go to your quarters and get all of your combat gear, ammo, medical supplies, FALs, cleaning gear, hand guns and anything else you can determine to be portable. Meet me back here in one hour and we will be transported to the short range shooting range and get our gear together. Don't be late.

# Chapter 60

McKenzie had provided us with a couple of grunts and I told him we needed vans to get to the range and we needed some sandwiches by 1200 hours for the group. They scurried off and Mike and I went to work.

What followed was an extremely busy day. We started with the basics and told everyone to field strip their FALs and reassemble them. That went off flawlessly. Lewandowski did it twice. I talked to Richter about breathing exercises to slow his heart rate down before the sniper shot, and he looked at me and said, "Yes, I understand that." Everyone shot targets at 300 yards with no problems. Richter and I fired the Mausers just to make sure the rifles were still zeroed. We then had the pilots explain what they knew about the encampments. They had a large easel with a chart on it that showed our facility and the two encampments to scale. They had plotted potential hides where they thought there would be a field of fire yet in a vegetated area where there might be decent cover. It was a good job and a good starting point. But the actual selection of the hides would take place in the dark and I asked them if they could take the shooting teams up in a Huey and see for themselves. No problem. We set it up for the end of the day.

The basic arrangement was that both encampments were 3000-4000 yards away from our facility and spread apart about 2000 yards. So the shooters could be relatively close, but firing at about a 45-degree angle away from each other. It would be about a two-mile hike back to our gate.

I then explained that this was a one or two shot affair and then to back out. We either scored or we didn't but there was only one chance. We didn't know if the troops would retreat or attack, so once the shots were taken, we should haul ass. We went back and forth over the pros and cons of different plans and locations and began to be comfortable with the strategy. In at night, cover up, shoot at 0900 and get the fuck out. We figured that even if the enemy came at us directly after the shot, there was a good chance that we could make it back to the gate before they did.

I asked about side arms and the Katanganese still didn't have them. Given their roles, I ordered that all team members be issued 9mm pistols with silencers. The idea was for them to be a hidden guard around the shooters just in case some odd enemy should happen by. Knives were OK but an unsilenced bullet could screw up everything. So we sent the grunts back to the base with the errand guy. Later in the afternoon the Katanganese practiced with their slightly used (and silenced) Browning Hi Powers, similar to Mike's. The silencers screwed onto the end of the barrels, and lengthened the gun by about six inches. I had seen a demonstration of silenced pistols before, and this was no different. When fired, you heard the gun's slide recoiling, but virtually no noise from the actual explosion of the cartridge. It was surprising how much mechanical noise there was from a gun firing, because in normal circumstances, the explosion of the cartridge was all you heard. The Brownings were not exactly silent, but probably 95% quieter than without the barrel device. The device also cut down on the energy of the bullet, but these guards were not going to be doing any long range shooting. Maybe 10 feet at the most, and with luck, they wouldn't be shooting at all.

Then I gave my speech about capture, which always was received in total silence. They knew then that this was deadly serious shit. All of them had heard rumors and stories just from living in the facility. But I went into some detail anyway. I explained that there were a lot more tribes than the Balubas, and some of them were reported to be a part of the Russian group. We were the common enemy. But what raised the hair on the back of their necks was when I described the ritual torture we had witnessed and the hopelessness of a rescue. "There are also reports of cannibalism among the Balubas, and other tribes as well. The Balubas seem to be partial to eating your heart. Opening your chest while you are still alive. I don't want to upset your appetite, but in one area, a prisoner or a slave would have their arms and legs broken, then placed in a stream or some other vessel with just their head above water for three days to 'soften the flesh'. Then killed and eaten." Predictably that always brought silence, but the lesson was a necessity. The real purpose of a pistol was for yourself.

I also explained that even though this was not what anyone signed up for, what was the alternative? It was a repeat of what McKenzie had said. Wait for 3000 troops to attack? Once the other side was on the offense, we were finished. There was no way to finesse a strategy against thousands of troops with the manpower available to us. And they seem ready to move. They couldn't just sit there getting psyched up for an indefinite period of time. Mike said that he was surprised that they hadn't already attacked. What were they waiting for? At about 1400 hours McKenzie showed up to assure them once again that the extra compensation would be 'generous' and wished us well. He allowed a few questions but most of the planning was done and it was clear what everyone was supposed to do. He had also arrived with a pile of sandwiches and cold drinks. McKenzie explained that he would be at the gate to see us off in the morning, and to try and get a good night's sleep. We would party tomorrow night! He was a good guy who seemed to be extraordinarily well prepared, and supported us in every possible way.

We had another session about the location of the hides, and we agreed on two tentative locations. I stated once again that this was going to be a one or two shot deal and the FALs or the handguns would come into play only in an extreme situation. I said "If someone starts flailing away with an FAL you'll have 3000 troops on your ass. On the other hand, if we leave this to the snipers, we can do our job and slip back to our camp before they know what the fuck is going on.

Also, it is looking like rain tonight so get your rain gear together and to dress warm. Get a good meal and then get to bed. We will see you in the cafeteria at 0230. Be ready to rock and roll."

I asked Richter and Lewandowski to stay behind for the Huey ride. The pilots took us over to the landing spot in a van, and along the way, we could see that the facility was beginning to button up. All of the heavy machinery was parked, and a lot of the employees had exchanged their Teamsters role for an FAL. It was a little like the National Guard going into action, and obviously they had trained for this possibility.

The Huey lifted off and through the headphones, the pilot explained that he would overfly the encampments at a high altitude not only to get a better perspective but also to avoid small arms fire that they had experienced the day before. It only took a few minutes to be over the camps and they looked very much like the presentation we had received. We spotted the two separate camps and they were very different. The Russian camp was well organized with rows of tents and latrines, but the Baluba setup was a hodgepodge of fires and jerry built huts. Still, it was clear where the center of each camp was, and that was our focus. The cover became less the closer we came to the camp and that was going to be dicey. Getting hidden while it was still dark, close enough to get a shot would be a challenge. We circled around twice and then headed back to the facility, setting down about 1700 hours. When we climbed out of the Huey, Richter pulled me aside and said in a quiet voice, "I want the Russian." I blinked and thought about that for a second or two and said "Done." It was the first time I had seen him smile.

We found McKenzie in the cafeteria having a bowl of soup and reading a stack of papers. As we approached, he waved us to sit down. He always seemed to have time for us, no matter how much he had on his mind. "So what is on your agenda, guys?" So I started. "It seems to me that we have U.N. troops scattered all over the Congo and my experience with them in Elisabethville and in Jadotville was that while we were on opposite sides, they conducted themselves in a professional manner. On the other hand, these guys on the other side of the fence act like rogue warriors. My question is: Can the U.N. do something to reign these guys in?" McKenzie leaned back in his chair and braced his hands behind his head and said, "That is a good observation and we have talked to the U.N. chaps about these things. It is damn unlucky that we happen to be in the crosshairs of something much bigger than us. But what this is about is east vs. west. The Russkies want a piece of the action and they particularly want a piece of the Katanga action because of the mineral deposits. There are rumors that there may be uranium deposits in the Katanga and that increases their interest. But anything that they can do to stir up an already huge mess they *will* do. And keep in mind, no matter the past mistakes Europeans have made, The Katanga was law abiding and peaceful, and run by blacks, not whites, until the U.N. got a hair up their ass and decided that secession was out of the question, the evil white man was behind all of this, etcetera. Now hear me on this: If this continues, and it looks like it will, all of the Congo is going to descend into a black hole for decades. Whatever is wrong with The Katanga it is 40 times worse in Leopoldville. But the immediate point is that here we are, isolated, and in the near term, no one is coming to rescue us. The Russians want an incident, and you can assume that they will market this as a fight against mercenaries. A fight to free the black man. Of course, all of that is bullshit but I cannot change any of it. What else?" So I started again. "I get the strategy and all of tomorrow, but what happens if things go sour. What is the game plan if thousands of these guys penetrate your perimeter?" McKenzie shook his head and said "It's a huge problem. We are a commercial operation here, not an army base. But we have cross trained a lot of our miners and we have a sizeable guard force. All together, we can place 400 men under arms, but they range in capability from excellent to rank amateurs. We also have the capability to retreat into several of the mines where we have supplies that could last for a month or so. But long range? We're fucked. We can buy a lot of time if you are successful tomorrow. By the way, this Hoare guy is creating quite a force, and we may cut a deal with him. But we can't compete with a real army and neither can he. What else?" Mike spoke up. "Our contract. We are supposed to be done the day after tomorrow." "I am well aware of that. I'd like to see you guys stay on, but I know that you have other plans. You have done so much more than what we asked for, and I intend to pay you well when you get back in tomorrow. We can get you both to Ndola the next day on the Huey, but that is about as far as I can get you. Things are very dicey there right now and I hear that the U.N is causing so much static at the border that there may be a halt to air traffic in a few days, so it looks like the day after tomorrow we can only get you that far."

I said, "That looks good to us."

On the way back to our room, I said "Did you notice that he said he'd pay us when we got back tomorrow? I wonder what happens if we don't get back?"

I sent a telex to Anne.

ANNE WARD-SCOTT- STOP % CAPITOL HOTEL STOP- LILONGWE, NYASLALAND STOP THREE DAYS WITH LUCK- STOP- TONY

# Chapter 61

It was tough getting any sleep. A thousand things were going through my mind and about 900 of them spelled catastrophe. There was also the beginnings of an electrical storm brewing a few dozen miles away. I could see the flash of lightning in the window and then count the seconds before the thunder arrived, and get a rough idea of where it was It seemed to be moving in our direction. That could be a blessing or a problem. When it rains in the tropics it rains in sheets. Buckets. Waterfalls. On the other hand, thunder could mask the sound of a .300 Win Mag. It might be a perfect cover. Gradually I dozed off in a fitful sleep until the phone rang at 0200. "Time to get up sir."

Not surprisingly, everyone was in the cafeteria when I got there. They were as hyped up as I was. Nevertheless, I had them line up like new recruits and Mike and I went down the line, checking their equipment. It all seemed to be in good order except one guy had no ammo in his pistol, which we quickly fixed, and one of the Katanganese had forgotten his knife, an important issue given their role. Embarrassed, he hustled back to his room and retrieved it. About that time, a support employee came into the room with a box and said "Mr. McKenzie thought these would be helpful." Helpful? They would be critical. In a small box were two pocket watches. I had just assumed that everyone had a watch, but what were they? Taiwanese junk? A major oversight on my part. The entire idea was to shoot simultaneously and why would we rely on junk watches? So I gave one to Richter and we set the times: 0237. I had asked for set of modern Walkie-Talkies which were also in the box. This would allow the two teams to talk to each other within a short range. I gave one to Mike and the other to Lewandowski with the admonition: Use it only when you need to. Preserve the batteries.

"One last check on what we are doing. When we leave the gate, I will lead with one of the guards and Mike will follow the group with another guard, and we'll proceed single file to the IP. At that point we'll split up and each team will be on its own. Our first job is to find a decent hide, close enough to get a shot. These guys are not going to assemble for our convenience so that we can shoot them. These groups have been in a tight area for three days, convening by 0900, and lasting till about 1400. So, while we are assuming a 0930 shoot, it is more important that we shoot together. Seconds after the shooting, they will either be on the run or running after us. At 0930, one of us may have a shot but the other may not. Even if we have to wait a few hours, we need to do this together. OK, let's be on our way, and good luck."

We left the gate at 0300, crossed the dirt roadway and into the bush. McKenzie was at the gate and shook each of our hands. We walked slowly and cautiously. We only had about a mile to go to the IP, but any sensible military operation would have defensive patrols about. As we proceeded, the lightning came closer and the lag before thunder was only a few seconds. Then the rain came. Not a drenching rain, but we were glad we had proper rain gear. In about 25 minutes we were at the IP and we stopped behind a large boulder and a lot of brushy trees. We checked our watches and the radios which seemed to be working alright. By this time, we knew what we had to do so there was no talking. I noticed that two of the Katanganese guards had their knives out of their scabbards and tucked in behind their belts. We shook hands all around and went our separate ways.

The terrain was not quite what we saw from the air, and was actually difficult at times. Ups and downs and small streams beginning to fill as the rain became more intense. The lightning now lit up the sky and probably us as well, but the thunder was our friend and I hoped that the storm would stay close by before we shot. When the lightning struck we could momentarily see the gathering place for the Balubas but it was deserted at this time. We crouched as we went forward, slightly spread out, stopping every 100 yards or so to reassess. We estimated that we were about 2500 yards away from our objective, still much too far away for a good shot. We crept forward and I asked Mike to use his range finder the next time lightning lit up the sky. "1960 yards" he said. Very close. Now we began looking for the hide and it was sparse pickings. If we got into an area with good cover, we might not have a decent field of fire. If we got too far into the open, we might be discovered. I whispered to the guards to spread out a little and look. They were very good at picking through the bush, and even though I knew about where they were, I could not see them or hear them. In a few minutes they came back and whispered that they thought they had our spot. I went forward with them and saw what they meant. The soil was sandy which would allow some easy digging, and while the bush was thick, there was a trail that led almost directly to the gathering spot. Of course, that was exactly where a patrol might be, so it was a double-edged sword. I chose a spot about ten yards off of the trail and we settled in. The next lightning strike was almost directly in front of us and Mike called out 1825 yards. If we moved any further forward, we would begin to lose our cover. I called them all together and said "This is it. I positioned the guards about 15 yards beside us and slightly forward. I put my finger over my mouth in the 'silent' position and we all broke out the netting to cover ourselves. The netting was a substitute for the Ghilley suits and seemed like a better solution given the lack of training. I checked on the guards once they were in place and then returned to look for a firing position. I had five guys to look out for while Richter had only four, so I placed the odd person directly behind us about ten yards. This would have to do.

Everyone settled in and made themselves as comfortable as possible, which was a misnomer as the rain increased. I took the Mauser off of my shoulder and unfolded the bipod. Mike arranged a first aid kit under the bipod legs as we didn't want any movement in the sandy soil. I removed the scope protective covers, and chambered a round. I checked my watch: 0407. Mike triggered the radio and Richter replied. Mike said "We are in place." Richter responded, "Give me five more minutes and I will be ready." I thought that this was getting to be too easy. That is, except for the rain. Lightning and thunder was all around us and the rain was heavy. The water crept down my neck and I could see that this was going to be a miserable several hours. Plus, there would be no 1800 yard shots if the heavy rain continued.

Time wore on and I could see the sky beginning to lighten on the horizon. 0615 hours. My target was a huge fire pit that was still smoldering despite the rain. This is where the Balubas and some other tribes such as the Batetela gathered, all known for past cannibalism and torture. The thought that we were all within a mile of being eaten sent chills up my spine, and I un-holstered my P.38, jacked a 9mm cartridge into the chamber and laid it alongside the Mauser. Whatever else happened, there was no fucking way I was going to be captured. How long would these guys continue to gather before they either attacked or went home? I had this sickening feeling that we might be a day late.

The time crept by as we shivered in the cold and wet morning. I looked around and could not see the guards. These guys knew the bush and they knew what their job was. They were somewhere close by. I nudged Mike and handed him a candy bar. He nodded back and went back to his complex optics, zeroing in on the most likely spot where a leader would be standing. "1820 yards." I knew the bullet drop chart by heart and I adjusted the scope. Actually there was something new. A dozen or so guys at the encampment started hauling in wood and stoked the fire. The rain seemed to be diminishing but there was still lightning and thunder close by, as the storm seemed to be crossing over us, turning slowly into an electrical event rather than a rainstorm. Things were looking up. It was 0745 when Mike shook me and pointed behind us. One of the guards was wiping blood from his knife on to his uniform. The guard pointed backwards and made a slicing motion across his throat. Then he disappeared.

I got on the radio and Richter answered in a whisper. "Yes?" I said "Be alert. Our guard just killed a guy on patrol." He said OK and triggered the radio off. I fiddled with the scope and made sure the bipod legs were firmly supported. Looking through the scope I could see people beginning to accumulate. What these guys could be doing for three days in a row was a mystery to me, but their leaders apparently had them all psyched up. If their intent was to capture the huge mining operation they *needed* to be psyched up. What they did not know was that the people in the mining operation were scared shitless of these guys. There were lots of nerves on both sides.

Mike had a much wider field of vision with his binoculars and whispered "These guys are all heavily armed. Everyone has an AK-47 and bandoliers of ammunition. They are looking as though they have something in mind besides sitting around a fire."

At 0845 the head guys showed up by the fire pit. It was a surreal sight as the lightning flashed, the thunder boomed and these two guys stood by the now-roaring fire, their bodies slick with oil or some substance. About five minutes later two tribesmen pushed a guy, obviously a hostage forward towards the leaders. The hostage struggled but was no match for those holding him, let alone hundreds of others who seemed to be applauding. One of the leaders seemed to nod and the guy was thrown into the fire! He tried to run out of the blaze but tribesmen around the fire pushed him back in. His clothes and hair afire, he finally dropped to his knees and was consumed. Mike was seeing this better than others, and he puked. I suppose all of this happened just to get the crowd active.

At 0900 I triggered the radio and asked Richter "What does your targets look like?" He said "The Russians just arrived, so I think we should wait till they begin talking and stand still. There are two of them. I'd say a Major and a Lieutenant. Oh, we just killed a guy on patrol. No noise." I said "Let's check in at 0915 and see what we have." The thunder and lightning interfered with the radio but I thought that the messages got through. I signaled the lone guard behind us to come over, and whispered for him to gather up the other two guards. We were getting close and I didn't want to be looking for someone as we hauled ass. I checked the scope again and took the Mauser off safety. Mike said "The two leaders are about ten feet apart but they have begun their tirade and seem stable as far as position is concerned. 0912. I triggered Richter and asked "Can you be ready to go at 09015?" He said "Make it 0920 and we'll have a go." I said that I would have Mike call Lewandowski for a countdown at 60 seconds and to try and hit his men at exactly zero. Thunder continued and I was glad to hear it.

At exactly 'fire minus one minute', Mike called Lewandowski and said 60, 59, 58, 57 and he could hear Lewandowski repeating the time for Richter. I told Mike I was going for both of them and hoped that the thunder came on strong. I began my breathing exercises and settled in. The closer I came to actually firing the more relaxed I became. 32, 31, 30, 29. Mike inserted "It's all go here." 17, 16. I engaged the set trigger, and touched the fire trigger. The targets were small but clearly in view. 9, 8, 7, 6, Thunder roared….5, 4, 3, 2, 1". The Mauser fired and I immediately focused on the second guy and fired. Mike said "Two down. You blew the side of the first guy's head off and it looks like the second guy got it square through the neck. The crowd is scattering." "Let's get the fuck out of here", and the five of us hustled into single file and headed for the IP. The thunder and lightning continued and I had no idea how that was being interpreted. Magic? A lightning strike? Voodoo? A bullet? We went ahead at a good pace but not in a panic.

We ran into Richter and his crew behind the same boulder and Richter said "I got the Major through the head and the same bullet went on through the Lieutenant's jaw. It was the first time I had seen Richter happy. I patted him on the back and we continued towards the facility. I thought, Not bad. Four enemies with three bullets.

We began to hear voices whooping it up behind us at the encampments and a few rifles being fired but it was surprisingly quiet.

We saw the gate in the distance and there were several dozen armed men outside of the gate, all armed, and just inside the gate was a M 60 machine gun with two guys manning it. Obviously they were ready for anyone chasing us back to the base. But there were none. We fell into a trot as we crossed through the gate and moved ahead for a couple hundred yards before we stopped. The only casualty I saw was one of Richter's guards who had apparently suffered a knife wound when he had dispatched his target. But he kept up and sagged a little as we stopped. A medic attended to him and it looked like a bad cut on his upper arm, but nothing of a fatal nature.

Now we needed to see what we had accomplished. McKenzie came over and shook our hands and said "Let's go up in the Huey and see what is going on back there."

# Chapter 62

I t only took a couple of minutes for the Huey to reach the encampments and what we saw was stunning. We first swooped over the Russian area and saw the two officers laying on the ground. The Lieutenant had actually crawled a short distance, leaving a blood stain behind him, but was now stationary. The Major was clearly dead, and the crows were beginning to circle. But the most astonishing thing was that there were only a few troops there, wandering aimlessly around. Hundreds had disappeared. We went on to the Baluba area and saw much the same. Laying there before the fire with bluish red brain matter scattered around the spot where the leaders had been speaking. There was a light rain, but the chiefs hadn't moved an inch. The encampment was deserted.

We landed back at the facility and the biggest surprise were enemy troops gathered by the gate asking that we protect them! Apparently they did not even hear our rifle shots due to the thunder. So far as they were concerned the instant deaths came from their God, punishing the leaders and sending the thousands of troops into a full- fledged panic. It was hard to believe. Here we had not only managed to scatter the enemy, but we bore no responsibility for the deaths. Their God had done it and they asked for our protection. The guards did in fact distribute food and blankets, but they were left outside of the gates, where they spent the night, moaning a strange chant that went on until morning.

McKenzie had different ideas. He told us all to get a little rest and be outside of the cafeteria on a small patio for steaks and beer. And that sounded damn good to us, even at 10:30 in the morning. I told the crew to gather up all of the gear and place it in the conference room and we could sort it out later. I said "Good job, guys. In fact, a fucking excellent job. I am very proud of all of you and let's have a steak blowout this afternoon!" Mike got a kick out of Richter and Lewandowski who were back-slapping and grinning like Cheshire cats. Fact is, this didn't end the threat of miscellaneous troops overrunning the place, but it seemed logical that the next group would at least be disciplined troops from a U.N. country. But that was all conjecture and in the future. For now, we savored the victory.

Later, in the afternoon, cleaned up and stuffed with charcoal cooked filets and beer, McKenzie and a couple of other executives made a toast to all of us and gave thanks to a mission that far exceeded their expectations. After all, the worst-case scenario was all of us tied up to stakes and tortured. Then the good part came. The finance guy handed out envelopes to each of the nine guys who participated in the maneuver. I could feel that there was cash inside. No checks or promises in The Katanga. Mike and I just slipped the envelopes into our pockets but the others opened them and were ecstatic about the generosity. Then McKenzie had another surprise. He announced that Mike and I would be leaving the next day and gave us each a box with a medal in it. He took them out and placed them around our necks. It was some kind of official thanks from the Belgium government and was very impressive. The crew all clapped and a lot of back-slapping ensued. Then another surprise: McKenzie said that the crew would stay intact as a permanent organizational unit and that Rolf Richter would be in charge, including custodianship of all of the special equipment including our beloved Mausers. Richter was overcome with emotion and tears rolled down his cheeks as he shook McKenzie's hand. This guy had faced more adversity than 20 normal guys put together, and finally, someone recognized his value. We all gave him a huge round of applause.

It was dark when we headed to our rooms, a little shit-faced from all of the beer, but everyone was happy as clowns.

# Chapter 63

After breakfast we packed our gear which didn't amount to much. Except for the money. In the envelopes was $10,000 U.S. Dollars for each of us which truly amazed us. That was plus the $6000 each of us had coming in the original contract. We each had almost $35,000 for our year plus in the Katanga. It was overwhelming but chicken feed compared to what had been accomplished. I also lovingly packed away Andrew Mkandawire's P.38 and reflected on the lousy deal The Katanga had suffered. As for my P.38, I kept it on my belt. After all, we were still in a war zone.

About 1000 hours we walked out to the helicopter with our small bags and the entire crew was there to see us off, including a lot of workers I didn't know, but they had heard what had been prevented by our actions. We climbed in and Richter came over and shook my hand again. I said "Look up Bakersfield, California and if you ever get a chance, come by. We have good beer there too." He nodded and gave me a slap on the back as the rotors began to turn. We lifted off and flew over the site of the encampments and were shocked to see the four bodies still there. In the case of the Balubas there were animals fighting over the remains, but the area was otherwise deserted.

Our destination was Ndola, which was as far as McKenzie was willing to take us. He had considered Lilongwe, but was unsure about safety issues and fuel availability because of the limited range of the Huey. That was alright with us. To us, Ndola sounded like Switzerland! I asked the pilot if it was possible to set down somewhere close to the American consulate and he said "No problem, mate, they have a landing spot right on top of their building!" Further along in the flight he contacted the consulate and they were ready for us.

We avoided the center of Elisabethville/Lumumbashi but from the outskirts we could see the tragedy from several miles away. Entire rows of house were on fire and vehicles were parked catty-whampus in the streets. I tried to make out the hospital where Anne had worked but it was unrecognizable from all of the other downtown buildings with people swarming around them.

It was about noon when we landed on the roof of the American Consulate in Ndola. Now to track down that Vinson guy and get the fuck out of the area.

# Chapter 64

We gathered our belongings and waved goodbye to the pilot as he lifted off, heading north. We walked down a steep set of stairs and entered the building and asked about Vinson. The answer? He was around the corner at the Mexican Restaurant. Mike said "That guy has a hell of a good job. Eating Mexican food and flirting with the waitresses." Which was exactly what he was doing. He waved us over and saw that he had two tacos and a giant burrito in front of him, covered with some kind of gravy goop. Between bites he said "Sit, Sit." We sat, and while he continued to eat, we ordered some food from his girlfriend. Or whoever she was.

Finally, he appeared to be through a 4000 calorie lunch and he said "Big surprise to see you here! What brings you?" First of all, I thanked him for getting Anne and our injured buddy on their planes and he just waved that aside like it was just part of the job. Which, of course, was true. Then I laid out our issue. "Mike here has an open ticket to Johannesburg and on to Capetown and we need your help in figuring out the plane schedule, getting him to the airport and all of that." He said "That may be a bit of a problem but I'll get right on it. The problem is that our proximity to the border has this city in a total uproar. Troops are spilling over to our side and the airlines have stated that they are discontinuing service. But as today, some of them are still flying, so lets' see about that. Now, how about you?"

"Regarding Ms. Ward. The lady who you gave a room to and got her on the plane to Lilongwe?" "Of course. I gave you the wedding ring, correct?" We all laughed and I said "Well, she is still in Lilongwe, and I want to join her." He said, "She is a lovely lady and I think she deserves a more proper wedding ceremony. But did you know that she has a very large revolver she keeps with her? It scared the cleaning lady half to death!" Which caused us to break out in another laugh but I quickly settled down. "So how about an exit?" "That is a bigger problem. I know for a fact that there is no air service to Lilongwe. It is basically a wide spot in the road by airline standards and there is little demand. And, the authorities in Nyaslaland are as concerned about importing problem people because they are having their own independence issues." So I asked, "How can I get there? What do you suggest?" He thought for a minute and said, "Well, you could fly all around Southern Africa and finally get there, but that is hardly a solution. I recommend a bus." My heart about stopped. "A fucking bus? Is there such a thing?" Vinson explained that yes, there was a bus that made the trip to Lilongwe and on to Blantyre twice a week, and in fact, it would leave tomorrow." All I could think of was an endless trip in a broken down bus. Vinson could see my disappointment and said, "Actually it is not a bad bus. A Volvo. They have both first and second class seats and the entire trip, as I recall is about 15 hours. It is a little like our pony express. They change drivers every couple hundred miles but the bus continues."

"Any other options?" "Well you could hire a car, but that is probably not a good idea. The cars are all junkers, and there is a problem with bandits along the way. In fact, some of the drivers are in cahoots with the bandits!" I thought about the thick rolls of hundred dollar bills I had and caressed the butt of my P.38. "Can you get me a tickets? First class?" "No problem. You can stay here tonight. But let me get on Mike's case. We may have to get him to the airport right now." So Vinson paid the bill and we walked around the corner to the consulate. It was a kind of thrill to see the Stars and Stripes flying above the building and I was beginning to feel positive, bus or no bus.

As it turned out Kenya Airlines had a flight to Johannesburg in three hours and after Vinson harangued an official who agreed to accept Mike's tickets for an 'administrative cost' of $100. "Is that OK with you?" Mike said that was fine and fingered his roll of money and pulled out a hundred-dollar bill and dropped it on Vinson's desk. Vinson was probably a lowly GS-7 and wasn't used to guys carrying around that kind of money, but snatched it up and said "I suggest that we get you to the airport right now before something else changes."

The airport was total chaos. People were camping out in the parking lot and the small terminal was overwhelmed with refugees, many with small kids crying and miserable. The government had set up a kind of soup kitchen but conditions were appalling. It looked like war had come to Northern Rhodesia which itself was going through the preliminary throes of becoming Zambia. Still, Vinson knew his trade. He stopped our driver at a side entrance and told us to follow. The door led to a hallway and then to a room that was reasonably well organized, where the pilots filed their flight plans and had a place to relax. We followed him into an office where he slipped an envelope to a 300-pound official with a thick cigar in his mouth, leaning back behind the desk. We assumed the envelope contained Mike's hundred-dollar bill. The guy peeked into the envelope, smiled, and said "Please sit down. Would you all like tea?"

We waited in the office for two hours as other people came by, some of them offering envelopes of their own. One woman, of unknown nationality, and with a small child, was angry about the bribe but what choice did she have? She was given a seat, and we all waited. We heard the plane coming in, which turned out to be a DC-6 propeller plane. We could see the plane circling in front of the terminal and the doors and the moveable ladder rolled into place. No one exited. No one was flying to Ndola. The fat official gathered up his retinue, including Mike and motioned for them all to follow. It all happened quickly, and all I could do was give Mike a hug and say "I'll see you in Bakersfield!" Mike grinned and followed the official. He was thinking of 1) getting the fuck out of here, 2) Rene, and 3) definitely not Bakersfield. Vinson said "Let's be going", and I followed him back down the hallway to the car. By the time the driver worked his way out of the traffic jam and people just wandering around, I heard the engines on the Douglas fire up. Now everyone was out. Except me. It was my turn.

Back at the Consulate, I was given a room with a bathroom and a bed and then I spent a little time with Vinson. He was intensely interested in what had been going on in The Katanga. Because of the very few Americans he had only sketchy information, plus the propaganda coming from the State Department. I didn't explain what Mike and I had been up to but I let him know that it was a travesty that our country was supporting a government that was far more savage and incompetent than Tshombe's dream of independence. He seemed sympathetic, but he was, after all, a bureaucrat used to doing what he was told, and not involved in anything of a strategic nature. But he did his job well and I was very pleased for his help. Which continued for dinner, of course, around the corner at the Mexican Restaurant. Back at the Consulate my tickets arrived and I was asked for $84.30 which I paid with a hundred -dollar bill. Vinson said "Sleep well and get breakfast here and pack a bag of food, eat well, because you will not have much in the way of nutrition on that bus. We'll leave at 0645."

# Chapter 65

I thought that the airport was bad. The bus station was many times worse. Vinson stayed with me as we wound our way through a crowd that included caged chickens. Vinson quipped, "They will go second class!" There were unsavory looking men everywhere, many dressed in rags and barefoot. Many held huge boxes and I wondered how all of this stuff would ever fit into the bus. The bus itself was decent and fairly new. It had a curtain that separated the elite like me, from the second class folks. I periodically felt my roll of cash and touched my P.38. No one seemed to care that I had a gun on board. I was dressed like a soldier and I suppose everyone thought that was what I was. Added security.

They began boarding and I said my goodbyes to Vinson, who accomplished magical things that I could not have done by myself. He may not have been a policy-maker, but he sure knew the ropes as to how this squalid city operated. I grabbed a seat directly behind the driver and stowed my bag beneath my seat. The seats had a fresh paper headrest covering a well-worn seat that was slick with many trips of dirt and grime. Then came the second- class passengers with their chickens and one with a parrot. The passengers were about half white and half black, and all of them had a harried look about them, having travelled God knows what path to simply get to this point. They sank into their chairs with relief, and many of them fell asleep before the driver stepped aboard. A station agent dressed in a dirty tee shirt and cutoffs came aboard and passed out a map for our trip with asterisks on where the stops would be. It also explained that there was a rest room on board but limited to 'emergencies.'

The driver stepped on board, looked around and made sure that everyone actually had a seat, then sat down and started the diesel. And away we went. He had to honk his way through a crowd, but in a few minutes he was headed out of town. I looked down at the map and read: 13 hours and 979 kilometers.

The trip was agonizingly slow. I figured that whoever owned this bus line thought that we would average over 70 km per hour. Which was a bad joke. First of all, the roadway was about twenty feet wide, but storms and no maintenance limited the pavement to about ten feet. On either side of the pavement there was a one foot drop off. So as we encountered an oncoming vehicle, there was a constant battle of 'chicken' to see who would pull off. We usually won the battle with cars and small trucks, but when a truck and semi-trailer came the other way, we usually lost. Being seated as I was right behind the driver, I could see these crazy fuckers coming right at us, intent on certain death. But at the last possible moment, either we or the oncoming traffic would drop off the pavement to safety. And, the drop off itself would create an uncontrolled situation that I thought at the time would cause the vehicle to roll over. But the driver took all of this as a matter of course and was unperturbed with the situation. Eventually, I gained confidence and began to look at the scenery.

What was most prevalent was that thousands of people walked. Occasionally there was a bicycle. That was a blessing because had there been even light traffic we surely would have had a fatal accident. Of the people walking, the women had impossibly heavy and unusual loads they carried on their heads, and usually an infant on their backs. As we had seen before, the men just walked, carrying nothing. We're talking about thousands and thousands of walkers going who knows where? There were small villages along the way that the driver just stormed through sending people, goats and chickens scattering. In the bigger towns he slowed and if we actually stopped, we would immediately be besieged by people trying to sell us everything from potatoes to tomatoes to wood carvings. Desperate people, trying to get a Kwacha or two so they could provide for their families. I noticed that there were no fat people in the countryside in either Rhodesia or Nyasaland. The other thing that was noticeable was that there was absolutely no trash anywhere. The population used wood and paper goods to cook and so there was no wood or paper along the roadway. And very few trees.

And so it went. We dodged cars and trucks, avoided walkers, and the driver tried to keep the bus under control for kilometer after kilometer. We continued across the Muchinga Mountains, finally stopping in the small town of Serenge. It was time for a driver change. This allowed the passengers to get off and use a deplorable bathroom, and wade through an army of sales people. I finally gave in and bought a small ebony carving of an elephant, which simply created more pressure to buy something else. I got back on the bus. The refueling done, our new driver climbed on, tipped his hat to the passengers, started the diesel, and off we went. We descended in elevation and crossed the border into Nyaslaland around Chipata where the climate changed to a tropical, high humidity condition. Heading south towards Lilongwe we had to head east to Nhakota Bay on Lake Malawi, which seemed like a detour, but was a scheduled stop. This was a well-developed city and the people there were decidedly hostile, especially to foreigners. I soon found the reason. We were to be there for about an hour and I walked over to the lake, and could see across the water in a haze to an indistinct Mozambique. On the Nyasaland shore was an elaborate Victorian style building, about three stories high with a jetty built out from the shoreline into the lake. This was a huge installation but it was in disrepair and abandoned. I approached a couple of fishermen and found that they spoke English and asked. "What is this place?" Unemotionally, the fisherman said "This is where they brought the slaves. They walked them out to the end of the pier and put them on Arab slave ships." I was shaken to be in this very place. I asked "And then where?" The man was cleaning a small fish, looked up and said "Zanzibar. Then they sold them in Arab countries." I was speechless. I thanked them and wished them good fishing, but the ghosts hung thickly in this place. Later, I found that the slaves that came to our country and the rest of the Americas came from the west coast of Africa, but the Arab trade continued long after the trade was out lawed in the west. In fact, it continues today in the more remote areas of the northern desert countries in Africa. I stumbled back to the bus, and now understood why a westerner was not particularly welcomed in Nhakota Bay. An Arab perhaps even less.

Heading south towards Lilongwe, I saw workers mowing the roadside lawns with machetes. A power mower would have done the job in no time at all, but that was not the point. There was plenty of labor in Nyasaland. Then, as we passed the Lilongwe airport about fifteen kilometers north of town, the sun was setting and I was stiff and sore from spending hour after hour on this bus. Finally, at dusk, we pulled into the portico of the Capitol Hotel and the bus wheezed to a stop. Here, drivers would change again and continue to Zomba and Blantyre to the south. But for me, I was home.

# Chapter 66

About ten passengers got off at the hotel and I gathered my bag and straightened up and tried to regain some circulation from endless sitting. I made my way into the lobby which was how I remembered it. Modern and clean. Like an oasis. I stood in line and when I got to the desk I said "I am Anthony Ward, Ms. Anne Scott's husband. Can you give me her room number?" The clerk said "Oh Mr.Ward, we have been expecting you! Your wife has been here at the desk at least four times this evening! Your room is #67, right down that hallway by the pool." I thanked her and headed towards heaven. 70, 69, 68 and then 67. I knocked and Anne's voice said "Who is it?" "Tony." "Tony!!" The door swung open and there she was, wrapped in a towel and wet from a shower. She held her arms out and the towel dropped to the floor, I said "Let me get into the room first." She laughed, jumping up and down, and I closed the door and swept her into my arms. I was at a disadvantage because I still had a military uniform on. She had nothing! But with her help, the buttons flew, the zippers unzipped and the clothes dropped to the floor in record time. Then, Anne and I dropped onto the bed. Between physical events, we recaptured our close calls just getting to Lilongwe. We knew that we had been very lucky. And happy.

The next morning, we woke up late and there was someone knocking at the door. Anne got up, and opened the tiny peek-hole. It was the housekeeping lady who said "Is everything alright here?" Anne answered. "Everthing is absolutely perfect in here!" .

# Afterword

<u>The Katanga</u> is a novel. The characters are my own invention. However, the story (generally)\ follows real events in the attempted secession of The Katanga province from the Congo in the early 1960s. This was a time when the chorus for independence in African colonies was like an uncontrolled stampede. The problem was (and still is) that the Europeans had so deliberately neglected the education of the indigenous people that they were totally ill-equipped to run a country. But world- wide politics, particularly at the United Nations demanded immediate independence, ready or not.

In the case of The Katanga, Moise Tshombe had a different vision. He was black and he created a black country but partnered with whites. His was a vision of a nation where whites and blacks could both operate a country. But the United Nations would hear nothing of the kind. It was black nationalism without exception. Now. And what was the Congo (Zaire) the U.N fought to keep intact? It was a country conceived at the beginning of the 20<sup>th</sup> century when Europe sat at a table and divided Africa. Why perpetuate that atrocity?

The end result was that Tshombe's dream was overcome by force. By the time that The Katanga experiment collapsed, Joseph Mobutu had assumed control of the entire Congo. What ensued was 30 years of savagery, corruption, starvation, and depravity. Three million Congolese died in the mayhem and bloodbath that followed Mobutu's insane, greedy, and corrupt rule. No historian doubts this fact. Think of it. Three million people! But it kept the Congo intact. Laurent Kabila followed as Mobutu was finally forced out suffering from terminal cancer and internal revolt, but the new regime continued the same pattern of corruption and insanity. Finally, Kabila was assassinated at the end of the twentieth century and his son assumed control. There is now reason for hope, but don't hold your breath. As for the guerilla venture, the last mercenary left The Congo in 1965.

So the question is: What would Tshombe's new country of The Katanga have yielded had it been allowed to blossom and grow? At the time of its' collapse, it was the only safe place in the Congo. Afterwards, the Congo endured 30 years of total lawlessness. It is the worst example of the collective might of the United Nations academic ideology and power politics over practical governance. It is a lesson that should be learned. When a world body with no inherent long- term responsibility attempts to dictate solutions, chaos and suffering at the highest possible level may occur. The cure was much worse than the disease. At least that is the way it worked out in the Congo.

But the final chapter of The Katanga has yet to be written. We now understand that the U.N. is going to probe (again) the '61 crash that killed Dag Hammarskjold. On that stormy night in 1961, the U.N. plane carrying Hammarskjold, the Secretary General of the United Nations, and 15 other people, were on their way to meet with Tshombe. But the four engine plane crashed minutes after the last radio contact in a stretch of bushland 8 miles from the airport at Ndola, in what was then the British protectorate of Northern Rhodesia. Its cause has never been determined. And now, six decades later, a U.N. panel will again look into the matter.

So the ghost of The Katanga still hangs over the farmlands, villages, bush and jungles of the province that once promised so much for a fresh start in central Africa. Had that meeting between the U.N and Moise Tshombe actually taken place, things might be different today. Perhaps Tony might be running the hardware store and Anne managing the hospital in Elisabethville.

Norman Kelley
Oceanside, California

# Technical Acknowledgments

**Jim X. Buck**
U.S. Navy, Pacific Theatre, Lieutenant Commander. Pilot on Lockheed Constellations and other transport aircraft; post retirement: private pilot for European and American dignitaries, flying Lockheed Jetstars and Gulfstreams.

**Michael Raymond Calendar**
U.S. Marine Corps, Pacific Theatre 1982-1986. Sargeant, Forward observer, mortars; Okinawa, Korea, Philippines.

**Michael Campbell**
U.S. Army, 2003-2014; Iraq, 2003-2006; Staff Sargeant; Tank Commander and section platoon Sargeant; M1A1 Abrams Main Battle Tank.

**Michael Robert Giles**
U.S. Army, Viet Nam, 1967-68. Corporal; Assigned to the 82nd and 101st Airborne, Special Operations and Medic.

**Leon (Pete) Hanna**
U.S. Army, Viet Nam, Dung Ha (near DMZ)1968-69, Corporal, High burst registration for the battalion firing batteries.

**Kenneth Jolly**
U.S. Army, Viet Nam, near Saigon, 1968; Sargeant; Chief Quartermaster, small arms.

# About the Author

Norman Kelley has managed large governmental agencies retiring, from the California Department of Transportation as the assistant director. He also served as the Director of Transportation at the California Public Utilities Commission. Kelley went on to direct a team of twenty American sent to the Kingdom of Saudi Arabia by the U.S. Department of Transportation in an effort to streamline their transportation organizational skills. He continued as a management consultant with Price-Waterhouse in Malawi, (ex-Nyasaland), Central Africa, on a World Bank funded effort intended to develop professional capability and introduce the concept of delegation and independence of action. He helped create the consulting firm of Development Management Associates in Malawi, and travelled throughout central Africa.

Kelley and his wife, Patricia Ann, live in Oceanside , California. Kelley writes, builds model ships and occasionally enjoys a single malt scotch in the late afternoon.

Kelley holds a Bachelor of Science degree from Excelsior College, State University of New York.

CPSIA information can be obtained
at www.ICGtesting.com
Printed in the USA
FSOW02n1555230117
29951FS